DIPLOMAT

Your Invitation T̶̶̶ ̶̶̶̶̶mbassy

William S. Shepard

For Georgette and Paul.

With best wishes,

William S. Shepard

iUniverse, Inc.

New York Lincoln Shanghai

Diplomatic Tales
Your Invitation To The Embassy

Copyright © 2006 by William S. Shepard

All rights reserved. No part of this book may be used or reproduced by any means, graphic, electronic, or mechanical, including photocopying, recording, taping or by any information storage retrieval system without the written permission of the publisher except in the case of brief quotations embodied in critical articles and reviews.

iUniverse books may be ordered through booksellers or by contacting:

iUniverse
2021 Pine Lake Road, Suite 100
Lincoln, NE 68512
www.iuniverse.com
1-800-Authors (1-800-288-4677)

This book revises and replaces **Consular Tales**, Copyright © 2001 by William S. Shepard, and **Foreign Service Tales**, Copyright © 2002 by William S. Shepard.

ISBN-13: 978-0-595-39100-4 (pbk)
ISBN-13: 978-0-595-83522-5 (cloth)
ISBN-13: 978-0-595-83489-1 (ebk)
ISBN-10: 0-595-39100-1 (pbk)
ISBN-10: 0-595-83522-8 (cloth)
ISBN-10: 0-595-83489-2 (ebk)

Printed in the United States of America

DIPLOMATIC TALES

4'

For Lois, and for our children Stephanie, Robin and Warren, and our pets.
We often lived overseas, but we were always at home.

CONTENTS

▼

PART II: FOREIGN SERVICE TALES

List of Illustrations

PREFACE
So You Want To Be A Diplomat?

Every year, the Department of State has a Foreign Affairs Day, when former career diplomats like myself are invited back to Foggy Bottom for a day of briefings. We often hear the Secretary of State, and insider accounts of what is going on in international affairs. And there is always a ceremony held in the Diplomatic Entrance, the C Street Lobby. Flowers are placed by the plaques dedicated to officers who have been killed in the service of our country during the previous year, and to their family members who have died overseas. There is a military honor guard, and often a message from the President. And we are hushed in our world of memories, of our life overseas and our experiences in the American Foreign Service.

Diplomacy is a traditional career that is evolving. Diplomats used to be largely confined to fine capitals, and perform traditional duties of representing their own nation, while keeping an eye on developments in the host country. These are still essential tasks, and the language training that makes them possible is crucial. And diplomacy is collegial. In several posts where I served, American diplomats were always consulted by our diplomatic colleagues before it was time to seal their bags of diplomatic reports, for we spoke the local language, and often they did not. At the same time, our consultations with friends from other embassies gave needed perspective into the local scene. I never went to a diplomatic reception without a mental list of colleagues to consult, and policy issues to discuss.

The word "diplomacy" is itself instructive. It means "having two eyes," one for watching the capital which sent you, and the other for observing the capital where you are serving. Both perspectives are important for the career diplomat, for as times change, at home and abroad, as they always do, so will ideas regarding the national interest and the profession of diplomacy.

It is therefore no surprise that, once again, diplomatic priorities appear to be changing, as they have repeatedly in the past. Nontraditional and even novel aspects of the profession seem increasingly important, at least to our elected leaders. We now hear that our 6,400 member American Foreign Service has a responsibility to "transform" other societies by easing the spread of democracy to the billions of people who lack its blessings. This sort of thing is not new. We have seen similar pronouncements before, such as those stressing the importance of narcotics suppression (Nixon Administration), and the value of monitoring human rights abroad (Carter Administration), and we will again in the future. Each of these programs has value, but as national priorities change, sometimes overnight, enthusiasm wanes for what previous administrations most valued. But meanwhile, the core work of diplomacy continues.

The largest diplomatic post we have soon may well be the Embassy in Baghdad. (It used to be the Embassy in Saigon.) And so my experiences in wartorn Saigon related here, which were quite novel when I experienced them, may well be more typical for future diplomats than the embassy world that previous generations knew. In any event, I hope that as the profession evolves, we will retain a decent respect for the values of other cultures, no less valid for being different. For as we respect others, so they value us, and not just for our military force.

In whatever form, the American Foreign Service is at the cutting edge of our national security. Adaptable young persons with a good sense of humor who are seeking a fascinating life, should explore diplomacy. This career is now as open from the bottom to persons of talent as it is at the ambassadorial summit to persons of means and the ability to predict winners of national elections.

And so I write, in the hope of interesting young Americans to embark on a career of adventure. In Part One will be found real experiences that my family and I have had during our American Foreign Service career. I place special emphasis on consular responsibilities and assignments, for that is where most beginning diplomats get their start in the profession. Also, since that is the part of our calling with the most human interest, it may be the most accessible guide to the ways of diplomacy. In Part Two, we move to the capital, to embassy life. This collection of short stories illustrates each part of a typical American embassy abroad. Is it all fiction? Probably not. I've found that fiction can be at least as real as what is said to be nonfiction. Perhaps they blend, in this postmodern age. Certainly, the truth about Foreign Service life is not found entirely in either part of this collection of experiences.

My last diplomatic assignment was serving as Consul General in Bordeaux, a consular post that was closed for budgetary reasons in 1996. Actually that has happened twice before, since the Bordeaux Consulate General, the first consular mission opened by the United States, was opened during President George Washington's first term, back in 1790. It was first closed briefly at the end of the eighteenth century during American fury over the XYZ Affair, when bribes were sought, reportedly by French Foreign Minister Talleyrand himself, as a condition for negotiations over shipping and commerce. The Consulate General was also closed during the Second World War, after the Germans took over previously Unoccupied France. Now it has been closed once again.

Why have consular representation in Bordeaux? The city, best known as the center of the world's most glorious wine region, is much more than that, just as the jurisdiction of the Consulate General extended far beyond the city. It included all Southwest France, more than one-quarter of the entire nation. This is a dynamic industrialized region, containing the heart of the French aircraft and defense industries, leading universities at Bordeaux, Toulouse, Limoges and Poitiers, important American investments, and a stream of American visitors, tourists and businessmen. Bordeaux is an important city politically. Two recent Prime Ministers have served as Mayor of Bordeaux. For that matter, French President Jacques Chirac hails from the region.

On the coast is also the French center for the ETA extremists in the Basque nationalist movement, a group cited repeatedly for its terrorist activities, and initially blamed for the commuter train bombings that rocked Madrid in March, 2004. Since the same State Department announcement that closed Consulate General Bordeaux also closed the American Consulate in Bilbao, Spain, that meant that the only two on-scene American locations for monitoring Basque terrorism and other ramifications of this explosive issue are both now closed.

There are management reasons beyond geography and politics for broad American consular representation. First, it was wrong to claim that other posts will fill the gap caused by the closure of Consulate General Bordeaux. That is simply not true, as American travelers who fall ill, or with expiring passports, will discover. Service as a Consul General is also training for higher management posts in diplomacy. That will be even more difficult to achieve in the future.

What work does a consulate general do, and where are they found? A consulate general operates under general instructions received from the embassy, in the host country capital. In our case, that meant the American Embassy in Paris. A consulate general provides a variety of services to Americans who travel through the region, or live there. In addition, a number of services, including visa availability, are provided host and third country nationals. Consulates have defined areas of geographic responsibility, called consular districts, and that of Bordeaux was extensive.

I always found the work fascinating. And I hope that some other young American reading these words will agree. We need good consular officers, people with a sense of adventure. Perhaps they will again serve in Bordeaux. I hope so. From Vice Consul to Assistant Secretary of State for Consular Affairs, the work requires dedication and experience. It varies, it matters greatly, and it cannot be done at arm's length, from someplace else.

But as the consular world is subject to the jurisdiction on an embassy, in Part Two we will proceed to the capital and explore an American embassy. With the diplomatic life of the career Foreign Service, though, there is a special need for a sort of road map. Embassies, the diplomatic profession, foreign assignments, all seem to belong to the realm of imagination. What can be real about this world?

First, it should be recognized that it is a world, with its own rules and traditions. In wondering how to access it more clearly, I decided that these stories should revolve around the typical personnel of an American embassy overseas. Within that context, other themes could be played out, including those lasting favorites, love, murder, jealousy and extortion. They happen in the best of families, after all. Here are the players.

The head of an American diplomatic mission overseas is, of course, the Ambassador, who is appointed by the President and approved by the Senate. In this collection we have several specimens of the breed. There is Bartleby the bureaucrat, soon to be replaced in "Two Track Diplomacy." Rather a more appealing example is Marcia Taunton, reflecting on family history at Reims while on route to her Embassy, in "A Glass of Champagne." In "Home Leave," Ambassador Clanton returns to the scenes of his boyhood, revealing some of the guile that has apparently helped propel his successful career.

The Deputy Chief of Mission, or "DCM," is second in command to the Ambassador, and is in charge of the mission when there is no chief of mission at post. That in practice is rather a tricky business, as diplomatic managers have discovered. If you leave a DCM in charge of an embassy too long, he has a very difficult time remembering that he is no longer in charge when the Ambassador arrives. The DCM in "Foreign Ministry Calls" does what a good DCM must do, weaving together different parts of his mission as the embassy tries to solve a nuanced problem with their host country before the arrival of the Secretary of State. By contrast, the DCM in "Twenty Years After" has his own problems to worry about. If he continues to annoy his Ambassador, the chances are good that he will be transferred to another post shortly.

There are four Foreign Service sections within a typical American Embassy, all supervised by the DCM. The Political Section follows local government affairs such as elections, and often is responsible for negotiating agreements with the host country. In "Buried Treasure" we see a Political Officer through part of his work, trying to arrange grants for emerging host nation political leaders to visit the United States. In the process he learns something about the workings of his embassy that staff meetings had failed to convey.

The Economic and Commercial Section follows economic trends and looks out for American commercial interests. Peripheral chores are also important, as Commercial Officer Bill Ketchum finds out in "Diplomatic Reception." The work can be unglamorous and demanding, and the source of resentment, as Larry Carter shows us in "Little Brown Jug." (I am grateful to Mary Higgins Clark for personally selecting "Little Brown Jug" the second prize winner in her 2000 Mary Higgins Clark Mystery Magazine Contest.) But there are many rewards, not least of which are the opportunities to find out more about local traditions and cultures, as in "Local Holiday." Sometimes what is most familiar can be the most exotic of discoveries.

The Consular Section, as we have seen, is the world of visas and human interest stories involving both Americans resident in the host country, and foreigners who come into contact with the embassy. Old family traditions and the visa world may even intersect, as a new Vice Consul learns in "Give Me Your Tired." And in "The Old Master," an experienced consular officer is nearly set up as an unwitting witness to an ingenious extortion attempt.

The Administrative Section handles the nuts and bolts of living overseas, from property maintenance to pay records. The General Services Officer, or GSO, is the action officer for such matters, handling the brunt of many of the more routine embassy chores. He or she also comes into repeated contact with local life, and in closed societies, probably has better and more informed local contacts than anyone else in the mission. In "Spirits," the GSO learns something of value about local traditions, once he stops interpreting what is going on in terms of his own background.

At this point, I should mention that there is of course a broader context for American embassies. The Department of State itself (always referred to by Foreign Service Officers as "The Department," as though only one existed) oversees all American embassies overseas. In "Control Officer," we see a new Desk Officer in the Department taking an official trip overseas with some irksome Congressional visitors. All Foreign Service Officers worry about their next assignments, which are handled by the Bureau of Personnel in the Department. In "The Golden Years," it has taken retired Foreign Service Officer Roger Irvin a long time to realize how much an early reassignment cost him. He is, one suspects, prepared to act on that realization.

The traditions of the Department of State itself are, of course, as old as the Republic. That is literally true in the case of "Who Stole the Treaty of Paris Desk?" There it falls to a career Foreign Service Officer and amateur diplomatic sleuth, Robbie Cutler, to discover what happened to a priceless national treasure, the desk on which American and British negotiators signed the treaty that ended the American Revolution and started our formal recognized existence as a sovereign nation.

Families are the key to successful life overseas, as at home. In "FSB," a candidate for the written Foreign Service Examination reflects on his family's life overseas as he prepares to take the test that will determine whether he will join the profession. And in "Nothing to Lose But Your Chains," a Foreign Service wife on holiday with her husband in rural England openly reveals the spunk that she has always tended to suppress in the name of his career. "The Extra" takes a retired Foreign Service Officer through a day as a film extra, when many incidents on the set conspire to remind him of events in his Foreign Service career. Finally, in "*Les Revenants,*" a retired Consul General takes matters one step beyond, and after speculating about ghost stories he has heard, finds himself a participant in one. The cameo appearance of that annoying Larry Carter in the same story may lead you to suspect that he got away with murder, after all.

The themes of bureaucracy, dedication, courage and careerism are all here, of course. Also we see the interaction with local cultures, the strictures of time and place, and the importance of diplomatic colleagues. One concludes by rather hoping that our young Commercial Officer will find true love with his lovely counterpart from the Embassy of Chile. That is certainly a possibility. But he had better do a good job of running the Diplomatic Tennis Tournament for his Ambassador first! And so as we begin to explore the diplomatic world, let my consular tales guide you along the human interest side of our international diplomacy.

PART I

▼

CONSULAR TALES

Credit Gerald Clayton, Copyright ©1984. Used by permission.

CHAPTER 1

▼

CONSULATE GENERAL BORDEAUX AND ITS CONSULAR DISTRICT

"Bondfield...James Bondfield." With apologies to 007, I like to think this is how the first accredited American consular agent introduced himself to Bordeaux in the 1780s. James Bondfield operated in Bordeaux as an agent for the Committees of Correspondence of the Continental Congress during the Revolution itself. Surely Mr. Bondfield's duties were important in keeping the badly needed supplies flowing from France to the struggling United States of America despite blockades, in the period when Beaumarchais struggled to supply the American revolutionaries and Lafayette set sail from nearby Pauillac to come to our aid.

With the end of the Revolution, and signature of the Treaty of Paris, then came our first official consular mission as a nation. The Consulate General of the United States in Bordeaux dates back to November 24, 1790, when President George Washington signed letters of appointment for James Fenwick of Maryland to be American Consul in Bordeaux. At that time, just after our Revolution had ended and as theirs was getting underway, the American Minister in Paris was Thomas Jefferson. This earliest link with American consular work is still remembered in Bordeaux by an imposing structure on banks of the Garonne River.

Named for our first American Consul, who commissioned the structure (and who served until his death in 1849), the Hotel Fenwick, a commanding structure that still exists on the city's formerly exclusive Quai des Chartrons, was built in 1795. About 30 years ago this historic structure was sold, and one of my predecessors as Consul General tried to interest the United States Government in buying back our first Consulate General. It was not approved for purchase, which was a pity, for the large structure, designed for warehousing commercial American shipping goods in safety, now could house both the offices of the Consulate General and housing space for American staff.

Now, three consular missions in France have been closed, including Bordeaux. That just leaves Consulate General Strasbourg (where the workload centers on reporting on the various European community organizations that are located there), and Consulate General Marseilles as consular missions outside of Paris. It is not possible that they will be able to offer American citizens proper consular services. They are too far away from American travel destinations, and their resources are already stretched too thin.

Let's consider Consulate General Bordeaux as it functioned just prior to being closed in 1996. It was located at 22, cours du Marechal Foch, in a residential townhouse downtown near Europe's largest open square, the Place des Quinconces, in earlier times the site of an imposing fortress. The Consul General lived in a leased townhouse residence in the suburb of Cauderan. By the way, the post of Consul General has, with very rare exceptions, been a career office in the United States Foreign Service. We have shied away from making it a political reward, with good reason. The work demands professionalism, good language skills, and there is often little or no margin for error.

Let us take a walk through the Consulate General together, to find out more about consular work on the scene. Going through the doors, there is a series of security gates, an unfortunate necessity in these days of terrorism, which were installed during my stay as Consul General, following two security surveys. You cannot proceed further into the building without the security gate being activated. Also, in off hours, you cannot leave, as I discovered one evening after working quite late. I was the last person to leave, and had left my overcoat containing the passkeys in my office upstairs! Trapped in the vestibule, I was relieved to see the Consulate General's neighbor leaving his office, spoke to him through the letterbox opening, and in high amusement he telephoned my security guard to come from the residence with the duplicate keys and extricate me from this embarrassing predicament!

Once admitted, continue down the hallway and you would find yourself in the Consular Section. Most people probably visit the Consulate General in connection with consular services. For Americans, this can involve the gamut from the routine (a passport to be issued or a notarization to be taken) to the urgent (a missing person to be found, or a sick or deceased American to be repatriated). For French nationals or other non U.S. citizens within the consular district, there is a wealth of consular services including visa issuance (with more than 5,000 issued annually even though the visa waiver program had eliminated the requirement for several categories of visitors) and notarials. The Vice Consul generally presides over this domain, supervising the work of several consular employees.

Proceeding upstairs, the visitor might note the historical plaque on the wall that my predecessor arranged listing all Consuls General from Fenwick to the present. He would then arrive at the office of the Vice Consul, or entering first through Executive Secretary Gillian Woehrle's domain, the Consul General's office. This is a spacious office, with enough room for staff meetings, and it lends itself well to smaller representational gatherings. Wall decorations depend upon the incumbent. Down the hall is a secure storage area, although we followed instructions to destroy classified material so conscientiously that it is doubtful that any stock of classified material remained.

The next flight up contains the commercial and cultural sections of the Consulate General. Commercial representation is important. Bordeaux, its immediate region, and indeed Southwestern France generally is one of the most productive, state of the art commercial regions in Europe, particularly in the automotive, information and aerospace sectors. In a Bordeaux suburb, the Ford Motor Company makes transmissions, and is a regionally important employer. (I had a nice personal connection as well. Learning that Ford's Manager, Gilbert Levy, was going to have his 50th birthday a week after mine, we celebrated together and invited our guests to our centennial instead!)

Commercial representation includes making a decent showing at trade fairs throughout the region as well. The Bordeaux Fair, held periodically, was scheduled to be held within the first year of my arrival. Most of the nations represented in Bordeaux's rather large consular corps would have booths, some rather elaborate. Of course, there were no funds for the United States to be represented, the Commercial Counselor at our Embassy in Paris regretfully explained. A cable that I sent to the Department of Commerce elicited the same doleful reply. This was not exactly aggressive national commercial representation.

What to do? My imaginative Commercial Attache, Roger Barthaburu ("like all great persons a Basque," he repeatedly explained to me) suggested that we spend the entire $200 commercial funds that the Commercial Section disposed of per year, and invite managers of the leading American firms to lunch, and see what happened. This was the first of a series of good ideas from Roger. The luncheon went well, and so did the loaned contributions of machinery and other equipment that we could display. Artisanal work by a highly skilled local staffer at the Consulate General (whom the State Department Inspection team that spent a week with us later wanted to fire on the grounds that his work was unneeded) put it all together with clever signs. Since this was, after all, the United States, the Bordeaux Fair Committee reserved the prime exhibition area, at the entrance of the enclosed portion of the fair, for our exhibit.

A borrowed Model A Ford (illustrating the length of our commercial association with Ford in the region) topped off the exhibit and attracted a great deal of attention, including a welcome visit by Mayor Chaban-Delmas and other dignitaries, and front page local press coverage with good photos. I was pleased to send back to the Department of Commerce a glowing report which asked that they contact the home corporate offices of American firms in Bordeaux who had made the exhibit possible.

Nothing like giving Commerce something constructive to do.

The same third floor at the Consulate General houses the work carried out by the United States Information Service (now thanks to former Senator Jesse Helms abolished as a separate agency), which expanded our reach exponentially. Classrooms gained new skills through workshops on the teaching of English. American performers of the highest quality reached audiences throughout the region, while lecturers on an extensive variety of topics were programmed. My own lectures on American history and politics at the Universities of Bordeaux, Limoges, Poitiers and Toulouse were facilitated by our USIS office.

A personal high of sorts occurred when USIS assisted the Director of the Bordeaux Municipal Archives to assemble an exhibit, "The Doughboys In Bordeaux: 1917," in which some of my father's photos from that year were used. The exhibit, which was opened by Mayor Chaban-Delmas in the presence of the American Ambassador, Evan Galbraith, underscored for many America's traditional role for freedom, with our oldest ally.

It also was an eyeopener to realize just how much of Bordeaux's infrastructure, from the airport (including the separate military portion from which General de Gaulle flew to London in 1940 to continue the struggle against the Nazis), to the shipyards, and much of the railways, was first put in by American military engineers to accommodate the American Expeditionary Forces under General Pershing which landed in Southwestern France in 1917.

The top floor of the Consulate General housed our administrative offices, and our clear telegraph facilities. Administration tends to be lowest on the Foreign Service totem pole. That is unfortunate, because good administration is crucial for post morale, and in some countries where the society is a closed one, officers working in administration have more contact with local people than do political officers. They also have to have initiative. I remember coming back from an American festival at Biarritz on the Basque coast, where the guest of honor was Senator Paul Laxalt. It was the Fourth of July, and preparation of the residence for the reception was in the capable hands of our Administrative Officer, Henri Katzaros.

As we drove up to the residence, I saw with horror that the furniture was being moved out the front door onto the street! It turned out, however, that Katzaros was rightly concerned by weather reports that predicted a downpour in the Bordeaux region. He knew that our garden party reception would have to be moved indoors, and that in turn meant that the furniture would have to be removed and trucked away for the afternoon. He was right to take this action, and I was relieved to discover that the Consulate General was not, after all, being burglarized just before the Fourth of July Reception!

A Consul General must personally be responsible for all aspects of his consular mission. But also, his responsibilities include representing the United States throughout the consular district. As a practical matter, one therefore has to make a judgment how time will be allocated between Bordeaux, and the administrative and representational responsibilities connected with the Consulate General itself, and the rest of the sprawling consular district.

In Bordeaux, proper running of the Consulate General means that finances must be planned to last the entire fiscal year, and that equipment works smoothly. It means that we must meet and get to know not only the current leadership, but also those aspiring younger people who are the leaders of tomorrow. It also means spending a lot of time with the media, both print and television. During my tenure, local television had a decidedly leftish tinge when it came to politics. It was something of a first when I was able to appear on television and hold forth on American presidential politics, in French. (Returning to the office I tried fishing for compliments and asked Gillian Woehrle how it had gone and was told "Not a bad half hour, but you did after all make two grammatical mistakes!")

At our residence, there were a cook and a cleaning lady. Both were fine workers, and I split their expense with the government. Each month I would ask

Henri Katzaros to compute their salaries precisely, and then would give him a check to be cashed to pay my share of their salaries. He would do this, then add the government's share, and I would deliver to the two employees their sealed envelopes containing their monthly salaries.

Receptions and dinners were something else, and had to be carefully budgeted for out of the year's representational allocation of funds. That meant hiring a cook and waiters, and in Bordeaux, good ones abounded. However, after the first few dinner parties, I began to notice that the leftovers were fewer and fewer. It turned out that the cook and waiters were taking them home! I consulted an experienced hand at the Embassy, and was told that this was indeed a delicate matter. I should have laid down the groundrules at once—leftovers stay in the kitchen.

Trying to change things now would carry a heavyhanded imputation of stealing! I took that risk, and the leftovers stayed in the refrigerator. I noticed, however, that the catering costs went up somewhat for future dinners!

The meals were generally delicious, judging from the 20 pounds I gained in two years! The only real disagreement regarding cooking came when we decided to have turkey for company. The cook arrived late by my reckoning, but on time by his, and instead of a mouthwatering slow-roasted turkey the good American way, the poor beast seemed to be boiled in its own juices! It was dreadful. No wonder Art Buchwald tries each year to explain Thanksgiving to the French. He should also add to his column a basic recipe for making turkey the American way!

Upon my assignment as Consul General, Lois and I poured over the pictures of the residence, and discovered that the very last expenditure for it had been an orange shower curtain, purchased in 1977! When the laughter subsided, and we also discovered that an interior decorator would be taking a look at American diplomatic properties in Germany and Spain and could easily stop in Bordeaux, we asked that this be done.

It didn't take much money, just some paint, curtains, patience, and good North Carolina furniture. The resulting effect united a New Englander's feeling for tradition with Southern quality. It greatly enhanced the use of the residence for representation. It is galling to think that this too has now been lost.

Representation and political reporting on events in Bordeaux are key responsibilities of the Consul General. But in addition to being a representative on the scene, the Consul General reports on political developments of importance throughout the entire consular district and must, therefore, know his region thoroughly. I made it an early priority to visit every single corner of this sprawling consular district, and call on the leadership throughout the widespead area of the French Southwest.

Who are the key political figures in each of the twenty *departements* of the consular district, and what are the important issues? To find that out I travelled everywhere, and reported on regional developments and emerging trends, holding talks with leading figures in government, politics, the regional press and television, the military, leaders in education and industry (including labor) and a variety of other fields, from historic conservation to aerospace.

Was the effort worth making? Absolutely it was. When I heard of a train wreck in a remote area of the Southwest, I was on a visit in Dordogne. The city's officials, whom I had already met, let me use their offices to establish contact with the national authorities who were gathering information on the spot about the train wreck. I was able to find out that no Americans were amongst the many injured, and so inform Embassy Paris and the Department of State before worried inquiries even began to reach them.

On another Sunday evening at my residence in Cauderan, I got a call from the Embassy's duty officer. An American tourist, skiing somewhere in the Pyrenees, had to be notified of a medical crisis back home. His father had suffered a massive heart attack. I telephoned a series of regional authorities I had met during my courtesy calls in their gorgeous, mountainous remote area. In turn they started checking, and in an hour I had located the American tourist.

The Bordeaux consular district then included four separate regions. The Aquitaine Region, of which Bordeaux is the capital, includes the Basque country, much of Gascony, the Dordogne and the Valley of the Vezere (where the world famous Lascaux caves are located), and of course, the world's preeminent wine regions near Bordeaux. One could spend a glorious time in the *Medoc* wine region alone, but it would be a shame to do so without at least glimpsing the Graves and Sauternes regions south of the city, not to mention St. Emilion and Pomerol east of the Garonne River. This is a world of its own, and one often full of American tourists.

There is so much to see, that that is hardly surprising. I'll just mention three little known attractions, all within an easy drive of Bordeaux. First is the Chateau de la Brede, in the Graves region south of Bordeaux, along route D 211. This pleasant castle, with moat, drawbridge and courtyard, was the home of the philosopher and writer Baron Montesquieu. He wrote *The Spirit of the Laws* in his library here, and his setting forth the theory of separation of powers became the guiding framework theory for the Constitution of the United States. If you can, visit Bordeaux during May, when a Music Festival will feature concerts in this same library.

Downstream along the Garonne River from Bordeaux is a litttle used route, D 10, which leads to Saint Andre du Bois. Here one finds Chateau Malrome, where the painter Henri de Toulouse-Lautrec died. His last home is worth seeing, and the careful viewer will note the official death certificate on a bedroom wall, for "Henri de Toulouse-Lautrec, *sans profession* (unemployed)."

A bit further down the Garonne is the imposing Chateau de Cadillac, where membership ceremonies for the wine society, the *Connetablie de Guyenne*, are held. The castle was the stronghold for the Dukes of Epernon. It has also entered American automotive history, by a rather curious route. While sailing down the Garonne River en route to the New World, Antoine de Lamothe, a courageous adventurer from the rural interior, saw the castle, and decided that the name Cadillac was just right to add a certain tone to his own name, so he appropriated it, and it was as Antoine de Lamothe Cadillac that he founded what became Detroit, Michigan, in July, 1701. A group of Michigan state legislators came when I was Consul General to put up a commemorative plaque at Lamothe's early residence in the Lot et Garonne. It was, I was informed, the only time that the State of Michigan had ever officially commemorated a site that was not physically within the state.

The neighboring Midi-Pyrenees Region, whose capital is Toulouse, contains eight *departements* and is an important and growing center for commerce and the aerospace industry. It doesn't resemble the sleepy area I first saw while on a bycycle and camping trip in the summer of 1955, except for the artistic and cultural treasures of Toulouse. The Toulouse leadership, justly proud of their city and region, used to ask me when we were going to move the Consulate General from Bordeaux to their city. I wonder what their reaction has been to the news that we had closed the mission entirely.

The rural areas of this region are fantastic. In the Lot is found one of the great pilgrimage destinations of medieval Christendom, Rocamadour. Situated in dramatic countryside where valleys and peaks alternate, Rocamadour is best approached by 216 steps up to the Place St. Amadour (which the faithful wanted to, and condemned felons were sentenced to, ascend on their knees). I have a pilgrim's staff from my last visit there. The Gouffre de Padirac, France's Mammoth Cave, is nearby. Locals say that the cave was just a gully when Charles Martel, Charlemagne's grandfather, stole a bag of souls from the Devil. The Devil chased Martel, but his donkey succeeded in leaping over the gully, although the bag of souls dropped during that leap. The Devil fell in, and started digging to recover the bag. No word on whether the Gouffre de Padirac is getting deeper with the passage of time.

We all have heard of Limoges and its celebrated porcelain (although the enamelware is just as fine, particularly "Limoges blue," and a much older tradition), which supplied the White House with porcelain for President Lincoln, amongst other administrations. Limoges is the capital of the Limousin Region, rich in history. Some of it is evocative, such as the fortress of Chalus, in the Haute Vienne on Route 21 about half an hour south of Limoges. It was here that Richard the Lion-Hearted was killed in a skirmish, at the height of his reputation, having just returned from the Third Crusade. Some of it is tragic, like the nearby ghost town of Oradour sur Glane, its inhabitants massacred by the *Das Reich* Division in June, 1944. And some of it reflects world famous artistry, like the little town of Aubusson, some 53 miles east of Limoges in the Creuse, where tapestries are still woven by hand, and past masterpieces may be seen at the Tapestry Museum, or modern ones at the Jean Lurcat Museum.

The President of France, Jacques Chirac, hails from the Correze Department in this region. And it is worth stressing that any diplomatic establishment which wants to know French leaders should know them not just in Paris, but in the provinces.

French political life tends to build on municipal and regional power bases, which are not abandoned when a political leader is elected to the French Senate or *Chambre de Deputes*. You can sometimes see Mayor Le Blanc in his home city more readily than you could see Minister or Senator Le Blanc in Paris. That capability is of course lost—and with it the feeling that we really understand the French political system—when missions are closed.

I had known Poitiers, the capital of the Poitou-Charentes Region, since my days as a Fulbright grantee teaching in a French boys' *lycee* in Chateauroux (where it appears that I missed having the actor Gerard Depardieu as a student by a year or two). The nearby ancient university, where Joan of Arc was questioned, was therefore already familiar.

But as a student I hadn't had the opportunity to visit the port city of La Rochelle, or the region of Cognac, for that matter. Both oversights were corrected, and I was rewarded by the discovery of an annual detective film festival held in March in the little town of Cognac, with American actors featured guests. One festival I attended featured the films of Humphrey Bogart, and the presence of Lauren Bacall.

For a little known treasure, visit Rochefort in the Charente-Maritime. I once paid an official call there on the Commanding Admiral of the French Atlantic

Naval Command, in the *Hotel de la Marine*. He observed that historians often say that the French Navy has never had a victorious engagement of first importance in world history. He said that was dead wrong, citing the French Navy's role under Admiral De Grasse in the Battle of Chesapeake Bay, which prevented British naval resupply of their beleaguered forces at the Battle of Yorktown, the culminating victory in the American Revolution.

Such visits from time to time strengthen and reinforce in a small way our alliances and friendship with key foreign leaders. This is worth preserving, even if it costs a few dollars.

But Bordeaux remained the heart of our consular work. It was always a pleasure (actually, I used to try to find an excuse) to have an official talk with Mayor Jacques Chaban-Delmas, former Prime Minister of France and Defense Minister. He was the young military representative of General de Gaulle in France under the Nazi Occupation, and after the war created his own political fiefdom in Bordeaux, ousting an entrenched Socialist politician to do so. After his retirement, Chaban-Delmas was replaced as Mayor of Bordeaux by Alain Juppe, former Foreign Minister and Prime Minister.

And so Bordeaux's national and international importance will continue for the foreseeable future, with or without American consular representation there to observe, to consult, to report, and to serve American citizens and be available for our many friends who live there.

With this overview in mind, let's get more into the detailed work of a consular officer, and the representational aspects of being an American diplomatic official overseas. Before Bordeaux, I served consular assignments in Saigon, Singapore and Budapest, not to mention five tours of duty in what has been described as "the most exotic capital of all," Washington. I also had earlier served in the three other Foreign Service specialties: political analysis and negotiation, commercial and economic work, and administration.

I relied on all of that background in Bordeaux, as examples from my working experience there will show. Whether the subject was visas, or missing persons, or repatriating American citizens, the work was always varied and interesting. See if you agree.

I'll start with a favorite activity, representing the United States at an official event.

CHAPTER 2

▼

MONTAIGNE, THE FRENCH RESISTANCE, AND "LA FRANCE PROFONDE"

During my first week at the Consulate General, my very efficient Executive Secretary, Mrs. Gillian Woehrle, announced an elderly visitor, a French former resistance fighter.

His errand was instantly appealing. He was a member of the very first Resistance group that operated in France during the Second World War. That group, the *C.N.D. Castille,* was formed before the German military occupation, and even before the flight of General de Gaulle to London in May, 1940, to begin the liberation fight. Operating out of the Bordeaux shipyards, the group was so accurate in its reporting that at length the Allies became convinced that their intelligence was genuine. The group was credited with supplying information leading to the destruction of at least eleven German submarines and twenty cargo ships.

So moved was de Gaulle that after the war he himself came to Mr. de la Bardonnie's chateau to commemorate the meeting room where a handful of Frenchmen began the French Resistance. Now, Mr. de Ia Bardonnie explained, a permanent memorial was being built to the Resistance, and to *C.N.D. Castille* in particular, in a field along the road at Selles de Castillon, a hamlet between St.

Emilion, the wonderful wine village, and Castillon la Bataille, where a French victory ended the 100 Years War against the English in 1453.

"Would the United States offer a commemorative plaque for the memorial site?" Of course I would authorize that. Arrangements were also made for me to attend the commemoration ceremony, which would be held in one month's time.

Then, of course. I found that there were no funds for such an expenditure. And so I did what any bureaucratically inclined diplomat would do. I reasoned that this was a representational expense if there ever was one, and found out that by postponing my initial entertaining I could quite nicely pay for the plaque from the post's skimpy representation funds.

It took more time to think of an appropriate inscription. All I could think of was the courage of the Resistance group members, many of whom were caught, deported, tortured and murdered. Since I am a student of what the columnist George Will has called "The American Illiad," our Civil War, at length an appropriate citation came to me. It was "Uncommon valor was their common virtue," and it was first said to refer to the Union combatants of Fredericksburg and Chancellorsville after their defeat at Lee's hands in 1863. With Gillian Woehrle's help, we carefully translated that into French, and I prepared to present the granite plaque at the commemoration.

Ever since I was a bit late for a national commemoration in Greece (and ended up driving through a military parade standing at the national route's sidelines in full attention for, I suspect, higher ranking participants), I've made a special effort to be on time for ceremonial occasions. On this Saturday morning I was half an hour early for the commemoration, and was therefore somewhat surprised when the head of the welcoming committee greeted me with a sad smile. "But you are late, *Monsieur le Consul General.*" Puzzled, I looked at my watch, while he explained, "If only you had been here in 1939!"

The Resistance Memorial that was being dedicated was an evocative structure. It rather resembled a gate that was opening away from the road towards the field and forest beyond. The effect was intended. This property marks the dividing line between the French *departements* of Gironde and Dordogne, and so also, during the early years of the Occupation, the border between Occupied and Unoccupied France. On this site was located a farm owned by a member of *C.N.D. Castille*, Mr. Etorneau (code name *Moineau*), and from this location Resistance fighters, downed Allied pilots, and others fleeing the Gestapo made their way South. *Moineau* himself, like so many other members of the Resistance, was caught and killed.

The Bordeaux Consular Corps was in evidence, including my British colleague, who was resplendent in his kilt. So were officials from both departments, former Resistance members. and of course, former Prime Minister Jacques Chaban-Delmas. He later told me that, representing de Gaulle in France during the war, he was able to travel throughout the country, owing to his position as an inspector in the Ministry of Finance On at least three occasions. he said, at the last minute he had had to trust unknown Frenchmen and women, once by passing to a woman his briefcase, which contained Resistance documentation. "Whenever that happened," he said, "I was never once betrayed."

There is in Bordeaux. between the Town Hall (a very inadequate translation for the *Palais Rohan*) and the Cathedral St. Andre (where Eleanor of Aquitaine married King Louis VII in 1137) a Museum of the Resistance, thanks to Chaban-Delmas. One can easily trace there the genesis of Resistance activity, and see their transmitters, and the newspapers that were slipped under doors, and the rudimentary military weapons that the early Resistance had. One is also saddened to see, not only the Nazi propaganda sheets, but antisemitic French political propaganda that had sullied the Fourth Republic. I reflected on that one evening while attending Rosh Hashanah services at the Bordeaux Synagogue as the guest of Rabbi Maman. From that synagogue during the Occupation, the Jewish population of Bordeaux, including a member of the French Cabinet, had been herded and then deported.

At the commemorative ceremony that Saturday morning, a particularly poignant moment was provided by Mme. de Gaulle Anthonioz, General de Gaulle's niece, who had been sent by the Nazis to the Ravensbruck Concentration Camp. She placed an urn containing ashes from the death camps in a prepared reburial site at the inner base of the memorial gate, forever swinging out to safety, for the *C.N.D. Castille* members who had not returned.

Mayor Chaban-Delmas also spoke and recalled the heroism that was being remembered that morning. It was good to recall that in a time of evil and corruption, the best instincts had also produced extraordinary men and women.

We had a luncheon following the ceremony, and I was able to speak with a number of the former Resistance group. One woman told me of the Nazi practice of running false parachute jumps of their own people, feigning to be British or American, in order to lure the Resistance to a prearranged site. It apparently was successful several times. As she recounted it I noted the terror in her eyes, still, over forty years later.

Another member told me that one of the most effective members of the Resistance group had been a mentally retarded young man who worked as a laborer in the Bordeaux shipyards. The Germans ignored him throughout the war because of his disability, but he had a good memory and could count as well as anyone. Many of the reports that he originated ended up in German battle casualties. He was never even suspected.

The wine provoked, as any formal French luncheon will do, some good-hearted speechmaking. I asked to say a few words, and did so. I had noticed that the Memorial that we had just dedicated was only a mile or two from the Chateau Michel de Montaigne, at Saint Michel de Montaigne, where the celebrated sixteenth century writer had written his *Essays*, virtually inventing the essay in the process.

Montaigne's *Essays* had been the first book that I had read as a college freshman. Its broad humanity needs no endorsement from me, and the desire to read it again in the original influenced my decision to major in French literature. When I rose to make my toast, to the surprise of those present, I began by talking about the *Essays*. Merely by taking a different turn in the road, a matter of perhaps five minutes, we would be at Montaigne's chateau. Writing in a time of enormous difficulty, and serving as Mayor of Bordeaux during the period of religious wars, Montaigne was an example of civilization for everyone. I continued that it was to preserve and extend that civilization that the *C.N.D. Castille* had formed and operated. On behalf of the United States of America, I was glad to be amongst them to offer our thanks. When I revisited the memorial site years later, I was pleased to see the American plaque, with its evocation of Chancellorsville, celebrating their heroism.

A year later the Bordeaux Consular Corps met for luncheon at the Chateau Michel de Montaigne, thanks to the owners, Franck (who is the Honorary Consul of the Netherlands) and Patricia Mahler-Besse. It was a memorable occasion featuring *coquilles St. Jacques*, Pauillac lamb, with white wine from the property and also Chateau Palmer, the celebrated Margaux property partly owned by the Mahler-Besse family, which is a neighbor of Chateau Margaux and occasionally surpasses it in quality.

It was pleasant then to visit the tower where Montaigne wrote, and whose ceiling features various sayings in Latin and Greek. The view from the tower window was excellent, and the atmosphere of seclusion must have been perfect for the contemplative author. He was inspired to turn to writing, legend has it, by the fact that he and his wife didn't get along very well, and so the tower became his escape from domestic strife!

A year later I was visited by Professor Norman Rudich, who was my professor of French literature when I was an undergraduate at Wesleyan University. It was a pleasure to be able to show the Montaigne tower to Professor Rudich.

So much history in such a small area. Within twenty miles, we had some of the best vineyards in the world, those of St. Emilion (including Chateau Ausone on the slopes of the town, and Chateau Cheval Blanc on the plain) and Pomerol (including of course Chateau Petrus). European history had been made at Castillon la Bataille, where for probably the only time in the 100 Years War the French were ahead of their English (and Plantagenet) adversaries in military technology, thanks to master gunners, the Bureau brothers.

Literary pilgrims come from all over the world to see the Chateau Michel de Montaigne, and they cannot fail to be impressed by the site, rustic and genuine. Learning of my interest, Mr. de la Bardonnie confided in me that there was another property with Montaigne associations in the region. It now belonged to his son. Later Lois and I drove to the property, which is set in a hamlet in the Dordogne, for Sunday dinner.

The countryside was set with russet autumnal colors that day. The village church next to the Andre de la Bardonnie residence was antique and charming. Their home was a sixteenth century house set in a garden. Basically it was one large room. It had been built by Montaigne for his son.

The ceiling beams were fascinating. They were massive oak, and carried the entire length of the house. By rough calculation, they had been living trees when Columbus set sail for America. Lois and I were delighted to be the guests of Mr. and Mme. Andre de la Bardonnie, and had looked forward to the occasion with anticipation. Driving there, one felt very far from modern concerns, and the substantial meal, with French country specialties, had nothing in common with *nouvelle cuisine*.

Dinner concluded with a special cognac, the last of six bottles of a family cache, we were told. It was deep, amber and delicious. The bottle was an oddity. It looked a bit lopsided, and was clearly not machine made. Mr. de la Bardonnie told us that it was from the '45 vintage, and had been taken to the Dordogne to prevent it from falling into German hands. A bit later he became more precise. The vintage was not 1945 but 1845, and the Germans in question had been the forces of Otto von Bismarck in 1870 during the Franco-Prussian War!

One surprise remained, a personal gift from Louis de la Bardonnie. This was a silver shoe buckle, which one of the de la Bardonnie ancestors had worn at the court of Louis XV. It was rare, because so many had been "donated" or otherwise taken during the French Revolution, when nobles divested themselves of their personal property in an effort to save themselves. We valued the gift, and after enjoying it for some time, returned it to the family when the donor's granddaughter married.

As we left our friends and that perfect little Dordogne town, I remembered what every American visitor to France with some knowledge of French hears at some point. People will say to them. "Yes, Paris (or Marseilles, or wherever you happen to be) is interesting, but it is not *La France Profonde*," an expression that I would translate roughly as "the real France."

After that splendid afternoon, as we took leave of our friends I said to them that it had been pleasant, after many trips to France, to finally discover *La France Profonde*.

It was their home in the Dordogne.

CHAPTER 3

▼

THE AMERICAN COMMUNITY

The American community, resident or just passing through, is a primary constituency for American consuls. Its size and importance in the host country is of course variable, but each member has something to contribute, or a grudge to vent, or a lesson to teach. Counting visitors, I've met and talked with the whole range of folks, from smugglers to Nobel Prize winners. This of course reflects our diversity as a nation. Each individual may require some consular service, and so that community becomes a constituency in miniature.

Travellers may want to renew their passports before they expire, or they may want to find out the latest travel advice about a risky area that they were planning to visit. The State Department periodically issues travel advisories, which are helpful in such cases. There may be questions about local requirements in a variety of legal or medical matters, and the consular section will keep up-to-date lists of English speaking qualified professionals in both areas.

Emergencies happen, as Americans get sick, or may become crime victims overseas, or occasionally may be picked up by the police. When catastrophe strikes, the first thought of many Americans, and rightly so, is to get in touch with the nearest American consulate. In extreme cases, when war or insurrection threatens, the consul and his staff may have to organize an emergency evacuation of American citizens in the consular district. A number of consuls have lost their own lives "under heroic or tragic circumstances," as the State Department plaque in the Diplomatic Lobby puts it, while organizing these rescue operations. It is sad to think that increasingly there isn't going to be an American consul available because that post has been closed, and the nearest American official is now hundreds of unhelpful miles away, and simply does not know the territory or the local officials.

The business that comes up is varied, sometimes complex, and always interesting. We could be talking about a question of an American's impending marriage overseas, or an adoption (and visa) situation of a child abroad, or notarials to make sure that local courts in the United States or overseas recognize your previous divorce. Perhaps it's a question of their honoring your claim to that piece of local property, left to you by your uncle, who never got around to seeking American citizenship.

Sometimes plans go awry, and an American youngster who is out of money will show up at the consular office in a panic but affecting a sort of bravado, expecting help to either continue the adventure overseas, or get home and back to school (preferably without his disapproving parents being informed). There are inventors who want to know about patent procedures and the like, and there are angry Americans who want to renounce their American citizenship.

And there are prominent visiting firemen. Every diplomatic or consular post will get its share of visiting Members of Congress, for example. To many, these "CODELS" (for "Congressional Delegations") were of questionable use, but I rather looked forward to them. You could find out a lot about what was going on back home from these visitors, and often their business really was legitimate and timely. However, my reputation as a judge of character took a severe pummeling after one CODEL in Budapest. It was a two-man trip, and while one Congressmen was a pleasant, easygoing sort, the other was your basic, obnoxious pusher and shover. We all liked the first and detested the second, and were considerably abashed a few months later when the first was indicted by federal prosecutors for forcing his office staff to give him kickbacks of their salaries as a condition of staying employed!

My great Hollywood adventure in Bordeaux began with a press notice in the local paper that the actress Meryl Streep, with a full company, was going to do some extended filming of a picture named *Plenty* in the Dordogne region of our consular district. On a Saturday morning I drove out to observe the filming. The Dordogne remains largely a glorious, rustic area, and its unspoiled interior regions could, with the occasional television antenna removed, be the background locations for a film set any time in the last century and a half.

This film covered the Second World War period. The day I was there, the story line concerned an intrepid officer of the British Army who was parachuting into the French countryside to link up with a Resistance unit (which included Meryl Streep). It was fascinating to watch the parachute (which was inflated from below with generator-powered fans, not dropped from the skies), and the film crew, which stopped traffic on the country road while the filming was going on, recreate 1943 before our very eyes.

Following the drop, Nazi soldiers (actually, French extras), hot on the trail of the British soldier and the Resistance net, were filmed roaring through the scene on their motorcycles. It was exciting stuff, and fun to watch. At one point in a break in the filming I asked the Director, Fred Schepisi, what happened next in the story. He replied that exhilarated by their narrow escape, Streep and the British officer race to the designated hiding place and make passionate love. I couldn't resist asking, "But who wins the war, Fred?" He polled the film crew to find out!

Another noteworthy visitor was Andrew Young, former Ambassador to the United Nations in the Carter Administration, and when I met him, Mayor of Atlanta. Atlanta and Toulouse are sister cities, and Mayor Young was in Toulouse to talk with Toulouse Mayor Dominique Baudis at the opening of the Toulouse International Fair. This was an important regional event, and I joined their discussion and served as interpreter. I'm sure that the fair, and Mayor Young's visit, resulted in increased sales of Ameican products. Any consul worth his salt will piggyback on the visit of distinguished Americans from home to extend our official reach, and get some good exposure for the United States in the process. And sharp visitors, like Mayor Young, will help you do so.

The resident American community overseas runs the gamut from "characters" to persons of great prominence. Both can enrich the community in which they live in unforgettable ways. For example, Bordeaux was said to be a closed community, rather standoffish towards Americans. I never found it to be that way at all. People in my native New Hampshire aren't all that gushing either. But the extent of my welcome, and the esteem in which Americans were held there, was a tribute to many of my predecessors, and to memories that the French people had of American troops fighting for liberty twice in this century. My welcome was certainly also due to the very high caliber of the small American community which had connections with Bordeaux, including Ambassador Douglas Dillon and his family, the owners of Chateau Haut Brion. The Dillons set the standard for the entire Bordeaux wine industry through their modernization of Haut Brion, and their well deserved reputation has been something of a door opener for other Americans as well.

The most memorable American source of local color that I ever met was Bill Bailey, who kept the Coconut Grove Bar in Singapore. Or rather, he kept what had once been a bar and thriving nightclub, when he was in his salad days. Hearing that his bar might finally close, Lois and I went over to the dimly lit place one night for a chat with Bill Bailey over the house specialty, San Miguel beer.

Yes, he told us, he really was the Bill Bailey of the legendary song. He seemed to know everybody, particularly those in show business, and told us that he had known Cary Grant when Grant was still Archie Leach. But he would never heed the advice of the song, and go home. Bailey even stayed in Singapore during the Japanese occupation, incarcerated in Changi Prison (the original for the prison in the film *King Rat*, which was set in Singapore, with William Holden playing the lead role).

As the ceiling fans turned, we sat perched on our bamboo stools at the bar while he poured us a second round of San Miguel and warmed to his memories. Bill Bailey told us that after a full year in Changi, the Japanese authorities had allowed each prisoner to write one postcard home. Not having a home or anyone to write to, the famous expatriate told us that he had thought a bit before sending his precious postcard to William Randolph Hearst with the message "Dear Bill, Here stuck in Changi Prison for the duration, Wish you were here instead of me. Bill Bailey". He never received a reply, and he never went home to the United States.

Contrary to popular belief, American consuls cannot perform marriages, although I have been a witness at several marriages involving American citizens, in Singapore and in Saigon. The marriage of Jeffrey Stone, the American film actor (and the original Prince Charming for the Disney film *Cinderella*), and Christina Loke in Singapore was a highlight of our stay there, our friendship with Jeffrey lasting longer than the marriage. He now lives in Penang, Malaysia, doubtless improving the local scene.

During my second Viet-Nam tour, my apartment was above the Embassy's outpatient medical clinic, and one fine Saturday morning a very attractive young Vietnamese woman knocked on my door to keep her (downstairs) appointment for her prenuptial medical examination! Alas, my doctorate is not in medicine…

Sometimes, an irate citizen will want to renounce his American citizenship (as Lee Harvey Oswald, President Kennedy's assassin, attempted to do at our Embassy in Moscow). This is a fundamental right, but not one to be indulged lightly. Too often the anger passes, and the person who made the renunciation is stuck with the consequences, and years of remorse. In Budapest one afternoon, an American whom I had seen from time to time around the city came in with a beef against the United States Government. He went on at length, while I listened with what I hoped was the appropriate mix of interest, solicitude and bureaucratic inertia.

Then he demanded to renounce his American citizenship right there and then. Believing he needed to have some time to think things over, I blurted out the first reaction that came into my head. "Sorry—I only accept renunciations of American citizenship on Tuesday mornings. This is Tuesday afternoon. If you are still of the same mind, come on back next Tuesday morning and we'll tend to it." Faced with this off the wall response, the young man retreated in total confusion. He did not return the following Tuesday morning, and although he continued to be seen around town, to my knowledge he never again pursued the idea of renouncing his American citizenship.

One of my other from-the-hip reactions in Budapest was less successful. An older American lady "of a certain age," as the French would say, came in one morning hoping for help with getting back to the United States. She was well dressed, wearing jewelry. I told her that there were no official funds for that purpose, and tossed in the gratuitous note that perhaps the jewelry she was wearing would be a source of funds.

I could have kicked myself later for that tactless remark. It was more than likely that the jewelry was not hers at all, and had been borrowed to show that she was a person of standing, down on her luck and worthy of trust. I hope she made it back safely, but if she did, no credit goes to anything I did.

Other consular officers who had preceded me in Budapest had set up a very informal and unauthorized revolving fund. It wasn't much and it was certainly unauthorized, but it was very helpful to give someone who was down on their luck the $10 or $20 they needed to get by. We were always repaid. I did the same thing in Bordeaux, adding toiletries that the airlines would give out during the course of my flights to and from post. A shave and a good meal were sometimes all that a young American needed to turn his luck around.

Divided families were heartbreakers, with their attendant overseas feature of child snatching, often from the parent with legal custody. We did what we could in the best interests of the child, but that is a very hard thing when the child has become the pawn in a larger and destructive emotional drama, played out by the very couple who should be looking after the youngster's best interests, and his or her physical and emotional health. My first day as American Consul in Budapest began with such a case, and we opened the office a half-hour early so that we could process free from harassment the case of a child who was returning with his parent to the United States. Later the other parent came in, and I've never seen a child so torn up and emotionally battered. If the object of using the child as an emotional shuttlecock had been to make him pay for his parents' stupidities, that was succeeding very well indeed.

In all of these matters, our local consular employees were invaluable members of the team. They were invariably loyal and hardworking, and supplied through years of experience the background in host country laws, procedures and customs that an American consular officer in a three-year tour could not hope to equal. Besides, American laws and procedures, in which the consular officer is trained, are quite complicated enough.

Adoptions are a case in point. While in Saigon during the war, I oversaw a number of successfully concluded adoption cases. They were a tribute to a fine and compassionate American impulse, and I hope that they worked out well. The paperwork was complicated beyond belief. It actually demanded full attention for half an hour after each interview just to record the status of the application, and what needed to be done next, to bring the visa application and the eventual travel of the child to the United States to a happy outcome.

In Saigon, there were two hard periods in my adoption work, one internal and the other external. The internal problem surfaced when an inexperienced visa officer took my place for a few days when I came down with dengue fever. He didn't understand immigration law or adoption procedures, and was too stupid to ask. Instead, he conducted cursory interviews, told the adoptive parents that all was just fine, and closed the files without recording what had taken place. This created chaos when one set of adoptive parents with a strict travel deadline appeared a month later, ready to take their child to the United States as promised.

In processing the case I stumbled upon what had happened, and with the help of a sympathetic Immigration and Naturalization Service officer in Manila I was able to work things out. Then I went on a hunt throughout my adoption files and found twenty other cases that had also been mishandled. Sorting them out properly to make sure that the adoptions, visa issuance and travel occurred in good order became the priority for my office, and a challenge that was successfully met. The young officer left the service.

The external problem concerned a fraudulent adoption scheme that had the totally unwitting patronage of a prominent antiwar United States Senator. His staff, doing their bit in the good cause, kept sending cables about the case. As a rule of thumb, all consuls know that when the pressure starts before you even see the applicant, something probably is very wrong with the application. So it turned out in this case. The application was fraudulent, and I denied it. My next dressing down from the Senator was answered by a cable from the applicant's sister, who had exposed the fraud and urged that the visa be denied. We never heard from the Senator in that matter again.

Notarials are a tricky matter, and are commonly attested to by American consuls. Usually, the consul is attesting that the seal on a foreign document is real, and made by a person with the authority to issue it. These attestations have value in American legal proceedings, but of course, it should be clear (and often is not) that a consul's notarial seal says nothing about whether the contents of a foreign document or its translation, are true or false. All we are doing is attesting to the authority of the office that issued it. On a more elaborate scale, I have also conducted legal examinations under oath for American attorneys of witnesses who live overseas. All of this is done according to the scale of fees that is publicly posted in every consular office.

We get our share of crackpots, both American and foreign. In Singapore, an American inventor came in to ask me about American patent law and procedures. That was on behalf of his invention, a Rube Goldberg contraption that he claimed was a perpetual motion machine. I took a look at his plans, and saw that some parts rubbed together. How could this possibly be a perpetual motion machine when he had not solved the problem of friction? Oh well, back to the old drawing board.

In Budapest, I left the Consular Section with mixed feelings to become the Embassy's Political Officer. After my last day as Consul, Lois and I had my consular replacement and his wife over for dinner. Over coffee, I briefed him on some of the more elaborate pending issues, and cases that he would inherit. Almost as an afterthought, I gave a little sermon about the importance of consular work, particularly to the public at large. Most visitors to an American diplomatic or consular mission are not carrying peace proposals or other high policy. They have some chore, routine to you but the most important thing in the world that day for them, that needs attending to by the American Consul. A small percentage of them will be unreasonable or even rude. The trick is to pay sincere attention, and to do what you can. In the rare event that things get out of hand, the Marine Guards can usually be summoned quickly. As it happened, I remembered to tell the young officer the story about my visitor with the perpetual motion machine, and the evening ended pleasantly enough.

The very next day, the young Consul's first day on duty in that office, a mentally deranged Hungarian came in and had a lengthy interview. Then he left the office, went to the visitors' restroom, pulled out a revolver (which would now be caught upon entry in this day of metal detectors) and shot himself to death. Shaken, the young Consul later told me that he had followed my advice and spent time with the visitor, heard him out, and treated him respectfully. The suicide was inevitable, and the Consul was glad that he had behaved appropriately. He thought that the suicide would not be on his conscience for a lifetime. I surely hope so as well.

Consuls know American citizens who retire in the old country, where often the cost of living is less than in the United States, so retirement can be an intelligent option. For many it works out well, although the consul must monitor the community a bit to make sure that those government pension checks, for example, are still going to the right persons. The retirement community abroad is I suspect getting larger, as many retired persons hoping to economize remember their dual nationality.

Older persons are also traveling more generally, a good thing in many respects. Sometimes, the trip of a lifetime, long planned and painstakingly saved for, provides the occasion for senior Americans to meet thair consul overseas. The occasions can be either funny or sad. I remember being gulled by a California group called People To People Tennis, which was visiting Hungary. There were no private Hungarian citizens then for them to play, so they ended up with exhibition matches against the diplomatic community.

A lady from the Dutch Embassy and I played mixed doubles against a California couple each of whom would never see 75 again. The match was held at the Air Free Golf Club, a small diplomatic club which then boasted one tennis court and a few holes of putt-putt golf in the Buda hills, and which now houses a secondary school for the diplomatic community. They beat us soundly, something like 6-2, 6-1. What ringers! The California lady (who began the game at age 65, she said, rubbing the salt in) told us after the match that we were totally predictable in our tennis, and they ran us ragged, our tongues hanging out while they stayed in center court and happily lobbed the balls back to us in the farthest corners of the court!

Other senior visitors abroad will inevitably require medical services. That is why we keep up-to-date lists of English-speaking physicians at the consular office, with notations of their specialities. And from time to time a traveling American citizen will die overseas, and the consular officer will help in a variety of respects, from taking possession if that is necessary of items that the American had with him, to assisting with arrangements for repatriation for burial at home, if that is what the family wishes. It is a sad thing, but it happens, that the consular officer will receive a call from a distraught surviving relative regarding their wife or husband, who has just passed away in a hotel in this foreign land, far from home.

That business of taking possession of a decedent's personal property always struck me as somewhat macabre, but it is required by our law when the decedent has no kin or legal representatives in the consular district. Often the arrangement is provisional, for a relative will turn up from the United States.

One rather Dickensian case in Budapest involved an elderly lady with few financial resources, who had returned with suitcases full of knickknacks, probably intending to sell them one by one, to live on. She died soon after her return, and our invaluable consular assistant Johnny Haar, a man of great patience and dignity, and I had quite a time making sure that those possessions were not stolen. We had her rooms sealed, conducted a proper inventory, and disposed of the possessions according to the wishes of her next of kin, sending back a full record under consular seal.

Several times, I counseled relatives that there was no need to make the trip from the United States, for we could sort out by telephone and cable everything that needed doing, including the shipment of the deceased home for burial. Sometimes that may have saved an expensive but unnecessary trip that grief or guilt would otherwise have impelled.

Surely one of the favorite career diplomats for all who served with him was Ambassador Phil Habib, President Reagan's Middle East Negotiator, a highly skilled and accomplished career Foreign Service Officer with whom I had served in Viet-Nam. Phil stayed with me in Bordeaux when he addressed a local conference, and it was a delight to accompany him on press briefings (which ended up with full page accounts of his missions and views). It pleased him, I think, to realize that given France's consuming interest in the Middle East, which then far exceeded ours, he was more of a household name in my region of France than he was in the United States.

I took him to meet Alexis Lichine, the guru of American wine for many connoisseurs, at his Chateau Prieure-Lichine, and watched the two hit it off beautifully. They swapped stories of "liberating" wine stocks from enemy control during the campaign for France, Phil for his unit advancing from the Mediterranean, and Alex for the table of General Eisenhower.

After so many years of service in so many diplomatic hotspots, from Saigon to the White House, a few years ago Ambassador Habib collapsed and died while visiting the commune of Puligny-Montrachet in Burgundy, where the world's finest dry white wine is grown and vinified. I would like to think that Phil's last moments involved sipping a glass of Montrachet. I also hope that this was before our Consulate General in Lyon was closed, so that an American Consul on the scene could have been there to attend to immediate needs, and ease somewhat the burdens of Phil's family.

His country owed him that.

CHAPTER 4

▼

SECURITY AND TERRORISM

You might say that Mignonne, our six-month old Siamese cat, had a highly developed sense of personal security. One morning she ran up the long staircase at our Bordeaux residence and started scratching the locked bedroom door. This kept up despite attempts to shush her so that we could go back to sleep.

At last I got up to see what was the matter. She ran down the steps, and looking behind herself frequently to make sure that I was following her, went to the front door. There, ringing for entrance, was the maid, and clearly, Mignonne was tired of waiting for her breakfast. What bothered us was that opening that door was the job of our contract security officer, who had his room just by the front door. He was supposed to prowl around the first floor and the grounds all night. On this occasion, he had instead gone to sleep in his room, and bolted the door so that he would not be disturbed. The security contract continued, although this guard was fired.

I still have a little booklet, "Guide To Living In Saigon," published by the American Women's Association of Saigon, that discusses security measures in some detail. (It was published before I arrived, for at that point, except for a few uniformed, or social welfare personnel, there were no American women in Saigon.)

The booklet gives a number of security tips, in English and Vietnamese, and has a tearout section so that household staff would have appropriate security instructions in their own language. In addition, daily precautions are listed in an attempt to instill a sense of security consciousness in the reader, newly assigned to Saigon. It was a helpful effort.

I do not expect to reclaim the benefits of my life membership in the *Cercle Sportif de Saigon* anytime soon, nor is it likely that I'll go shopping again at Thanh Le's or have another comfortable shortsleeved linen walking suit made, but I will remember the security lessons of this little book. They have served me in good stead since then, and are still needed, as attacks on our diplomatic missions, and subway bombings in London by various terrorists still show.

Security and terrorism were mentioned almost as an afterthought when I joined the Foreign Service, but have become daily preoccupations since that time. Now we learn, for example, not about defensive driving, that mainstay of the American road, but instead how to take the offensive in driving through a terrorist ambush.

Just before I arrived in Bordeaux, extremist groups had targetted American diplomats in Paris. During our Bordeaux assignment, it occurred to Lois and me that a closeness of diplomatic views on Lebanese policy between France and the United States might trigger an assassination attempt on an American diplomat in France. Not only was there a potential target, but also, it seemed to us, the opportunity for terrorists to act, since at that time there was virtually no professional security surrounding American consular facilities in the field.

Our schedules were not closely held, our houses lacked guards, and the consular premises themselves were not even equipped with metal detectors, let alone security personnel.

Lois was an appointee of the Secretary of State on the State Department's Council on Overseas Schools, which met every six months in Washington to try to increase corporate funding levels for American schools overseas. After the next meeting at the Department of State, she decided to raise our theory on security with Under Secretary Ron Spiers, who listened carefully, smiled, and said there was no such causative link, and no cause for alarm. He was smug, patronizing, and wrong.

Two months later our Consul General in Strasbourg, Bob Homme, was gunned down as he left his residence. Bob, who was in his car, retained the incredible presence of mind when the shooting began to drop to the floor and ram his fist hard onto the accelerator The gunman continued firing at him through the car window and hit him superficially five times. Bob's car lurched across the street and crashed into a fence. He survived to tell the story, and an extremist group, the Lebanese Armed Revolutionary Faction, claimed to have fired the shots.

I was not in Bordeaux on that Monday morning, although I should have been. I was supposed to leave on a trip to La Rochelle from my residence that Monday morning. However, I left Bordeaux a day early, and drove to La Rochelle on Sunday afternoon instead. It is hard to say quite why, although security was an element. Since my first assignment in Saigon, I had thought that being somewhat unpredictable in movements from place to place was an important security precaution. There, I would vary my routes to the Embassy, and leave both my appartment and the office at different times. It occurred to me to do the same thing that afternoon in Bordeaux.

Calling on the Prefect in La Rochelle at his magnificent office late Monday morning, I was told before my scheduled meeting to call immediately the security office of our Embassy in Paris. The Security Officer told me what had happened in Strasbourg, and he was glad to hear that I would be away from Bordeaux for about a week travelling, and that my schedule was not published.

Lois was in the Far East on a trip, as Chairman of Republicans Abroad, a group that organized American Republican voters overseas. (Since she was not a U. S. Government employee, the Hatch Act strictures forbidding political activity did not apply to her.) Returning to my hotel I received a rather frantic call from her Executive Assistant in Washington, Anne Botteri. I could have kicked myself for not calling Lois immediately.

It seems that Lois had returned to her hotel in Hong Kong, flipped on the room television, and the final news item was, in its entirety, that "the American Consul General in France was just shot." It took some sorting out, particularly since nobody was home at the residence in Bordeaux, for Lois to learn what had happened.

After that, belatedly, our consular security became more professional. Surveys were taken, with teams of visitors, and expensive structural measures were undertaken to protect the Consulate General office building itself (all of which, of course, has now been lost with the closure of the Consulate General). I received a round-the-clock security guard service at the residence (which usually worked well without Mignonne's intervention), and an armored car with professional French security officers as escort when I drove to or from the office.

The drill was professional and unvarying. As we returned from the office, an officer in my car called the security guard at the residence. When we pulled up, the guards in the car behind me (all of whom were cross-trained in at least two different martial arts, in addition to firearms) would exit first, and flank me as I walked to the front door. At the last moment the security guard inside would open the door, and I would enter, my back covered by the guards outside.

One evening while we were performing this drill, an attractive young woman wheeling a baby carriage neared the front door from the left. I automatically leaned forward to have a look at the baby. Instantaneously several things happened. One security officer shoved me aside and stood between me and the baby carriage. The residence front door was opened by the contract guard. The second outside guard literally shoved me sprawling through the front door, which was immediately slammed shut behind me.

My first reaction was astonishment. The thought that that situation could have posed a threat had never crossed my mind. The second thought was appreciation for my guards and for their training. I think of that episode sometimes when I read that politicians use security guards for personal errands. The next time that the same guards were on, they happened to mention that the Bordeaux Girondins, our nationally ranked soccer team, were playing a crucial match that night. It was bound to get a bit rowdy, so they would be free to accompany me if desired.

We went, and I was the guest of Mayor Chaban-Delmas at an evening where we all enjoyed ourselves greatly. It may have been the first time in weeks that the Mayor's entire cabinet was present at the same time! The guards knew that I had drawn the right conclusions from their rough and tumble handling. And the home team won.

The measures that were taken helped diffuse one explicit threat to the Consulate General from a European radical extremist group. Aside from that, a bomb explosion that leveled one wing of a hotel I usually stayed at on the Basque Coast the day before my arrival was probably aimed at the hotel's owner, who had refused to pay the protection money which Basque ETA terrorists living in the region had levied.

The armored car was surprisingly maneuverable for a car its size and weight. It compared more than favorably with the car that Ambassador Henry Cabot Lodge had in Saigon when I was his Aide there during the war, in 1968. That car just had the weighty armor specially attached to an ordinary car. Tires were a constant problem. They always seemed to go flat from the extra weight.

My armored car in Bordeaux handled much more easily, and it really didn't look like an armored car at all. I found that out while on a trip in the provinces, when I was calling on the Mayor of a small town. Emerging from the meeting, I was surrounded by a mirthful group of fellows from a nearby cafe. It turned out that I was parked in the wrong place (actually it should have been the right place, but the Embassy Security Office had overreacted and we were not using diplomatic plates).

Half an hour after I arrived, the cafe loiterers told me, the police came and tried to tow my car away. They couldn't do it. Then they went away and came back with the municipal tow truck—which clearly had enraged more than one of these fellows in the past. They attached my armored car to the back of the tow truck, and then started to drive away. The onlookers, I was told, by this time filled the street. They were absolutely delighted when the weight of my car won the tug of war, and the back of the police tow truck collapsed!

At that point the police gave up in disgust. I think that I could have been elected to the local Town Council very easily on the strength of that episode, which was certainly worth a round of drinks for my new-found friends!

Every consular post has security responsibilities for the local American community, and for handling the evacuation of Americans from other posts in times of danger. Those plans are updated regularly, and occasionally must be implemented. In Singapore, we nearly had to manage a full-scale evacuation of Americans from Indonesia, during the civil war period of the mid-sixties. The fact that that time coincided with Indonesia's policy of Confrontation with Malaysia (which included Singapore) was an added complication.

One of my earliest assignments in Singapore, as General Services Officer in the Administrative Section, was to negotiate and then implement a security guard contract for the Consulate General. It seemed endless, but at length, all was in place. The very first night that the contract was in effect, the newly hired watchman found a pipe bomb that would have destroyed the front half of the Consulate General. According to ordnance experts, the mechanism in the pipe bomb was of Czech manufacture.

Security and terrorism on a grander scale became my fixation for one strenuous week when I was the Malaysia and Singapore Desk Officer in the Department of State, a number of years later. As it happened, Lois and I had just returned from a traditional Malaysian wedding, and wedding banquet, that was held at the Malaysian Embassy. It was a Sunday night, just time to catch the news and turn in.

That is when we became the Sunday news.

A thin-lipped telephone call from the State Department Operations Center crisply informed me that terrorists from the Japanese Red Army had taken over our Embassy in Kuala Lumpur, Malaysia. Would I come immediately to the State Department and put together the crisis task force in the Operations Center that would deal with the situation?

This was my third Operations Center Task Force crisis, following a spell as Executive Secretary first of the Cyprus Task Force in the Johnson Administration, and then of the Pueblo Task Force that was convened when the North Koreans seized our vessel. So I knew the territory. Driving in, I was relieved that there were very few American citizens involved. The terrorists had struck at the consular section of the Embassy, the most accessible part of the mission, separated from other parts of the Embassy, which was located in a commercial highrise office building. Their prisoners included several Americans, a number of Malaysian nationals who had been awaiting visa interviews, and a Swedish diplomat who happened to be visiting the Consular Section to revalidate his American visa.

The Task Force that I assembled was small, and worked around the clock, in premises on the Seventh Floor of the State Department just off the Operations Center. From that aerie, one has access to all of the instantaneous communications facilities of the Operations Center, plus access to decision-making principal officers of both the Sixth (regional bureaus) and Seventh (the Secretary and Under Secretaries) Floors.

The reason for the Japanese Red Army takeover in Kuala Lumpur soon became clear. The Japanese Prime Minister would be making an official visit to Washington shortly, and the terrorists thought to use that occasion for the United States to put pressure on him to release Japanese Red Army terrorists who were being held in Japanese prisons.

Our working group was select and few in number. I remember Under Secretary Larry Eagleburger, Assistant Secretary for East Asian and Pacific Affairs Phil Habib, and a consultant, Steve Pieczenik. who later collaborated in Tom Clancy's television program and book, *Op Center*. A consulting psychologist, he gave us invaluable insights into the mind of a terrorist, and how their decisions were affected by sleep deprivation. Without his help, a successful outcome to the crisis would have been a very doubtful proposition.

At one point, the terrorists threatened to kill their hostages, one by one, each hour that the United States did not agree to their demands. Eagleburger and Habib were able to maintain the American policy of not negotiating with terrorists, and eventually the terrorists seemed to realize that their main problem was saving their own necks, which would be impossible if they carried through with their stated threats. Eventually they were flown out of Kuala Lumpur to a Middle Eastern destination where their politics were more appreciated, and the hostages were released unharmed.

The fact that few Americans were involved as hostages simplified the operation. I and my relief called the hostages' relatives to brief them whenever we had something to tell them, and sometimes, when we did not. One evening I was called from Stockholm for an official briefing, that was immediately relayed to the Swedish Cabinet, concerned about their diplomat.

And the first evening, very late at night, Assistant Secretary Habib asked me to call the Japanese Ambassador, so that he could brief him on the situation. The Ambassador's Aide stalled, not wanting to put his boss on the phone, prompting Phil to wonder aloud whether the hapless Aide was the same fellow who had spent so long typing out the Japanese communique at the time of Pearl Harbor! We laughed, cutting the tension we were feeling.

The problem of terrorism is increasing. Not only officials, but also private businessmen are targets for terrorist attack or kidnapping. Sometimes, a consular officer can provide information on the subject to Americans living within his consular district, or can advise tourists who are travelling through unsettled areas. And so I'll offer a word of advice to Americans travelling or working abroad. Check the State Department website for security information before you travel. Then, while abroad, keep in touch with the nearest American consular office. If living abroad, find out and implement security measures appropriate to your region, vary your usual travel routines, and do not publicize your schedule. A little paranoia can be a healthy trait now and then.

It has been recently announced that a number of one-person consular listening posts will be established in areas without present American consular presence. If that scheme works, absorbing the reality of what consular work is actually needed in important regional cities, and evolves into consulates opening and reopening, with appropriate attention to security, so much the better.

But if instead terrorists realize the opportunity that is now being handed to them, then I suspect that the State Department officials who announced this harebrained scheme will be the first to denounce it as a very bad idea.

CHAPTER 5

▼

SOCIAL SECURITY

American consular officers take field trips from time to time, to verify records, check on conditions in remote parts of their consular district, and show the flag for American citizens. These are often retirees or students resident in the area. Sometimes instead they are confined by accident or illness.

Whenever possible, a field trip will be scheduled to serve a variety of purposes. One summer week in Hungary, for example, I observed the trial of an American citizen charged with negligent operation of a motor vehicle, then visited an American couple in a regional hospital, and then did an errand for the Social Security Administration. Since the Iron Curtain was in full effect, that made the trip rather an adventure.

Unlike most trials which I attended, it seemed that my attending this one in Miskolc, a rather ugly industrial town northeast of Budapest, was probably a tactical error for the defense. Jail time seemed unlikely given the facts of the case, which included property damage only, and a dispute as to insurance involving the rented car. However, Embassy Budapest policy was quite rightly that a consular officer should attend every criminal trial of which we were informed. The defense counsel were, of course, told that I would monitor the trial, and word spread rapidly.

Had I not been there, I suspect that the prosecution would not have pontificated so much, in what seemed like a routine case. But their arguments droned on, and the three judges (two of whom had not been corrupted by legal training) nodded their heads in agreement at the prosecution's forensic flourishes. In response, the defense stressed the banal nature of the offense, the fact that the American defendant wasn't wealthy, and—with a knowing nod in my direction—the need to attract, not scare away, American tourist visitors and the welcome dollars they provided the economy.

The last argument prevailed, for it underscored to the judges that they didn't really know what the school (or rather, the Party's) solution would be in this case. And there was that American Consul from Budapest to consider! Finally, the judges reached a Solomonic decision. Drawing themselves up after a short conference, with as much socialist dignity as the musty provincial courtroom would permit, they announced a sentence for the defendant that was at least twice what anybody in the courtroom (much less the prosecution) had expected. Then they suspended every bit of it, provided that a rather small and reasonable fine was paid instead. Following the trial, as a courtesy I introduced myself to the judges and told them how interesting it had been to observe the processes of socialist legality at work! Meanwhile the American defendant, having already deposited his fine with the clerk of the court, was making immediate plans to travel back to Budapest and then, to Vienna and safety!

The next morning, I visited an American couple in the Miskolc hospital. They had been the victims of a traffic accident, which was not terribly serious, and they were being well treated. I promised to call their daughter in the United States and give her a first-hand account, to allay her fears for her parents.

While waiting to see them, I had an insight into how tough Hungarians can be. In the ward adjoining the American couple's room, I saw a fiftyish Hungarian farmer, who I learned was only two days out of ulcer surgery. He was having luncheon, or rather, refusing to take the unappetizing liquid diet that his doctors had prescribed for what remained of his digestive system. "None of this junk," he snorted. "I want real food!" He smiled with appreciation as his daughter obediently gave him smuggled sandwiches from home that met his definition—rough bread with slabs of lard and hot red peppers for filling!

Driving that afternoon from Miskolc, I saw for the first time the Hungarian secret police car that was assigned to tail me for the trip. Either I hadn't noticed it previously, on the main roads, or the fact that I was now headed for an area near the Russian border made increased surveillance necessary in their view. It was considered very bad form at the Embassy to try to fool surveillance, and so I never tried to do so. Besides, they were by and large bored fellows just doing a routine job, not politically attuned *apparatchiki*. On occasion they would be helpful to a stranded diplomat and even help change a flat tire, or radio for a repair truck from a nearby town. We used to pack sandwiches for them too, I recall.

The small farm village that I was headed for lay just inside Hungary's northeastern frontier with the Soviet Union. Except for the incidental economic benefits that sluiced over the town by virtue of its location near that border, few concessions to the twentieth century's concepts of mechanical progress could be seen. Even the occasional political slogan that one sometimes saw in Hungarian towns (rather than advertising, which was never seen) would have been jarringly out of place, amidst the few short streets whose paving seemed a recent affectation. There was a store where articles in common use were sold (at fixed prices, of course). There was a tiny village church, well tended with fresh flowers at the door, which was kept open for the occasional visitor, and for the rest, one-story houses lined the streets, clearly sufficient for the needs of the town's few hundred souls.

The small scale of existence in this little village suggested that the visitor was an intruding Gulliver. The town was located in a slight declivity, which separated it from its surroundings and minimized its scope. As I drove into the town, it was clear that no directions would be needed, for the streets only bore the names of Hungary's great nineteenth century statesmen, and nothing more recent. One sensed that with the names of those long dead heroes of past causes, sufficient concession had been made to what outsiders might expect of the town. Leave us alone, it seemed to say. There were two or three automobiles parked along Kossuth Street, older cars that were spotlessly kept, giving the impression that like tethered horses they belonged just where they had been parked.

The town was perhaps a four or five hour drive from Budapest, but the lack of any forest of television antennas implied that the actual distance was far greater. It was mid-afternoon, a languid mid-August day. One or two well-wrapped persons of indeterminate age slowly prowled to or from the store. There were no young people to be seen. Perhaps they were all working in the fields that largely surrounded the town.

Abruptly I arrived at the day's destination, a one-story house. I briefly took out my notebook and reviewed the substance of my errand there, before leaving the car and presenting myself at the front door. The old woman, the very old woman, who lived here had a probable claim for benefits under our Social Security law. I was there at the request of the Social Security Administration to ask a number of questions that would help determine whether her claim was allowable.

Astonishingly, the woman would now be one month past her one hundredth birthday.

I went up to her gate, but there was no need to ring, for she was pruning the rosebushes in her garden, and saw me as she peered towards the gate from the bushes near her front doorway. For my part I stared at her as, thin and slightly bent, she straightened her shawl, peered at me a second or third time, and then with a sniff remembered the purpose of my call. "*Zsuzsa!*" she cried in an excited voice, and Zsuzsa shortly appeared, a woman of nearly seventy, to open the gate and welcome me into the house.

It was apparent wihout words that the old woman and Zsuzsa were mother and daughter. Zsuzsa actually seemed rather older than her mother, and her responses were like obedient, cooed replies, in which the habits of a lifetime seemed displayed. I doubted that Zsuzsa had ever married or left the little town, or for that matter even this house, in which I now sat while the news of my arrival was absorbed by the community.

It was a one-room house, and at this time of day, the primary purpose emphasized by the room's arrangements was that of a sitting room. I sat in a chair by the wooden table and wished that I had brought something for them. Zsuzsa sat near me while her mother sat in a chair near the doorway, a participant and yet a spectator. Then the official appeared, a large man whose sullen conversational sallies suggested that his attempt to avoid a career of physical labor by political loyalties was a loss for both the fields and the Party.

Shortly another man appeared, perhaps a neighbor. It was clear from his talk that he was a schoolteacher who wished to be of some help to Zsuzsa and her mother if he could. He had received some university education, including some English at the University of Debrecen before the war. For his part, he was relieved that I spoke sufficient Hungarian so that translation was not really necessary. For my part, I was pleased that in this little town, a friend took an interest in Zsuzsa and her mother.

Gently I explored with Zsuzsa and the schoolteacher the simple facts of the matter, and they provided answers to my inquiries, or corroboration of known details. Yes, the old woman was the widow of a man who had left this town and this very house over seventy years before. He had worked in America, become a citizen, and had died there over thirty years ago. No, the old woman had never remarried. Signatures were affixed and attestations made.

"Why had her husband left?" I asked the schoolteacher, official business now completed. I then heard something of famine, of poor and insufficient distribution of food, of living in the ebbwaters of autarchic empire, of the recollections and traditions of people which did not in the least match my nostalgic view of the Habsburg Empire in the days of the Waltz King.

And then, I heard them speak with force of America, sometimes glancing at the sullen official who sat nearly dozing at the other end of the table. It was not done for my benefit, but seemed to pour forth from their hearts. I have never heard the United States and its opportunities so earnestly complimented on the floor of the United States Senate as I did in that poor village setting in eastern Hungary.

A bottle of wine was produced, and we each had a glass, including the old woman. Thus animated, she went to the cupboard and returned with the house's rarest treasures. These were the last letters from her husband, and his picture, a sepia-toned photograph of a man in his early thirties, sturdy "like you," the old woman said. Then, lost in her world of nearly seven decades gone, over and over she murmured the talismanic word, "Pittsburgh…Pittsburgh…Pittsburgh…," the city from which the letters had come, less and less frequently, until no more could be sent.

Zsuzsa went to prepare a cup of tea for her mother, and the schoolteacher briefly sketched the rest of the history of the family for me. Two sons now lived in another town, much like this one. Zsuzsa, the only daughter, was born shortly after her father left, driven away by hunger and the wish to banish it from his house. Or perhaps he simply couldn't face it in another child. Zsuzsa, of course, had never left home at all.

The old woman had barely left the town during her entire life, although she had once visited Budapest, where she had "seen the Empress" passing by in a coach. The old woman's husband had regularly sent a little money, which had been a great help, but somehow never the windfall that they had planned. A later photograph from Pittsburgh showed him at a picnic, shaved, smiling, hoisting a glass of beer.

That was all, really, except for the death certificate that had somehow arrived after the war. Silicosis. And then, years later, a single check from the United States Treasury for benefits under the Social Security Act. Should there be reciprocity from the Hungarian Government, qualified relatives of deceased American citizens might begin to receive their benefits regularly under that law. I was there to verify the old woman's right to those checks.

As I left the old woman became animated, and eyes shining, she called out "Honored sir! Welcome guest!" These were the words that she had been muttering to herself repeatedly since I arrived. The light of vindication seemed to shine from within her very being.

Driving towards Debrecen and a good dinner, I wondered how the old lady now would find the spirit to continue to hold onto life, until her checks started to arrive.

And then I realized that it really didn't matter at all now, not at all.

CHAPTER 6

▼

THE RED AND THE BLACK

One afternoon a letter arrived at my Bordeaux office that awakened a lot of memories from my previous assignment in Hungary. The letter, from Father Julian Fuzer in Detroit, Michigan, representing the "Committee For The Canonization Of Cardinal Mindszenty," asked my cooperation and testimony.

I was glad to oblige, and Father Fuzer was kind enough to write me subsequently to say that my recollections had been useful. Cardinal Mindszenty, the Primate of Hungary, had of course been imprisoned under the communist regime and subjected to a show trial, and eventually sentenced to life imprisonment. He was briefly released during the confusion of the 1956 Hungarian Revolution, but as that epic event neared its tragic end, Cardinal Mindszenty appeared dramatically at the door of the American Embassy (then Legation) in Budapest and asked for refuge. It was granted, perhaps by President Eisenhower personally. From that day on, His Eminence resided in the Embassy, in the corner office that had been the Ambassador's office (and is now once again).

We had two duty rosters at the Embassy then. The first was the routine duty roster that all Embassies have, which puts someone in charge of fast-breaking events concerning the mission that happen during off-duty hours. The second roster was composed of Hungarian speaking officers such as myself who walked with Cardinal Mindszenty in the Embassy Courtyard during his late afternoon exercise period.

I was formally introduced to Cardinal Mindszenty before our first walk, but before that I briefed myself on his history. One fine point that stuck with me came from the Embassy's Political Officer who knew him well, Ross Titus. Ross told me that the Cardinal suffered from chronic arthritis in his feet, owing to tortures that he had sustained while in prison. Whenever it rained or the weather was particularly cold, I therefore would ask the Cardinal whether he wanted to walk outside as usual, or would prefer to stay indoors.

He always seemed to appreciate the question. Once he did stay indoors, and that was when I told him that it was bitterly cold outside. "So cold that the wolves are howling?" he asked. The vivid Hungarian expression was new to me, which he could tell by my puzzled expression, and so he elaborated a bit. "You know, Mr. Shepard, we Hungarians say that when it gets extremely cold that the wolves desert the forests and come into the towns and villages in search of food. Is it that cold?" I understood that life in that part of Europe had different cultural reference points from my New England upbringing!

During our first walk back and forth in the Embassy Courtyard, which was surrounded on three sides by a building controlled by the Hungarian *AVO* or Secret Police, windows flew open and five photographers took our pictures in a frenzy of picture taking that went on for the full half-hour of our walk. Even when I later became a statewide political candidate, I never had my picture taken so persistently. "They already have me on file many times," the Cardinal explained. "This is for your benefit. You are supposed to be intimidated."

During our walks, we covered many conversational topics. The Cardinal wanted to talk mostly about Hungarian history. He could be nearly as indignant at the failure of the French, at the time of Louis XIV, to come to Hungary's aid during a seventeenth century Hungarian rebellion, as he was about contemporary times. I once asked him whether Nazi or Communist imprisonment (for both regimes had imprisoned him in turn) was worse. He thought for a moment and simply replied, "The Nazis usually remembered to give me something to eat."

For his part, the Cardinal remembered the children of Embassy staffers. It once happened that it was my turn to walk with him on Christmas Day. I brought our daughters Stephanie and Robin along with me for the occasion, and sure enough, he brought forth little chocolate bars and blessed each child, then aged 8 and 7. Years later, driving Stephanie to school in Washington one morning, I asked her what she remembered about Hungary. The first thing that popped into her head was "that nice man in the long red robe who gave me a chocolate bar in the Embassy courtyard."

As I told Father Fuzer, I was impressed by Cardinal Mindszenty's courage, beginning with his comportment when the Nazis entered Hungary years earlier. A number of Hungarians at that time Germanicized their names, hoping perhaps to curry favor or at least to mitigate expected ill treatment from the German soldiers. Father Joszef Behm, in protest against Nazi barbarism, took precisely the opposite course, changing his name to Mindszenty, from the little village of Csehmindszent, where he had grown up.

Cardinal Mindszenty felt deeply for his people and concerned himself with their welfare. He was extremely suspicious of any moves by the Communist Kadar regime, and especially those that the West would interpret as liberalization, in turn possibly justifying policies that he thought would accommodate the communists and prolong their power in Hungary. I still recall one lecture he gave me on the Hungarian Government's subsidies for alcoholic beverages, making them cheap and widely available. He said that cheap alcohol dulled the people, and that was the government's intention.

In 1971, negotiations were concluded which allowed Cardinal Mindszenty, over his strong and stated objections, to leave the Embassy and, indeed, Hungarian soil. He said goodbye to the Embassy staff, and left the building for the first time in fifteen years.

Surely he had planned that moment in his imagination for a very long time. He must have imagined the crowds that would be there. Looking out from an Embassy window, I could see that of course, there were none. The Hungarian Secret Police had cordoned off the square. The only couple I saw in the early morning sat on a park bench halfway across the square, their backs to the Embassy. Perhaps they were police spies, monitoring the far end of the public square. However, they seemed to be arguing, and although they might have been witnesses to history, they missed the entire departure.

My wife Lois did not. She had assumed that the streets would be blocked off around the square. Therefore she drove me to work. We arrived just before the square was cut off from traffic, and Lois parallel parked the car directly opposite from the Embassy's doorway.

Shortly thereafter, the car of the Papal Nuncio to Austria arrived, along with a Hungarian police car or two as an escort. Cardinal Mindszenty left the Embassy with his clerical escorts, pausing for a moment to salute the crowd with a broad wave.

But there was no crowd at all. There was Lois Shepard waving a friendly goodbye to His Eminence. After a moment or two Cardinal Mindszenty saw her, gave her a friendly wave back, and then got into the Papal Nuncio's car. The shades on the car windows were drawn, and the procession began its drive to Vienna.

During a trip to Budapest in 1989, we spent a welcome return week in Hungary and had a chance to see how that nation and its tough-minded people were evolving as communism began to disintegrate. It was somewhat disconcerting to talk with Ambassador Palmer in what had been the Cardinal's quarters, but I saw a plaque on the wall that recalled that the Cardinal had lived there during his 1956-1971 internal exile in our Embassy.

A large book of woodcuts on my coffee table recalls an official visit that, as American Consul in Budapest, I paid to the Martonvasar Orphanage in early 1971. The children, who ranged in age from 7 to 14, were very excited to see an American diplomatic official in those Cold War days, particularly one who, judging from their good behavior, had some power to change their lives for the better, to make them perhaps a bit more comfortable, with a greater variety of food, and perhaps an outing now and then.

The outings would come because the orphanage officials wanted to buy a bus—but I am getting ahead of my story. That happens when you see those young expectant faces still, over the course of the years. Not that I would have used the money for a bus, you understand, but that was hardly my decision to make.

Shortly after the Second World War, an American citizen had died in New Jersey, an immigrant who had been raised as an orphan at the Szekesfehervar Orphanage. He had left his property to the institution that had raised him, with an important proviso. That condition was that the Bishop of Szekesfehervar (one of the most important and traditional Roman Catholic regions of Hungary) and the Mayor agree on the disposition of funds for the municipal orphanage.

During the War, the Orphanage had been damaged by bombings aimed at the Szekesfehervar railroad yards, and the institution had been moved to the small rural town of Martonvasar, near Lake Balaton. The case had been continued in the state court for some time. Finally, the New Jersey state judge, while reserving the ultimate decision, had asked that an assessment be made whether the decedent's wishes could be carried out properly. Everyone seemed aware that there were some forces for change in Hungary. It didn't seem likely now, for example, that the dollars would simply be manipulated by foreign exchange authorities without a reasonable value in forints going to the orphanage, but that was a point for the Embassy to consider. I had the more interesting task, prior to visiting the Martonvasar Orphanage, of seeing whether the Bishop and the Mayor could as stipulated cooperate in administering the bequest.

Szekesfehervar lies between Budapest and Lake Balaton. It became an important royal city when Hungary's founding monarch, Saint Stephen, built a royal basilica there in the eleventh century, said to be along the pilgrimage route that he had opened which led to Jerusalem through Constantinople. The city became the burial site for the founding Arpad dynasty, and still contains important associations with medieval Hungary.

For me, however, the city more nearly recalls the Austro-Hungarian era, with its wealth of late baroque buildings, often in yellow, with classical facades. It takes little imagination to conjure up horse drawn coaches darting along the streets to taverns and restaurants where Hungarian spicy food and Balaton white wines go down well.

I was welcomed at a baroque mansion (whose facade was disfigured by a tacked-on addition, proclaiming it to now be the *Varosi Tanacs*, or Town Council) by the Council President and Mayor of Szekesfehervar, Dr. Istvan Tilinger. Like a Billy Wilder film set of East Berlin in the 'fifties, the furniture didn't fit into the mansion, the accomodations were clearly rundown, and one wondered when the real owners were going to return and sweep out this crew of usurpers.

None of that, however, affected the Mayor's welcome. He even presented me with the city's bronze medallion, which shows Saint Stephen on horseback. (Turning the medallion over when I had returned to Budapest that evening, I saw that it predated the Communist regime, in fact commemorating 900 years since Stephen's death, with the dates 1038-1938 stamped on it.) He seemed knowledgeable about his city, and about the bequest and the reasons for my visit.

It seemed that the Mayor and the Bishop were old acquaintances and antagonists, who had probably each decided long before my visit what mutual accommodations were tactically necessary as they pursued their very different goals. Mayor Tillinger gave me a straightforward account of the history of the Orphanage, adding the telling detail that the reason for its being moved from his city to Martonvasar (while retaining the legal succession to the earlier institution) was because it had been American bombers which had levelled that part of the city! Therefore, according to him, this bequest would be a sort of welcome retribution for damage done to the earlier institution that the Hungarian-American decedent had once known.

I reserved my main question for the end of our conversation. "Yes, I can work with the Bishop," the Mayor said. Then, lapsing into Hungarian slang, he added almost as an afterthought the observation, "You know, for a priest, he's really not such a bad guy."

I then met with the Bishop in the Episcopal Palace. We had sweet coffee and some cookies, while he savored the visit from an American diplomat, made even more unusual by the fact that the Primate of Hungary, Jozsef Cardinal Mindszenty, was in refuge at the American Embassy in Budapest. I made no mention of that fact to the Bishop (nor had I mentioned the fact of my forthcoming visit to Cardinal Mindszenty during my walk with him in the Embassy's interior courtyard the previous week), nor did he inquire after the Cardinal.

The Bishop, a tall, angular and rather intense man, deplored the fact that religious instruction was no longer given at the Martonvasar Orphanage, which had formerly been the case. However, he said that the children were well treated although lack of funds was a problem. He said that he could work with the Mayor, who was "a better man than most of them, and he does have an education." I started to pursue this conversation a bit but was stopped by a nearly imperceptible pursing of the lips by the Bishop, and a nod towards the corner. Such gestures were not uncommon at the time, and I understood that he was telling me that his office was bugged by microphones.

In the corridor I did pursue the matter. He reassured me that he could work with the Mayor, although the moral context was far from ideal. However, with something like an emerging grin of an experienced boxer who looks forward to the ring, he added that the bequest would give him some influence over the affairs of the Martonvasar Orphanage, from which he was totally excluded now. His moral position favoring the bequest was therefore quite clear.

With this earlier trip to Szekesfehervar as background, I was quite looking forward to seeing the Martonvasar Orphanage. It was a plain set of buildings in an unremarkable town, but there were fresh air, plain food, dormitory living and the rudiments of an elementary education. The children, who were all scrubbed and waiting in their classrooms and refectory, seemed well looked after and excited by our visit. Their administrators seemed well meaning if somewhat pedestrian. We greeted the children individually, and their shy smiles were irresistible. Lois whispered that I should make a little speech then. I know that I should have said a few words as any career diplomat can do at the drop of a hat. Surely the effort of speaking in Hungarian publicly was not insurmountable. I had done that before, and had even managed the translation for the conversation between the American Ambassador and Hungarian President Pal Losonczi at the Hungarian Parliament.

But the words wouldn't come, to the orphans who would go back to their dormitory and classrooms after our afternoon's visit, while we headed back to our busy diplomatic schedule. All I could manage was a heartfelt thank you for the book of woodcuts portraying Hungarian national heroes which the older orphans had made in their art class for presentation to visitors.

It was several years later, while at a diplomatic reception at the Hungarian Embassy in Washington, that I learned from their Consul that my report, which had been forwarded to the New Jersey state judge by the Department of State, had been instrumental in his decision to fulfill the intended bequest. The Consul added that the money was now being used for the benefit of the children at the Martonvasar Orphanage, doubtless after long discussions between the Mayor and the Bishop.

The first portrait in the oversized book of woodcuts is, quite fittingly, that of Saint Stephen, wearing the royal crown which he received from Pope Sylvester II in the year 1000, the traditional starting point of Hungarian national history. The cross on top of the crown is slightly askew, a mishap that took place centuries after Stephen's death. Meanwhile the Crown of Saint Stephen has had an existence of its own, as befitting the very personification of the nation.

As the Second World War ended, the Crown of Saint Stephen, and other royal regalia, came into American hands. It happened in May, 1945, as advancing American Army units came across a group of Hungarian officers and men in Austria. The Crown of Saint Stephen had fascinated me for years. It was said to be kept by the United States Government for safekeeping at Fort Knox, Kentucky. The Crown signifies the very existence of Hungary as a Western nation, emerging from the Hungarian people's tribal and nomadic origins.

I have seen the British crowns of state, which are kept in the Tower of London. I have seen Empress Farah's Crown, set with 1646 precious gems, in Tehran. And I have seen the Crown of the Andes, bedecked with emeralds from Colombia. But I must say that I have never seen any object like the Crown of Saint Stephen. Its value is intrinsic. Its workmanship may have been ornate under the standards that prevailed in the tenth century, but it appears naive to eyes that have seen the elaborate creations of later goldsmiths and jewelers.

That adds to its power. It virtually radiates back from its millennial old panels and pearls the veneration of an entire people. If there is a sacred object in the history of any people anywhere, it is the Crown of Saint Stephen of Hungary. Its hold on that people can hardly be overestimated.

In addition to the Crown, the regalia included a sceptre, an orb and a sword, all fitted into a sixteenth century ceremonial chest. Although not officially admitted by the United States during the time that they were kept there, these objects, together with Gisela's robe, the coronation garment that was said to have been made by Queen Gisela for her husband King Istvan (Stephen), were in fact kept at the Federal Depository of the United States Mint, at Fort Knox, Kentucky.

From the beginning, this regalia was understood to be held for the Hungarian people, in a sort of trust. They were always treated with the utmost respect, and when they were transported to Fort Knox by military motorcade, the Air Force arranged a flyover in honor of the Crown of Saint Stephen, an appropriate ceremonial gesture, since the Crown legally personified the Hungarian nation. In fact prior to the communist era, legal judgments were rendered "in the name of the Crown."

American stewardship was of a high order of excellence. Fearing deterioration, United States fiber and textiles experts in the Department of Commerce recommended that a special container be built for Queen Gisela's Coronation Robe. Following that advice, an aluminum case was constructed which allowed the Coronation Robe to lie flat rather than remain folded, which would have caused the fabric to deteriorate.

As Hungarian Desk Officer in the State Department following our return from Budapest, I became *de facto* custodian of the Crown of Saint Stephen and the regalia, and in fact examined them in their Fort Knox repository (The external appearance of the Mint's Depository at Fort Knox, as portrayed in the movie *Goldfinger*, is quite accurate. Since the filmmakers were not allowed into the building's interior, however, those scenes are fanciful.) I was struck by the obvious respect and high-level care that had been shown by American officials to the Crown and the regalia, and hoped that some day, that would be known.

The return should have been better handled than it was, particularly since the announcement of the Holy Crown's return to Hungary was made officially on the 21st anniversary of the day that Russian troops had swept into Budapest in 1956, crushing the Hungarian Revolution! They had been invited into Hungary by Janos Kadar, still the head of the Hungarian Communist Party at the time of the return of the Holy Crown!

I had left the Hungarian desk two years earlier, and following an assignment as Malaysian and Singapore Desk Officer in the East Asian and Pacific Affairs Bureau of the State Department, was in Greek language training preparing for assignment as Deputy Political Counselor at our Athens Embassy.

I attended the special session of the Committee of International Relations of the House of Representatives that was held on the transfer of the Crown. They were riveting, as the consultations that the Carter Administration had evidently hoped to avoid were held publicly.

Busloads of Hungarian-Americans descended upon Washington, at their own expense, to be present at the hearings, and to offer testimony. Also heard were representatives of the Carter Administration.

As the Congressional hearings ended in the late afternoon, two eminent Hungarians, former Prime Minister Ferenc Nagy and General Bela Kiraly, who had led the Freedom Fighters in 1956, testified in favor of the return of the Crown of Saint Stephen and the regalia. They said that these precious objects were doing no particular good at Fort Knox, but that properly displayed in Budapest, they could be striking reminders of Hungary's culture and history as an independent and proud culture and nation.

It was probably my imagination, brought on by hearing long hours of testimony, but for a moment it seemed to me that at length the largely Hungarian-American audience all turned to the last two speakers in a gesture of group consultation and solidarity that seemed to echo back through Hungarian history. For a moment there I nearly saw something of the ancient tribal ways. Certainly those Members of Congress who were holding the hearings became irrelevant. All of the side conversations were in Hungarian. A group consensus emerged and seemed to ratify what respected leaders had had to say, and that decision, largely unpopular, would now be carried out.

In 1998 I saw the Crown of Saint Stephen and the regalia properly displayed at the National Museum in Budapest. They were well and respectfully shown in a separate exhibit room. I was pleased to see that Gisela's Robe had been rewoven where necessary with extreme skill, and I hoped that young Hungarians would take the opportunity to become familiar with their national heritage.

In early 2000, the peripatetic Crown and regalia were moved yet again, this time to the Hungarian Parliament for permanent display. The post Communist era elected government was trying to associate itself with the very symbols of the nation.

If they earn that association, who could object?

CHAPTER 7

▼

JOLLY TARS AND THE SPIRIT WORLD

The days of American shipping along the Gironde River to Bordeaux, that preoccupied my American consular predecessors since Fenwick stored American goods at his consular establishment, the Hotel Fenwick, in the eighteenth century, are long since past. But years earlier as Consul at our Consulate General in Singapore I had a full range of consular responsibilities with sailors, none of them routine.

We had arrived in Singapore by flight from Hong Kong, following a cruise on the President Wilson from San Francisco to Hong Kong. Our daughters Stephanie and Robin, then toddlers, still remember their friends, the Cookie Man and the Jello Man, who gave them treats aboard ship. Lois turned out not to be a sailor, which meant that Stephanie, Robin and I had breakfast together each morning, followed by a gallop on deck. Unfortunately that gave the girls ideas, and Lois and I at luncheon one day were appalled to see our children, intrepid Stephanie in charge, on a lurching deck by themselves and headed for the railing to see the sights! They had managed to leave the nursery and climb a flight of stairs before I spotted them.

We arrived in Singapore with 17 pieces of luggage, and Robin with a 102 degree fever, just in time for Chinese New Year. Thank heavens that Roger and

Margie Sullivan of the Consulate General had realized that all stores would be closed for the holiday, and stocked the refrigerator with food and brought over two cribs for the children.

Our first social event after Robin's recovery was a luncheon held in a Singapore restaurant in a private dining room. While a great treat, the luncheon was somewhat long. After three hours, I began to wonder about the vaunted Singapore reputation for business efficiency. When did they find time to do anything other than have luncheon? After four hours, the host began to look very nervous. Maybe he was planning dinner. After five hours, we saw some of the same courses served that I dimly recalled having seen earlier.

Our host asked the restaurant owner what on earth was going on. It turned out that several hours previously, the waiters had changed shifts. Our waiters for luncheon had left, and the afternoon waiters had come in and seen us in our private room, with the table cleared. They took us for a wedding party that was scheduled to use the room, and was unaccountably late. Since the luncheon was prepaid, there was no bill presentation when "our" waiters left. We saw no need to stay for dinner!

Singapore in those days had much to fascinate the visitor. An evening visit to the Temple of the Monkey God is indelibly fixed in my memory. As the incense burned, a slight woman, perhaps a Temple worker or priest, went into a sort of trance, then jibbered while an interpreter passed along questions from anxious persons and interpreted the replies.

"Will my husband get the job?" "Will my sister find a husband?" "When will our luck change?" The inquirers seemed generally soothed by the results. It certainly beat waiting for months to see if Ann Landers has picked your problem to answer.

We remember vividly such local color as Change Alley, Cad's Alley at the Raffles Hotel, and the Death Houses, where those persons thought to be incurable were left to be cared for, a sort of traditional hospice. But we read of several cases when physicians had come to the Death Houses and treated persons there who had then gotten well. Their reinsertion into their homes must have been interesting. When the residents of Death Houses passed on, an elaborate funeral ceremony was customary, with paper houses, cars, and other possessions burned to accompany the departed's spirit, and perhaps provide more comforts in the afterlife than he had known in this life.

In this fascinating atmosphere, the American shipping presence was still important, and as American Consul I had a number of dealings with seamen and masters. American consular regulations regarding American flag merchant vessels seemed to have been written by a landlubber under the influence of Gilbert and Sullivan's *HMS Pinafore*. The Consul's signature, required for the dismissal of a sailor from his shipping articles, meant a lot of business for us in Singapore. It was, of course, required that we make sure that the sailor actually had consented, for under the rules then prevailing, the master's responsibility for repatriation of the sailor came to an end when the sailor was signed off the shipping articles.

Of course, that could work both ways. Occasionally a sailor wanted to leave, and that could be ascertained fairly regularly. But compensation had to be fairly given, and the sailor's rights respected. I had one captain in three times at the Consular Section discharging sailors. Each time the transaction looked valid enough, but a pattern began to emerge. Perhaps he was merely trying to reengage a new crew at advantageous terms, leaving his original American crew high and dry, without sufficient funds to make it home. I raised this possibility with the captain, and the procession of removals of sailors from his crew abruptly halted.

Then there was the machinist's mate, a burly Wallace Beery type of pronounced paranoid views and great strength, who failed to sail with his ship. A police tip led me, bar by bar, to his whereabouts, in a series of waterfront areas full of colorful characters who wouldn't have passed inspection in a Bordeaux drawing room. Eventually, following a physician's examination, he was pronounced fit to travel, and funds were secured from his shipping lines for his return trip. Then he disappeared again. I was called by the ship's local agent on a Saturday afternoon and told that our sailor had holed up in a Singapore hotel, and so I abandoned plans for a quiet afternoon at the Singapore American Club (where a businessman's wife once told me that she was sure that I worked for the CIA because I always wore sandals—which surely contained a miniature transmitter—around the pool).

Now, the great operating principle of a consular officer is that any problem that is out of his consular district is no longer his problem. Once my sailor left Singapore, I blush to say, he was therefore no longer my concern. I went to the sailor's hotel room to check out his health. Physically, he was fine. Mentally, he was fragile. At one point he started to come after me with one of the biggest wrenches I had ever seen. I extricated myself from that predicament, and located his examining physician, who eventually got him calmed down for the night.

I discreetly arranged for his flight out of Singapore with the aid of an airline official who owed me a favor, and who passed the word to flight personnel along the way. I sent a cable to every American consular officer within reach, and notified the sailor's relatives at his stateside destination.

That after a while bothered my conscience. What if he had acted up during a flight? Well, flight personnel were prepared, the sailor was sedated, and his family was waiting for him. It was the best compromise that I could puzzle out in a situation with only bad alternatives. Furthermore, other officers at the Consulate General would not even have wanted to hear about the problem. It was not a "foreign policy" matter. Still, it bothered me. And so I was considerably relieved when I checked with my airline contact a day or so later and found that the flight had gone smoothly, with no problems from this passenger, and that he had indeed been met by his family in California.

The constant presence of American merchant shipping did have one nice bonus, though. Every consular officer sooner or later faces the problem of indigent American citizens who need help in arranging the transfer of funds from home for their repatriation (or travel to somebody else's consular district). When there isn't any responsible person to ask, the problem is much worse. Very occasionally, a consul can work something out with an American ship captain, and I did so in the case of an American of college age who had run out of money.

He seemed a decent fellow, and as far as I could determine, was indeed going back to college, but had underestimated his travel expenses, and had nobody at home to whom he could turn. He was now broke, and "How can you help me, Mr. American Consul?" He seemed reasonably athletic and fit, and so I suggested the possibility of his working his way back to California on an American merchant ship. He jumped at the idea, and kept in touch with my office on a daily basis staying, as I recall, at the Sikh Temple, which was respectable and safe, but hardly the Hotel Bellagio.

In about a week, a captain came in with a sailor to discharge, who was being sent back home for illness. It was not a skilled position on ship, and I brought in the young college student. On my say-so the captain agreed to take the young man on his return voyage, for the ship was leaving Singapore in two days, and so I formally signed him onto the ship's articles.

Six weeks later I received from the young man a very nice letter of thanks that we have kept. The voyage had been interesting and the work, although arduous, had been nothing he couldn't do. He had earned his way back, made some money in the process, and now was about to begin his next college year. Thank you, Mr. American Consul.

At that, the college student surely was a moral cut above the next sailor that I had to research. This fellow had lived in Singapore following his discharge from ship's articles for a few months. Now he was applying for a job with the federal government that required a security clearance, and so I was asked to check out what he had been up to in Singapore.

That led me to the Erin Hotel (not its real name). The manager indeed remembered the man, who had paid his bills regularly, and not caused a fuss. Actually, the place remained popular amongst the seafaring crowd, judging from the men in the dingy lounge. It was hard to see one's way through the thick cigarette and cigar smoke, but it didn't take too long to figure out that the female help at the Hotel Erin was young, reasonably attractive, not given to overdressing, and had a penchant for sauntering up the stairs with the clientele.

And so I turned to the manager, noting that his hotel was full of sailors of all different nationalities, and yet it was nowhere near the docks where their ship landed. How did they ever hear about the Hotel Erin, and what had attracted them here in such numbers?

"It must be our wonderful Italian food," he deadpanned, as I declined his invitation to stay and try the specialties of the house.

The spirit world, perhaps given the animistic beliefs of some Singapore residents, seemed to be evident from time to time. Our introduction to this aspect of things came just after we arrived in Singapore, when Lois interviewed as a maid Ah Wah, clearly one of the finest people and cleverest employees we were ever fortunate enough to employ.

Ah Wah had worked for the Consul General, at the imposing residence on 53 Grange Road. However, a murder had occurred in the servants' quarters shortly before our arrival in Singapore, and so Ah Wah flatly refused to live there. "There were spirits," she said, shuddering.

Perhaps there still are. I once helped with the administrative planning for the Fourth of July Reception held on the fine lawn at 53 Grange Road. To keep the dust down for the evening reception, I put on the sprinklers, to water down the lawn. Unfortunately, I overdid it, and throughout the evening, ladies in high heels found themselves slowly but irrevocably sinking into the lawn!

In Singapore, I soon became acquainted with the Dean of the University of Singapore Law School, a natural development since I had taught law before entering the Foreign Service. At the Dean's request, I was asked to lecture on international law, and did so before a good and motivated student body. I also helped establish their moot court competition.

Icing on the cake was my selection as an honorary Member of the Law Faculty. A colleague was Vice Dean Tommy Koh, a fellow graduate of the Harvard Law School, who I suspect was looking for someone to help him enliven the otherwise insufferable law faculty meetings. We started making them more interesting, but not before I had a tiff with the Consulate General's Budget and Fiscal Officer. She urged disapproval of my voucher for a luncheon with Tommy. I argued, on the contrary, that this was an important man who would become even more so in the future. The Deputy Principal Officer sided with me.

Ambassador Tommy Koh later became Singapore's Ambassador to the United Nations and to the United States, and my friend "Punch" Coomaraswamy, who taught evidence and enjoyed coming over for dinner to argue forthcoming criminal cases, became Singapore's Speaker of Parliament, and later also Ambassador to the United States. I was the only officer at the Consulate General to know either man, when Singapore was in effect expelled from the Malaysian Federation.

That event, now celebrated as Singapore Independence Day, took place on the first week that I ever pulled duty as Duty Officer at the Consulate General. Looking back, I should have taken far more seriously Ah Wah's warnings "not to leave the house today—there may be trouble." But at the time we were far more concerned with events at home. Lois's father had just had a heart attack. He did not survive. There were no official funds for compassionate travel, and we couldn't afford it ourselves. We tried to make plans for Lois to go home for the funeral. Our Naval Attache, Commander Heiderer, even booked Lois on a military flight to Baguio, The Philippines, with a connecting flight home. Then, security concerns closed the military airport, and it reopened too late for Lois to make connections in time for the funeral.

More pleasant memories from our tour in Singapore included the birth of our son Warren Burke Shepard, and the welcome visit of Lois's mother. But I am glad that State Department pursestrings have become less miserly, and in these circumstances, a flight home would now be officially authorized.

We did have occasions to travel across the causeway to Malaysia even after the political separation. We both wanted to see the fabled private zoo of the Sultan of Johore, but when we did, it made us both sick. The animals were magnificent, but they were kept in small cages, or paced endlessly back and forth in what amounted to prison holes in the ground. Later, when Lois became President Reagan's Director of the Institute of Museum Services, with responsibility also for federal grants to zoos throughout the United States, she remembered that, and funds were provided for natural habitats that were appropriate for the animals and more interesting for the visitors.

Malacca was a fascinating coastal town, with little left from its colonial past except for an enclave where descendants of the Portuguese settlers made a meager living as fishermen, supplemented by Malaysian governmental programs. The remnants of St. Francis Xavier's Citadel may still be seen, but if you want to copy a British gent of the last century and buy a Malacca cane, light and flexible, the wood probably now comes not from Malacca but instead from near the border with Thailand.

We went swimming off the Malaysian coast from time to time. On one memorable occasion I sat for a shave in a Chinese godown near the water, and it became a contest of wills that I hadn't experienced since Fort Benning. "Am I really going to go through with this?" I asked myself, particularly when it became clear that the barber, whose razor was extra sharp, didn't bother with frills like shaving cream!

A few miles down the road we parked the car in a secluded spot, took out our towels and picnic lunches, and had a nice day on the beach. We returned to find the driver's side window slightly open, and quickly discovered that an enterprising burglar had managed to get into the car and rifle through my wallet, which had been left in a coat jacket on the back seat. He had taken half the money, not all of it, perhaps figuring that I wouldn't bother to report the loss if I had enough gas money to get home. Malaysia is a highly civilized country, it seemed. Even the thieves have standards!

In neighboring Kuala Lumpur, it was well known that the Political Counselor's residence was haunted. It got so that visitors refused to come, a disaster for official political representation by any standards. When I held the Malaysia and Singapore desk in the State Department, the house's occupant told me that he had arranged a full-scale exorcism of the residence, conducted by a Malaysian Government official who had been active in the antiterrorism movement during the Emergency of the 1950s against the communist insurgents. After several days, the final exorcism was in fact broadcast!

That was not the case with a house in Saigon. My very last night in Viet-Nam during my first tour was spent at a dinner party given in my honor by an Embassy officer. Since the house was really quite grandiose I couldn't resist asking my host how he had happened to get it. He said that the house was haunted by the ghosts of two Frenchmen who had been murdered in their beds, throats slit ear to ear in the earlier, Viet Minh uprising against the French. Sure enough, whenever a servant broke a glass, it was because he had seen one of the murder victims! At the end of the dinner I was pretty close to seeing them too, and I was doubly glad to be on the plane the following day.

Haunts of diplomatic premises are not confined to the Far East by any means. The Defense Attache's house in Budapest is part of Castle Hill, and comprises a tower section which is said to be haunted. This is a rather recent haunting, we were told, in fascinating detail during a Washington dinner by a recently returned Army colonel, a rational sort who had spent a lot of effort trying to find out what caused those disturbances in the tower, and why nobody could spend the night there undisturbed.

Some psychic disturbances could be explained rather easily. The officials of the British charity which got such a reasonable rental on downtown real estate in Singapore, and who later wondered why nobody came near their premises, would have done better to check out the house's history before signing the highly favorable lease. They would have discovered that they were leasing what had been the headquarters of the Japanese *Kempetai* (Gestapo) during the Occupation. Locals could still hear the screams.

As Country Officer for Malaysia, Singapore and Brunei in the Department of State a few years later, I had the opportunity for a return visit to the region. Singapore seemed even more modernized, and very prosperous, and Ambassador John Holdridge hosted a reception at 53 Grange Road. This time it was held indoors, so there was no problem of visitors sinking into the dampened sod. In Malaysia, I visited the Thai border regions, as well as Kuala Lumpur, and Ipoh, for an exposure to a variety of Malaysia's ethnic and commercial concerns. As usual, it was fun visiting the markets, and buying some colorful cloth material to be made into dresses for Stephanie and Robin, with a batik shirt or two for Warren.

The highpoint of this trip, though, was my side trip to the island of Borneo. I visited the Sultanate of Brunei, and was regaled by a locally based British banker who told me about the old days of court etiquette, when the Sultan had to be addressed through the circular Official Ear Trumpet, so that his royal ears would not be profaned through direct discourse from a commoner. I attended Easter services in Kota Kinabalu, Sabah, in a beautiful Anglican church overlooking the harbor, where the services began with prayers for a congregation in the State of Washington!

In Kuching, Sarawak, I visited a former Land Dyak headhunters' long house, toured the Sarawak Museum and later had dinner at a country club that was right out of the prewar colonial era, with the welcome change that everyone was now welcomed for membership. Worth taking a look at also in Kuching is the *Astana*, or official residence for the Sarawak Head of State.

When I had earlier left the Consulate General in Singapore for assignment to Saigon, on the last day I entered my classroom at the University of Singapore Law School, I was touched to see banks of flowers, largely orchids, in every corner of the room. I started to express my gratitude, but a blushing student shot up her hand and got up to explain. "But Mr. Shepard, the flowers are not for you. They are for Prime Minister Lee Kwan Yew, who will be addressing us here in the next hour!"

That reminds me that on my last visit to Singapore, quite by accident I ran across and recognized the government agent who had been assigned to monitor my international law classes at the Law School. He was immediately noticeable then because he was ten years older than the other students, and seemed also to be taking notes more conscientiously than his younger colleagues. I went over and introduced myself, and he acknowledged that he had been my former student. "But your classes earned me a civil service promotion," he beamed. "Six months after you left we had a written examination and there was a section on international law, which I knew well because of your course. I was the only one to pass the test and be promoted!"

I wonder if those who had been assigned to my case in Budapest could have said as much!

CHAPTER 8

▼

CRIME AND PUNISHMENT

One of the main tasks of an American consular officer is to assist American citizens who have run afoul of local law. Since this was a very farreaching responsibility, I didn't at first limit my intervention to classic cases of American citizens on trial. In the beginning, I probably went overboard in a case or two, substituting eagerness for good New Hampshire common sense.

In my first consular position, in Singapore, local police authorities were short of Caucasian males for a lineup. I agreed to stand in, in a case where an American was suspected of a crime. I probably owed the local police a favor. There were seven or eight of us in the lineup, including the suspected miscreant. Instead of just filling in, it suddenly dawned on me with growing apprehension that, well, the suspect in police custody was about my height and weight. Then the witness went up and down the line several times, eyeing me suspiciously.

That's all I needed, with Foreign Service promotions grinding to their customary halt. I could see the Associated Press treatment of the lineup now…"Witness Picks American Consul As Thief In Singapore Police Lineup!" At length, the ordeal ended, and the witness fingered one of my fellow suspects (who was not, as I recall, the chap that the police had in custody at all). Then and there I stopped volunteering to take an active role in host country police procedures.

However, the host country's police authorities are key people for a consul to know. They are every bit as important as elected officials, or people in the education or legislative heirarchy. They shouldn't be forgotten when a consul is entertaining. And yet, time and time again, I would hear from police officials that they had never before talked with, let alone met socially, an American consular officer.

Of course it also helps if you are assigned to a country with a fair and decent legal system. It probably won't be the same as our own, with the full protections of a jury trial, legal representation at all stages, and the presumption of innocence. But fundamental fairness must be present throughout, and a consul can help assure that. If not, there are grounds for official protest, and perhaps securing better treatment.

I got to know the Prefect of Police in every jurisdiction of the broad Bordeaux consular district. Sometimes, they would call me when an American citizen, usually a youthful indigent, seemed to them to be having problems. Then I could step in *in loco parentis* and help the young person sort himself out before trouble arose, with a small loan of money from the revolving fund, or a cable back home for funds.

Sometimes I heard about a problem long after it was over. Two American girls sent me a tape and transcript about their outrageous treatment by French customs authorities along the Spanish border. I sent a letter of protest to the ranking regional customs authority, citing what had happened. A month or so later I received an official reply from that official, who had looked in cursory fashion into the incident, and satisfied himself that his officers had acted properly. With that in hand, I sent him the full tape, a rough transcript of what they had said to the young women, and an angry official protest. That quickly changed matters.

What is a crime, of course, depends upon where you are and what the local authorities say is a crime. One of the saddest stories that I heard in Budapest concerned a young woman in the grim days just before the 1956 Hungarian Revolution, who had taken the bus along the same route that I sometimes used going to the Embassy. (Until security became a problem, I always preferred to take local public transortation wherever possible. This offered good insights into what people were experiencing, and gave me a chance to read the local papers without interruption before I got to the office.) One day, she wore a silk scarf that a friend had sent her surreptitiously from Italy. She was apprehended by police on the public bus, and condemned by a "people's court" to three months of imprisonment for this "anti-social behavior."

Sometimes, all was not as it seemed. One Saturday evening in Budapest, I was called to the telephone, and picked up the line to hear a frightened American citizen. He had just arrived at the Budapest Airport that afternoon, and had been separated from others who had arrived, then isolated. Demanding to speak to the American Consul, at length my number had been dialed for him.

The entire business was rather puzzling. Hungary at that time was desperately trying to encourage tourism of all sorts, and incidentally earn badly needed hard currency. From time to time the Hungarian Secret Police, or *AVO*, would try to coopt an American citizen, but invariably those were Hungarian-Americans, with some family connection to the old country that could be used as a pressure point. We took strong official exception when we found such a case. This was different, for the visitor was a Californian with no previous connection with Hungary of any sort, family or otherwise.

I calmed him down with a few minutes of general orientation, and told him that either there was more here than met the eye, or I would have him out of custody shortly. Then I asked him to pass the phone to the most senior Hungarian official in the room. He did so. I could tell by the voice, even if I hadn't heard the title "Doctor," that I was dealing with an educated professional man, not a secret policeman.

We spoke in Hungarian, and the matter was soon sorted out. The visitor had come directly from an African nation where there was a cholera epidemic, and he had no record of immunization. They were required to keep him in isolation for a few days. We would have done the same thing if he had landed in the United States. I asked to speak to the American again, and briefly explained matters. His relief was obvious.

Then I asked what he was doing in Hungary, and he said that he had come to attend an economics conference. He had wanted to see something of Budapest, but the conference itself was sure to be a crashing bore. He agreed with me that as compensation for missing the city, he would have an adventure to dine out on when he returned to his campus that fall!

Of course, not all consular cases in this protective services area ended so quickly. One criminal case in Budapest lasted the entire year of my tour as American Consul.

When an American gets into legal or criminal difficulties overseas, the first reaction is to ask the Consul to recommend a good local attorney. Actually, consular officers are precluded from recommending anybody in particular. Even your local bar association in the United States probably wouldn't go that far. But a list of attorneys who represent American citizens is kept, with comments on their abilities to speak English, and a notation of particular legal specialties. In Hungary, I put together a new lawyers' list, carefully making sure that those on the list didn't mind. They did not—and that small detail in itself told me something about where matters stood in Hungary at that moment.

Lawyers, there as elsewhere, had their different strengths and specialties, and I got to know a number of them. One, a real *prima donna*, was a clothes horse who just loved his own arguments, which often succeeded. Another was a rather courageous attorney who took politically difficult cases involving Ameican citizens. I wondered why, and was told by a mutual friend that this attorney had never forgiven himself for not taking an active partisan role in the 1956 Hungarian Revolution. And so, he was now making up for it by representing Americans at the bar. Another lawyer was a convinced communist, who thought that it was her duty to represent any client in need. She was probably the ablest of the lot, provided one didn't contest her political blind spot.

Cleveland is the world's second Hungarian city after Budapest, surpassing Miskolc in Hungary for that distinction. And so it was not surprising that many of our Hungarian-American visitors to the Consular Section were from Cleveland. One was a popular radio announcer, who was apprehended while escorting a tour group back to Hungary. The offense charged was currency manipulation.

The Szappanos case had legal aspects, and other protective features. Specifically, I worried about Mr. Szappanos's health, and as time went on managed to plant that thought with his Hungarian captors. It took a while, but it worked.

The charge tried to make Mr. Szappanos into a currency profiteer, but such was not the case. The Hungarian forint was mantained at an artificial premium within the country, while it circulated at its true (and sharply reduced) value overseas. Furthermore, foreign exchange had to be given up to Hungarian state banking authorities, and exchanged for forints at the artificial rate. I am sure that those who had given dollars to Mr. Szappanos to pass on to relatives within Hungary would have applauded his efforts to obtain forints at their real value in Vienna, thus multiplying what their relatives in Hungary would receive, by comparison with the official exchange rate.

These allegations hardly showed a criminal, and his counsel portrayed Mr. Szappanos as a likeable man who had chosen a manner forbidden by Hungarian law to help people. The case might have been dismissed with a fine and a suspended sentence, except for the fact that Hungarian authorities wanted to make him an example, in order to stop the currency manipulation. The prosecution's attempt to portray Mr. Szappanos as John Dillinger was hollow. Even so, he was convicted and sentenced to prison.

I visited this American citizen as frequently as possible, first in the waiting room of the holding prison in Budapest (an infamous prison from 1956 and its horrifying aftermath), and then in the provincial prison where he was to serve his sentence. Each time, I could bring him some cigarettes, and a basket of food that Lois put together at our expense to supplement his monotonous and unimaginative prison diet. He was forbidden *deli gyumolcs*, or "southern fruit," such as oranges, these being generally unavailable in Hungary, unless of course one happened to be a member of the ruling communist heirarchy.

As each visit concluded, I told him that upon my return to the Embassy I would send a full report to Washington, and that I would immediately request my next consular visit. The important thing was to try to keep his spirits up, to have him get a bit of exercise if that was possible, and to understand that he would be returning to the United States. I did worry about his health. However, he kept his spirits up, and was eventually released and expelled from Hungary prior to the time that his full sentence would have expired. He returned directly to the United States, and I never heard from him again.

The grizzled fellow with the regional accent who presented himself in my consular office in Budapest one morning, refusing to state his business with my consular clerks, was quite a different matter. He wanted money. He could, he said, offer precise details regarding a heroin shipment now proceeding through Eastern Europe, bound for Western Europe and then the United States. He gave the names of several American narcotics control officials with whom he had had previous contact.

Given the time constraints of the impending heroin shipment, there was little time left to do anything but cable an immediate report, by the highest precedence. Clearly he had planned it that way. Still, I did what I could to flesh out his identity with linguistic evidence. He said that he had lived in the Far East, and in response to my questions, he was knowledgeable about that area. I placed his accent to within 100 miles of his stated hometown in France. On the chance that the story might be true, and in order to hear the details of the shipment itself, I put together what he had to say, and sent it off to Washington and elsewhere.

To my astonishment, and that of our Budget and Fiscal Officer, a cable came back authorizing the payment requested, and citing payment fund details by appropriation. This was real stuff, for Washington was telling us that his payment would come not from Embassy funds, but from a special allocation. As we had arranged it, the man returned, and was not in the least surprised that authority to pay him had been received. I took down the details of the heroin shipment, which would have done credit to an Eric Ambler novel. The heroin was being moved on the Berlin Express, that connected Western troops on normal rotation through the East German corridor, to West Germany. I absorbed the story, paid the man his money, and quickly informed both Washington and other posts on a need to know basis.

Then, nothing happened. We were not informed of the result of my reporting cable. "Oh well," said the Budget and Fiscal Officer, "his story was so good that you wanted it to be true." As part of my duties, it happened that I was Embassy Narcotics Control Officer. This involved occasionally sharing information with Hungarian officials, an odd position to be in, with the Cold War still our predominant fact of life there. As with Hungarian soldiers that I met and talked with in Viet-Nam, these officials seemed reasonable and competent, and I thought that some contact of this sort was useful.

Then out of the blue, a telegram was sent to every American diplomatic post stating that a meeting would take place in Washington to coordinate narcotics control efforts worldwide. All post narcotics control officers would attend. This might be an opportunity to find out what had happened to the heroin shipment that we had reported. Was it for real? What was the result?

I returned home for the meetings (complete with Christmas shopping lists for the children), and heard and took part in interesting discussions on drugs, where they came from and how they were processed, their addictive qualities and their human cost. The conference was coordinated by an energetic White House thirtysomething named Egil "Bud" Krogh. (Whatever the political administration, the White House always seems to produce a raft of youngsters who confuse assertiveness with judgment. It never seems to fail, and it is not a matter of liberal or conservative, or Republican versus Democrat. Something of this is captured in the television series, *The West Wing.* Perhaps it is something the White House Mess puts into the food.)

The Narcotics Conference, I must say, was well organized, and produced useful information in a fine cause—the suppression of the international drug trade. During one of the intermissions, I approached a senior official from the Drug Enforcement Administration, identified myself and alluded to the information I had passed on from Budapest. Had it produced any worthwhile results?

He told me that that cable had been received just in time to coordinate a major heroin bust, precisely along the route that my informant had outlined. It was, in fact, the biggest heroin interdiction ever successfully undertaken in Europe, he said.

It surely was only coincidental that, as we all later discovered, the leadership in the interdepartmental effort against narcotics was the White House Watergate gang. It has been said that the meetings gave them a defensible reason to get together from time to time to plan their strategies for political subversion. Oh well, at least most of them paid for their crimes.

CHAPTER 9

▼

SWIMMING OUT TO SEA

The very day I arrived in Saigon, where I was assigned as consular officer in 1966, I saw a revealing incident. I had just checked into my transient quarters and started walking downtown. Stopping at an intersection, I watched the traffic policeman (called "white mouse" from his uniform). He was directing traffic from his perch above the busy traffic circle. With sharply pressed uniform, gloved, the policeman executed crisp turns, beckoning traffic to stop or start. He looked very efficient. He had probably been through the Military Police School at Fort Gordon, Georgia, or the equivalent here.

Then my eyes glided down to the traffic itself. I saw that not one car was paying the slightest attention to what the policeman was signalling. They were darting pellmell across the intersection, colliding or nearly so, their klaxons screaming. Motorcycles and pedicabs added to the confusion, trailing dust and going every which way. It struck me that if this was an example of the South Vietnamese Government's authority with its people, we had problems.

I remember the *An Loc* Orphanage near Saigon. I visited this orphanage for young girls from time to time, first in connection with my consular duties, which included numerous adoption cases. As American Consul, I would be asked to go to the orphanage to be sure that the child concerned was healthy, before the visa was finally approved. After the third or fourth visit, as the father of two girls who enjoyed shopping for them, I noticed that each time I visited with a child, she seemed to be wearing the same white dress. And so I asked the supervisor, who admitted that was the case. They only had one nice dress, and that was used for a child when visitors came, to increase the prospects that the orphan would be taken into a new family.

Another sort of dress story stirs in my memory. My roommate, Jay NcNaughton, and I were driving downtown on Christmas Eve to get something to eat when he glanced down the street and said "Migawd...It's Miss World!" Sure enough, Miss World, a gorgeous young *sari*-clad Indian woman who was travelling with the Bob Hope Show, was there. Jay was driving our jeep, so I was dispatched to tell her that her "official Embassy escort" had arrived for the evening.

That worked, and briefly we basked in the company of this beautiful creature. Trying to make conversation, I asked what she thought about the Vietnamese national costume, the *ao dai*. She frowned slightly. "Excuse me, but I can't answer that. I'm not supposed to discuss politics in Viet-Nam!"

Military investigators, largely U.S. Army, sometimes kept in close touch with consular officers. They were concerned that Amrican citizens under investigation for criminal activities might try to leave the country. An American consul could get wind of that, either through a passport renewal application, or possibly through a visa application for a girlfriend.

And so I became very interested, as it developed, in one of the series of black market investigations that Army CID was running, against a PX official who was siphoning off official goods and selling them on the black market. It was quite a complicated operation, lucrative, and involved a number of accomplices. We kept tabs as the evidence grew and probable felony indictments accumulated.

Then one Monday morning, having some coffee before heading for the consular section of the Embassy, I read the Saigon *News*, which usually took five minutes cover to cover, allowing for the mysterious English that was often used. The PX employee's car had been found miles north of Saigon, in an insecure area. He was nowhere to be found. I mentioned this to a CID investigator later in the week. He replied that the man was surely aware that the dragnet was closing in on him, "and this was his way of swimming out to sea."

The man would probably be killed. But if by luck he were taken captive, possibly an eventual liberation would mean that he could come home with no conviction whatsoever. He might even be considered a hero. Which made some sense, given his alternatives.

After a few months I was transferred to the Embassy Political Section, which included a number of able young diplomats, including John Negroponte, now Director of National Intelligence. I spent several weeks there before being appointed Aide to Ambassador Henry Cabot Lodge. One staff meeting is etched in my memory. Political Counselor Phil Habib, a burly man with excellent political judgment who reached the highest levels of the diplomatic service and became an advisor to Presidents of the United States, was holding forth about the quarterly report that had just been submitted about the political and military situation in the Mekong Delta region.

The report maintained that progress was being made. Phil ripped it apart, citing an addendum that showed that not one voluntary report had been made in the entire region by a local inhabitant regarding the enemy's activities! "How can you guys say that we are winning in that crucial region when, with millions of inhabitants and enemy cadres all over the place, in three months not one single person feels secure enough to volunteer to us what the enemy is doing?" It was unanswerable.

My selection as Aide to Ambassador Henry Cabot Lodge put me in a line of Aides including Tony Lake, Peter Tarnoff and Dick Holbrooke, that had served that distinguished American during one of his two tours as Ambassador (which we referred to as Lodge I and Lodge II). As it turned out, I was Lodge's last Aide in Saigon, and the first for incoming Ambassador Ellsworth Bunker. My selection to work for Lodge had something to do with my fluency in French (which he sometimes preferred as a diplomatic language), but probably more to do with my proficiency in Yankee. I could usually predict his reactions before they happened, which helped things run more smoothly in the small office that directed the Mission in Saigon.

The assignment was an eyeopener beyond Viet-Nam, offering an opportunity to meet constantly a real American Who's Who, from Charles Lindbergh to General Omar Bradley. The most genuine celebrity I ever met, soft-spoken Bradley was the sort of man who made you rise instinctively when he entered the room. The assignment also made me critical about the press, particularly those who wrote their articles before the event they described had taken place.

We are all familiar with the end result in Viet-Nam, but the bravery of those Americans who served there, both military and civilian, was incontestable. And in the longer view, I think it entirely likely that time was bought for Thailand, Indonesia, and the balance of Southeast Asia, so that the "dominoes" never fell. So you can put me down as one who sees Viet-Nam in the overall Cold War context. Now, the problem is to engage the Vietnamese, and through economic leverage influence peacefully that country's emergence. It won't be easy, and it won't be quick.

As we used to say in Saigon, "Sorry 'Bout That!"

Seven day weeks, eighteen hour days were routine in the "Old Embassy" in Saigon, which was configured like a twelfth century Plantagenet fortress. I developed at close hand the deepest respect for Ambassador Lodge, whose weekly "Letter to the President" (actually a cable) summarized the conflict as he saw it. Lodge was a master of the English declarative sentence, that supreme instrument of communication and persuasion, and his legendary vanity had substance behind it.

By contrast, working for Ambassador Ellsworth Bunker, the same seven day weeks and eighteen hour days seemed like a vacation. It was not that Bunker was any less demanding, but the stress was gone. I really only annoyed him once, when a White House message arrived in the middle of the night, for which I was routinely summoned to the Embassy, for the Aide screened all cables. I then went to the Ambassador's residence and was shown in to breakfast. Bunker himself appeared at seven thirty and said hello, as though my unaccustomed presence at his breakfast table was the most normal thing in the world.

After we had breakfast and some talk, I gave him the cable, which as I had imagined outraged him. Then I made things worse. What better way to calm him down than to discuss college football. So I said that my Father had been at Harvard while he had been at Yale, and that I was often told about the epic Harvard-Yale football games of those years. Alas, I remembered too late that the reason that Father had trotted out those stories was that those were the great days of Harvard football under the legendary coach Percy Houghton, and that Bunker's cherished Yale football team had been skunked every year!

A better episode was Bunker's R & R trip to Kathmandu, Nepal, to see his wife, Ambassador Carol Laise. While on the flight I asked the pilot to bring us close enough for a good look at the Himalayan peak Annapurna. It was pristine and majestic, the most glorious natural sight that I have ever seen. When we landed in the Air Force plane, the Nepalese had no landing gear or ladders to get us off the plane, so they wheeled up a wooden platform that missed the plane door by four feet. Meaning a joke, I told Bunker that protocol demanded that he exit first. And so the Ambassador, well into his seventies, did so with a big grin. If there were a word for Ambassador Bunker, it would be imperturbable. He was the premier negotiator of his time, and a twenty year "political" ambassador so distinguished that the career Foreign Service made him an honorary career officer.

Nepal in those days had been visited by very few Westerners. It was before the plague of hippie truthseekers, and it was, and I hope still is, beautiful. As the birthplace of one of mankind's great religions, it was sometimes awe inspiring, with a light that recalled the legendary light of Greece, still sometimes visible when the industrial pollution in Athens lifts. I wandered the rough, unpaved streets of Patan, one of the smaller urban neighbors of Kathmandu, and went into a food shop. I may have been the very first American to do so. And by the corner wall the incense was burning to a shrine for the martyred President John F. Kennedy.

I remember one Sunday in Saigon, just before I started to work for Ambassador Lodge, when another officer in the Political Section asked me if I wanted to go out onto the Saigon River. I said sure, and was surprised to discover that the excursion included some waterskiing. After a while I tried it without much success, my mind dwelling on the fact that the enemy was on the other side of the Saigon River. Clearly we were within the range of highpowered rifles. Why weren't we all targets? "Because they don't think that way," was the unconvincing reply.

Returning to Saigon a few years later as principal staff officer for Secretary of State Rogers, I was struck by the tension at the Embassy towards Washington. It was nothing that they said, but rather what they did. Each visitor's office, including mine, had been fitted with individual wooden nameplates, hand painted. Why go so far to please?

Maybe I'm reading too much into it, but there were growing divergences of view between official Washington and our Embassy in Saigon. This visit was Embassy Saigon's attempt to plead its case on the direction that our efforts there should take. But what it told me was that the Embassy wasn't going to prevail. If they had to try that hard, it wouldn't work.

I also looked once again for a well-known Indian soothsayer, but couldn't find him. In my previous tour, this fellow was known for his uncanny abilties to predict the future, and I had visited him one evening with a good friend, an American businessman whom I suspected of working for the CIA. As we walked into his living quarters, the soothsayer looked at my friend and said "You are not what you seem!"

With that opening, we were a spellbound audience. My friend's fortune was not good, but the soothsayer told him that it would be an entirely different matter if he had been born in the afternoon rather than in the morning, as he had supposed. The next day my hardboiled friend called his mother in New York to make sure!

I was reassigned to Saigon in 1973 when Henry Kissinger's Paris Peace Treaty went into effect. Hungary, Indonesia, Poland and Canada formed the quadripartite International Commission of Control and Supervision (ICCS) to police the agreement. A number of Foreign Service Officers with previous Viet-Nam experience were assigned back to Viet-Nam for this purpose. Since I spoke Hungarian and had served in Viet-Nam, I was on the short list. Such an honor!

This time we were in the "New Embassy," the one where the helicopter liftoffs took place two years later. I looked up some old chums, and was told how the enemy had managed to carry its offensive so strongly into Saigon five years previously, in 1968, six months after my first tour there had ended. It turned out that there had been more funerals than usual in Saigon, where there were a number of large cemeteries, in the months preceding the offensive. Accompanied by fireworks and mourning relatives, the funeral corteges came repeatedly into the city. But the coffins contained not bodies but the weapons needed for the *Tet* offensive.

Our four-man unit in the Embassy each specialized in one of the four ICCS nations. Arriving in 95 degree heat from 25 degree Budapest in early February (I left after Lois's birthday, which infuriated everybody involved whose birthday it wasn't), it was exhausting for all concerned, not least for the Hungarian military in their heavy wool uniforms.

The night of my arrival, I was in the elevator of the Majestic Hotel down by the Saigon River, a Claude Rains location if there ever was one, when the Hungarian military commander, Major General Ferenc Szucs entered the elevator with an aide. A portly man who was clearly very uncomfortable, he proceeded to let fly some expressive oaths in earthy colloquial Hungarian about precisely what he thought about the weather, those who had sent him there, Viet-Nam, the food, the mosquitoes, and life in general. Here was a quandry, since I was going to pay an official call on him the following afternoon. I hadn't met the man yet, although I knew Ambassador Imre Uranovics, their civilian delegation head, from calls on him at the Foreign Ministry in Budapest, and I didn't want to start off our working relationship with the suspicion that I had eavesdropped on his conversation.

What to do. Before I got off the elevator, I turned and said to him in Hungarian "My sentiments exactly, General. I look forward to our meeting tomorrow afternoon." I introduced myself, and left the elevator. Then in the surreal Saigon world I went to my room, dropped off immediately to sleep, and woke up at two o'clock. There was just enough time to make my meeting with General Szucs, so I raced out of bed, dressed, and flew down stairs to the lobby, only to discover that my internal clock was still running on Budapest time. It was indeed two o'clock...in the morning.

That assignment, with John Helble (from Embassy Jakarta, who handled the Indonesians), Vern Penner (who handled the Polish contingent) and Steve Johnson (who was to handle the Canadians) was the most difficult diplomatic assignment I had undertaken. (Amongst the military delegations, there were several suicides.) But it did buy some time for an orderly American military withdrawal.

To do this, we had to establish four regional centers, and twenty-three sub-centers, for the four-nation ICCS throughout Viet-Nam, and we had to do it at the very time when our military effort was, of course, drawing down. When I left that assignment in July, 1973, I had been preceded by the last American combat forces in country. Everyone else had returned long since to "the world," as we used to refer to that part of the planet that excluded Viet-Nam. Astonishingly, and with the help of a resourceful American Major General named Jim Fairfield who was assigned to help our little unit, we did it.

As I look back on it, we can well compare this strenuous period, when we had to put together a working military observer peace agreement throughout South Viet-Nam, with more recent peacekeeping efforts. The lessons learned are still valid, although it seems to me that they have to be relearned each time. In Iraq and Afghanistan, I empathize with the peacekeepers, surely too few in number, who are trying to maintain law and order and build a nation before it flies apart. They are always under fire and there was insufficient advance planning for their civil affairs mission. That reminds me of the lack of preparation for the ICCS in Viet-Nam before we got there.

Shortly before the Paris Peace agreements were signed, Canadian External Affairs Minister Sharp had given a rather prescient speech, in which he voiced the hope that this time, some groundwork would be laid for military peacekeepers. Details like that were presumably beyond Secretary of State Kissinger, so shortly after my arrival, I got to cope with the fact that the furious Canadian military contingent was threatening to leave. They were right to be angry. They were "housed," if that was the word, in a huge metal quonset hut that radiated tropical heat at Tan Sohn Nhut Airport in Saigon under a constant low-level Republic of Viet-Nam Air Force flight plan. There wasn't even any air conditioning.

I helped sort that one out fast, and the Canadians stayed. I developed an enormous respect for the professional competence, both military and diplomatic, of our North American neighbors. Let nobody ever take the Canadians for granted. Neither were they there to slant any reports our way. They weren't. They were reasonable and fair, and in any scrape I want them on our side. If they are not there, there is a problem.

And they are definitely not Americans! I found that out in a godforsaken hamlet near Cu Chi a few months later, where the communist tunnel tours now run, when I was talking with a Canadian officer who with his ICCS fellows was keeping track of a very difficult sector. He had actually gone to high school in the Washington, D.C. area, and spoke American English with no Canadian twang whatsoever. I listened to what he had to say about their months in virtual isolation in the unfriendly countryside. Then, trying to commiserate, I muttered something about this being a very rough assignment He bristled, then threw his shoulders back proudly and said, "I shall go and serve wherever it is Her Majesty's good pleasure to send me!"

Putting the entire peace machinery in place summoned all sorts of diplomatic skills. I have an indelible memory of being asked to move an armed Viet Cong contingent from their encampment, to take part in monitoring as the agreement stipulated. They, of course, assumed that they would all be killed as soon as they left.

One American military officer and a Vietnamese interpreter and I entered the area, which was ringed with barbed wire. We were seated at a table in the open sun, and served a cup of tea. I talked with their leader in French for a bit, and tried to establish some points of trust and, failing trust, of reference. That effort worked, and the unit became integrated into the overall peacekeeping machinery. But I was very, very glad to leave that armed perimeter, mission accomplished.

The euphoria of being there, in the news and on the spot, didn't last long, and soon the Hungarians and the Polish contingent had their orders to be unhelpful. The ICCS produced reports which were painful to read, and a disgrace to the professionalism of the two communist military contingents. But there were various subplots to enliven the situation. Knowing zero about Southeast Asia, the Polish and Hungarian military would sometimes slip into Russian as a common language. Of course during the days of Sukarno in Indonesia, a number of Indonesian military officers had received some military training in the Soviet Union, and so understood Russian. They would tell the Canadians, and our debriefings from them were most helpful.

One of the reports that was produced can be taken as a typical ICCS result. In Two Corps north of Saigon, a bridge had been blown up, and a busload of Vietnamese civilians had been sent to their screaming deaths in the gorge below. The report was written by the Canadians, and concurred in by the Indonesian observers. It cited what could be unassailably shown. Parts of the exploding device had been found. They were of Czech manufacture. The area was one which had always been in the hands of the South Vietnamese Government, with some Viet

Cong activity. The bus had been blown up by the device and been destroyed, causing the driver and twenty-two civilian passengers to die. Draw the obvious conclusion.

There was, of course, also a Polish-Hungarian accompanying report. It said that buses often broke down. Possibly that was what had happened in this case. One never knew.

My last field inspection trip was by helicopter to the notorious Parrot's Beak region near the Cambodian frontier. My visit for many years later was the source of nightmares. Our preflight military intelligence briefing could not be held, because the last briefer had returned to the United States the day before. We did know, however, that the communist forces in the region now were possessed of heatseeking surface to air missiles. Have a nice day.

We flew out anyway to a small village, passing as we did a ruined French colonial villa that could have been a setting for the Catherine Deneuve film, *Indochine*. Somebody's dream had become a nightmare, and we were intruding. The children from the little town's elementary school had been carefully dressed and outfitted with flags to greet us. Probably they had been led to believe that peace and gentleness would now be the rule. I am sure that they were unprepared for the mortar shells that killed so many of them, twenty minutes before our arrival.

The local authorities tried to clean the square up, but of course they couldn't succeed. Walking across the square, I slipped and fell in what had been the blood of a child. Our pilot ducked small arms fire from the adjoining hillsides as we left the hamlet. And so the killing continued, long after our departure from that hamlet and later from the country itself, as wave after wave of Vietnamese took to the boats and themselves went out to sea.

My last drive before flying out of Saigon was to the *An Loc* Orphanage. My letters to Lois, and memories of the orphanage from my previous assignment, had produced some practical help. She had organized the diplomatic colony in Budapest, and sent me a generous shipment of new clothing for the orphan children. The Hungarian military ICCS contingent, always very resourceful and decent when they were given half the chance, reflecting their nature as Hungarians rather than the official communist ideology which they hated virtually to a man, flew the shipment over as free cargo on a troop replacement flight. They will now be staunch NATO allies, with greater belief in their mission.

And so I left Viet-Nam, glad at least to have taken a strenuous part in the predominant foreign affairs issue of the times, but overjoyed to rejoin my family.

CHAPTER 10

▼

IRON CURTAIN

When we lived in Budapest, much of the overt terror had disappeared. The memories of the heroic 1956 Hungarian Revolution were still fresh, and nobody believed official propaganda that it had been a "counterrevolution." Also nobody believed the Party line that the shell marks on buildings in the city were all still from 1945.

The New Economic Mechanism, a form of state economic control with some private incentives, had been worked out as a means of trying to revive a failing economy, while giving a needed safety valve for private enterprise. A number of Western diplomatic observers saw these developments as wholesome signs of a "Hungarian solution," but others including myself enjoyed the goulash and understood that the Kadar regime was detested.

There were ways of showing our annoyance. One of the wiring devices in our home worked through the telephone, and it had to be activated every morning. The early shift really was early. The phone calls came punctually at 6:30 every morning. We would growl upon answering, and the same voice would always say that they were trying to reach the Central Statistical Office. Then we struck back.

One morning our daughter Stephanie answered the phone in Hungarian with a cheery "Good morning. This is the apartment of First Secretary Janos Kadar." Whooping with delight, Stephanie came racing into our room and announced "Mommy and Daddy—you'll never believe what those idiots said....'Oh excuse us, Comrade, we must have misdialed. We're trying to bug the phone of the American Consul!'"

We never again heard from the "Central Statistical Office."

One evening, though, annoyed because my closet was humming, I said loudly to Lois while fetching a fresh shirt, "You know, Lois, the salaries in New York are getting out of hand. I've just heard that a verbatim Hungarian to English translator at the United Nations makes $10,000 every month, with a free apartment thrown in!" I could have sworn that the humming grew louder, and I may have been ultimately responsible for a closet defection!

The diplomatic community, of course, was spied on all the time. It was a job, I suppose, although what they expected to learn of substance was beyond me. Budapest was hardly Tokyo, Moscow or Bonn in terms of diplomatic secrets. It was not really a very healthy city, either, but that was because in their command economy, there was no environmental movement. Our first Embassy apartment was downwind from a hospital, which disposed of its infectious refuse by burning the bandages. That is why our daughters got to enjoy a summer at a mountain camp in Switzerland.

We gave a dinner in that apartment for some members of the medical profession. At that point, the public television extended series from Great Britain, *The Forsyth Saga*, was playing on local television in period Hungarian, and our guests were fascinated. I too became fascinated as they discussed the television series. They slipped into polite, prewar Hungarian, echoing the speech patterns that they had seen on television, even using titles that would have been theirs by professional right in a different Hungary.

That, of course, is how one hopes that diplomatic entertaining will proceed, without a hitch. In order to make sure that they did, the custom was to first book Lajos, then plan the rest of your dinner party or reception. The finest headwaiter who was approved to work the diplomatic circuit, Lajos was widely known to be a full colonel in the Hungarian military intelligence service. I can't vouch for that with certainty, but I do remember barking "Colonel!" in his general direction at one dinner party, and both Lajos and the British Defense Attache whose drink he was pouring answered me! His intelligence work aside, Lajos had a kindly side with children, and he painstakingly taught both of our daughters how to set a table properly for a formal dinner party.

Lois still recalls with horror a dinner party that we gave in our apartment for our consular staff. The two waiters arrived late, and tanked. They proceeded to get everything absolutely wrong, and refused disdainfully to carry out Lois's directions, which had been carefully explained to our parttime cook. It got so bad that it became, to me at least, hilarious. I couldn't wait to see what disaster was going to take place next.

The high point was probably the roast beef and yorkshire pudding. Since they didn't know what a yorkshire pudding was, they disregarded the horrified protests of our parttime cook, boiled it down and served it as a sauce over the salad. By this time, I was helpless with laughter. They couldn't have been more comic if instead of a Karl Marx economy they had been in a Marx Brothers film (which, come to think of it, their economy closely resembled). Lois was not amused.

One December, we were the targets of a badly coordinated program of harassment. We had moved to a house on *Roskovits utca* on the hilly Buda side of the city. The house had been built by a Hungarian military attache who had made money in the pre World War One period. Legend had it that he privately sold to an arms manufacturer the plans for a military proximity fuse. Our residence was grand, constructed with oak interiors, and is surely the finest diplomatic residence that we had in the Foreign Service. However, it was heated by a coal furnace, which needed constant firing.

For reasons that were never made clear, the Hungarian Secret Police began harassing every visitor to the house. The maid was allowed to come, but the coal stoker was not. Meanwhile, the temperature started to drop The saddest case was a Sunday cook, an elderly lady who earned a little money, and as we looked the other way took away enough food to last her through the week. She was badly frightened by these official thugs and never reappeared. We missed her, and her superb chocolate souffle.

It got colder, and the Embassy supplied room heaters, and made provisional arrangements for the children, who had fallen ill, to leave.

Outside our house, across the street, in the early fall there had been repairs done to the cracked sidewalk. For no particularly apparent reason, a portable warming room complete with wood-fired potbellied stove had appeared on our side of the street the week before our harassment began. It was on a direct line of sight with my first floor study. It was of course too late for the facility to be connected with the genuine workmen whose sidewalk repairs had been finished three weeks earlier. But it was from this little structure that our visitors were harassed.

Then I got mad and decided, after our official protests proved unavailing, to take more effective, and personal action. I went out to the structure, knocked on the door and went in and talked a bit with the astonished "workmen" within.

That same evening, there was a national day reception with the entire diplomatic corps present. I went up to one of my favorite Foreign Office heavies, who everyone knew was really a security service official, and started a conversation.

Tipped off, friends from the British, French, American and Austrian Embassies gathered around. I told the official that maybe he was right, that Hungarian socialism was the wave of the future. He was curious but interested. Certainly things were getting measurably better in Hungary, and I appreciated the work that had been skillfully done on repairing the sidewalk outside my house that fall. He beamed. Unfortunately, I continued, the little heated house that was supposed to provide for their comfort in the cold weather wasn't erected until after their work had been completed, but one can't have everything. He began to smell a rat. However, I had visited the structure that very afternoon, and could now testify to the real concern of the Hungarian Socialist Workers Party for the workers. Now he was beginning to sweat.

"There were six men in the little structure warming their hands when I visited them this afternoon. I must say that even in the United States, I would not expect four of the six laborers to be wearing jeans that had been freshly drycleaned—and five of the six to have manicures!" Everyone exploded with laughter. The little structure was gone the next morning. The harassment stopped, and was never resumed.

Of course it was one thing to be a foreign diplomat, and quite another to be Hungarian, hoping that things would change for the better. Still subject to socialist "law" and the secret police, Hungarians became self-policing. Sometimes we would go out for dinner, and it was chilling to see Hungarians out enjoying themselves at the next table. They would then have another glass or two of wine, and start to relax. Suddenly, they would realize that they were calling attention to themselves. Then they would stiffen, call for the check and immediately leave, probably hoping the police would leave them in peace.

On Sunday mornings I would often go to church on Castle Hill and enjoy the music in particular. Singers from the Hungarian State Opera were required to sing in the choir, in an effort to attract tourists. One day, curious about Protestant churches, I found my own denomination, and attended a service. It was not a good idea. I was of course not known, and my shoes gave me away as a Westerner. More people spent time staring at them than, I fear, concentrated on the sermon. At that, at least there were parishioners. At Budapest's Grand Synagogue on *Dohany utca*, since renovated through the generosity of the actor Tony Curtis in memory of his father, the holy books still awaited the faithful, but now there were many more books than there are worshippers.

The matter of defectors was a constant and preoccupying topic of conversation amongst our Hungarian acquaintances. Lois and I had met a very nice Hungarian professional couple, had dinner and parted with promises to get together again soon for a pleasant evening. But they never called, and were evasive when we tried to be in touch. Finally, Lois said that she had run into the woman at Vorosmarty's Pastry Shop in Pest. To her astonishment, the woman had been quite rude. The incident was puzzling, but only because we put it into a personal context.

Months later, we mentioned that incident to another Hungarian friend, with good contacts throughout the city. She informed us that the couple had successfully defected to the West. The plan had been carefully worked out The husband was on an official trip, and his wife and their son managed to get tourist visas approved for travel to Switzerland, where all three met and defected. When Lois had seen the woman, it was after her husband had left, but before her own visa and that of her son had been approved. "That is why she was so rude to you at Vorosmarty's. She couldn't take the chance that she was not being watched. That might have spoiled the entire plan. Surely she would be the first to apologize for her behavior if she ever saw you again," our friend said.

From time to time I would leave the Embassy office and just walk about, learning more about the city and something about what the people were thinking. Lois and I went out to the theater whenever we could, and very frequently were the only diplomatic couple in the audience. That was a shame, not just because others were inadvertently cutting themselves off from real Hungarians, but because Hungary enjoys a fine theatrical tradition that still shone, even in those days. The *Mikroszkop Szinpad*, a satirical review, would give us some idea of how far the Hungarians thought they could safely go in twitting the Russians.

The puppet theater was also of excellent quality, and the children always looked forward to going there. When I went to Viet-Nam, I carried a little drawing that Robin made, from The Wizard Of Oz, quoting the song "Follow The Yellow Brick Road" in its Hungarian language version, *Mindig A Sarga Ut*, for good luck.

Scanning the weekly program of coming events in Budapest, I was very interested to note that there would be a lecture on the works of Solzhenitsyn. It seemed rather a daring thing to do at a time when Solzhenitsyn was officially banned in Soviet Russia. I put on some old clothes and went along to the lecture, which was held in a smallish room of the university portion of Pest. Not many people were in attendance but the small room, which quickly became too warm, was filled to overflowing, mostly with young people.

Everyone had heard of *One Day In The Life Of Ivan Denisovitch*. The point of holding the lecture, which was actually more of an expanded seminar meeting, became fairly apparent, as the lecturer said again and again that the evils set forth in that book had been entirely addressed. So instead of being an exercise in daring curiosity, the point of the seminar was to put the lid on questioning the regime. Eventually, those present began to question themselves. "Have you read *Cancer Ward?*" The gossip spread around the room as, by word of mouth, the young people present informed each other of books that Solzhenitsyn had written. The young people slowly filed out of the seminar room, little wiser than when they had entered, and somewhat puzzled to understand why the evening had been scheduled at all.

We would occasionally hear about attempts to coerce a member of the diplomatic community. None seemed to have been successful. What may have been my opportunity came late one Friday afternoon, when a startlingly attractive young Hungarian woman came into the consular section, and with a mysterious air asked to see me. She carried with her a postcard said to be from an American somewhere in Viet-Nam, that had come into her possession. Perhaps we could discuss the entire matter at a nearby cafe, she said. I made a copy of the postcard, passed the copy along, and returned the original to her, saying that my wife was due to pick me up for dinner soon, and wasn't it odd that the postcard had made it to Hungary with the wrong Vietnamese stamps attached?

The young woman made a face at that, and stalked out of my office. That may have been the last time that our consular section was used as a test course for an intelligence service training mission.

Very often, I heard stories from Hungarians applying for visas to visit the United States about what their nation had come to, in the days before the 1956 Revolution. "You've probably never heard of me," one distinguished gentleman began, "but I was the Hungarian Walter Cronkite." He had been picked up by the secret police for that reason, and spent years in the camps. He even traced the Hungarian gulag for me, camp by camp.

Another gentleman virtually announced himself by his sonorous voice before he even entered my office. This American citizen had been a leading soloist with the Hungarian Opera, and he had fled in 1956. I asked him when he had decided to leave. He said that he had made that decision during a performance of Wagner's *Parsifal*. The dictator, Matyas Rakosi, was at the opera that night, and when the long first act ended, the applause was torrential. Pleased but puzzled, my visitor took a number of bows. Then the house lights were turned on. He saw that the backs of the audience were to the stage. Everyone was applauding the dictator, and nobody wanted to be the first to be seen to stop!

"When my people have come to this, I must leave," he said. When he came to the United States, he left Camp Kilmer, New Jersey, where many Hungarian refugees received transit housing, and took a train to Mississippi, where he had an acquaintance at the University of Mississippi's Music Department. As it happened, there was a party that night, and his hostess, intrigued by his accent, asked where he had come from. He told her about the Hungarian Revolution.

Her reply was "Honey, I don't know anything about politics. But if you are a rebel you had better stay with us in Mississippi!" And so he did.

That Christmas we had a glorious, huge tree that took up most of the stairwell at our residence. I learned that most Hungarians had small trees, and asked why. Friends told me that in the pre-1956 period, one risked prison by having a Christmas tree. Many people did anyway, but the trees were small, so that they could be smuggled under an overcoat. In memory of that period, many people still preferred to celebrate with small trees.

When we were in Hungary, there had of course been some easing from the terrible earlier days, when official murder of brave dissidents, and particularly those who had participated in the 1956 Hungarian Revolution, was the rule. As diplomatic officials, we still could not have much contact directly with Hungarian people, but as the American Consul, I probably got to speak with more Hungarians than anybody else at the Embassy. Sometimes valuable insights came from my own consular staff.

One day I was reading the mail after hours in the office, when Mrs. Livia Grusz, our senior consular employee, came in to say goodbye for the day. She saw me looking at a school catalog, and asked what it was. I explained that we had to start thinking about Stephanie's schooling if we stayed longer in Budapest, since the British Embassy School was only a primary school. I had therefore sent for some catalogs from schools in the United States, and if we stayed, Lois and I would have to make choices regarding Stephanie's next school. That seemed to summarize what had been lost in her own country, and the very distinguished Mrs. Grusz started to cry. "We don't have any choices in Hungary anymore," she said.

Our entire family gained impressions of the system. Warren, nearing his fifth birthday, when asked if he had any special request for his birthday cake, replied that he wanted one "like that, Mommy," pointing to a red star on a building in downtown Budapest.

Stephanie had a very practical view of the system. One day back in Washington, she remarked that it was good to be back in a country where you didn't have to bribe people to wait on you in stores! She explained that she remembered that when you went into a store in Budapest, the clerks sat behind their little counters, and since they were state employees and had no financial motivation, would rather drink their coffee and gossip than wait on customers. So you had to give them a 10 forint coin in order to get them to sell you what there was to buy in the store!

For the 25th anniversary of the 1956 Hungarian Revolution, Robin recited my translation of a Tibor Tollas prison poem at a gathering in Washington. There were no dry eyes in the audience, as people remembered their own experiences in Hungary, or those of loved ones they had lost.

Hungary was of course not an isolated communist country, and in some respects was better off than its communist neighbors It was instructive to travel about, and see what was going on elsewhere. One such trip was taken to Vienna, Austria, by Lois and a friend from the British Embassy. My birthday was coming up, and a friend at the American Embassy in Vienna had two Siamese kittens, just six weeks old, that would be just the thing for my birthday.

The ladies returned with Minou and Minouette in a cat carrier in the back seat. When they came to the Hungarian border, Lois realized that there might be problems, so she did the same thing that our Singapore friend Helen Ling had done when leaving Communist China with her own porcelain collection hidden in her luggage—nice smile, no local language. The border guards, actually decent enough youngsters, moved their metal detection devices around the car with the diplomatic plates as usual, all the while keeping up a line of chatter in Hungarian about the kittens.

"Did you see those cats in the back seat?" "Sure, what about it?" "Do you suppose that she has any papers for them?" "No, of course not. If she did, she would have given the papers for inspection with her passport." "Do you still see those cats in the back seat?" "What cats?" And that is how Minou and Minouette joined the family.

Lois and I drove to Czechoslovakia for a visit, just five years after Prague Spring, and the Warsaw Pact clampdown. It was wonderful seeing the old city, and a thrill to see an opera, Madame Butterfly, in the *Tyl* Theatre, where Mozart's *Don Giovanni* was first performed, and where several scenes for the movie *Amadeus* were filmed. It was good to taste genuine Czech pilsener and see something of the countryside. We drove out to Karlsbad, then a dreary place but formerly an elegant European spa, where the noxious waters still bubbled.

We were the only customers in a faded restaurant, where the staff seemed glad to see us, and anxious to please. The waiter steered us towards good choices, and suggested that we try Baked Alaska for dessert. We agreed with his suggestion, and time seemed to stop as we enjoyed a leisurely luncheon. As the plates were cleared from our luncheon entrees, we were served a perfect Baked Alaska. The cake had obviously been freshly made for us.

Driving into Austria from Czechoslovakia, the Czech border town was named *Hate*, and the atmosphere was in keeping with that name, as snarling dogs patrolled the Czech side of the border. On the Austrian side, a single, bored customs official waved us through, and the total absence of police machinery was its own statement.

We took a family vacation trip one Easter to Yugoslavia and Italy from Budapest, and it was sad to remember during the Serbian conflict how those picturesque Yugoslavian towns, such as Mostar and Sarajevo, used to look. Picturesque stone bridges from the Renaissance, architectural gems in small villages, and the fortified promenades in Dubrovnik which looked out on scenic ocean views, all were damaged and needed extensive repair. Returning to Belgrade from Athens several years later, we stayed with Harry Dunlop, the Embassy Political Counselor. He cautioned us about the gasoline shortage as our stay ended, and so we got up early, and drove to a station near the outskirts of town. There was a half-hour backup of cars at the one service station, and no guarantee that any gas would be available when we got to the head of the line.

Squinting, I thought that I saw another service station about five hundred yards down the road, on the other side of the road, the side for cars returning to Belgrade. I had the odd notion that just perhaps, that service station might have some gasoline. So I drove the car out of the line that we were in, drove up the road, made a U-turn, and sure enough, the service station was open and they had gasoline. I filled up the car, and we were on our way. No other car followed me to do the same.

Lois and I had an unforgettable experience with Russian officialdom during our tourist trip to Moscow and (then) Leningrad. While in Moscow, I stopped at the lobby ticket kiosk at our hotel, to ask if by any miracle there were two tickets available for the Bolshoi, where Maya Plisetskaya was dancing in *Anna Karenina*. The woman said that she would do what she could. Come back later. I did as bidden, and was pleased and quite surprised to receive two fine seats for that evening's performance.

The next morning, still recalling a brilliant performance, I went back to thank the woman, and found her in tears. "It's all your fault," she said. The manager had just bawled her out good and proper for selling me the tickets when they had in fact been reserved for another couple, who had flown to Moscow from New York, with this performance the main reason for their trip. "No matter," the woman said, "I saw them and I saw you. You and your wife would appreciate the performance better. You are *kulturni*. That's why I sold you the tickets instead!"

There were, for us, compensations for living behind the Iron Curtain at the time. If DVDs were unknown, we had films and projectors that the Embassy supplied. We were largely spared the searing disintegration of drugs and schools and protest that scarred the United States at that juncture, and the children had good schooling. The children had activities at home. They put on some rather clever puppet shows for us, and occasionally got to stay up late when American visitors came to dinner. Warren once explained to a guest, who was taking a third helping of turkey, that the turkey "was good for leftovers too!"

Nobody at that time could foresee the collapse of the communist system, although perhaps we should have made that connection, from the obvious fact that it was a hated, alien imposition on Eastern Europe. More to the point, time and again we found that it didn't correspond in the least to the desires of the people, was inefficient in the supplying of goods and services, and starved people of exercising their own initiative.

What was really important to people, though, regardless of the ruling system, was their personal life—their homes and families. For the old lady that I visited near the border on my social security errand, something much more lasting and fundamental than politics or ideology was at work. To others, like the ticket sale-slady in Moscow and the waiter in Karisbad (or Karlovy Vary), something else seemed to be at play. Of course they appreciated good tips. But they and many others that we met seemed to be saying to this American couple that they, too, had their own traditions of which they were justly proud. We shouldn't judge them by a detested regime over which they had neither control nor influence. We learned not to do so.

It was, however, equally clear that the Iron Curtain was also a shield that rewarded conformity and inefficiency. Its removal would mean that people would now have to work out their own national and personal concerns without a system that supplied the answers. We have seen that freedom is not its own panacea, and we understand the cost of keeping it. We are also beginning, I hope, to see the blossoming of peoples under new freedoms that will make them better off, with greater security, than they have ever known. When I think of my friends, in Hungary and elsewhere, it's worth it, for them and for us.

CHAPTER 11

▼

MISSING PERSONS

Finding missing Americans is a traditional and very important role for the American consular officer. Of course you must rely upon local resources. We do not replicate the police or the fire departments, or the Red Cross overseas. But it is vital to know these and other officials, and to have a clear understanding of how the local government works.

As Consul General in Bordeaux, my jurisdiction extended over twenty French *departements*, roughly several good-sized American states, which represented one-quarter of the entire nation. I made it an early priority to get to know each *departement*, both the leading political figures and the university people, as well as the French military and the police. My main contacts of course were the French administration, both elected and appointed, in each region, not only at the local level, but for the dozen or so leading cities in the region too.

Knowing the territory and its officials is worth the investment in time. You never know when the phone will ring, and what it will bring. Serving as a consular officer is like being a duty officer one hundred percent of the time. I've alluded to one missing persons case earlier, but it's worth spelling out here.

One Sunday night I was watching the late news on French television when the phone rang. It was the duty officer at our Embassy in Paris, who had an urgent message from the Department of State. It seems that an American citizen who had just arrived in the Pyrenees region for a skiing trip had to be informed that his father had just suffered a heart attack back in New York. Because I knew the region very well (and had the private home numbers of its officials), I was able to get through to the French *Sous Prefet*, the ranking figure in the small community where the American had gone to ski. She in turn, through the police, located the American, and within an hour or so I had spoken with him, and so informed our Embassy in Paris.

However, not all missing persons cases can be handled that quickly. I found that out when an urgent cable from the Department of State relayed a message from a United States Senator. It arrived on my desk, punctuated by exclamation marks from the Deputy Principal Officer, when I was a first-tour Vice Consul stationed at the Consulate General in Singapore. The Senator's next door neighbors were planning a wedding. Their other daughter and her husband were travelling in Singapore, and must return home immediately. The tone of the cable was formally polite, magisterial, and brooked no excuses The couple would be found, or the Senator would know the reason why.

This was the first of a series of cables from Senator Saltonstall on the subject, which lost politeness and gained intensity as the days wore on. His cables were answered, not defensively but factually, by messages that I drafted which detailed the steps that we were taking to find his missing neighbors. The paper trail was being established. If and when I found the missing couple, my cables would detail the steps that had been taken to achieve that result. If they didn't turn up in timely fashion, the Senator's staffer would be able to prove his or her diligence to the Senator. But all of that took a back seat to actually finding the couple.

Americans travelling overseas are encouraged to register at American diplomatic and consular missions along their route. By doing so, they let American consular officers know where they can be located in case of urgent need, ranging from an emergency at home, to a natural or political disaster in the foreign land. Of course, practically nobody actually does this, and our lost American couple had not done so.

They had arrived by ship one week earlier, and had left no indication where they were going from Singapore, or indeed, whether they were going to stay on the island, and if so where and for how long. And so we began by calling the usual places where Americans congregate, starting with the American Club. They had not been seen. Then I and my small consular staff started the laborious business of calling all of the hotels in town, to see where they might be registered. (We excluded the Hotel Erin, despite its reputation for tasty food.) Anticipating a gloomy cable from the Senator, we also checked with the police and the local hospitals, which thankfully were also without result.

As the days wore on, and the cables, now daily, arrived from the Senator (with helpful admonitions added before dispatch by officials in three separate offices of the Department of State—the East Asia and Pacific Bureau, the Congressional Affairs Bureau, and the Consular Affairs Bureau), the life of the Consulate General began to revolve around the missing couple. Staff meetings began, not with a political roundup by the Political Officer on the Prime Minister's latest speeches, as would have normally been the case, or even by the Economic and Commercial Officer on Singapore's latest foray into Jay Gould capitalism, as the Consulate General's pecking order would ordinarily have dictated.

No, sirree. The ordinary staff meeting rules had been suspended, and all that was required for opening formalities from the Consul General was for that daunting senior officer to peer down at Vice Consul Shepard across the long table and say "Well...?"

It struck me from the beginning that the missing couple was probably no longer in Singapore at all. After all, Singapore is a small island. Either they were making a side trip and would return, or they had long since moved on. With this in mind, I had suggested by cable to the Department that they copy their information to neighboring diplomatic and consular posts, so that my colleagues at neighboring embassies could join in the search, and broaden our chances for success. But before I had even sent that cable, I had called my colleague and counterpart, the Vice Consul at our Embassy in Kuala Lumpur, Malaysia, since Singapore at that point was still a constituent part of neighboring Malaysia, to make sure that the Embassy was also involved in the search.

By this time, we had informed every Western church, club or social institution on the island, and been in touch with all car rental firms and airlines. I was about out of ideas on where to look, and had come to the conclusion that the couple had long since left the island, when an excited staff employee opened my office door and interrupted an immigrant visa interview to tell me that the missing American couple was on the telephone.

They were in my office an hour later, calling her family. They were safe and sound. It turned out that they had left the island by bus the day of their arrival, and had then gone hiking and camping in Malaysia. When they returned to Singapore for some badly needed hotel rest and cleaning up after their tropical camping adventure, an alert hotel registration clerk had remembered my call, and had put them in touch with me.

They made arrangements to fly back for the wedding, and in the fullness of time a gracious cable arrived from the Senator. It is probably quibbling to add that they were rather grouchy about having their holiday interrupted for the wedding, and that consequently they made life as unpleasant as possible for the staff of the Consulate General while waiting for their flight. Didn't we know that their neighbor was Senator Saltonstall of Massachusetts?

I knew that the bloom was off the rose for my exploit when at the next staff meeting, Consul General Lacey peered over at me and said, "Shepard...Did you *have* to find those people?"

Then everybody laughed with us both, and we went on to the next item of business. So far, Tom Cruise hasn't called to inquire about the film rights.

Probably the most celebrated missing American has been Jim Thompson, who disappeared from a cottage in the Malaysian hills in 1967. Thompson lived in Bangkok, and had been a moving force in energizing the Thai silk industry. His disappearance was major international news, as he was well known and admired by many, and his home is still a shrine in Bangkok.

The area from which Thompson disappeared, the Cameron Highlands, is a well-known and very pleasant hill station in central Malaysia, a five hour drive from Kuala Lumpur, the Malaysian capital. Turning eventually into the mountains from Tanah Rata, one arrives at the Cameron Highlands and the coolness of the place, a verdant jungle by location and little Scotland by the architectural efforts of homesick expatriate British settlers, is a very welcome contrast to the heat and monsoon rain of the tropics.

Lois and I had become friendly with Dr. and Mrs. T.G. Ling in Singapore, where Mrs. Ling had an antiques shop. The outspoken Helen Ling, daughter of American missionaries, was an authority on China and its art. Over time, we persuaded her to come to our home for a series of informal talks on Chinese antiques. We combined those evenings with nocost potluck suppers weekly for members of the American business community. It was one of our first official entertaining ventures, and for the thousands of dinners and other entertainments we have given over the years, it is hard to think of one as successful. We all had good dinners, and learned valuable things about Chinese antiques and indeed about the Orient generally from an authority, and didn't have to spend any of the taxpayers' money in the process.

That is not to say that the evenings were without incident. On one occasion a businessman, an inveterate cigar smoker, inadvertently used one of Helen Ling's discussion pieces, a priceless low basin from the Ming Dynasty, as an ashtray! We watched in horrified fascination across the couch while this process was repeated several times. Helen Ling was in full oratorical flight, and it took her a few moments to connect our guest's actions with her antique. When she did, she told off the transgressor in no uncertain terms and then twisting the screw, remarked that she had known the young man's father in China, and "He didn't have any sense either!"

At length all was forgiven, and I seized the opportunity to ask about her escape from China as the Communists had taken over. Her antiques were well known, and there had been a death sentence put into effect for anyone taking antiques out of China, even though it was one's own property!

Helen was in a reminiscing mood, and she told us that she had indeed left behind most of her collection. She had decided to take her miniatures, which then formed the basis of her collection and the start for her fashionable antique shop in Singapore. Although her Mandarin (and, I think, also her Cantonese) was fluent, she packed her antique miniatures in a steamer trunk and covered them with layers of female foundation garments When the outgoing customs inspection officers started to go through her trunk, this tough-minded lady turned kittenish, pretended not to understand a word of Chinese, and watched while the redfaced customs officers went through several layers of girdles and such before stopping and waving her impatiently through the line. She had faced a possible death sentence, and a minimum of certain long imprisonment and the confiscation of her property, but she had managed to leave China with some of her own property after all.

The Lings had purchased a property in the Cameron Highlands, a Tudor style cottage they called Moonlight. It was said to be a very advantageous purchase when they bought it, for property values were depressed during the Emergency in Malaya, an armed communist insurrection centered in the interior. Thanks to Helen Ling, Lois and I had a delightful holiday there, enjoying the beautiful surroundings, the cooler air, and an outing or two at the Smoke House Inn, where bountiful afternoon teas were served and roast beef was the specialty of the house, not to mention steak and kidney pie. Possibly the only jarring note was the tiger trap that was set less than one hundred yards from Moonlight Cottage. We were told by the gardener that a tigress had been shot on the property a few months earlier, and that the male had been seen occasionally prowling in the vicinity.

It was the following year that Jim Thompson disappeared, while a guest of the Lings at Moonlight Cottage. There are a number of trails in the region through what is essentially highland jungle, and those trails crisscross and vanish suddenly in the dense overgrowth. Despite a thorough organized search, Thompson was never found and remains missing to this day. The theories that followed the minute reconstruction of Thompson's last days spun into tales of espionage, kidnapping or murder, and decades later the mystery remains.

Except for me, that is, for I see a personal tragedy, not a convoluted mystery. I think it quite possible that the tiger found his prey and avenged its own loss. Actually when the Thompson disappearance made the headlines I was serving in Saigon as Aide to Ambassador Henry Cabot Lodge, and had mentioned to him this idyllic retreat in the Cameron Highlands. His interest in a holiday there stopped rather abruptly with the news of Jim Thompson's disappearance!

The Cameron Highlands episode in Malaysia reminds me of a disappearance in quite another dangerous mountainous region, the area near Delphi in central Greece. It is an area for experienced climbers, and Mount Parnassus, for which Montparnasse in Paris is named, is a center for excursions of all sorts. The region is, however, rather dangerous, and is given to temperature shifts and the onset of fog.

Early one Saturday morning I was the Embassy Duty Officer in Athens and had just poured a cup of coffee and was starting to read the cables when an urgent message came in from the State Department reflecting the concerns of a United States Senator for one of his constituents. Here we go again, I thought. It seems that the young man had been reported lost from a tourist group in the mountains near Delphi.

This was a potential crisis, and I checked with the Ambassador and notified Greek police and military authorities before calling hospitals and hotels throughout the region. Our search lasted throughout the day. A later cable informed us that the young man's father had booked a flight to Athens. I called the family in the United States to tell them of the steps that we were taking, and to try to get some understanding of the young man. I learned of this vacation trip, which had long been planned, and heard that he had something of a history of stressful incidents. It rather sounded to me as if the family was feeling some guilt for letting him set off by himself on such an extended trip.

As the day wore on, the weather in the region worsened. I was able to locate the tour group, which by this time had left Delphi and was in another part of Greece, and talked with a group member. She said that the young man had seemed rather preoccupied. She added the detail that cars had been plentiful in the mountainous region where the group had been sightseeing.

The Greek search and air helicopter mission that I had requested on behalf of the Embassy had scoured the mountainous countryside without result. Greek military authorities called to tell me that they could perhaps put in a bit more time, but the fog was beginning to roll in, and while it was always possible that the missing young man could be found in that region, the search in that mountainous area would be largely repetitive, with reduced visibility.

I thanked the Greek military liaison officer and suggested to them that they stand down for the day. I thought it wrong to endanger the lives of rescue workers, and something troubled me about both the disappearance and the family's reaction. On a hunch I looked up various train schedules from the region and sent an urgent message to every American consular mission within a few hundred miles.

The next day I was called by one of our consular officials in Germany. The young man had showed up there, broke, and was asking for financial help to get home. He had wandered off from the group, hitchhiked to the nearest town, and then taken public transportation north, leaving Greece even before we had been notified that he was missing.

I briefed my colleague in Germany, and then called the young man's family with the news that their very lost young man had been found. And I was glad that my hunch had turned out to be correct, and that no searchers had crashed in the fog on a fruitless quest to find him.

CHAPTER 12

▼

VISAS

Visas are the essential business of an American consular office. Although their necessity may be waived from time to time by agreement between the United States and the host country for certain classes of visitors, most visitors require visas, and all immigrants do.

The difference between an immigrant visa, for someone who intends to stay in the United States and become a citizen, and a nonimmigrant visa, for a tourist, a student, or a businessman, for example, is essential. Many persons who are refused nonimmigrant visas fail to get them because the consular officer believes that they are really intending to be immigrants, and stay permanently in the United States. It would not be fair to allow someone who intended to do so to come as a nonimmigrant, and then file a petition to change his or her status, while others waited their turn for immigrant visas.

Visa law tends to be complex, and has bred its own specialty at the bar. Some ineligibilities may be waived. In Hungary, for example, where many persons were unwilling members of the Communist Party before the Iron Curtain crumbled, that ground of ineligibility could be waived for a visitor upon application to the Immigration and Naturalization Service.

Probably all consular officers, and most American Foreign Service Officers, regardless of their eventual specialization, will start their careers with a tour on the visa line in a consular section. At a small post, the consular officer will encounter nearly every type of visa application. At a larger one, there may be specialization, with different officers handling nonimmigrant and immigrant visas. Here, the aspiring diplomat meets the public for the first time, again and again, and does his or her best to apply what Congress has decreed.

It is interesting work, and can be wrenching when refusals are inevitably involved. One develops a feel for people and their character. I have investigated cases that looked great on paper and turned out to be fraudulent. I have also authorized the issuance of immigrant visas to people with very few assets, but a willingness to work hard that was unmistakable, and a view of the United States that I sometimes wish was more broadly shared by native born citizens.

What I have never done is give anyone a special favor because powerful voices could be raised in the applicant's favor. There is a rule of thumb that the more the consul hears about a visa application before the applicant shows up in person, the higher the probability that there is something wrong with the visa case. You can go overboard with that, of course. The best course is not to prejudge any case for any reason.

That is why I had to inform a fellow consular officer in Singapore who had urged issuance of a visa that I would be glad to reconsider the case—after the young lady's infectious eye disease had cleared up. (It did, and she later got the visa.) That is also why in Bordeaux I told several officers in the Political Section at Embassy Paris to back off or I would report their attempted interference on behalf of a visa applicant, the son of a prominent French politician, to the Deputy Chief of Mission, the Ambassador's second in command. In Saigon, an AID employee had developed the habit of bringing his girlfriends around the consular section from time to time to prove that he knew the consul and presumably, could arrange the young lady's visa to the United States at the appropriate time. I was pleased to play a role in throwing that worthy out of the country, and I suspect, out of government employment entirely.

Several of my experiences in Budapest underscored the importance of judgment in handling visa cases. They also had a political component. In one of my first cases, a Hungarian man was applying to come to the United States as a visitor, to see his family. The application was straightforward enough, except for the fact that he had been convicted and served time for a crime. Even that, given all the circumstances, was not necessarily fatal. He was visiting his immediate family, and an appropriate waiver could probably have been arranged.

The more I talked with the man, however, the less I was convinced that his conviction would have passed muster in an American court of law. It seemed political and trumped up. The man was not in a great hurry to travel, and so I pieced the case together, and saw that he had been railroaded by the Communist Party via a phony conviction, to lose his job and home, before a kangaroo court.

I put the entire case and surrounding circumstances together, and sent my research off to the Legal Advisor's Office, Department of State, with my opinion that this had been a "political offense," pure and simple, and should not even be counted as a conviction under our visa law. The Legal Advisor agreed with my assessment. The applicant himself was stupefied that someone who worked for a government would have helped him clear his record in this way. It was a nice feeling to have done so.

About this time, I read in the local Hungarian press about a bizarre criminal case involving the manager of a small local grocery store. The case was "political," but not in the same sense as the injustice that had been shown to my visa applicant. Technically a state employee, all of his prices were fixed by law. What the man had done was astonishing. Each day, he simply memorized the hundreds of prices for his commodities that were charged elsewhere, and tacked on a small increment. Each evening, he pocketed the difference between the "legal" price and what he had skimmed. This went on for some months before he was caught. I couldn't help but wonder what he might have done in a free economy.

One weekend, the Hungarian Communist Party was stirring up protests over the jailing of the American radical figure, Angela Davis. I was the designated recipient of protest petitions. The wireless file distributed by the U.S. Information Service that weekend happened to contain copies of excerpts of a press conference that Angela Davis had been allowed to hold from her jail. I made copies of them and handed them out to the protesters, all of whom were members of the Young Communist League, dutifully handing over their mimeographed petitions.

Two reactions from the Hungarian youngsters who had been bussed in from the provinces for the occasion were memorable. One, looking over the Angela Davis press conference extracts that I had just given him, got the point immediately and blurted out to a friend, "Look at this, Janos. She is freer in prison to say what she wants than we are outside of prison in this country!" And a bit later, a group leader delivered himself of a pat little speech for the benefit of his fellows and then, after they had left the room, stayed behind. He turned to me and said "Mr. Consul, this isn't going to be a problem for my student visa application, now is it?"

At least he realized the potential problem, unlike the applicant who forgot herself and kept referring to me as "Comrade Consul" throughout the visa interview!

Visas are entirely possible for people who are ill, provided that the stipulated medical procedures are met, and provided also that they are close relatives of American citizens and will receive medical treatment in the United States I have several times arranged the travel of such persons, with their medical attendants.

One immigrant visa case provided the most dramatic of all of my visa cases. It happened in Budapest, and the applicant was a Hungarian man, who had married an American citizen. The difficulty arose due to the man's mental disorder. He would be all right for a while, and then go off the deep end, requiring hospitalization and treatment. We kept waiting for appropriate medical attestation of the man's medical condition, and so the visa process stretched on and on, while his American wife waited, less and less patiently.

One evening, I received a telephone call from the distraught woman in the United States, wondering why I was holding matters up. She seemed to think that the problem was that I thought that her husband was an active member of the Hungarian Socialist Workers (Communist) Party, which he was not.

The conversation went on and on, and I was sympathetic to the delay in what I euphemistically called "this difficult case." But we weren't communicating. Clearly the lady and I were just talking past each other. Finally, inevitably, I mentioned something about his doctors, and how they hoped that he might have improved enough to travel by the summer.

"Improved from WHAT?" his wife wanted to know.

It dawned on me that she didn't have a clue about her husband's mental illness. And that proved to be the case. Apparently they had met and married during a trip that he had taken to the United States a few years earlier, during an interval of lucidity. Then he had returned to Hungary to finish his studies, and the problems had flared up again, and the poor woman that he had married, who had stayed in California, had been entirely ignorant of her husband's actual condition.

There was a sharp intake of breath on the other end of the line, followed by at least a full minute of dead silence. Finally, a subdued and resolute voice said, "I love my husband, and will do what I can to help him. Where do we go from here?"

I described the procedures for visa issuance, including the option of travelling with a medical attendant to privately financed hospitalization in the United States. Resolution of the case came after my transfer from the Consular Section, but I gather that with patience on all sides, it was satisfactorily resolved.

The most serious management issue that confronted me as Consul General in Bordeaux began as a visa issue. At that time, Iranian applicants hostile to the radical Khomeini regime were desperate to leave Iran and find sanctuary in another country. Inevitably, the United States became a favored destination. Not only Embassy Paris, but consulates in France as well as our diplomatic and consular missions in neighboring countries became little by little deluged with Iranian visa applicants.

Returning late from a trip within the consular district, I saw an unprecedented line of visitors to the consular section outside our office door. The next morning, I asked the Vice Consul for an explanation. He admitted being overwhelmed by a rash of Iranian visa applicants, who were not residents of the consular district. I told him to restrict the hours of visa issuance for Iranian nationals for the time being, and prepare a full report.

The consultations with Embassy Paris then began. Ugly rumors started to be heard that somewhere in Western Europe there was an American consular official on the take. (Later, following investigations, an indictment was issued, based on the conduct of a consular employee at a mission in Spain.) At the request of the Embassy, for the time being, I personally signed off on each visa approval for Iranian nationals within the consular district, following the Vice Consul's determination.

It wasn't long before an aggressive immigration law attorney from California, who had received large fees advising this flood of applicants, came to my office and tried to try to push me around. In preparation for the interview, I had had the American flag placed behind my desk, and my own degree from the Harvard Law School prominently displayed.. He tried to argue the law with me, which wasn't a very good tactic, since I knew the law better than he did.

I also told him in no uncertain terms that it had taken me twenty years of professional discipline to become a Consul General, and he was trying to destroy that, for his own profit, and I was having none of it. I told him that his applicants had told us that he had told them that they needed his help to apply for visas (which is, of course, not the case). To remedy that misrepresentation on his part, I would have prominently posted, in French, English and Farsi, the statement that no legal representation was needed to apply for an American visa.

I also said that according to the Vice Consul, several applicants whom he had refused had seemed to understand that moneys paid to this lawyer had included "a little something" for the visa itself! I rose, so that he got the full picture, with flag, and then threw the lawyer out of my office.

That settled one problem, more or less, while it created others. I advised the apprehensive Vice Consul to request, in writing, a full security investigtion from the Embassy of these events. Then, at the direction of the Embassy, I assumed total control over all Iranian visa cases, and began by limiting them to a reasonable proportion of my overall daily schedule. The Vice Consul took a needed rest, and I cooperated fully with the security investigation, which cleared the Consulate General of all of the rumored allegations, which I had brought to the personal attention of the Deputy Chief of Mission.

While this was going on, I was interested to reflect that the task that I had thought most important—getting to know the farflung consular district—had clearly taken second place to a looming visa application problem at the Consulate General, which had suddenly emerged. It was a good lesson in management. I knew that we were understaffed, with just two American officers, and was pleased when my successor succeeded in having a third officer, a Consul, assigned to oversee things at the Consulate General during her necessary absence in the district. I had had no such help available.

In a fairly short period of time, things returned to normal. The Iranian visa line dwindled and vanished. I never heard again from their lawyer, dire threats to the contrary. The visas that we did issue were entirely justified under the law. No genuine applicant was seriously inconvenienced by my slowdown policy. Several, as a matter of fact, indicated a measure of relief that we were proceeding cautiously rather than just denying them a fair opportunity to be heard. The lack of such consideration, after all, is why they had left Iran in the first place.

The local press, after one cursory article, dropped the matter. Their interest had been piqued by the fact that French applicants were for a time unable to get their applications processed in a timely fashion. This was a valid point, although there was no rule requiring that a visa applicant be a resident of the consular district. Meanwhile, the security investigation that we had requested was concluded, and in the bargain I had learned some valuable lessons about management.

CHAPTER 13

▼

VISITORS AND REPRESENTATION

The great thrill of consular and diplomatic service is representing the United States. Despite these jaded days when patriotism sometimes seems suspect, and a virtue is often made of selfishness, there is something to be said for representing an idea, an aspiration. Although there is no serious money to be made in a consular career, representing our nation counts for a great deal. Selling soap or lawyering are worthy pursuits, but it's not the same.

I mention this because one can give up a lot financially in a Foreign Service career. It was galling to realize, for example, that with regular promotions, I was always far below the median in annual salary surveys of my law school class. Indeed, it was fifteen years before my Foreign Service salary equalled what I would have earned, as a brand new law school graduate, simply by signing on with a major law firm as a junior associate!

However, there is another financial consideration. When one starts a career, one is immortal. There are few searching thoughts about pension benefits. There ought to be now, with private company pension schemes failing right and left. The fact of the matter is that an earned government pension, with annual cost of living adjustments, is a very fine financial inducement indeed. And so is the medical insurance, which may be kept in retirement.

My first actual representation of the United States was memorable. It took place when we served in Athens, when I was asked to represent the Embassy at the annual celebration of the breakout at Missolonghi. This was an incident during the Greek Independence War in the early nineteenth century, when an international brigade of volunteers, including men from the young United States of America, broke through the Turkish encirclement of the city at great personal cost. It was at an earlier stage of the Missolonghi affair that Lord Byron died of disease.

The ceremony began in the village orthodox church, at night, lit by candlelight, as hymns were intoned and prayers said. Then we proceeded on foot with a torchlight parade through the town and to the area, now profuse with statues, where the breakout had taken place. Consular and diplomatic officers from every nation that had sent volunteers to Misslonghi were represented. It was a strange mixture, from the Soviet Russian Consul to the French First Secretary.

We each, in turn, posed wreaths to the cenotaph of the fallen, by torchlight. It was impossible not to reflect on what had happened there, and the brave men that we were celebrating. It made me very proud of what those Americans had done there, hopelessly outnumbered, less than fifty years after the Declaration of Independence. I was very conscious of what an honor it is to represent the United States of America.

Years later in Bordeaux, as a picture on my study wall now recalls, we commemorated Americans who died in the Second World War who are buried in a small cemetery in a Bordeaux suburb. I stand there with Mayor, and former French Prime Minister Jacques Chaban-Delmas, the British Consul General, several Deputies and the Commanding General of the region. The crosses and the Star of David in that place reminded me of the names of the fallen that I had taken note of just before the picture was taken. They seemed to represent, in that small cemetery, our many traditions of religion and race, all resting now together in quiet nobility.

Bordeaux is a rather formal place, I was warned before arriving. That didn't bother me very much, and I found that the comparison I had made with my native New England was quite appropriate. People wouldn't gush over you, but there was a great measure of acceptance, provided that one spoke French and understood their rules. It was probably best not to emulate one of my distinguished predecessors, who turned the residence wine cellar into a pool room, and invited one of the *grandes dames* of Bordeaux downstairs after dinner to play snooker!

Since I had majored in French in college, this was a real opportunity to move to fluency. I looked forward to public speaking opportunities, and there were many. My secretary warned me about a previous consul, who read from a typed speech, slipping without being aware of it from the first page to the fourth, then back to the second! I once was invited to lecture on our constitutional doctrine of separation of powers before the Montesquieu Academy of Bordeaux, and was then honored to be voted their first American member.

Dinners and receptions were frequent in Bordeaux. I decided to serve American wines, having inherited a good representative sampling of fine American wines that had been left at the Consulate General following a *VinExpo* that Bordeaux holds every other year. I discovered that the more the Bordelais understood good wines, the more they appreciated our own. At one dinner, for example, Profesor Ribereau-Gayon, a wine authority then serving as the Director of the Institute of Oenology at the University of Bordeaux, was a guest.

A fine American red wine was served. As was customary. the waiters masked the label while serving the wine, but several guests asked to see exactly what was being served. They realized at once that the American Consul General was serving a California red wine. *Quelle scandale!* As they sipped the wine in disbelief, Professor Ribereau-Gayon gave his verdict. "This is a perfect wine. How lucky we are to taste it. It is absolutely the equivalent of one of our Bordeaux first growths!" With that pronouncement, everyone else fell into line and praised the wine extravagantly.

On another occasion, I was serving an American white wine, and the scenario was similar. Guests hadn't heard of the wine before. The authority at the table was Count Alexandre de Lur Saluces of Chateau D'Yquem. He was very pleased with the wine and surprised to taste it, noting that "This is a private reserve, and I thought it never left the owner's own estate!"

After those two early dinners, I had no problems serving American wines in Bordeaux. But I did learn something about French social castes when the wife of a Socialist Deputy turned to Corinne Mentzelopoulos, owner of Chateau Margaux, to ask "Why don't you rip up those expensive vines at Margaux and instead plant something cheap, that the people can enjoy!"

Anyone who knew me in Bordeaux also knew Mignonne. Lois gave me that enchanting Siamese cat for Christmas, and at breakfast the next day the cook, seeing her for the first time, said *"Qu'elle est mignonne, celle-la!"* Whereupon Mignonne was named, and if the name was right out of a Colette novel, so was Mignonne.

At one dinner party at Chateau D'Issan in the Margaux, I was seated next to probably the only person at the table who didn't know about Mignonne. I had been on a trip around the region, and Mignonne hadn't been consulted. When I returned to Bordeaux, she made it quite clear that she hadn't approved of my absence. Since Mignonne stories were frequent, I started telling this one, and halfway through, it dawned on me that the lady seated next to me didn't know that Mignonne was my Siamese cat! So in a roguish mood, I asked her advice on how to placate Mignonne and get beyond the present state of pique. She sighed and suggested flowers. (Actually, a platter of canned salmon would have been more to the point.)

The table rose for coffee, and the ladies went in one direction, the gentlemen another. I shall never forget the expression on that lady's face when the ladies returned. Frosty is a mild word, not near her actual mood. Glacial would be closer to the mark. No sooner had she embarked with the other ladies and started to tell them about the American Consul General's indiscretion than they informed her that Mignonne was not some *demimonde*, but instead my cat, as everybody knew!

We had many official visitors, in fields ranging from finance to the fine arts, and each provided an opportunity for me to open up the official residence and invite new people in. The same was true around the region, as the stay of Senator Paul Laxalt in the coastal Basque country proved. As probably the most prominent Basque in public life, those who met him were very proud of his achievements. Distinguished men and women reflecting our country's diversity were always the best walking advertisements for the United States. Members of Congress, Nobel Prize winners, journalists, literary figures, all travel abroad, and can enrich the local scene.

The most important visitor in many respects was the American Ambassador in Paris. His trips in my region were carefully planned, and required a great deal of advance work, and cooperation with local authorities. Ambassador Van Galbraith, President Reagan's representative, charmed the Bordelais. His French was excellent, and he knew France well. I planned two trips for him. On the first, he flew to Toulouse, where I met him, and he toured some of the industrial facilities of that most important industrial and aeronautical sector, and addressed the Chamber of Commerce at a luncheon. We planned ceremonial occasions, as well as a visit with the press. With a few minutes to spare on the schedule, I also showed him, to his delight, the perfect medieval abbey courtyard where Saint Thomas Acquinas is buried, now near the busy intersection of downtown Toulouse.

At Bordeaux, Ambassador Galbraith was the guest of honor at my reception, and at a superb luncheon given by Mayor Jacques Chaban-Delmas at the *Hotel de Ville*. He opened the exhibit on the "Doughboys in Bordeaux: 1917" at the Bordeaux Archives that I mentioned earlier, noting that like my father, his parents had both served in the First World War, his mother as an ambulance driver.

On a later visit to Limoges, we had to rip the schedule to shreds and start over again several times. The Mayor of Limoges, Senator Louis Longuequeue, I liked at sight. He was a burly man and clearly in charge of his city. He had also been described as an "old-line Socialist," and I asked him what that meant. He told me, "That means that I remember when American parachute troops came into my city and rescued us all from the Nazis." He had been an orphan, and his education had been aided by an American scholarship fund. It was a pleasure to visit with him, and to plan the Ambassador's trip.

We had hoped to visit the Haviland porcelain factory, whose long association with the United States was well known. Their exhibit room marked the White House china that they had furnished, including the service for President Abraham Lincoln. However, labor difficulties, I was forewarned, might erupt, causing public embarrassment and marring the Ambassador's visit. With regret, therefore, I informed Haviland that probably we would not be able to include the factory in our visit.

Instead we went to a modern factory producing other goods. Ambassador Galbraith was right at home, and interested in what he saw. Back in the armored car, I saw that we had managed to squirrel away enough time to have an abbreviated visit to Haviland after all. I called the Limoges President of *France-Etats Unis*, the Franco-American Friendship Society, who had been standing by for my call. She cleared the visit immediately with a top Haviland executive, and minutes later the visit took place. Those who had hoped to embarrass the Ambassador were totally unprepared, and the visit was a good success. With a small official staff, it only was possible because of the goodwill and quick reactions of our friends.

With this incident in mind, it occurred to me to suggest that each American diplomatic or consular mission around the world be entitled to award, in the name of the Ambassador or Chief of Mission, some few medallions to nationals of the host country who had volunteered and been helpful to the activities of the mission. I actually pursued this in Bordeaux, and awarded some medallions to a variety of helpful people from a schoolteacher who had helped with bilingual exchanges, to a Socialist Deputy who had been friendly to our efforts.

The suggestion didn't proceed very far at the time, but it might be worth reviving, particularly in these days of budgetary lacerations and diplomatic and consular drawdowns. We could call them the Benjamin Franklin Awards, after our first Minister to Paris, and a medallion shouldn't be hard to design or cost very much. Such a gesture would win us new friends when we need them most.

Relations between the Consulate General and the Embassy are important. In theory, I could consult the Ambassador if I had to do so. In practice, the Consul General at Embassy Paris was responsible for supervising the Consulates General in France. However, for matters of substance, very often it was the Deputy Chief of Mission, the Ambassador's second in command, who had the final say.

Consuls General met formally at Embassy Paris twice a year. We discussed topics such as the allocation of leader grants to the United States, which always went disproportionately to people the Embassy nominated, and reporting functions and responsibilities. These were important occasions to pull together the entire American diplomatic and consular mission in the host nation. The perception of the people of Bordeaux was another matter. Before one trip to Paris I was invited to a dinner in Bordeaux, and called the host to regret, saying that I would have to be in Paris at the Embassy. "Sorry to hear that you are leaving France for the week," was his reply.

The Consul General who first supervised us was a fine professional, with good experience and advice which he would share in a manner that went down well, itself a real skill. He was a pro, and like any experienced Consul General, as you've gathered by this time, enjoyed telling or hearing a good story. He was replaced by a self-important prune, whose leadership qualities we were all slow to grasp. He came to visit me in Bordeaux once, and didn't really seem to like anything he saw.

I developed a mental block which prevents my recalling his name. But I do recall his final gesture. When my driver came to take us to the Consulate General in the morning, he bolted up from the breakfast table, and raced as fast as his portly legs could carry him, past security and out to the car, where he proceeded to plunk hmself down in the back seat, right-hand side, the place for the ranking official. All in all, it was not a gesture that Omar Bradley would have thought it necessary to make.

Part of the point of having a Consulate General is to sharpen those management skills that are needed to run an Embassy, or comparable levels of executive responsibility within the Department of State One learns to manage people and resources, to stretch limited money, and most important, to establish priorities.

How much time should be spent in Bordeaux, and how much should be allocated to the remainder of the consular district? Should there be a new position sought to handle the expanding workload in the consular section, or the commercial section? How should representation funds be allocated to get the best value for the money? What are our goals as far as political reporting are concerned? It may be well to tie visits within the consular district closely to the French election schedule, to get the freshest feel for evolving political events.

All of these questions, and many more, are matters that a Consul General must juggle. They are important to the professional development of a career consular officer, because only rarely do consular work and diplomatic reporting involve any management responsibility at all. When we lose a Consulate General, more than just the services that Americans and host country citizens have come to expect is lost. A rare opportunity for learning management skills, essential to running successfully an even larger diplomatic enterprise, is also lost.

One also learns some of the pitfalls of management. It is fun to be feted, and to have one's sterling qualities recognized by all and sundry. But there are risks, including those who would take advantage of the situation. For example, once in the southern portion of the consular district, I was invited by a French company to spend the night at their corporate chateau following the dinner that they had given for me. It was late, and the countryside was isolated, so I did so, of course deleting that day from any *per diem* claim for official reimbursement. It seemed that all was well, and I promptly forgot the matter.

Never again! The next time I saw that company's representative, he wanted preferential treatment, and the law bent, for visas for their representatives to travel to the United States. The inference was obvious, a favor for a favor. I showed him the door. From this lowcost learning experience, I learned better the dividing lines for official conduct, and what "favors" might actually end up costing. I sometimes have the feeling that official Washington has yet to learn that elementary lesson of management, ethics and discretion.

Bordeaux had a sizable consular corps, about equally divided between the career consular service, such as myself for the United States, and honorary consuls, such as Franck Mahler-Besse for the Netherlands, Paul Duret for Bolivia, and Lionel Cruse for Finland. Amongst the career diplomats, several nations viewed being Consul General in Bordeaux as an assignment interchangeable with ambassadorships. The Canadian Consul General, my neighbor in the suburb of Cauderan, had just been an Ambassdor in Eastern Europe. Others, like the British, used their Consulate General as an ambassadorial training ground.

The Dean of the Consular Corps was the Spanish Consul General, Count del Campo Rey. He once remarked to me that he was sorry that Americans did not study their Spanish colonial heritage more thoroughly. With a year spent in high school in Florida, where we did learn that subject, I agreed with him. I also once had the occasion to call on his brother, Spain's Consul General in Pau, and a former Spanish Ambassador to Czechoslovakia.

Happily there was never been the occasion for a united representation, as is occasionally the case with a diplomatic or consular corps. That usually means a problem of some sort with the host country. We had such *demarches* from time to time in Hungary, usually concerning the official Diplomatic Service Bureau, which we all had to use to find "help." The Bordeaux Consular Corps was therefore social in orientation, while as is always the case its members exchanged notes on the local political and economic scene.

I recall with pleasure the luncheon the Consular Corps held at Chateau Margaux, which marked my departure from Bordeaux and the consular service. It was an elegant sendoff.

CHAPTER 14

▼

NEGOTIATING A
CONSULAR CONVENTION

Gradually, as the Iron Curtain gathered some rust, American citizens, particularly dual nationals, began to travel to East-Central Europe. But they wanted to do so as American citizens, with some measure of personal security. They wanted to be assured that they would not be harassed by the police, or locked up, and they wanted above all recognition from largely unwilling local governments of their new status as American citizens.

This was particularly difficult in Hungary, where divestiture of Hungarian citizenship was a rare and complicated process, requiring high government approval. That meant that someone who had fled Hungary in 1956, for example, and settled in the United States, becoming an American citizen, might be astonished to discover that he was still considered to be a Hungarian national by Hungarian authorities, even though that dual Hungarian citizenship had been formally renounced by the new American citizen!

The consequences were farreaching and important. A young man, for example, might risk military service in Hungary if he returned for a visit. Taxes might be claimed. And worst of all, perhaps a former Freedom Fighter might be arrested by Hungarian authorities many years after the event.

One of my responsibilities was to begin the negotiation of a Consular Convention between the United States and Hungary, that would regulate these matters in a way that protected all American citizens. Although it was a matter of urgency, there is no hurrying a Communist bureaucracy that doesn't want to be rushed. And so I first presented the American draft convention, answered some preliminary questions, and then every few months, when either the Hungarian side had a point to raise or Washington grew impatient, I would talk with officials at the Foreign Ministry and from time to time get very preliminary agreement to an article or two. At the rate we were proceeding, it would take twenty years before the convention was agreed to and took effect!

I was therefore very pleased when I was called by Ambassador Puhan into his office and told that a possible visit by Secretary of State William Rogers was in the wind. It would be the first visit ever made to Hungary by an American Secretary of State, and therefore it was a significant occasion and, if it took place, a chance to advance our bilateral relations. The Ambassador asked me what the prospects were for the convention, and I said that the Rogers visit would make possible either completion or significant process on this important treaty.

"Fine," Ambassador Puhan replied, "and now I want you to draw up a cable saying what you need to get this done before the Secretary of State gets to Budapest." My cable was short and to the point. We needed three things. First, we needed an experienced executive secretary, whose only responsibilities would be to our consular negotiating team. Second, we needed whatever supplies were customary, such as treaty paper and official seals. I didn't know exactly what they were, but I figured that those reading my message would know. Third, and most important, we needed as head negotiator an experienced consular attorney with broad discretion who would not have to refer every comma back to Washington for approval.

Each item on the wish list was granted. Our executive secretary, Mary Pappas, was unflappable, and her last assignment had been as executive secretary for the four-power Berlin status negotiations. The State Department Legal Adviser dispatched Assistant Legal Advisor for Management, Security and Consular Affairs K.E. "Gene" Malmborg to head our two-person delegation, and he brought with him the necessary treaty supplies.

To save time Gene stayed as our guest in our residence, and we cut the social amenities to a minimum. In the evening when we did some informal consultations, it was in the garden, hopefully out of reach of the house's listening devices. Consular employee Johnny Haar was our very helpful interpreter (rendering into English what the Hungarian head of delegation had said in his own language).

However, since there was no time for the certification of the Hungarian language version of the convention by an approved American linguist, it became also my responsibility to certify that the final Hungarian language version of the convention was in all respects an accurate rendition of the English version.

Our consular relations with most nations are governed by the multilateral Vienna Convention, but with the those Communist East-Central European nations (at the time including Poland, Czechoslovakia, Hungary and Bulgaria) that had arrived at the stage where the safety of American travelers in sufficient numbers required a consular convention, the general provisions of the Vienna Convention were insufficient. They just didn't grant enough protection to our citizens who might find themselves facing a trial or imprisonment. We needed tougher provisions that protected our people, and without them, there would be no consular convention. We wouldn't agree to anything less.

Whereas our negotiating team was efficient, the Hungarian side was cumbersome, with five ministries represented. Their representatives had sharply differing points of view on a number of topics in the convention, which they would argue amongst themselves, sometimes at considerable length. When tempers rose they had a tendency to forget (if they knew) that I was a trained Hungarian speaker. Nobody would ever mistake me for a native Hungarian, but I could understand most conversations in reasonable detail. The State Department got its money's worth for my language training in that negotiation! The Hungarian side often called coffee breaks to settle their own positions, and several times I was able to tell Gene what their different points of view actually were, from which ministry. On one startling occasion in the fourth or fifth day of the negotiation, I went one better than that, and was able to tell Gene not only what their different positions were on a key article under discussion, but what they had agreed, if pressed, to settle for as a fallback just in case we didn't buy their initial negotiating position.

Needless to say, we did not!

As a personal matter, I wanted to make absolutely sure that American consular officials could attend trials throughout Hungary, despite the fact that they, like the United States, had areas that were closed to our officials. That provision had been used once to bar me from attending the trial of an American citizen, and I was determined that that would never happen again. We prevailed on that important point as well.

A consular convention must address many matters, which are a virtual summary of what consuls actually do, and their rights to take steps on behalf of their own nationals. How to establish a consular office, the rights and duties of consular officers, and their immunities must be spelled out in some detail. Consular officers do not have the same standing or immunity as diplomatic officers, and may even be subject to civil lawsuits in some cases.

At the same time, they must have the untrammeled right to communicate with their embassy in the host country's capital city, sending privileged communications. This "right" I found myself exercising every week in Bordeaux, when either I or the Vice Consul would put together the classified diplomatic pouch, seal it, and acting as our own couriers, run it over to the railroad station, exchanging it with the incoming diplomatic bag from Embassy Paris, with their designated courier. I was really quite hyper about this responsibility, ever since the fear of the Almighty had been put into me as a junior officer when I was given a one-time diplomatic courier commission—which I kept as a souvenir—and brought the Secretary of State's toplevel cables personally from Saigon to Bangkok.

As might be suspected, the rules are also quite specific about consular property, including real estate, and the inviolability of that property, and of course official files, from the local government. In Bordeaux we once had occasion to call the police authorities to the Consulate General in connection with possible terrorism, and the French authorities were absolutely punctilious about respecting this principle. I am sure that in the event of a fire in the Consulate General, I would have personally had to call the Fire Department, and given appropriate identification before they would have entered the mission, which is just as it should be.

On my wall as treasured souvenirs, there are two documents which were issued by the United States and France regarding my assignment to Bordeaux as Consul General. The first, bearing the Great Seal of the United States and the signatures of President Ronald Reagan and the Secretary of State, is my commission as Consul General, requesting the cooperation of the French authorities as my responsibilities are undertaken.

The second document, personally signed several months later by French President Francois Mitterand and countersigned by Foreign Minister Claude Cheysson, is an *exequatur*, or document recognizing my authority to act as Consul General of the United States in twenty specified French *departements*. I have similar *exequaturs* signed by President Thieu of Viet-Nam and his Foreign Minister, Dr. Tran Van Do, and by the Paramount Ruler of Malaysia, for my stay as Vice Consul in Singapore. Alas I just missed receiving a handsome certificate signed by Queen Elizabeth II, for during my stay in Singapore, we lost consular jurisdiction over Brunei, then a British protectorate as to foreign policy.

Of course, a receiving nation is not obligated to issue an *exequatur* and allow a consular officer to enter onto his or her functions, nor is it obligated to give any reasons for refusal. That happens when they believe that the consul is actually a spy under cover. Also, the formal document now is rarely issued. Diplomatic notes are exchanged instead. There was a nice touch of formality about the *exequatur,* and I am sorry that is being lost. My *exequatur* from Hungary, for example, was issued by simple diplomatic note, in response to the Embassy's routine notification of my arrival. Probably somebody received $50 from the Department of State suggestion program for suggesting that we save paper by downgrading assignments of consular officers, and skip the issuance of appropriate commissions. But something of the dignity of the process gets downgraded as well.

Our convention set forth in some detail what duties a consular officer may be permitted by his sending state to undertake. A consular officer is entitled to protect and promote the interests of his nationals, including corporations, and to gather information regarding economic, commercial and other matters. He is entitled to be in direct contact with appropriate local officials, hence my visits around the four regions of my consular district as set forth in my commission and acknowledged in my *exequatur* by the French Government.

The convention also acknowledges the right of the consular officer to charge such fees for the performance of his duties as are prescribed under the laws and regulations of the sending state. In any American consular office, those fees are posted, and may be clearly seen by the public. In the old days, a consul was actually expected to support himself not from a salary, but from the collection of consular fees, and that is what Fenwick did. I doubt very much that anyone ever disputed any fee that was charged by the "grey ghost" of the Confederacy, John Singleton Mosby, when he served as our Consul in Hong Kong many years after the Civil War ended. Now, of course, all fees go directly to the U.S. Government.

A consul may authenticate and serve various judicial documents, and also take testimony if the law of the receiving state so permits. He may also keep a roster of nationals within his consular district, an important right that helps with notifying the American community of important events, from cultural matters to warnings in the event of political unrest and the necessity for evacuation from the host nation. Actually tourists ought to keep their nearest American consulate also informed of their whereabouts as well. It comes in very handy when they are being traced by anxious relatives in the event of emergencies at home.

Consuls can also give a consular attestation to the host government's registration of birth of an American citizen abroad. We have as a treasured momento the consular attestation of the birth of our son Warren in Singapore, issued by my successor as Consul. They may record marriages and divorces that have taken place under local law, and of course, notarize a variety of documents, or attest to the seals of American or local authorities on legal documents.

The extension, issuance, and revocation of passports from the sending state is a prime responsibility of the consular officer, as is the issuance of visas to foreign nationals. The routine work of most consular officers is devoted in large part to passport and visa matters, which are of crucial importance to the applicants directly involved, and rightly so.

Many of these matters were either mutually understood, or posed no serious problem between the United States and Hungary during our negotiations for the treaty. It sometimes seemed that we were making great progress, when what we were actually doing was clearing out matters that were essentially noncontroversial. We got to the hard provisions soon enough.

There were good reasons for this, and as I had said to Ambassador Puhan before the negotiations started, I could not guarantee that a treaty would be ready for signature when the Secretary of State arrived. But we would make significant progress, and as the list of agreed articles accumulated, if it came to just one or two serious disagreements, the very fact of the high-level visit might prove sufficient incentive to find common ground. If the treaty could not be concluded, we would still have accomplished in two weeks what might, at the rate I had been proceeding with the Foreign Ministry, have taken two decades!

The first disagreement was something that I would never thought of, and yet, from the Hungarian side, it made a certain sense. They were very anxious to give their consular officials in the United States authority over the estates of Hungarian nationals who died here. Basically, they wanted their consuls to usurp the authority of American probate courts! They were motivated by several concerns. First, there might be a fair amount of hard currency at stake. Second, I gathered that a Hungarian consular official was considered a person of central importance for his expatriate community, representing as he or she does a homeland with a unique language and culture. Third, the Hungarian legal system, in common with other European legal systems, accords great importance to the notarial function. It is a profession in and of itself, with quasi-judicial features. What the Hungarian side was attempting to do was to wrap these various elements together, and give their consular authorities in the United States an authority that was far greater than we could accept, and a power that would be unacceptable to the American legal profession.

Our Hungarian negotiators kept returning to this matter, again and again, both in formal sessions and in coffee breaks. As the session continued, day after day Gene and I would return to the Embassy, and either write cables to Washington summarizing the day's negotiations, or prepare new drafts for Mary to type and make ready for distribution at the next session, or both. We began to mention this unexpected problem in our reports as a potential sticking point.

What was so bothersome to me was that they were really asking for something that could not possibly be granted. They seemed very sure, blinded by their political view of things, that the Executive Branch could agree to whatever it wanted, and then the Senate would go along with whatever had been negotiated. Besides, it was such a small matter for the United States, and such a major concern for the Hungarian side, why couldn't we yield on this point?

Of course, there are times when a consular officer has the right to step in when one of his or her nationals dies overseas, but such occasions are largely provisional in nature, such as sealing off property pending court proceedings, or taking physical possession of personal property when a tourist dies in the consular district. But neither situation involves the consular officer himself stepping in and performing legal or even quasi-judicial functions. The disagreement grew, and eventually threatened to disrupt completion of the agreement entirely.

Gene argued the law and precedent forcefully. Still the Hungarian side wouldn't budge. It struck me that much had been lost during communist rule in Hungary. It occurred to me that no Hungarian diplomat in the 1930s would have made the argument that the Hungarian negotiators were making. They would simply have understood, as a matter of general knowledge about the United States, that what they were seeking was not possible. That nobody on their negotiating team could fathom this was, I thought, striking evidence of what had been lost in communication during the communist years.

Finally, during a dinner that the Hungarian side gave for us towards the end of the negotiation, I talked turkey with the chief Hungarian negotiator on the point at issue. Now, some have said that the definition of a successful diplomat is "a good man who is sent abroad to lie for his country."

Precisely the opposite is true, and the value of being respected for honesty is nowhere more important than across the gulf of different political systems. I told the Hungarian chief negotiator, an icy man of utter probity who was one of the few totally convinced communists that I ever met in Hungary, that what his side was insisting upon was just out of the question. I said that I would not agree to any such power for consuls in our draft consular convention. If it went in over my objection, I would recommend that the Secretary of State not sign the document. If he did, I predicted that the agreement would never be submitted to the Senate for its advise and consent to the President's ratification. If it were sent to the Senate with such a provision, every bar and judicial association in the United States would oppose the treaty, and it would fail. Those were the facts of the matter.

Our Hungarian host was stunned to hear this said so bluntly. Eventually, the day before the Secretary of State arrived in Budapest, the Hungarian side withdrew their position regarding this power for their consuls in the United States. They had argued so hard and so elaborately for it, that it must have been a bitter pill for them to swallow. I had the distinct impression that they did so, not entirely convinced that I was correct, but knowing that I held that honest belief and had the certain opinion that their position if adopted would prevent the treaty from ever becoming operative. And that, I think, is why they dropped it.

The second, and to my mind far more serious and substantive matter, I saw no means of resolving. That was the Hungarian insistence on treating Hungarian-Americans, even those who had renounced their Hungarian citizenship, as Hungarian nationals. This was of critical importance, because of the general rule of international law that a consular officer may take up the cudgels for his or her own nationals, provided that the person involved is not at the same time the national of the other state. This dilemma meant that in virtually every case of importance to the United States, an American consular officer would be powerless to act. Hungarians could say that the defendant was still their own national under Hungarian law, and it was unassailably not for an American consular officer to claim who was or who was not a Hungarian citizen.

Gene Malmborg spun several different formulas at the Hungarian side in an effort to resolve the impasse. At length he succeeded with a masterful draft declaration, agreed to by the Hungarian side, that for purposes of this treaty they would recognize the American citizenship of persons who were dual nationals, not raising the dual nationality issue. That meant that we could protect our nationals after all. It was a subtle way out of the dilemma, and one that to my knowledge was never broken by the Hungarians.

Of central importance to me, as an experienced consular officer, was timely access to Americans who had been taken into police custody. Under any circumstances this is a bad situation to be in, but when compounded by the fact that the police were communist, and judges often unprofessional, quick access by an American consular officer was of prime importance. Gene thought so too. We were pleased to have the right of access to American nationals taken into custody explicitly recognized by Article 41 of the consular treaty. It stipulated that best efforts would be made by the detaining power to notify the consular officials of the person detained quickly, and at latest, within three days of that person's being taken into custody.

At length every article had been agreed to, and the Secretary of State would be in the position, shortly after his arrival in Budapest, of signing the first bilateral treaty between the United States and Hungary in nearly forty years. I was proud to have played a role in this result and, eager to dot every "i" and cross every "t," took it upon myself to get the Secretary of State's official seal and take it to the ceremony. This, of course, would be the portable one, not the more elaborate seal that is used in Washington.

I skipped lunch to drive over to the Secretary's hotel quarters, and was given the portable seal by, I thought, an unnecessarily officious staff officer. Driving back across the Danube I decided to double check. The package I had been given looked after all suspiciously like a jewelry case. It turned out that I had been given a pair of Secretary Rogers's cufflinks by mistake! I doubled back and got the seal, and returned his cufflinks in good time for the signing ceremony. It struck me as incongruous that members of the Secretary's official party, who had done nothing at all for the treaty, shoved and pushed to get themselves into the official event picture. That left no room for Gene Malmborg, Johnny Haar, Mary Pappas or myself. But we knew who had actually done the work.

So it was with mixed feelings that, removed from the negotiating pressure, I waited for Lois to pick me up at the Embassy to go home for dinner. We had to stop along the way at the outdoor market for groceries. As usual, there were long lines, and so we split the chores. After days of arduous legalistic Hungarian I realized that I couldn't remember the Hungarian word for "eggs" and had to get out of my line to go ask Lois!

It was two months later that a cable arrived. My certification of the Hungarian language edition of the treaty had been accepted, with just one question. It was a point that I had wondered about, and had posed a question to clear up the matter during the negotiations. The answer satisfied me, and so did my linguistic certification of the treaty satisfy the Department of State.

The Convention on Consular Relations Between the United States of America and the Hungarian People's Republic set some sort of fast track record. It breezed through the United States Senate and became the law of the land one day less than one year after it was signed in Budapest.

Shortly after that I became Hungarian Desk Officer in the Department of State. In my first month on the job, a cable was received from our Embassy in Budapest, detailing an arrest of an American citizen. I picked up immediately the fact that it been four days, one more than allowed by Article 41 of the Consular Convention, between the American citizen's arrest and notification of that arrest to American consular authorities. I shot off a cable to the Embassy citing this violation of Article 41 of the treaty. Within days an answer was received. The Hungarian authorities admitted error, and had released the American without trial or other action. They had kept their word.

The issue of consular access has also arisen here. I followed with interest a comparable case before the International Court of Justice (ICJ) at The Hague that arose here in the United States. The LaGrand Case (*Germany v. United States of America*) was a murder case. However, the State of Arizona had not given consular access within the specified time limits to a German Consul, in a case involving one of his nationals. On November 17, 2000, the ICJ rendered its verdict. The United States lost the case, apologized to Germany, and formally stated that steps would be taken to prevent any recurrence. It was too late, however, to provide any relief for the accused, who had already been executed.

And in 2005, in *Medellin v. Drake*, the Supreme Court heard arguments based on an ICJ ruling that the United States had violated the Vienna Convention on Consular Relations by failing to tell Mexican nationals charged with murder that they had the right to meet with Mexican consular officials. Seeking to diffuse the issue, the Bush Administration accepted the ICJ decision and instructed that new judicial hearings be given in these cases. I was interested to note that intervening in this case with briefs before the Supreme Court were retired American diplomats, including those held so long at the beseiged Tehran Embassy, who wanted international consular standards upheld, as a safeguard for our own citizens held in jails abroad.

On the 25th anniversary of the 1956 Hungarian Revolution, I was honored to be made an Honorary Hungarian Freedom Fighter by the World Federation of Hungarian Freedom Fighters, in a ceremony marking the event on Capitol Hill in Washington. Those present made special note of the Consular Convention, which they said made it safer for Americans of Hungarian background to travel to Hungary with dignity and safety.

CHAPTER 15

▼

A FOREIGN SERVICE FAMILY

Looking back now on our years in the Foreign Service we feel nostalgic for a lost world, far away and no longer reachable. But from time to time memories let us return. We know that we cannot, really, ever do so, because diplomacy is itself so sensitive to time. As Foreign Service Officers overseas we think of the government where we are assigned when we were assigned there, and that is by its nature changing. We can and do return to other countries where we once lived. The buildings where we lived and worked may be the same, but everything else has changed. Friends have moved on as well. But sometimes a memory will return, strong and sensory, on the wings of an anniversary, a remembered song or a treasured family recipe.

I became interested in living overseas quite young. As I grew up in New Hampshire, again and again Father told about France, where he had served in the Signal Corps during the First World War. But he never talked about the war itself. For that, I had to wait until my first visit to France, now fifty years ago. Sitting at the *Pied de Cochon* restaurant in *Les Halles* eating onion soup late one night, I struck up a conversation with my French neighbor at the next table. His lapel rosette, he said, was that of a veteran of Verdun. I told him that Father had never told me what the Western Front had been like. This eloquent and earthy stranger told me.

After the Armistice, Father had stayed in France and studied chemistry at the University of Besancon. He loved to tell how, after the word had gone out that French-speaking soldiers would be eligible for university courses if they had $100 and a good service record, he and his friends had pooled their money and had come up with exactly the sum required. Those were the days when university men saw it as their duty to fight for their country and now, the war being over, here was a chance to stay in France for a semester before classes began once more at home.

Some fifteen men went before the board, one by one, got a cursory oral examination in French, showed the identical $100, and left the room. Father was the last in the alphabetical line, and as he showed the $100 which had been slipped to him by his predecessor in line, all of a sudden the light dawned and one of the officers on the screening board gave him a very fishy look. But he and his friends were admitted regardless. Many years later, it was a pleasure to forward to our Consul General in Strasbourg, my colleague Bob Homme, photographs and a flag from Father's student detachment, which he in turn presented to the University of Besancon for their archives.

Having grown up with tales of overseas, my interest in diplomacy as a career was fixed in secondary school, when I happened across a book on the subject in the library. There was never any career question in my mind. Representing the United States was a grand career, and participating in the great public events of our time was the challenge. The Foreign Service notion of spending a few years in one country and then moving on had specific appeal to me, far outweighing the financial advantages of working for a Wall Street law firm.

Forty years later, a law school classmate remembered at our reunion that I had told him that I was going to enter the Foreign Service "because I didn't want to wake up one morning late in life and wonder what living in Singapore would have been like."

International affairs always intrigued me. The major international event of my years at Wesleyan took place thousands of miles away, with the outbreak of the 1956 Hungarian Revolution. Too young for service in Korea, and just too old for my military service to be spent in Viet-Nam (to repair that deficiency, the Foreign Service sent me there for two tours anyway), the Hungarian Revolution showed the world the bravery of the Hungarian people. Time Magazine got it right when they named as "Man Of The Year" for 1956 two young Hungarian Freedom Fighters, a ragged boy and girl. We look forward to celebrating the 50th anniversary of those heroic events on the scene where they took place, in Budapest.

I raised money for the Hungarian Freedom Fighters who had been able to flee to Austria that terrible winter. The following year I had a Fulbright grant in France and spent Christmas in Vienna, where I vividly recall a Christmas Eve midnight mass at St. Stephan's Cathedral, the Primate of Austria evoking the sad fate of the Hungarian nation just across the border. In hindsight, the 1956 Hungarian Revolution looms even more important for our age, as it presaged the fall of the Iron Curtain and the Soviet Russian empire.

As a college student, now I had two goals. I wanted to have a career in the United States Foreign Service, and I wanted to serve in Budapest and in France.

My first few years in the Foreign Service, including tours in Viet-Nam and then in the Executive Secretariat of the State Department, were exhausting, but I certainly couldn't complain about missing the action. I did the staff work for the secret negotiations that led to the Paris Peace Talks over Viet-Nam, and for the recovery of the *Pueblo's* crew from North Korea. I was senior staffer for Secretary of State William Rogers's 18-day trip around the world, with stops in Viet-Nam, Thailand (for a SEATO conference), Afghanistan, Pakistan, India and Iran (for a CENTO conference). The last five countries we fit in during one weekend!

As in any Foreign Service career, the hours were often long and separations due to assignments still happened. But somehow, except for my Viet-Nam tours, whenever the children were having a school night, I was always able to join Lois and be there. This is worth pondering, to make the point that grandiose career plans tend to ignore the very real aspects of family life under the best of circumstances. So, of course, do the announcements of State Department officials which do not take family life and the schooling of our children sufficiently into account.

For example, I had always enjoyed travel, and had even changed high schools from New Hampshire to Florida, and so I made the easy assumption that transitions are easy for families. Wrong! Overseas, I would go into the American Embassy as a newly assigned consular or political officer and be at home. I knew the organization and how the Embassy worked, and perhaps already had a friend or two on the staff. There would be a learning curve as far as the local country was concerned, but that was always interesting, and part of the job.

For my family, it was quite a different story, and each move became harder as the children got older. Lois took to the Foreign Service with interest, and her contacts and political instincts were right on target. We had a running joke that we would leave a meeting or reception, and I would tell her what had been said, and she would tell me what had really been going on.

Whenever we were assigned to a new diplomatic mission overseas, the practical chores of dealing with school registration, new and lost friends for our children, the welfare of our cats, and making that Embassy residence our American home fell to Lois. Fair enough, I suppose. She in some measure had joined me in choosing the Foreign Service, unfair though that service was at the time in many respects to Foreign Service spouses. Our children, of course, had not done so. We had chosen for them. And when they had to leave good friends, or arrive home with irrelevant skills, like a knowledge of soccer rather than baseball, that was hard for them.

Over the years Lois had to establish (and leave) successful careers as a teacher, real estate associate, and Dean of Women at a Maryland preparatory school, as we were constantly uprooted It must have been for her a source of constant frustration. It was even more difficult for the children to be uprooted frequently, just after they had made new friends.

Our son Warren may have expressed it best in an essay that he wrote in Athens. "Returning to school in the United States in 1973 was a shock for me. It was much different from the British Embassy school. To be popular, you had to be a muscle-bound, All-American Superstar. Intellectuals did not seem to fit into the picture, and I was miserable during my second grade year as well as my third and fourth grade years. As time passed, things started to pick up. By the sixth grade I started to grow taller and more athletic. I worked hard all year and got all As in every quarter except one B in math. I was a leader of a group of Kids who had generally the same interests, such as The Beatles, *The Lord of the Rings*, and other fantasy-adventures as well as baseball. Then I found out that we were going to Greece that summer."

To begin with, Lois and I and our toddler daughters Stephanie and Robin became a Foreign Service family, straight from our years in Charlottesville, Virginia, where the girls were born during our assignment with the Army's Judge Advocate General's School. One of my nicest memories is that shortly before our departure, I walked around the block of our residence on Virginia Avenue with Stephanie, then a toddler. The walk was a delightful revelation. She seemed to know everybody, and had a smile or greeting for everyone.

Our younger daughter Robin proved something of a linguist in her early days in Singapore, where Warren was born. Robin mastered the Hokkien dialect of Chinese virtually as a toddler. One day her *amah*, Ah-Siew, was walking around our residence area with Robin when a small group of children from a nearby *kampong*, or settlement, yelled something rude at Robin and Ah-Siew. To the amazement of Ah-Siew, Robin gave better than she got, yelling right back at them in Hokkien! "But she didn't learn those words from me," Ah-Siew insisted.

Our security in Singapore was guaranteed by a singular incident. Ah-Wah came racing to Lois one afternoon to tell her that a Chinese baby had died. Sure enough, a mournful cortege crossed in front of our house, and Ah-Wah had raced out to see what had happened. The baby, a little boy named Tiong Keng, had fallen into a water cistern. By the time his parents had fished him out, he was no longer breathing. Lois instinctively held out her arms, and the boy's mother confided her son. Lois then started emergency mouth-to-mouth resuscitation and after an agonizing few minutes, Tiong Keng threw up water, let forth a loud cry, and started to breath once again.

Shortly after that, small baskets of oranges began to appear on our doorstep. And then there was a series of robberies in our diplomatic neighborhood, as athletic burglars came into houses from the rooftops, sometimes even while the families were at dinner in the same house! But we had no such problems. It was as though our house was exempted from burglary.

We all have some very nice family memories from our various assignments overseas. High on my list is the year that we spent Hallowe'en in Transylvania during our later assignment in Budapest. Stephanie and Robin were then 8 and 7 and their brother Warren was 4. We had managed to locate some "real" Hallowe'en corn candy at a PX in Germany, plus some assorted costumes and skeletons. That year, Hallowe'en was on a Saturday night, and so I arranged visas for the weekend stay in Romania, and we loaded up the car and drove towards the border.

It was a beautiful region, hilly and countrified. One could see why those who know it are so fond of it. Vowing to get settled before dark, we found our little town, settled into rooms which were complete with a sitting room featuring a couch made of plastic and reinforced cardboard, and set off for Dracula's Castle, the *Vajdahunyad*.

To get there, we crossed an industrial park, in a town that was overindustrialized. But at last there it was, a medieval, forbidding pile, one of the two or three castles that Bram Stoker is said to have used as his model for Castle Dracula. We were just on time, and our family was the final tour group of the day. We saw the tower, the great hall, the courtyard and the dungeon. The dungeon created the greatest impression, with its massive walls and hopeless aspect, and a massive oaken door leading below that creaked in a solemn drone that I can still hear.

As we left the castle to return to our hotel, I asked the guide whether he thought there was anything to the Dracula story. He smiled and, as he closed the door, glanced at the children and said that of course there was nothing to it, provided that you are all home before dark. The children raced to their room, and woke up the next morning to Hallowe'en candy and decorations, and stories to tell their friends at the British Embassy Elementary School the following week.

By the way, you don't really have to believe that business about garlic warding off vampires if you don't want to. It turns out that garlic has another purpose, well understood by rural Hungarians for many centuries. That is the prevention of storms. Lois and I discovered this when we decided to splurge, and planned a dinner dance for our anniversary. The trouble was that a major storm was predicted for that night. Our maid, Erzsi, had the answer. All we had to do was to tie batches of red *paprikas* and garlic together, just on the outer ledge of every window of the house. Dutifully, we did so. To everyone's astonishment, there was no rain.

One must take these matters as seriously as the locals, after all. Once in Nepal, I asked a man why the wooden statues at temples in Patan were so erotic. He replied that was so to save the centuries-old temples which were carved of wood from being struck by lightning. They believed that the goddess of lightning was a prude. The carvings were therefore to ensure that she turned away, and so would not loose her thunderbolts on the wooden temples.

Everybody who knows us also knows that we keep cats, or perhaps the reverse is true. Dogs have owners, it is said, while cats have staff! Minou and Minouette came from Vienna, as has been said. Mignonne was our Bordeaux cat. In between, I missed the blessed event of Minouette's delivery of five kittens, for that came during my half year duty in Saigon. Lois was giving a dinner party at our *Roskovits utca* residence in Budapest that momentous evening, when Stephanie and Robin came racing downstairs to announce to the assembled diplomatic party that Minouette was delivering kittens in Robin's room, in the chest of drawers.

Drawing himself up to his full dignity, the Ambassador of Chile reminded one and all that he was a medical doctor, and the dinner party adjourned upstairs. Minouette, doubtless pleased by the expert backup, still did the necessary and presented Minou with five beautiful Siamese kittens. I wish we had kept one of them, a handsome klutzy male named *Choi-Oi* (a Vietnamese expression that roughly translates as "What, me worry?"), but when old enough they were given away to enrich the lives of diplomatic colleagues.

It was Stephanie who discovered the secret room at our Budapest residence on *Roskovits utca*, up the street from Moscow Square in the Buda hills. Always an inquisitive child who wanted to understand her surroundings, taking nothing for granted, she was pleased one day to discover that an alcove in her bedroom on the third floor had a concealed door that led to another, hidden room. Within it there were old springs and mattresses.

The mystery was solved a few years later when Associated Press correspondent Endre Marton came to see me when I held the Hungarian Desk in the State Department. Endre was the only Western correspondent in Budapest during the 1956 Hungarian Revolution. As he tells the story in his book, *The Forbidden Sky*, it was to our house on *Roskovits utca*, then occupied by political officer Tom Rogers, that he, his wife Ilona and daughters fled in January, 1957, following an anonymous tip that their arrest was imminent.

Robin and Stephanie had many friends at the British Embassy School, and as the diplomatic community was allowed by the everpresent authorities some contact with the local community, they also took ballet lessons. The training was rigorous, and I remember that their practice sessions, all in Hungarian of course, used to last hours at a stretch. I took fencing with a fencing master at the British Embassy. We used to clear away the movable bookcases and the class would fence in the library reception area. It was exhausting, but superb exercise.

Warren, our youngest, had the gift of being liked and respected by everybody. When we lived in Greece, he was elected President of his Middle School, running against the most popular Greek-American boy in a largely Greek-American school. Once he greeted visiting Greek youngsters from a public school in an address in their own language, just to make them feel welcome.

One of our favorite family excursions in Greece had been to the island of Skyros, in the Aegean Sea, where the traditional goat dances are held the first Sunday of Lent. The origin of these dances has been lost over the centuries. The goat-man, or *geros*, wears a goatskin mask which must be stifling, and a shepherd's jacket worn inside out, over long baggy white woollen trousers. His belt is decorated with goat bells of varying sizes. He has two companions, the *korella*, or young man disguised in a traditional bride's costume, and a *frangos* or Frank, which means a European male, freer in costume. The three whirl in dances to the ruined castle on the summit of the island, while other trios continue the dancing all day.

Some believe that the disguise aspect of the dancing recalls the disguise of the hero Achilles as a girl, prior to his leaving the island for the Trojan War. Nobody really knows. But the sound of those bells remains haunting, and they call back former inhabitants of Skyros every year as surely as the bagpipes summon highland Scots for their clan reunions. It would be fun to take our grandchildren there for the annual ceremonies.

On other family excursions, we saw as much as we could of the wonders of ancient Greece. We visited ancient Olympia in the Peloponnese at Greek Easter, and Warren ran the ancient footrace with joy. We visited Delphi and the treasures of Meteora. We travelled to Corinth, and read on the engraved stone of a nearby church St. Paul's celebrated epistle to the Corinthians. We saw Greek classics at the ancient theatre at Epidavros, where the acoustics are still miraculous. And at Mycenae, we saw the remnant capital of the cursed House of Atreus.

One fall weekend when his sisters were planning for a social function at their school, I arranged to go on a climbing expedition with Warren, to Mount Olympus in northern Greece. It was a good climb, sticking within the tree range for the most part, and required an overnight stay in a hut, then a quick breakfast early the next morning before the final climb. It was a beautiful morning perfect for the climb, and I treasure a photo of Warren and me with the summit just beyond.

Warren's fatal illness a few months later, from a form of hepatitis, probably contracted during a school trip to Egypt, was a blow which we still cannot understand. Before we left Athens, a memorial service was held at the American Academy, where Stephanie had graduated the week before. Ambassador McCloskey read the poem, "To An Athlete Dying Young." A memorial was ultimately dedicated for Warren there, and prizes are annually awarded in his name at the American Community School in Athens, and at Phillips Exeter Academy, which he was to have attended that fall.

All of this came to mind as I returned to Athens for a visit several years later, wearing pinned to my lapel a cloth red poppy, the symbol of remembrance. I was met at the airport by Stelios Papadopoulos, from the Embassy Political Section. We had some talk about the forthcoming Greek legislative elections. We drove directly to Halandri, a suburb north of Athens, to visit the American Community School. Arriving at the Middle School there, we were met by Superintendent John Dorbis, and by the Principal, Dr. George Pimenides. There was a ceremony at Warren's monument, and I thanked the youngsters who were there for remembering our son on what would have been Warren's nineteenth birthday.

In Stelios's company the good memories from Greece returned. I remembered the monastery at Daphne, with its magnificent frescoes, and Eleusis, where Stephanie, Robin and Warren once stood by the grotto that traditionally leads to the other world. Then across the hills from Kifissia I could see again the fragment of the first theater at Dionyssos, where Thespis himself is said to have begun the traditions of Western theater.

I remembered family trips to Marathon, and to my favorite site, Rhamnous, with its Temple of Hera and side by side, the Temple of Nemesis, Goddess of Vengeance, which was erected to mark an earlier sack of the Temple of Hera by invaders. One of these days I really will walk the famous Marathon route to Athens.

The enclosure at Hera was sheer perfection during that weekend, the sky a rich deep blue, and wildflowers in profusion everywhere, whether camomile, or blue or yellow wildflowers. But within the open sanctuary of Hera itself, there were thousands of red poppies, poppies everywhere, against the blue sky and the water far below, and against the blanched white marble of the temple walls, red poppies bloomed in every nook and cranny. It was a nice way to remember Greece, and our family excursions.

I remembered that Stephanie had saved our house in Athens once. It was during the Christmas season, and a maid before leaving for the day had emptied ashes from the fireplace into paper bags in the kitchen. Of course, they smoldered and then caught fire. Stephanie arrived from school and saw the smoke, and would not have entered the house had she not heard Minou crying. She went in, saved the cat, then grabbed the fire extinguisher, and put out the blaze just seconds before the flames would have started up the kitchen wall. The Athens Fire Department commended her quick action.

Walking down from Kolonaki, we saw the King George Hotel in *Syntagma* Square. That is where where we had held Robin's sixteenth birthday party in the Tudor Room. It was such a nice birthday, as all of Robin's friends dressed like young ladies for the occasion, and as a bonus the view of the lighted Acropolis from this top-floor restaurant was memorable.

Lois and I remembered these things as a plaque, "In Memory of Our Foreign Service Family Members Who Have Died Abroad," was unveiled by the Under Secretary of State at the Diplomatic Entrance of the Department of State in May, 2000. The message from the President paid welcome tribute to Foreign Service families, his statement recognizing that such tribute was long overdue.

I had suggested the plaque, remembering all the joys we had experienced as a family. It seemed appropriate in that setting, for while Lois and I and our daughters had moved on, Warren in a sense never left our diplomatic life. Family members, who have not chosen that life, should receive more recognition for their many contributions to it.

CHAPTER 16

▼

POST SCRIPTS FROM BELOW THE CAVIAR LINE

Before you leave, I am reminded of a final story or two, not worth separate treatment perhaps, but still illustrating diplomatic life and travels.

Some rather indelible memories took place when I accompanied Secretary William Rogers as chief staffer, when he made that eighteen day trip around the world. After an initial stop in Saigon, I must have set some sort of record for international travel. That was because we had two staffing teams which leap-frogged each other. The idea was for one team to prepare for the Secretary's arrival, and then leave for the next stop as soon as the Secretary (and the next staffing team) arrived. The procedure worked efficiently, but we were exhausted.

That is how I began one weekend in Thailand, and then worked in Afghanistan, Pakistan and India before arriving in Iran on Sunday evening. When I was with the Secretary's party, and not advancing it by commercial flight, it was also possible to work on the plane. Ever anxious to see a famous site, even from the airplane, I had the pilot announce when we were overflying the famous Khyber Pass before landing at Kabul, Afghanistan. And since a call from Air Force Two to Washington via the White House switchboard was a "local" call, I once got to call Lois back home in Bethesda, from the Bay of Bengal! I never did get to leave the Embassy in New Delhi, but a thoughtful Embassy wife managed to get for me two Indian dolls to bring back for Stephanie and Robin.

At Kabul, our stay was only for a few hours. The Embassy was highly organized. The control officers had postcards of local scenes ready, with the correct international postage in stamps already stuck on. And I will never forget the superb Afghan hound that belonged to an Embassy family, who had brought it to the Embassy grounds so that we could see this splendid animal. They told us that in those days, the King himself approved the rare export of purebred Afghan hounds, one by one.

In Tehran, I had hoped to have an entire day off, but I awoke the morning after arrival with an exploding jaw. Instead of the planned trip to Isfahan, I spent the morning instead as an emergency dental patient. With the afternoon free, I took a car to a bazaar near Tehran and bought cloth for a traditional *chador*, or dress with head covering, for Lois, who failed to appreciate the humor.

Then I went to a large mosque for a respectful look around. I had rarely seen such misery expressed. There were, in those days of the Shah, religious leaders or *mullahs* at the mosque, engaging in lamentations that were real and unforgettable. It was a great contrast to the reception that the higher ranking members of the Secretary's party were receiving. However, since Farsi was not one of my language skills, I could only guess at the meaning of what I had seen.

That it did have meaning I had no doubt, but I couldn't seem to interest either the other members of the Secretary's party, or any member of the press contingent which was travelling with us, in exploring the matter. They did, however, all seem to enjoy the gifts of caviar which the Shah had bestowed. I bought some caviar at dinner in a Tehran hotel and quite enjoyed the real thing, absent the oily, fishy taste of the product that comes in little glass jars.

Some years later, Lois and I took a vacation trip to Moscow and Leningrad. It was evocative to be in Moscow the anniversary of the blustery day that Napoleon began his retreat. But we were less concerned about that than we were about using our limited time to see something of the city and surrounding countryside, which our Intourist escorts seemed doggedly determined to prevent.

Spike Dubs was our *charge d'affaires* in Moscow at the time, and he gave a cocktail reception for us. He gave a gracious little speech of welcome, and ended it by asking my impressions of Moscow. At that point, the wall behind him actually started to hum! I said "Well, Spike, I can tell you one thing. The surveillance equipment that the Hungarians use in Budapest is more sophisticated than what has been installed in your wall!" Spike was a fine officer who became Ambassador to Afghanistan, where he was murdered.

I was actually on duty in the Executive Secretariat of the Department of State when I first met Spike, a couple of years before that Moscow evening. It had been a grinding day, and basically, I had had it, and made some offhand remark to my duty secretary that I was going to catch forty winks, so "Don't wake me up unless the Russians invade Europe!" Half an hour later she did wake me up. My stipulation had been met. Our United Nations Ambassador, Bill Buffum, was calling me with the news that the Warsaw Pact was in fact moving into Czechoslovakia. I notified the Secretary of State and kept other key persons advised of developments as we heard them throughout that night, and those that followed.

In those days, a movement began to collect excellent pieces of furniture, reflecting our national heritage, for the State Department's reception rooms on the Eighth Floor. Under the skilled leadership of Clement Conger, that project has been realized, and visitors may admire such fine items as the very desk where the Treaty of Paris was signed, the peace treaty ending the American Revolution.

The movement has, however, gone too far, and has spread to the formerly operational areas of the Seventh Floor, where State Department principal officers have their reception area, now also guarded and cordoned off from the Department as a whole. The net effect is to separate the career Foreign Service from the political leaders of diplomacy, when their respective skills should be integrated.

I remember once sitting on duty for the Executive Secretary, when a furious Secretary of State Dean Rusk, in the open and adjoining office, said some injudicious things about the possibility that the Nixon presidential campaign, then in a deathlike struggle with Hubert Humphrey for the White House, had contacted the South Vietnamese Government, and told them not to agree to certain peace negotiation terms. Rusk backed out of that office and saw to his dismay that I must have heard what he had said, which would have been nationwide news. He looked at me carefully, and decided that he was dealing with a man of discretion. Nothing needed to be said, or was said.

But then, perhaps Secretary Rusk had learned his lesson and understood the need for caution in dealing with the Shepard clan. Some weeks earlier, as duty officer, I heard that Secretary Rusk was returning unexpectedly from the White House. Therefore, we couldn't close up shop and go home. It was about nine o'clock at night, too late to call Lois to tell her I'd be late. She was already on her way to pick me up, and when she arrived at the Department, in that more innocent time, she was allowed to come upstairs to the seventh floor, where I was on duty in the Executive Secretary's office.

The early Sennett comedies couldn't have improved on the timing of what followed. My duty secretary went down the hall to send some cables over to the

White House. Lois came in, we chatted and then she sat at the duty secretary's desk, to call our baby sitter to let her know that we were going to be late. And as she put down the telephone, Secretary of State Dean Rusk appeared, marched purposefully over to the desk where Lois was sitting, and announced that he wanted to dictate and send a cable.

Lois graciously gave the Secretary of State her opinion that that was just fine with her, after all, it was his Department! Never defeated by the Senate Foreign Relations Committee, Dean Rusk retreated in total confusion into his office. My duty secretary then appeared, and I sent her to the Secretary's office to retrieve the situation and take the cable! It's probably better for the security of the Republic that such scenes will not happen in the future. Henry Kissinger might have broken off diplomatic relations with some unoffending small nation, at least!

Speaking of the Senate Foreign Relations Committee, since I had just returned from service at our Saigon Embassy, it was my job to assemble all of the briefing materials used by Secretary Rusk on that subject over a period of time.

During one period, we received a number of earnest inquiries from Senator Fulbright's office, all of which Secretary Ruak was well prepared to answer with the help of messages that were sent to Embassy Saigon. We would get the inquiries, and I would plot out what we knew in house, and what we needed to ask Embassy Saigon. It was like matching wits with a determined opponent, intelligent but inexperienced. I have since wondered exactly who that new staffer in the office of the Senator from Arkansas might have been.

My own direct experiences on the Hill came as the result of a Congressional Fellowship, when I did foreign policy for Senator Robert Dole. He was the only boss I have ever had who made me stretch. Usually, it was a matter of doing the job and trying to exceed it because I wanted to do so. With Dole, there were new areas of interest. When the matter of arms control came up, Senator Dole told me to prepare a new proposal for him. That became my assignment for the fellowship year.

It was very challenging and of consuming interest. I produced and he approved a START proposal for the reduction of nuclear strategic arms that advanced the debate. When Senator Dole testified on his proposal before the Senate Foreign Relations Committee at a packed hearing, he did something most unusual. He looked around and saw me, then invited me to come to the witness table with him. Then he began his testimony by introducing me to the Committee, and giving full credit for my portion of the work that led to the proposal. You are going to look long and hard for a politician with the character to do that, in my experience.

My relations with the press were sporadic in my Foreign Service days, but as Sherlock Holmes would say, there were occasional points of interest. An always thoughtful Secretary William Rogers arranged for our epic eighteen day trip around the world to end in Scotland, where, after an interminable flight from Tehran, we caught our breath before returning to Washington. I arranged with a courier from Embassy London to receive important cables, and then, held a weird burning ceremony in the hotel rear courtyard, there being no secure facility for these messages after they were read.

It was a slow news day, and so some of the giants of the media graced our staff with their presence in the pingpong room. Little did Marvin Kalb, when he issued his rash and public challenge to me in a voice known to tens of millions of evening news television viewers, realize that he had taken on the Fast Eddie of the diplomatic table tennis world. I beat him two games out of three, and he left the room a shattered but I trust a better man. Eventually he left television journalism and took refuge in one of our academies up north. But as Paul Harvey would say, now you know the rest of the story.

Speaking of Sherlock Holmes, you'll remember that from time to time, Dr. Watson alludes to a story that hadn't yet been published. I particularly liked his reference to "The Adventure of the Giant Rat of Sumatra, for which the world is not yet prepared." Therefore, when I left the Indonesia, Malaysia and Singapore desk in the State Department, Sumatra being part of the island nation of Indonesia, I couldn't resist leaving a sealed folder in the back of a safe in the Indonesia part of our office bearing Dr. Watson's inscription. We'll see if that helps develop a sense of humor at the State Department!

Sometimes I recall fragments from our diplomatic life.

I remember the New Year's Day tradition in Greece that garbage collectors be given money, and the grinning face of the black toothed fellow who rang our doorbell at seven in the morning after New Year's Eve shouting *Skoupidia* ("Garbage").

I remember in Ipoh, Malaysia, having breakfast at my hotel when a seedy salesman appeared. and called his employer, a British firm in the capital city, Kuala Lumpur, to report progress in sales. The man stood up erect, and his sing-song voice was recalibrated to affect the cultivated cadences of James Mason. His report filed, the man shuddered, seemed to actually shrink in size, and he slunk off to the bar for an early pick me up to restore his courage.

I remember the Hotel Continental in Saigon, and the verandah area where sometimes, in the early evening, I would sit with my friend Peter Glick, an American businessman. Peter had a master's degree in French literature, and helped me compile a list of classic novels that should be read, from *Les Liaisons Dangereuses* to Andre Gide. A peddler used to haunt the verandah, selling smutty magazines. Peter, however, knew that the man was a reputable book dealer. When he came to our table, Peter would discuss first editions with him in Vietnamese. I found out from the peddler where to have books bound in Saigon. Periodically visiting the bookstores, and then the bookbinder's shop, today I have a collection of bound volumes of the classics that Peter had recommended.

About that word "verandah" just used…after a conference on Guam, Ambassador Lodge wrote a personal note to the Navy Captain whose home he had stayed in there. Lodge wrote that "It was pleasant to sit out on the verandah after dinner." I remarked to the Ambassador that perhaps this Captain hadn't been raised in New England, and so wouldn't understand the term verandah. He might call it a porch instead. Lodge took a moment out from the war to ponder this fine point, and then said "Let's send it as it is. If he doesn't know what a verandah is, it's about time that he learned!"

During that second tour in Saigon, as all of our military forces left, the night of Ho Chi Minh's birthday was the occasion for terrorism in Saigon. All of the electricity was cut, and in our little apartment compound, the Vietnamese guards ran away. It was very, very hot and, sweat drenched, I kept recalling the chatty letter that I had just received that day from Lois's sister Myrna. It helped me keep my nerves under control until dawn, when the shouts, cries and movements outside finally ceased.

I remember that after the fall NATO summit in Brussels one year, which I attended as a staffer for Secretary Dean Rusk, we stopped off in Madrid and Lisbon on the way home after the conference, in order for the Secretary to give briefings to the Spanish and Portuguese governments. This attention to detail for the period when both nations might be more integrated towards Europe and the common defense was striking. So was the magnificent *fado* singing in Lisbon, and the roast suckling pig dinner that I relished at *Casa Botin* in Madrid.

I remember listening to short wave radio in our patio backyard in Bethesda one beautiful spring, listening to democracy being crushed in Prague.

And then, who could forget that Sunday morning in Budapest when, in bathrobes, Lois and I sat on our back patio having breakfast and reading the papers, when to our distress a man appeared in front of us, snapping photographs left and right. I ordered him off the premises. Embarrassed, he admitted that he was the American Ambassador to the Soviet Union, Mac Toon, visiting Budapest. He had wanted to see once again the house on *Roskovits utca* that he had occupied as a young Embassy political officer years previously! He had incorrectly been told that we were away, he lamely explained.

Recently, Lois and I went back to the Department of State for a conference on doing business abroad, which was followed by a reception in the glittering eighth floor reception rooms. During the conference, I had been struck by how much had seemed to change politically, but how a knowledge of diplomacy helped make sense of this newer era. Whatever the political changes, people will have to be helped, missing persons located, visas issued, and the United States represented with decency and dignity. As a Foreign Service Officer one can be a participant, not an observer, in one's own times.

As for myself, as we left the State Department to drive home that evening, I had just one wish. I wished that I could be a junior officer taking the L5 bus from the Department of State to Chevy Chase Circle. There I would be met by Lois and then we would drive home to Bethesda, to see Stephanie, Robin and Warren once again.

PART II

▼

Foreign Service Tales

LE CONSUL GÉNÉRAL DES ÉTATS-UNIS D'AMÉRIQUE
ET MADAME WILLIAM SETH SHEPARD

VOUS PRIENT DE LEUR FAIRE L'HONNEUR D'ASSISTER
A UNE RÉCEPTION (FRAISES & CHAMPAGNE) DONNÉE
POUR FÊTER LE 209ᵐᵉ ANNIVERSAIRE
DE L'INDÉPENDANCE DES ÉTATS-UNIS D'AMÉRIQUE

ET

POUR FAIRE LEURS ADIEUX
LE JEUDI 4 JUILLET 1985, DE 13 H A 15 HEURES.

51, AVENUE CARNOT
CAUDÉRAN

R. S. V. P.
52.05.95

Veuillez présenter cette invitation à l'entrée.

Your Invitation

CHAPTER 17

▼

WHO STOLE THE TREATY
OF PARIS DESK?

The workmen all wore identification discs on chains around their necks, just like everyone else who worked in the Department of State. Security had thoroughly investigated every firm that did business with State, and then, doublechecked every employee who would enter the building. That was especially true for those who would enter the Diplomatic Reception Rooms on the Eighth Floor, State's ceremonial layer where Ambassadors are sworn in, the Secretary of State gives diplomatic receptions, and dinners and luncheons are held for high ranking foreign dignitaries. This is also where a number of America's national treasures are kept, as securely as possible consistent with making them available to be seen on scheduled guided tours for visitors.

For a dirty job such as refinishing the floor of the Benjamin Franklin Room, a huge room that could accommodate several hundred seated guests, as happened from time to time for state dinners, the precautions had been extensive. The room's elegant carpet, whose design includes the Great Seal of the United States as well as 50 stars, had been carefully rolled up and removed. All of the furniture in the adjacent John Quincy Adams and Thomas Jefferson suites had been covered, wall hangings further reducing any possibility that dust would settle beyond the Benjamin Franklin Room, and every door leading from the Benjamin Franklin Room had been kept shut throughout the week necessary for the work.

As the blue jeans clad workmen came into the building through the garage entrance reserved for them each morning, they went individually through Security. They retreated to the downstairs basement for luncheon, and the occasional break. The arrival security drill was reversed each evening. Finally, after all the work was finished, they carried out their bulky wall hangings and furniture coverings, loaded them with the floor refinishing and buffing equipment onto a previously inspected truck, and left. In due course the firm's accountant would count the days until a sizable U.S.Government check arrived in payment for his invoice, duly submitted in triplicate.

The cry of alarm began with a security guard, and it didn't stop until it reached the ears of the Secretary of State. The Secretary called the Assistant Secretary for Diplomatic Security, responsible for all matters affecting security within the building since a laptop computer filled with industrial strength diplomatic secrets had been stolen, igniting the Senate Foreign Relations Committee. The Assistant Secretary called Robbie Cutler, a career Foreign Service Officer now back in Washington taking language training at the Foreign Service Institute prior to his next assignment, at the Embassy in Athens.

"Robbie," he said, "I may need your help. We all know about your cases, those murders in Bordeaux and Budapest, and that counterfeiting ring in Singapore." That was nice of him, buttering up a midlevel officer before asking for his help. Robbie Cutler, the "Diplomatic Detective," was known throughout the State Department as a career diplomat with a rather different specialty. He solved criminal cases in his spare time. An amateur, he sometimes saw what the professionals had missed. It wouldn't hurt to ask him for help now, rather than later, the Assistant Secretary had reasoned, when the Secretary asked why he hadn't done so earlier.

"This is a touchy matter. It can't stay out of the press very long. Everyone will be reading about it tomorrow. Grand larceny. No, worse than that. Grand larceny of our country's history. Someone has stolen the Treaty of Paris Desk from the Eighth Floor. So you better stop your language exercises and get familiar with the case. Please."

Robbie gulped as he hung up the phone. The Assistant Secretary had not exaggerated. The Treaty of Paris Desk was a prize exhibit of the Department of State. It was the very desk upon which Benjamin Franklin and other American Commissioners in Paris had signed the Treaty of Paris with Great Britain in September, 1783, which ended the American Revolution and began the recognized existence of the United States of America.

Was it a valuable piece of furniture? It was distinctive and of good quality, containing four pull drawers and a low rolltop. But what happened on it, attested by paintings that showed the peace envoys affixing their florid signatures to the peace treaty at this very desk, made it priceless. Also, Robbie assumed, unsalable. It would be instantly recognized by anyone familiar with the period.

Either it had already been sold prior to being stolen, or it would not be sold at all. It would simply disappear.

The shuttle bus ride back to Main State from the Foreign Service Institute in Virginia gave Robbie needed time to think things through. By this time, not just State Security, but the FBI and Virginia police were all over the contractor's office and warehouse. Inevitably, Homeland Security also got called in, as several undocumented, broadshouldered aliens were found in the warehouse. Who could blame the police for not believing the story of the driver of a dusty SUV blocking the suburban lane forcing the truck returning from State to stop, then with brandished pistol ordering three workmen to unload bulky furniture drapes into the SUV? No, the license plates were covered. No, we didn't get a good look at the driver. No, we weren't carrying a desk in the first place.

"Care to go over to the warehouse with me, Robbie?" the Assistant Secretary asked. "We're going to get the truth out of those workmen, and their driver."

In a way, Robbie would later recall, they succeeded in doing so. While the police grilled each workman in turn about the hijacker, the stories became more practiced, more pedestrian. The truck had had to stop at that narrow turnoff, the driver insisted. Take a look at it yourself. If that was true, Robbie thought, that absolved him of any complicity. Or did it?

The Virginia police investigator said hello to his colleague from State. The Assistant Secretary was a fellow professional, an experienced law enforcement officer prior to his appointment, who had been very helpful in a recent hostage case. He was well within his rights to ask questions too. But who this other man was, this diplomat, was anybody's guess.

The Assistant Secretary went through his questions, while extensive notes were taken. Those notes, plus the transcription of the tape being made, might reveal some inconsistency, however small, that could be pried open later. Sometimes the process began just that way, and eventually the inconsistency would become so gaping wide that you could drive a truck through it. That was when you were lucky. More often, the process was a blind alley that led nowhere.

Robbie had two questions to add. "What did the man's voice sound like?" The men shrugged their shoulders. "Really, I couldn't say," one man answered. "It was muffled, deliberately. Phony. Sounded gruff. I couldn't tell you what his real voice was like."

That wouldn't help, or would it?

Then Robbie asked his second question. "Did you notice anything that surprised you about the man? What he was wearing, shoes for example?"

The men remembered nothing in particular. The hijacker had worn nondescript clothing, which they described. Nine out of ten men in an SUV at any given time would be wearing corduroys or jeans and a longsleeved sports shirt.

"Anything else? Anything that struck you as different in any way?"

"Yes, there was one thing," the driver finally remembered. "It struck me as odd at the time, but I'd forgotten about it. Funny how you jarred it loose, so to speak."

"What was that?" Robbie and the Assistant Secretary asked in unison.

"Well, I was staring at his gun, of course. Anybody would. And his hands were very dirty, too dirty, as though the dirt had been rubbed in, on purpose. That didn't go at all with the ends of his fingers. They had been manicured."

The all points bulletin went out for the SUV, with the driver's description. The afternoon papers carried headlines announcing the theft, and the six o'clock television news would be sure to cover it as a lead story. Probably the Department Spokesman was beginning to take questions from the State Department press corps right now.

"You look pleased with yourself, Robbie," the Assistant Secretary said as they drove back over the Theodore Roosevelt Bridge and turned towards the State Department on Virginia Avenue. "What's going on?"

"I'm pretty sure of a couple of things," Robbie said.

"Shoot. I'm all ears."

"First, what the hijacked workers couldn't say. They couldn't tell us what the man's voice sounded like."

"So?"

"Look at it this way. Sure, it's a normal impulse to disguise your voice. But unless there was something really odd about the voice, people wouldn't remember it anyway. It would only be distinctive if it were unusual, high-pitched, for example. Or if the man had a foreign accent of some sort. Anything that would help us narrow down the class of persons sharing the man's vocal characteristics."

"In other words," the Assistant Secretary began to follow Robbie's train of thought, "it could have been an unusual voice. Or perhaps," his eyes narrowed, "it was an ordinary one, but unexpected for a hijacker."

"Exactly right," Robbie said. "A cultivated voice, to go with the manicure. He'd think to disguise his voice, and to put dirt on his hands, but he just forgot about his fingertips. They would go with the voice, I think."

"So the hijacker was a cut above the usual thief?"

"More than that. He was the thief. He wanted us to think that with accomplices, he had stolen the desk, then hijacked it from them. Meanwhile, he already had the desk. This whole hijacking episode was to throw us off the track."

"So where is the desk?"

"I think it's never left the Department of State. If you're prepared for a very long night, and can secure the combinations to every suite of offices in the building between now and then from the regional security offices in the bureaus, let's meet back here at midnight and, gently of course, tear the place apart."

They found the desk at four o'clock the following morning. It was in an office used by a midlevel officer. Some old magazines were scattered on top of the desk. With the rolltop and legs shrouded by drapes, the desk was unrecognizable.

Robbie grunted in satisfaction. "I expect we'll find the dolly that he used to load the desk on, plus his workclothes, at his home, if he hasn't already destroyed them. What he did the final afternoon the workmen were there was to pose as a workman himself, changing clothes in a men's room, and using his own identification badge. Security was used to them at that point. He helped remove the drapes, then he slipped into the adjoining John Quincy Adams Room with his dolly, and waited for the other workmen to leave. Security swept the Benjamin Franklin Room, found nothing wrong, and left.

"Then our thief tilted the Treaty of Paris Desk onto one side and loaded it on his dolly. It's not overly large or heavy. One man could just handle it. He then took a service elevator back to his office floor. There was a reception that night in another part of the Eighth Floor, so the elevators hadn't been turned off. They were needed by the catering staff. I'm sure the thief had some anxious moments. Probably he had some cover story dreamed up about moving office furniture, in case anybody spotted him. But it was after hours, remember, and who notices furniture movers closely, anyway?

"Then came the hard part. I don't really think that it was part of his original plan. That was, of course, to arrange the phony hijacking the following morning. The point was to hide from us the fact that the Treaty of Paris Desk had never left the building at all! He'd noticed that the workmen hadn't finished loading their equipment and drapes. That meant that they would have to return the next day. So he had an inspiration, the hijacking. If we believed that, we would lose precious time interrogating the workmen. While we were doing that, sometime during the week he would work late one night, and then wearing old clothes load the desk onto his dolly, and take it down to a remote corner of the parking garage, loading it onto his repainted SUV."

"So, what was his motive?"

"Who knows? Repeated missed promotions, probably, and a sense of grievance, all internalized. And so was his vengeance. After all, he could never show the desk to anyone. Like most stolen art that is recognizable, he would have kept it to himself."

"Well done, Robbie. The Secretary will be pleased."

"How about some practical help. Just get him to tell the Foreign Service Institute to reschedule that language quiz I'm otherwise going to flunk tomorrow!"

"Done!"

CHAPTER 18

▼

TWO TRACK DIPLOMACY

Rogers Bartleby was a cautious man. He was given to a precise calculation of the small steps needed to reach the goals he had in mind. The wonder to his college classmates was that he had sought a career in the Foreign Service. But then, they believed in Hollywood's glamorous version of diplomacy. Those who encountered Bartleby in the exercise of his profession would never make that error.

Step after cautious step, the framework of a solid career had been erected. "Solid man, Bartleby," was the universal opinion, as Bartleby learned his craft in carefully selected assignments. While others veered off the straight and narrow, cultivating interests in the host countries where they were assigned, Rogers Bartleby kept his goal (an Ambassadorship) and his audience (the Department of State) ever in view.

Not that there was always smooth sailing. Here and there, a younger colleague's memorandum had, regretfully, to be sent back for reconsideration while Bartleby whispered its main ideas into the ears of appropriate higher-ups. Bartleby still shuddered when he recalled the Incident Of The Security Violation, when Marine Guards on a training exercise through his bureau in the Department of State had swept through his own desk and discovered a top-secret classified cable, seven months old, buried in a desk drawer. Dimly Bartleby had recalled stashing it there when he had been called for an urgent meeting with the Office Director.

No matter. Bartleby had researched the rules carefully, and proved that the Duty Officer, an untenured junior officer who was anxious to please, should receive the security violation. That young man irrefutably had been the last person in his office before the classified cable had been found, after all.

At last, the reward had come. Not that this ambassadorial assignment was much of a reward. It was to the sort of place that even Bartleby might have shunned while on his way up. But never mind, it was an Ambassadorship, and Miriam would like that, he supposed. It was a way-station for the real Embassy that now lay in his future, if he played his cards carefully.

For a moment only, Bartleby wistfully reflected that it might have been nice to have had children, young Bartlebys to bask in his day of triumph. The moment of reflection passed. They had made their decisions, despite her lingering doubts. There was only Miriam, after all.

Dutifully Bartleby regurgitated the answers expected of him at his confirmation hearings before the Senate Foreign Relations Committee. He had splurged on a new dark suit for the occasion. Well why not, the other one was a bit shiny, and possibly the $225 could be written off as a business expense. The favorable vote of the Senators seemed a foregone conclusion. They were too busy savaging another nominee, a political appointee whose politics they found reprehensible, to care about Bartleby.

Rogers and Miriam Bartleby got a ride back to the State Department from Capitol Hill with the Assistant Secretary for Legislative Affairs, who had accompanied the group of nominees. "Piece of cake for you, Bartleby," she observed as she let them off at the Diplomatic Entrance. "They'll confirm you easily."

Miriam waited expectantly. It was just noon, and she had worn her best dress for this festive day. She wondered what treat her husband had in mind to celebrate the Ambassadorship. She had read about a nice French restaurant not far from the Department, and of course there were those fine steakhouses on K Street. Her suspense was short-lived. "Great special in the cafeteria today," her husband said over his shoulder. "I noticed it this morning when I went downstairs for coffee after the final briefings before the hearing."

The years had made their difference. Miriam could disguise her feelings well now, except for a certain miniaturization of emotions near her eyes. A passerby would therefore have had to look very closely to see mutations in her expression, from hopeful expectation to incomprehension to the dawning realization that there would be no special treat.

She wondered what life would be like at their new post.

*   *   *   *

The Trade Fair was going well. Greg Barnwell, the Embassy's Commercial Officer, had planned carefully, and now he allowed himself a moment of satisfaction.

To begin with, there had been a great deal of bureaucratic inertia to overcome. Part of the problem had been financial. Commerce had said that trade fairs were not a good use of resources in this part of the world, that already was saturated with American commercial advertising. On the other hand, Washington had conceded a certain value in showing the flag, if it wouldn't cost much. With this reluctant and ambiguous endorsement in hand, Barnwell had been creative. Anticipating resistance, he had already saved most of the scant official commercial budget allotted annually by the Embassy. He had earmarked it for use at the Trade Fair. Then he had supplemented these funds with donations of material from American firms near the capital city. Mostly, he would have admitted, he had cornered businessmen one by one who wanted Embassy invitations and convinced them over canapes to help with Trade Fair preparations.

The Embassy had finally weighed in with Commerce, which gave the final approval for participation, when Barnwell had succeeded in wheedling this help locally. Official reluctance to participate then collapsed. Nobody was really for it, but nobody took the project seriously enough to oppose it, either.

That meant that the United States would participate, as it had done for nearly fifty years at past Trade Fairs. Commerce Deputy Assistant Secretary James Hopkins, who had been lukewarm towards the project, pointing out the needless expense involved, now instructed his secretary to make travel arrangements so that he could be present at the official ribbon cutting.

The Trade Fair opening highlighted the fruits of Barnwell's rummaging. There was, for example, a vintage car from the 'forties, loaned by the Production Manager of the local General Motors assembly plant. The car was the Production Manager's pride, and he carefully kept it in shiny new condition, driving it on occasional weekends, when fine weather permitted. Then Motorola had kicked in with its display. So did IBM. The local subsidiary of an American furniture rental firm donated offices, files and furniture for interviews.

The miracle was that it had all fit within the rather tidy assigned exhibit space that the United States had been allotted.

Then Barnwell had had a real stroke of luck. Dreamworld Productions, a Hollywood spinoff movie production company posing as an independent, was making a film in the region. They had great hopes that *You'll Never Believe This* would turn a nice profit, and the availability of Lola Bontemps to star in the film seemed to assure that those hopes would be amply realized.

To drum up interest for the film, and also to keep tourists away from the actual production site, Sam Jordan from Dreamworld had agreed to set up a small set at the Trade Fair, not far from the American exhibit. The film set was a smash hit from the start. A cameraman on loan from the production company took pictures of visitors to the set, instantly running them through a digital projector and modem. This allowed the pictures to be emailed back to the States at the double-click of a computer mouse, or anywhere else within reason. The lines formed quickly and remained constant.

The first official visitor to the American exhibit had been President Campos, when he opened the Trade Fair. Trained at Wharton, he was not easily impressed. He nodded graciously at the coterie of visiting Washington dignitaries, shaking hands with Deputy Assistant Secretary of Commerce James Hopkins. He was about to leave when he noticed the mock film set.

He asked what it was, and Greg Barnwell, thrust into the foreground by higher ranking officials to answer specific questions, explained that it was the duplicate of a film set where a movie was being made near the capital at that very moment.

President Campos led his entourage past the machinery, cyberspace exhibit and office space towards the film set. He made a beeline towards the Lola Bontemps poster that introduced the exhibit. Campos was entranced, and said so to the local press corps, which responded by fanning out and taking more photos of the American exhibit than their political convictions would otherwise have dictated.

Sam Jordan greeted President Campos with a gladhanded Hollywood welcome. Campos privately asked Jordan when he could visit the film set. He had a great interest in film-making, and was a big fan of Lola Bontemps.

Hopkins noticed Jordan's hesitation, and guessed the reasons for it. "The shooting schedule is pretty tight, Mr. President, but I'm sure we can work something out," Jordan said. Thinking quickly, he added, "The Embassy Commercial Officer, Greg Barnwell, whom you've just met, is our contact man here. Your office can check with him."

That would fend off this leering politician for a while, Jordan thought.

"Young Mr. Barnwell has a fine future," Campos kindly remarked to Ambassador Bartleby.

"I'll monitor your request personally, Mr. President," was Bartleby's assured response. Perhaps after all, with some goodwill from Campos, Bartleby would get credit for improving relations here so greatly that a civilized Embassy might be offered to him. Heaven only knew that he had paid his dues here!

Barnwell wondered how soon he could call Jordan.

Jordan wondered how he would deal with Lola.

Bartleby made a note to goad Barnwell.

Hopkins made a note to update his resume.

＊   ＊   ＊   ＊

"That was a great little country," Commerce Deputy Assistant Secretary James Hopkins remarked to his colleague in White House Personnel, over luncheon at the White House Mess. "I really enjoyed the visit. When will it come open? And shouldn't the President have one of his own people there?"

His friend, who was really tired of personnel work, rose to the bait. Replacing Hopkins at Commerce should be quite doable. It would take about six months to maneuver Hopkins through the process, including his hearings. Then a spell at Commerce would increase his own salability in the real world of commercial activity, if he parachuted out of the Administration. Mid-six figures would be about right, and a nice cushion no matter what happened in the next elections. Better fudge his answer for appearances sake, though.

"Well, unless he makes a mistake, Bartleby should be there for a while yet. But you'd be a good candidate after that, actually having been there, I mean."

Hopkins smiled accordingly. It was all, he thought, quite doable.

＊   ＊   ＊   ＊

Lola Bontemps was in a rage. Of all the benighted backwater dumps she had ever seen, this place was the worst. She knew, because Sam Jordan had carefully explained the matter to her, that her own salary was the reason that the production company was seeking to realize economies elsewhere. That explained why they were in this low wage-scale paradise in the first place.

"But dammit, Sam, why do we have to interrupt production for hours just so this Campos can come and leer at me! Really, he gives me the creeps."

"No more than he does his fellow countrymen, darling, but that's the problem. It IS his country. Just this once, I promise."

"Well, keep the old bastard out of the way."

Sam conveyed a gracious rendition of Lola's reaction to Greg Barnwell, who gleefully relayed the news to his Ambassador. Bartleby, of course, had reserved the right to inform President Campos personally of his appointment at the film set. The filming that day was of a crowd scene. Lola had to make her way through the crowd, in order to deliver a petition for her lover's freedom to the Prime Minister. She did so, again and again, losing patience as the local temperature mounted, and a series of lamentable miscues dictated that the scene be reshot.

And so the first thing that President Campos and Greg Barnwell heard when they arrived at the set was a screech from Lola Bontemps. "Can't you dumb bastards do ANYTHING right?"

Sam Jordan shot forward to save the moment. "Artistic differences, Mr. President," he cooed. "It often happens with major film talents." The visitors stood behind a boom cameraman and watched as the scene unfolded.

It was then that Barnwell had his inspiration. He whispered it to Jordan.

Sam Jordan was entranced. He asked President Campos if he would be willing to enhance their effort by actually appearing in the film. This very scene, as a matter of fact, briefly featured the film's fictional Prime Minister for the only time. Why didn't Campos play that role?

President Campos was enchanted. He would fulfill a boyhood dream by being in the film, and what's more, he would actually be appearing with Lola Bontemps!

During a short break, Sam Jordan put the matter to Lola. She glared at him, but Sam had had the sense to mention the matter in the presence of their visitors. She smiled graciously, a Borgia out of her time that would have made the astute cover their wine glasses had she worn a poison ring. Her ladylike internal reaction may be supposed.

The scene involving Campos and Lola went surprisingly well. There were only two takes, neither of them very long. For clothing, Campos was perfect in the clothes that he wore. So was Lola, in the brief costume that wardrobe had provided.

The more reflective might have said that the brief filming was no surprise. After all, President Campos had been playing roles all of his professional career. More perceptive observers of feminine reactions would have seen that the quicker the scene was finished, the sooner Lola Bontemps, Sam Jordan and Dreamworld Productions would be rid of their visitor.

As it happened, Campos was far enough away from Lola in their two takes that he never had any time for private conversation with her. Such a pity. Well, we'll always have *You'll Never Believe This,* he said to himself happily.

When the day's shoot ended, Lola wasted no time in having Sam Jordan call the White House. "Tell the President that he's represented here by a total turkey," she shouted. A major fundraiser for the last political campaign, there was no doubt that Lola's voice would be heard soaring well above Pennsylvania Avenue's pedestrian din.

*   *   *   *

A week later, Ambassador Bartleby was reading with satisfaction accounts of the press conference by President Campos, who praised the United States and its excellent representation in their nation. Bartleby could not doubt that a promotion to another and grander diplomatic assignment would soon be his.

He was astonished when a shaken staff assistant entered the ambassadorial suite. It seemed that the White House had just announced that the Honorable James Hopkins, Deputy Assistant Secretary of Commerce and a foremost authority on this small nation, had been nominated to replace Ambassador Bartleby, for whom no further assignment was announced.

Barnwell took the news with equanimity. He knew that a new chief would also appreciate his talents, as he went up the bureaucratic ladder of professional diplomacy, and after all, this man Hopkins had been a Trade Fair ally. All in all, the future looked bright indeed.

CHAPTER 19

▼

<u>FSB</u>

Bob Irvine sat at the assigned desk. Vaguely he was aware of the several hundred others who were filing into the large conference hall. He was early, as usual, and had followed his parents' advice for once. No cramming. "What's to cram for, anyway?" his father had insisted. "You've lived this life for twenty years and more. Just get a good night's sleep." "And a good breakfast," his mother had added. "Not too much. Just stoke the fires. Don't snack, either."

That had started a cavalcade of advice over the phone. "Just answer the questions that you know," his father added. "Don't spend time trying to figure out those you don't." His mother, on the extension phone, of course advised the contrary. "But if you have some idea, it's probably based on something. Go with your instincts."

He was glad they were so involved, so concerned. That probably meant that the teenage revolt stage was not only over, but forgotten. Not that it was their fault. But when they went overseas, Dad always had a job that he understood to go to in the Embassy. If it hadn't been so easy for Mom, at least she had her own routines and support system. Beyond that, they had chosen the Foreign Service life. His father had looked forward to it, and his mother had found it rewarding as well.

They didn't have a clue, really, what it was like to be in school and then transfer repeatedly. They didn't understand how kids thought and reacted, how important it was, particularly in junior high and high school, to know what music was in, what clothes to wear, what the team was doing.

Bob had felt like a total alien, coming back from the American Academy in Athens, to start Winston Churchill High School in Potomac. A soccer fan, he and his father had watched *Panathenaikos* at their Stadium whenever they could. Men only in the roaring crowd, the long dance of passes, the graceful power of extended legs, the scoring kick and futile lurch of the goalee, the rise of the crowd and screaming applause. Bob had a numbered *Panathenaikos* sweater that his father had bought for him after a division championship match. He was very proud of it. He wore it to his new American school the first day, and could hardly believe the snickers in the halls were for him.

"What's that gooky thing?" somebody said.

"Kids are dumb," he had said, on returning home that first day.

He never wore the sweater again.

It had taken a while, but after his father had worked up several doubles sessions at the school's tennis courts, Bob had regular partners from school. From there to the tennis team wasn't such a stretch. Tennis was a diplomatic sport, or rather, he thought, it was a sport that diplomats had played in each of the overseas posts where his family had been assigned. It was something you could take with you, and he had grown up with the game.

Ten minutes before the start of the Foreign Service exam. Bob knew all the stories. About five in a hundred would get through the written examination and then came the dreaded oral examination, when you had to go before a board of senior officers. Now there was a role playing exercise, too, at a government facility that was supposed to be a Consulate General. Candidates assumed roles within that mission, Vice Consul, Political Officer, Security Officer, whatever. Problems came up, and you had to handle them. Well, he'd seen his father do that for years. So what if only a handful actually made it into the Foreign Service? At least since the star years of Colin Powell and Condoleezza Rice there had been appropriations from the Congress to cover the annual expenses of an entering FSO class.

Some years before that, the State Department had taken nobody in at all.

At the current success rate, just two of the people taking this test today would make it. Two out of two hundred.

A young brunette woman took the seat diagonally in front of Bob. She sighed. Beaten in advance, Bob thought. Attractive, probably bright enough, but beaten in advance. How to limber up and relieve the tension? He remembered his routine on long flights. A few isometric exercises would tone him up and be good for his circulation. First, the arms. He strained one palm against the other in a lifting exercise, and felt the pressure in his biceps. Then he lifted each leg in turn a few inches against the weight of his hand pressing on the knee. The circulation rush made him feel more alive, more ready for the test.

Bob remembered Strasbourg, where his father had been Consul General, after they had left Potomac. It had been his father's last post, his retirement post. Bob had loved the city and its location. You could be across the Rhine in Germany in minutes, or in Switzerland after a short drive, or spend weekends in the beautiful Alsatian countryside. And then there was Annette.

Annette was a student at the University of Strasbourg. They had met one evening at a disco, when Bob was trying out the latest dance routines. Actually he never thought that he was very good, but since he was an American, after all, everyone assumed that what he was doing was the latest disco dance from New York. All he had to do was make something up and give it a name.

She had a warm, wonderful smile, and she didn't seem to care that she was a year or two older than Bob. Pretty quickly they were spending their free time together. Her soft, long brown hair...he could almost feel it against his cheek even now. If only he had been a few years older, so that they could have planned something together. But he had had to leave Strasbourg after two years to come home for college. His parents had insisted on that. "You spend so much time overseas, Bob. There's a danger that you'll forget who you are. Better get your college training back home. You can always travel later. You know how to do that."

He had seen her during school vacations, of course, first eagerly and regularly, then less often. She was a popular girl, and had new friends, but as time passed they had less and less to talk about. She also had decided that she wanted to stay in Strasbourg. She loved the city, its beautiful old section, half-timbered houses, the restaurants, and the wonderful hilly countryside that led through a storied wine district. And it wasn't possible that Bob would make his life and career in this corner of France.

Bob guessed that was a cost of living overseas. You made friends, sometimes intensely, for a short period of time. Then they were stuck in your memory, while time moved on. His father had once talked with him about that when they were driving to New England for a college admissions interview.

"It's the biggest cliche in fiction, but it's true. You can't go back again," he had said. "There are lots of reasons for that. First, we have a diplomatic community. That's always our base, after the Embassy itself. It doesn't make any difference where you are, in New York at the U.N., or in Accra. There's the diplomatic mission, and you know the people from other diplomatic missions and their families. That's half our Christmas card list, even now.

"But it's more than that, much more. You just can't ever reproduce the exact time and place, the circumstances of where we have lived abroad, even when you go back to the same city for a visit. Take Budapest, for example. When we were there, it was still behind the Iron Curtain. Now, there isn't one.

"That's the down side, I guess, unless you're a literary sort who enjoys those memories, and the isolation they impose. But there's a real plus side. Foreign Service life keeps us interested, looking forward to what's next. It's a fact that until we leave the Department, there's always going to be the prospect of another assignment overseas, a new country to get to know, a new capital city, not to mention another language to learn or brush up on. For me, that's always been a real plus."

Bob thought of Budapest. He remembered their house on the hill, on the Buda side. He remembered Marika their housekeeper, and the fact that Hungarian children wouldn't play with him. It was forbidden. School was upstairs at the British Embassy on *Harmincad* Square. *Harmincad.* Holy Trinity. A few Hungarian words still came back, from time to time. He had always liked Castle Hill, the *Var*, with the ice cream sellers and the wonderful statues and the view of the Danube and the city from the Fishermen's Bastion. It would be fun to go back to Budapest. Odd, he hadn't thought of that before. Perhaps he'd even get a Foreign Service assignment there. He'd heard that the Embassy had ten times the number of American personnel now, compared with when his family had lived there. Surely the fact that he once had known Hungarian would be a plus. It would make it easier to pick up again.

Well, maybe that wasn't true. He had been a toddler in Singapore. The family legend was that he had spoken Hokkien Chinese before English. He couldn't remember any now, of course. His *amah*, Ah-Siew, was Hokkien, like many of the Chinese majority on the island. She used to take him for walks around their residential neighborhood. Apparently one day, some kids from a nearby *kampong* village had called them names when they were out, and the very proper Ah-Siew had been shocked when her charge had answered them in very earthy Hokkien.

"I didn't teach him those words!" She had insisted later.

"We got him the same year we got you," his father used to joke. He meant their Siamese cat, Minou, the family pet for nearly fifteen years. Minou was their continuity, from post to post, and then back home. There were plaques all over the State Department lobby now, Bob remembered. They commemorated Foreign Service people who had died overseas. Now there was one for Foreign Service family members, too, spouses and children, FSBs. Foreign Service Brats. There probably should also be a statue for pets, Bob thought. They're the ones that keep us all sane. Nobody would ever have the nerve to suggest it. But it's true. Particularly when you're a kid yourself. It's good to have a pet to look after.

He remembered that afternoon in the Cameron Highlands, the hill station an hour or so from Kuala Lumpur. They had gone there for a vacation, a respite from tropical heat, when his father had been the Embassy Commercial Officer in KL. His parents had gone for luncheon to see some friends and explore the hill station, and he had gone for a walk into the small town area, the few shops that supplied what was needed for the hill station's British style homes. A fire had broken out in their rented house, when a servant had emptied ashes from the fireplace into paper bags. The fire had started up a kitchen wall when Bob had returned from his walk. He might have ignored it even then, but he had heard Minou cry. "We'll take him, of course," his mother had said. "He needs a vacation too from all this heat." Bob had quickly taken the kitchen hand fire extinguisher and put out the blaze.

It was just minutes before the fire would have spread, devouring the house, said a pleased Malayan Fire Brigade Captain, flashing a genuine smile.

"Don't touch the materials until we give the word," the test supervisor announced. Bob looked down at his desk, and saw that he had mechanically passed the test booklets along to neighboring desks, keeping one for himself. They were doing this by the clock, of course. That meant a few minutes before the booklets could be opened.

Bob took a last look around the room as the test supervisor watched the clock. Yes, there were about two hundred candidates now waiting for the test to begin. He wondered just who would be the other candidate to make it all the way and be commissioned into the Foreign Service.

CHAPTER 20

▼

DIPLOMATIC RECEPTION

Bill Ketchum carried his 3X5 card in his pocket, but he didn't really need that crutch. There were just four entries, listed in cryptic detail, matters that he had to check out at this reception at the German Embassy. In listing them, he had memorized them. In the order listed, the first item was "Trade Mission: Worth it?: Ask Georg."

Ketchum fingered his invitation and looked for the reception line. He thought just in time to slip the invitation into his pocket. It was all right to have it with you, but actually holding it might imply that he wasn't sure of his welcome. That was really gauche. Practiced diplomats like Sean Urquhart from the British Embassy and Tomas Santa Clara from the Spanish Embassy would rather be caught shaking hands with car keys still in their palms than go through a reception line with an invitation, as if you didn't really belong. What if Elena saw such a thing?

He shrugged off that nightmare and got down to business. Georg Munchner was his counterpart, the German Embassy's Commercial Officer. That was the reason for this reception, introducing a German Trade Mission to this sleepy capital. The stated justification, the promotion of exports, seemed anachronistic in these days of fax and e-mail, and corporations with global reach. Still, perhaps an official push made a difference for a collection of middleweight companies who couldn't afford export programs on their own. At least, that was the usual rationale. Georg could tell him how it was going, and then he'd decide whether this was something he could recommend to State and Commerce. There hadn't been an American trade mission here in three years. A successful German effort might be worth emulating.

He could start checking that out right away. There was Georg with a well fed, overdressed businessman near the entrance door of the main downstairs reception room, where a crowd had already gathered. This was probably as close to a reception line as they'd have. Ketchum sauntered forward, extended his hand and gave his best Main Street smile.

"Nice turnout, Georg. How is the trade mission going?"

"First rate, Bill. Let me introduce you to its leader. Heinrich Gardrein, Rhine Master Products, here is Bill Ketchum, Commercial Attache, American Embassy."

They exchanged pleasantries. "First visit, Mr. Gardrein?"

"First business trip here, yes. But I've known about this hidden paradise of yours for years." He gave Georg Munchner a poke in the ribs. "Can't expect to keep it for yourselves, you know. But you asked about the trip. It's going well. We've been here a few days and made a number of business contacts. Tomorrow we travel outside of the capital for the weekend, so it's not all business. But it's been worth it. I may have even located a local distributor. Can't let you Americans have all the business opportunities here, now can we?"

It was time to move on. Over there was Michel Artand, from the French Embassy. Just the man to see.

The second item on Ketchum's list was more important than trade mission minutiae from the standpoint of Embassy politics. His own Embassy, that is. And this was crucial. A doubles tournament was about to be scheduled at the diplomatic club. The tournament, for the Ambassadors' Cup, paired ambassadors with other players from the diplomatic colony. Ketchum had to scout out who was going to be on leave of the best tennis players in the local circuit, so that Ambassador Clanton stood a chance of getting a decent partner, and the other ambassadors who played would have less possibility of snagging one. Since Ketchum was also arranging the tournament itself, it was possible to juggle the schedule accordingly.

There were three superior players in the entire diplomatic colony: Sean Urquhart, Tomas Santa Clara, and Michel Artand. The very best was Artand. By anyone's standards, Clanton wouldn't be one of the three. Or one of the top twenty, for that matter. Neither was Ketchum, but that didn't prevent his having been named Morale Officer by the DCM as soon as he had arrived at post. "In case the title confuses you," the DCM had confided, "just remember your main task. You've got to get tennis partners for Ambassador Clanton so he stands some chance of winning a doubles tournament now and then." So he was stuck with being Embassy Tennis Attache.

"*Bon soir*, Michel," Ketchum began.

"*Tiens*, William. Surely there's going to be another tennis tournament. I can just feel it in my bones!"

"That's what you get, old chum, for playing such good tennis before you joined the *Quai d'Orsay*. Too bad your Ambassador doesn't play." Ketchum imagined for a moment that rotund gourmet playing any sport. It was like seeing Charles Laughton attempt to run a marathon. He grinned, and Artand joined him.

"Again with Ambassador Clanton. Why doesn't he take a hint from your American history, that charming Myles Standish and Priscilla Mullins fable, and speak for himself if he wants a doubles partner?"

Ketchum smiled. "When were you going on leave? We were hoping to start things off in a few weeks, and hold the tournament in April."

"Sounds all right to me. My leave's in early May."

Ketchum smiled more expansively. Time to close the deal. "Only fair that you help Clanton out, Michel. You owe it to us. After all, you learned your tennis at Stanford."

"As you always remind me. But the Turkish Ambassador has already asked. I haven't answered yet. He's such a competitor. I'd hate to be on the court when he succumbs to his high blood pressure. Let me think it over. You know, I'd like to help if I can."

"I appreciate it, *cher ami*. You've just made this a successful reception. Ambassador Clanton will be calling you in a day or so, to set up a practice match. Perhaps you can let him know then." Only fair, Ketchum thought, to make Clanton close his own deal.

"*Ciao*."

"*Ciao*."

Third on the list was a rumor concerning President Siguiera. Ketchum had heard that Siguiera was ill, and might step down, leaving office. There was probably nothing whatsoever to it, but the DCM had asked Ketchum to monitor anything he heard that could relate to the subject. Siguiera had seized power as General Siguiera five years earlier, and then had astonished observers three years ago by actually holding the elections that he had promised. That he had won handily was less surprising. That feat had even been accomplished played against the fanfare of an international observer corps. "No hanging chads here!" Siguiera had announced to a bewildered electorate, upon winning 73% of the vote.

Ketchum then remembered that rumor of a government reshuffle that Sean Urquhart had been trying to confirm. A couple of cabinet ministers might be getting the axe. That was worth running down. Another good rumor source, of course, was Tomas Santa Clara, Urquhart's rival as the longest serving political officer in this capital. He might know something. At the same time, Ketchum could also find out when they were going to take their vacations.

"Evening, Sean. What's all this about a reshuffle?" Urquhart, a no nonsense red brick university graduate who despised what he called "diplomatic fluff," enjoyed straight talk and the immediate use of first names.

"That's what I hear, Bill. Justice and Interior will be out within a fortnight. For some reason, they've blotted their copybooks with Siguiera. The internment policies, I hear."

That made sense. The latest Human Rights Report issued by the State Department had faulted this nation's quaint habit of rounding up illegal immigrants who crossed the southern border and then putting them in internment camps without hearings, sometimes for months, before trucking them back across the same border. Siguiera, who had been putting on a charm offensive with the new administration in Washington, had been offended when the annual report had been made public the week before his latest official trip there.

"So he's firing the chaps at the head of Justice and Interior as a way of signalling a change of things. The question is for you to answer: will that improve relations with the United States?"

"A little iffy, I think. Depends upon whether he backs up that action with appointment of more humane ministers." This was standard first secretary speak, safe pronouncements on a politically hypothetical subject. Couldn't get into trouble that way. Not like failing to arrange a winning scenario for the Ambassadors' Cup Doubles Tournament.

"By the way, Sean, I haven't seen you on the tennis courts in months. Given it up, have you?"

"Not at all. Just busy. I wouldn't miss the Ambassadors' Cup for the world. When are you going to hold it, Bill? A moment of maximum convenience for Ambassador Clanton, surely?"

"How could you ever think that? Still, it would be a good thing if he won."

"In several vital respects, I'm sure. My Ambassador may want to play this year. I'm not sure yet."

"To answer your question, the timing's not set yet. I'll let you know, Sean." So Urquhart might be part of another team. That shifted him from potential ally to rival. This must be handled with care. Of course, if Clanton could win without Urquhart, that would be all the better. And Clanton's winning with a Frenchman would doubly annoy the Brits.

Ketchum could almost picture the scene. A becomingly (and unrecognizably) modest Ambassador Clanton called to the rostrum of the diplomatic club to receive the Ambassadors' Cup. His only problem, Ketchum was sure, would be to share the stage with Michel Artand, if he could be talked into playing with Clanton rather than the Turkish Ambassador. If he did agree, Ketchum had no problem picturing whose name would be listed first on the cup. It would be displayed on the firepace mantle of the diplomatic club for the entire winter. He was sure that Ambassador Clanton would even look forward to bringing visitors to the club then, to admire the view of the city.

"Hello, Tomas. Nice reception. How are things at the Spanish Embassy?"

"First rate, Bill. This is a night off for me, really. I don't usually cover commercial receptions like this one, but Diego is on leave. He said he'd cover for me next month. I'm looking forward to seeing Madrid again. But the Germans do this sort of thing well. No bar liquor, just the good stuff."

So he'd be away in May. That was worth hearing. Tomas was a skilled player, and he didn't fool around. Unlike some others, he was not in the least above smashing the ball at Ambassador Clanton rather than his partner. It wasn't done, really, but it scored reliably. Yes, it was a far, far better thing for Santa Clara to be on leave when the Ambassadors' Cup was contested.

"Have you heard anything about changes in the government?"

"Such as…"

"A government reshuffle of some sort. I've been checking it out with Sean. He hasn't heard anything definite. I thought you might have heard something."

"Yes, I have, actually." He paused, waiting for Ketchum to continue.

"Why would there be a government reshuffle if President Siguiera himself might have to resign? They'd be better advised not to rock the vote until Siguiera's health looks clearer, wouldn't they?"

"My information is that his health will determine whether he has to resign or not. But those two ministers he wants out of the way in any case. If he stays, he doesn't want them in the cabinet. If he can't, then he wants them fired, to limit the possibility that either might succeed him as President."

This was heady stuff. Tomas sounded authoritative. "And just what have you heard about his health?"

"A lot, from a pretty good source. Actually an excellent source. The best. Known to our Embassy. A friend of the Ambassador. By the way, Ambassador Fuentes has a new enthusiasm. Perhaps you hadn't heard."

Ketchum mentally tabulated the enthusiasms that Ambassado Fuentes had exhibited during the past two years. Vintage wines, female second secretaries, antique furniture. That was the list, to his knowledge. The progression had seemed a bit illogical to Ketchum.

"What's he interested in now?"

"Tennis. He remembers that his Morroccan colleague won the Ambassadors' Cup last year, playing with Sean. He thinks that he and I might stand a good chance to win this year. There is no rule about which embassy the partner must come from, so we were thinking of teaming up."

He paused. "I hope you weren't thinking of postponing the tournament this year, Bill. We were quite sure that it would be held in May, as it was last year. My leave, you know," he confided. "Reservations. Tickets. Everything set for April."

Ketchum hemmed and hawed.

"Well, let me know, Bill. I do think you would be most interested in learning more about our source on Siguiera. He's really quite sure, closely connected and all that." Santa Clara leaned forward, a fellow conspirator. "No reason we shouldn't share what we know, after all." Then he wandered off to the bar in search of another drink.

Fourth on the list, of course, was Elena. She was the Second Secretary of the Chilean Embassy, and Ketchum had first seen her a fortnight ago, at a welcoming reception at her own mission. She was the most gorgeous creature Ketchum had ever seen, at least in this capital. Was she here at the German Embassy? Was she married? Did she remember him? Was she even aware of his existence?

"Hello there. Mr. Ketchum, wasn't it?" There she was. "We met at the Embassy of Chile a few weeks ago. I had just arrived."

She was taller than he had remembered, and just as stunning. She had buoyant grace, and seemed to glide towards him. Dark hair, dark eyes, and a film star smile, she was the sort that other females hope had a schedule clash. Permanently.

"Of course. You had just arrived." Imagine, this gorgeous creature remembering *him*!

"I noticed you going around talking with several people, Sean Urquhart, Michel Artand, Tomas Santa Clara. It was almost as though you were checking topics off a list. Were you?" she asked suddenly.

Candor might impress this straightforward woman. "Yes, I was, as a matter of fact. Rumors concerning President Siguiera. Trying to see if there was anything to them."

"Oh. You looked too intense for that. For a moment, I thought you were arranging the Ambassadors' Cup Doubles Tournament."

"That, too. Do you play?"

"I was national amateur champion, singles and doubles."

"Women's doubles, or mixed?" He couldn't believe what he was hearing.

"Actually, both."

"Have you played here yet?"

"Actually, no. Too busy settling in, and my tennis outfits haven't arrived yet. The shipment is expected in a few weeks."

"Too bad you came here, rather than going on to Wimbledon." It was a dumb thing to say, Ketchum knew, but sometimes trying so hard you just couldn't be Cary Grant. But did he have to sound like Larry, Moe and Curly instead?

She rescued him. "Not this year, certainly. For next year, that's an open question. It depends upon a number of things, including the prospects for extended leave and of course, lots of practice. That's why I wondered about your tournament."

"We were thinking of sometime soon, April, possibly, or May. Would that suit you?"

"The sooner the better. Of course, I'll need a partner."

Ketchum pretended to give the matter deep consideration. "I don't think that will be a serious problem," he said. "Just don't promise anyone else until we talk again, OK?"

She smiled agreement as he got drinks from a passing waiter for them both, and then headed off to talk with Santa Clara. It was time to deal, and find out what Santa Clara's source was on President Siguiera's health, and precisely what he had told the Spanish Ambassador. It was turning into an interesting reception after all.

CHAPTER 21

▼

TWENTY YEARS AFTER

Jack Sanderson turned right off Vassilias Sofias Boulevard, drove up the short side street and eased his car into the Embassy parking lot. He looked critically around the lot. Where were the security men positioned, and how many were on duty? How was the open lot secured during the working day? Were any more barriers needed?

He made a mental note to talk with the Post Security Officer. A good Deputy Chief of Mission should be on top of everything, and it helped to have a reputation for keeping everyone on their toes. That created a ripple effect of efficiency throughout the mission. No nonsense Sanderson, that was it. He even preferred to drive his own car, although Admin had told him that a chauffeur would be justified. Athens was a tough post from the standpoint of security, after all.

It had always been that way, it seemed. While walking through the Embassy entrance to his office adjoining Ambassador Boynton's suite, he passed the offices of the Political Section. There on the left was his old office, where he had reported on internal Greek politics, twenty years earlier. Jack nodded at the occupant, an earnest young officer on his first overseas political reporting tour, and proceeded up to his own office.

Ambassador Boynton of course had not yet arrived. He wouldn't arrive for another forty minutes at least. That gave Sanderson enough time to sort through the incoming cables which his secretary had placed in a folder on his desk. He would look through the other cable traffic later, before the staff meeting. Sanderson was an orderly sort. On this Monday morning, he would go through the State traffic first, including messages authorized over the weekend by the Embassy duty officer.

He had already gone through the USIS reading file, skimming through it over breakfast along with the Greek newspapers. He had the USIS reading file of items from the American press delivered to his residence each morning, as soon as it was ready. Nine times out of ten it contained the only items that interested Ambassador Boynton.

For a political chief of mission that was perhaps understandable, but it still annoyed Sanderson that he had to spend so much time on these extraneous matters with the Ambassador. You would think that after six months, he would begin to catch onto what was really important. After a few minutes, Sanderson's secretary carried back to the Political and Economic Sections his Greek newspapers, with the daily request for translations, summaries and comments.

His eye fell upon a stack of invitations on the left hand side of his desk. Polly would be pleased. She liked this sort of thing, and never seemed to quite grasp the idea that a reception meant work after hours. He remembered once in Djakarta, when he had added up the evenings they had spent either in official entertaining or at receptions. According to his datebook, that had consumed three hundred and forty evenings of the year!

That meant that an evening alone at home was a rare treat, a movie rarer still. No wonder the twins, Jocelyn and Sandra, had begun to seem like strangers, even before they were whisked off to their colleges in the United States.

There was an opening of a play at the Herod Atticus, with tickets enclosed, courtesy of the Foreign Ministry. That would be worth looking forward to. His Greek was adequate to the task, and Sanderson enjoyed the classic theater. It was *Oedipus at Colonnus*. The actors were unfamiliar names to him, but the play was a familiar continuation of the legend. He still remembered the thrill of recognition during his first tour in Athens when he had driven over the hills to Delphi, and recognized the "threefold way" where Oedipus had killed his father.

Two national days were coming up. He would bargain with Ambassador Boynton about that. Probably Boynton would go to one. He thought they were important, after all. As to the other, Sanderson would make sure that Political Counselor Jim Reavis, James Harrison Reavis that is, attended. That would free him from two decidedly marginal obligations.

There was a nicely scrolled invitation from the French Embassy. Sanderson picked up the envelope, and opened it with interest. He had last served as Consul

General in Marseilles, and fancied himself something of an authority on matters French. It was a cocktail reception. Obviously. For a dinner party, the hostess would have called first, and then sent the invitation later, to remind. It was to introduce his counterpart, just arrived, Marie Laure Cambon.

So Marie Laure was back in Athens!

He remembered her so clearly from that simpler time when they had both served here, in the Political Sections of their respective embassies, twenty years earlier. She had flaxen hair, unusual he thought for a Frenchwoman, and blue eyes. ("The Vikings were everywhere" had been her laughing explanation.) She had, he remembered, the trim figure and perfect balance of a natural athlete, without making a fetish of it.

She had enjoyed riding and sailing, and had almost, but not quite, shamed him into attempting the Marathon run, the original one of course, from Marathon across the hills at Dionyssos, down through Kifissia and into Athens towards the Agora. the ancient market where Pheidippides in all likelihood had finished the original Marathon.

He wondered whether he should call her, and dithered away several minutes before his secretary interrupted his reveries. Ambassador Boynton was in his office, and wanted to discuss the morning staff meeting. Bother Ambassador Boynton! Sanderson made the call, then rose from his chair and wordlessly left the office.

It was a glorious morning, just perfect for a leisurely stroll to Kolonaki. There was enough time to walk along and admire the fashionable neighborhoods, before he met Marie Laure. Her voice had trembled, and she had not hidden her pleasure at hearing from him so soon after her arrival in Athens.

Kolonaki was full of small tony shops bursting with expensive merchandise. Perched on a hillside, it contained restaurants fashionable among the diplomatic set. Sanderson was pleased to see that it hadn't changed, and that their favorite restaurant, L'Abreuvoir, was still there. It would have been so awkward to meet on the corner, having belatedly discovered that "their" luncheon rendezvous spot was now a postcard and souvenir emporium.

But that had not happened. Even the waiters seemed familiar, as Sanderson looked around with approval. Inside the restaurant, discrete booths made a contrast to the displays of fish and meats arrayed along an interior wall. It was customary to be seated, then, waiter in tow, saunter over to that counter and point out what you wanted. Eminently practical, Sanderson had always thought, particularly since his Greek vocabulary could never hope to cope with the immense selection of fresh fish on display. He doubted if even native speakers knew the name for every variety, come to that.

Since the weather was so fine, an outside table seemed preferable. These were shaded by the restaurant's ample awning, and the tables were arranged in tiers, so that from each one, the diners would enjoy an unobstructed view of Athens below. He chose a table that they might have sat at twenty years earlier, and remembered what they liked to order.

She was not a finicky eater, and neither was he. That might have put him off at the start, but her request for *steak au poivre* had fit his mood perfectly. They enjoyed *dolmades* first, flavored rice wrapped in grape leaves, and discovered that neither of them cared for retsinated wine. She had had a glass of chablis, while he had indulged a weakness for *ouzo*, that Mediterranean smoky aperitif that he later would enjoy in Marseilles, calling it *pastis*. It hadn't dawned on him until now that his lifelong defection from gin and tonics to *pastis* probably had stemmed from their luncheon meetings.

The *steak au poivre* had been perfection then, served hot and spicy, but not too spicy, accompanied with a superb fresh green salad and golden shoestring potatoes. She had been astonished by the wine, a fine vintage Greek red Boutari that could have been a Bordeaux. The view had been perfect. There hadn't been any dessert, not at the restaurant, in any event.

Sanderson sighed at his memory, then sat at the table and studied the menu and wine list. The *steak au poivre* was still featured, in case she remembered. His chair faced the entrance to the outdoor section of the restaurant, along one of Kolonaki 's sauntering streets. He needn't stare to make sure that he saw her immediately.

He ordered an *ouzo*, and when it came, plopped the smoky liquid into a glass of cold water, added ice and stirred the result. He sipped his drink. It was strong and refreshing.

He tried to remember all that had happened, but it was not possible. There had been so many pleasant times at first. He could hardly even remember their sequence anymore, although for a long time he had seemed to remember each day like a dancer would commit to memory a beautiful and intricate choreography. Now it all seemed somewhat jumbled together, not linear at all, a few peaks that were evergreen, and valleys of course.

He and Polly had gotten along fine in their first year or so, but then their separation had taken a toll. Polly had insisted on finishing her advanced degree at George Washington University, and so he had proceeded to Athens alone. Polly would come the following summer, when her degree work had been finished. In the meantime, he had flown back to Washington for their Christmas together. It was all that he could afford. He hadn't been in Athens long enough to be eligible for home leave back in Washington, which the government would have paid for, and so there was nothing to do but wait out the year.

Nothing to do, that is, until he had met Marie Laure early that spring, at a French Embassy reception.

The only honorable thing to do, he knew, was to make a clean breast of it to Polly, and seek a divorce as quietly and quickly as possible. That is what he had told Marie Laure, and he had meant it too, every word of it. His courage had held right up to the last minute, when he had met Polly at the Athens airport, and when her surprise, based on their Christmas week together at home, had leapt to his eyes.

"I wanted to surprise you," she had said. "Aren't you pleased?" Afterwards he had searched through her letters, and found that there had been oblique hints of her pregnancy, but he had been so caught up in his own maelstrom of feelings for Marie Laure that he had not deciphered her meaning.

Now the twins were in America in college, and he was meeting Marie Laure once more. It must have been the longest pause in emotional history. For him, it was all rushing to continue as before. Perhaps they could even begin again.

What was she like now, he wondered. Had she forgiven him for the way that everything had ended so suddenly, twenty years ago? They hadn't spoken except formally for most of their remaining time together in Athens, following that emotional scene. He had even, after sporadic attempts at correspondence, lost track of her over the years.

Well, not entirely. She was an excellent linguist and had a fine sense of humor, and came from a prominent family. Put together, those attributes had ensured that her colleagues at other French diplomatic missions could unknowingly help Sanderson chart her career. Someone always seemed to know where she was assigned, and how she was getting on.

Interesting that she had never married, Sanderson had thought. The predictable rebound had either never happened, or she had contained its effects. Smart woman. Then he saw her at the entrance to the restaurant. It was quite sunny out now, and he could study her for just a moment before her eyes became accustomed to the shadows. Then she spotted him, smiled and came into the restaurant.

They went through the kissing routine of the French, kisses on each cheek, with an American handshake as well, just as they used to do, and then sat down at the table.

Marie Laure looked at him closely. She hadn't remembered that Sanderson was quite this good looking. Of course he was older now, they both were, but she had always in a way been attracted to men of his present age. His French was still good. He had acquired diplomatic mannerisms that she found attractive, and she was pleased that he had seemed to remember every detail of their luncheons there.

Once he said them, she remembered. Yes, she had liked the *steak au poivre*, and she had liked it rather rare. "Cannibal!" he said, repeating the old joke, and she laughed, then again, more easily as the luncheon proceeded. He remembered dresses that she had forgotten that she had ever possessed. It was rather nice, and certainly flattering. She found herself warming to what he had to say, which was largely inconsequential banter, meaning trapped in nothings.

He hadn't really remembered that she was this much fun. There had always seemed to be something on his mind before.

Sanderson basked in the memories of the past, and in the pleasant smiles with which Marie Laure responded. What a fine audience she was, really. It was flattering. Perhaps they would be able to resume their friendship after all, if not on quite the same terms, then certainly with more discretion. His voice rose with a bit of anticipation, and he put his hand over her own.

The luncheon revealed some secrets to him.

Marie Laure Cambon had never quite forgotten Jack Sanderson, and their adventure in Athens. He had been amusing and fun to be with, and for a brief while, she must admit, she had been quite taken with him. It couldn't have lasted, of course. Americans were such Puritans at heart. He had volunteered the fact of his marriage with his name at their first meeting, almost at the same moment they had shaken hands. It was as though he had decided to offer her a rulebook for a game that he didn't know very well, but thought that he had invented.

He had been thoughtful and affectionate, she remembered. Their last private meeting had been a shock, and she admitted it. But then, such conversations, predictable though they were, always had an element of pain and loss.

They had of course talked over then what would happen when Polly, Sanderson's wife, came to Athens. Marie Laure had never doubted in the slightest that he would go back to his wife. That, in her experience, is what husbands did.

Sanderson (she realized that she had always thought of him by his last name) had never quite caught on that she had not encouraged him in his protestations that he would divorce his wife. No matter. That, in her experience, is what husbands said. To be absolutely fair, she observed that at the time that they said it, they probably even meant it. Still, she had been half listening.

Her career was her life. She had never had the least intention of becoming part of someone else's career. That was unusual when she had first passed her examinations for the *Quai d'Orsay*. Now it was less so, but still not commonplace. Still, as she had supposed, the fact that she was an attractive single officer wedded to her career had not harmed that career at all. In fact, she could probably write her own ticket for the future.

There were good opportunities at the Ministry, and her political connections remained excellent, even with the change of government. She had mastered the American trick of being thoughtful to politicians who were out of favor, knowing that even in France, the pendulum of *l'alternance,* or the alternation of power, would swing them back into office. There were also possibilities to head her own embassy, and she was intrigued by that. The point, she thought, was to avoid becoming a token *Madame l'Ambassadrice* at some small, unhealthy place. If an unhealthy climate was to be in her future, she might as well set her elegant *chapeau* to be Ambassador in Washington.

Sanderson's call had been a complete surprise. So he was also a Deputy Chief of Mission, and at this important American Embassy at that. He must be doing rather well.

When the Ambassador had cabled the *Quai* where she was taking an immersion course in recent Greek politics, he had kindly offered to host a series of introductory receptions for her. Marie Laure had asked only that her fellow deputy chiefs of mission be invited so that she could meet them early on.

And so, in addition to several receptions involving Greek public figures and artists, a special interest that she shared with the Ambassador, he had set up a reception for the "number twos" at the diplomatic missions in Athens. It was an original idea, and it had produced Sanderson, after all these years.

She had quite lost track of him, although she had wondered what had become of him from time to time. It was a natural curiosity. Then he had called, and with the midday free, she had surprised herself by agreeing to have luncheon with him in Kolonaki. Finishing the morning's staff meeting, she had taken a taxi to the restaurant rather than an Embassy car. That much was owed to propriety in any event, she said.

His concentration in her talk was almost complete, but not so total that he missed Polly entering the restaurant with her shopping friend, Joan Florigan from the British Embassy. Joan was a funny lady who was also, Polly always said, the biggest diplomatic gossip on the entire Athens circuit.

✳   ✳   ✳   ✳

"Didn't you hear me, Mr. Sanderson?" his secretary asked, with an unprecedented raising of her voice. Ambassador Boynton wants to see you before the staff meeting."

"Oh yes, thanks. I was thinking of something else."

"What would you like me to do with those invitations?" She asked. He had almost forgotten that he was still holding them in his hand.

"Accept for the French Embassy and the theater. I'll talk with the Ambassador and with Jim Reavis about the two national days."

She moved to mark his schedule accordingly as Sanderson coughed, straightened his tie, and went into the Ambassador's office for their usual Monday morning meeting.

CHAPTER 22

▼

LOCAL HOLIDAY

"It's like the Army. Young second lieutenants have the rank, and they are in command, but if they have any brains at all they'll listen to senior noncommissioned officers. Not that you would understand that from experience. Your generation didn't serve, after all." The effect was softened with a smile and a self-deprecating toss of the hands.

Commercial Counselor Stan Pettit was holding a section staff meeting. He'd covered the month's commercial trends, and touched on who was expected on the island during the next month. Now he was trying to explain to the newest Embassy arrival, Phil Ingraham, a junior Foreign Service Officer, just what Foreign Service Nationals did, and where these local hire career employees fit into the scheme of things.

"It's particularly important here in Singapore. On the surface it's a modern place. But unless you can figure out the background, and that often means what's important to the mix that makes up the local population, you'll miss a lot. They're good people, largely Chinese of course, but Indian and Malay too. Not to mention Eurasians and others I've forgotten."

"I think I get it, Stan. What you mean, I think, is that locals know the work and of course the territory. They're from here, after all. We come and go. So the trick is to tap what they know and use that knowledge correctly. I mean, they can also be a clue to understanding their broader community. Miss Tan for the Hokkien Chinese, for example."

Pettit nodded. Perhaps this new fellow could be developed into something over time. After all, he had just managed several consecutive sentences without using the word "like." That was promising. "Yes, Phil, but don't call them 'locals.' It doesn't sound respectful."

"OK. What do I call them?"

"By their names. Miss Tan, Mr. Singh, Mr. Salah, for example. Remember, they are colleagues. Treat them as such, as you would like to be treated. And, of course, there's also Mrs. Twitcham."

"Who's she?"

"She doesn't work here regularly. Just comes in from time to time. She's a retired British lady, with the finest handwriting I've ever seen. A real calligrapher. She said in her day, that was taught in the public schools. Just imagine! Her late husband was RAF, I think. We employ her to address our invitations and envelopes. Her work adds a nice touch."

✳   ✳   ✳   ✳

Phil Ingraham drove across the causeway that separated Singapore fom the south Malaysian state of Johore Bahru. The passport control was perfunctory. It was a nice night, and he had spent the hour's drive talking with his passenger, Mr. Salah, about the evening.

"My *kampong* or village always has a special celebration for the Sultan's birthday," Salah had said when Ingraham had first approached him about wanting to understand Malay customs. "That would be a jolly occasion, a feast day. You should visit us then. I always go back home for it. As a matter of fact, we could leave for the evening celebration from the Embassy, right after work. Just wear some casual clothes. Your suit won't be necessary." Salah had mentioned the date a few weeks later, and Ingraham had pencilled it in on his calendar. As the diplomatic round became more and more predictable, a routine rather than something to look forward to, he found himself looking forward more and more to the *kampong* evening.

A few miles after the causeway, Salah directed a turn off the main road. It was a sultry, starry night, and Ingraham had the top down. He followed the narrowing road half a dozen miles, then parked the car at Salah's direction and followed his host into a torchlit clearing. Almost as soon as he had stopped the car he had felt the sweat begin to drip down the inside of his sports shirt. It was not an unpleasant feeling, and the scent from the wild blossoming trees was strong and sensual.

Friends and family members spotted Salah and came running to meet him. Ingraham was introduced. He sputtered a few words in Malay, and kicked himself for not knowing more. He determined that he would learn at least enough to carry on a rudimentary conversation. "It's not really necessary," said an obviously pleased Salah. "Nearly everyone speaks English, except the old ones, who never learned or who have forgotten from lack of use."

There was music from the *gamelan* band, flutes and a stringed instrument accompanying this sort of Malayan xylophone. Lionel Hampton would have been proud, Ingraham decided. The melodies were haunting and repetitious. They sounded the same, but Ingraham guessed they wouldn't if his ear were more discriminating. Perhaps that would come in time. Lanterns were strung from trees, shedding light and atmosphere as they swayed whenever a breeze stirred them, forming a perfect backdrop for the music.

Ingraham and Salah joined his family at a table, with much ceremonial embracing for Salah and formal handshakes for Ingraham. These people were beautiful, he decided. No, they weren't. Well, some were. Their carriage seemed perfect, graceful. Most were in traditional Malay dress. The men wore shirts with long sashes. Some had curved daggers by their belts, a *kris* Ingraham remembered. The *sarong kebaya* that some women wore, which Singapore Airlines had now appropriated for its stewardesses, was really attractive. He wished that more of the women wore that glorious fitted top with the evocative skirts. Ingraham took a sip of the drink that had been poured for him.

Then the loudspeaker squawked. "That's my uncle," Salah whispered. "He's welcoming everyone. Then he'll read the birthday message from the Sultan. All very orderly. It's hard to believe that these same people, every generation or two, will run *amok*. That's a Malay word for a Malay custom, you know. Better not be around when that happens."

The message was read, the music resumed, and organization dissolved completely, as people from different tables came and greeted each other. Salah then led the way to tables where meat was placed from the barbecue pits. The evening went on and on, and Ingraham loosened up to the point where he could even venture a dance with Salah's sloe-eyed cousin.

"So this is getting to know the locals," he said to himself. "I'm all for that."

*   *   *   *

Miss Tan was a harder sell. "You say you really want to know something about our customs and folklore?" she said dubiously. "Isn't the Chinese New Year enough for you?"

"I know that from back home," he had replied. "Even when I was in Washington, doing the Basic Officers' Course at the Foreign Service Institute, I went to Chinatown for the New Year. Lots of fun. I really enjoy the dragon dance. But I want to see more." He didn't add that as the District's Chinese population migrated to the suburbs, increasingly the dragon dance was undertaken by lithe African-Americans.

"Just watch," she said. It was evening, and they were at a Singapore Taoist temple devoted to the Monkey God. Candles and incense sticks burned, and a line of Chinese watched a young woman gyrating. She seemed to be under a spell. Finally she spoke. It didn't seem to Ingraham to be Chinese, and it wasn't. To her side, another woman stepped forward and spoke to the first person in the waiting line.

"It's the translator," Miss Tan said. "That first person is now in a trance. She has absorbed the spirit of the Monkey God, and it is the words of the Monkey God that the translator is putting into Chinese. These people are consulting the Monkey God about their problems. They make small donations, and then they ask their questions." And so they were. Some wanted luck in finding a job. Another hoped her lover was true. Several asked insistent follow-up questions, and got further answers through the translator. Obviously the Monkey God did not stand on ceremony. "Well, it beats waiting for Ann Landers to handle your problem in the newspaper," Ingraham said.

"There isn't much of this tradition left anymore," Miss Tan said, as she steered Ingraham to a narrow street. Although past ten at night, the street had the light of day. They sat at a sidewalk restaurant and ate noodles and curried chicken and drank beer.

"What street is this?" Ingraham asked.

"It's the street of the death houses," Miss Tan said. "There they are, across the street. When an old Chinese person is going to die, the family takes their relative here. It's not sad at all. The old person is very well looked after, and as for the family, they are spared the terrible bad luck of a death in their house. Look at the large paper car there in the street," she said. Ingraham did. It was a paper Mercedes, very well made. There were paper sacks of money piled near, and paper clothing, furniture, even a small house. As they watched, it was all set on fire.

"The family pays for all that too. When their relative dies, the bonfire is lit. That means the dead person will be assured of all of those possessions in the beyond, the next life, all of the things that they never had here."

Ingraham was intrigued. "What happens if the old person recovers?"

"It has happened. Sometimes a member of the family, more modern in outlook, hires a doctor. A year ago there was a famous case, when a young person was removed from a death house just in time, before the appendix burst. The life was saved."

"So that was a happy ending."

"For the most part, yes. It helped that this was a young person, with an explanation that people could understand. With the older ones, there is an expectation that they will die here, in the death house. They expect it almost as much as their family. And everything is done for them. It is an honor, really."

*   *   *   *

"This isn't the custom of my people, you understand, Mr. Ingraham," said the tall, formidable Mr. Singh. "You asked about Indian customs. You said you wanted to understand something, and the Feast of Lights of *Thaipusam* is the most celebrated Indian festival here. But it's not Sikh, of course. It's largely South Indian, from Kerala State. That's where many of the Indian people resident in Singapore came from originally. By the way, call me 'Singh.' Everyone else does. It's a Sikh designation. Despite what Mr. Pettit seems to believe, it's not my family name."

Indian men filled the square and side streets, with an attitude of intense concentration. "They have been preparing for weeks, you see, Mr. Ingraham, fasting and praying, mortifying their flesh for this occasion," Singh explained. The Indian men seemed totally unaware of their surroundings, so rapt was their concentration on something inner. Relatives stood nearby, whispering support and encouragement. Like people on the sidelines at the Boston Marathon, Ingraham thought, holding bottles of Gatoraid for the runners to grab and gulp as they passed by, quenching their thirst and getting some strength back.

There seemed to be some sort of course here too, leading down through side streets off the square. And then it started. There were wooden cages with spikes which helpers put over the torsos of the Indian celebrants. The spikes dug into their flesh throughout the upper body, the more so because the men deliberately leaned on them, forcing the spikes downward, into their shoulders and hips. Ingraham thought he was going to pass out. He couldn't believe what he was seeing. And yet, there seemed to be no bleeding.

Singh pointed silently towards another man a few yards away. A spike was driven through his cheeks. Some ashes had been put on his face, and he joined others going along the route. This man, though, first stopped to walk, ever so slowly, along a path of white hot coals that had thoughtfully been put along the way. "He'll have no burn marks at all," Singh said. "By the way, I know him. He's a clerk at my bank."

*   *   *   *

"So you're getting to know something about the cultures of Singapore," Stan Pettit said to Ingraham over poolside drinks at the American Club.

"Yes, and I've enjoyed it a great deal. Many thanks for putting me on to that, Stan. It's really helped my understanding of the local culture, too. Just last week, for example, Mrs. Twitcham asked me to join her at the British High Commission."

"My wife was there too. The Queen's Birthday, wasn't it?"

"Yes. They served curious refreshments. Watercress sandwiches, as I recall. And odd drinks, with cucumber slices to stir them. It was held outdoors, which surprised me too, due to the extreme heat. All the ladies wore long floppy hats and long sleeves, despite the blazing sun. The men were in three piece suits. There was a long speech from the High Commissioner. And you know, Stan, the odd thing was, Mrs. Twitcham told me that it wasn't the Queen's real birthday at all."

Ingraham thought for a moment, trying to summarize the experience. "It was, you know, like, weird!"

CHAPTER 23

▼

GIVE ME YOUR TIRED

Vice Consul Maureen Appleby parked behind the Embassy, locked her car, and entered the Visa Office by the side door. The day promised to be sunny and pleasant. Everywhere but here, she thought glumly. This may be a tourist paradise, but it's my two-year sentence on the nonimmigrant visa line.

If this was their idea of a diplomatic career, they could shove it. Every day there was a visa line full of dreary people, sometimes the very same ones that you had turned down the week before, hoping to get into the United States. Recent fighting in the interior made matters even worse. They all lied to you, trying to find out what you wanted to hear. Anything to get their precious visas.

Careerwise, this was a first tour rite of passage, the State Department's Parris Island. You had to toughen up. That meant listening to all these lies. Those really qualified for visas were instantly obvious. Their papers were in order and they weren't desperate. It just wasn't credible that so many people from this desolate flyspeck of a country were going to the United States for a visit, and would return. Anyone who believed that would believe anything. But what was their option, given the even more stringent requirements for an immigrant visa?

And so the nonimmigrant visa line remained steady and long, day after depressing day. Two years of this, and she would transfer to someplace else. Anyplace else.

Now it was time for the Consular Assistant to open the sluice gates and let the day's hopeful applicants flood into the Visa Section. Maureen sighed, found a couple of letters from home on her desk, and put them aside to read later.

She sipped her cup of coffee, glowering at the front door, willing it to stay shut. It opened defiantly, and twenty-five people poured in. They took numbers from the Consular Assistant, and sat in the waiting area, peeping hopefully at the three Vice Consuls. The Consular Assistant called each applicant in turn by number. Just like the Motor Vehicle Department at home, only less friendly, Maureen thought.

Her first visa applicant, a well-dressed young man who was going to spend the summer with friends in New Jersey, produced their letter of invitation and a round-trip air ticket. He also had a letter of acceptance from the island's School of Journalism beginning that fall to prove he would return.

His paperwork was in order and Maureen granted the visa. It all seemed a little too pat, but why look for trouble in a good case? There weren't that many. The young man grinned his thanks. Too smooth, probably a bad case, but she couldn't prove it.

"Hello," the next applicant began. "I'm Feliciana Gomez. I want to visit my sister in Arizona and her baby. She showed a photograph of the month-old infant. Maureen smiled in spite of herself. She liked this well-dressed young woman. There were the round-trip air tickets. Maureen idly wondered what the penalty would be for cancelling the return plane ticket.

Maureen signalled the Consular Assistant to prepare the visa stamp. She sipped her coffee and frowned. It was now cold. One more visa interview, and she'd take a break.

The nervous, deferential old woman was wearing a dress that was still carefully pressed, although the dust along the skirt showed that she had probably had a long walk from her home in the interior just to get to the early morning bus that had brought her to the capital. Her nephew was there to serve as interpreter. Probably he would coach her with the right answers, too.

Maureen ignored the nephew and directly questioned the old woman in Spanish. This flustered the applicant. She couldn't seem to understand what was being said to her. Then the nephew intervened. "You must understand, Vice Consul, that Aunt Maria does not know this city and your customs. She is perhaps a little afraid."

He had a point, and Maureen backed off a bit. She put staccato questions to the old woman through the nephew. Had she left the country before?—Never. How could she pay for the trip?—Her other nephew was arranging all that. Maureen half expected to see the photograph of the baby that the last applicant had showed her. As a matter of fact, she could have sworn that somebody else had used that same photograph two months ago, before the last applicant's mythical niece had even been born!

The questions continued, and the tired old woman became confused. Finally she misspoke, giving the wrong state for her nephew's residence. That did it. Maureen denied the application.

The old woman didn't understand. Maureen repeated what she had said. The stunned nephew translated. There was a moment of silence. Then, with surprising dignity, the old woman stood up, stared at Maureen, and noiselessly left the room.

More visa applicants kept arriving. It was time for a quick break. Maureen decided to take a brisk walk around the Embassy and have some coffee.

She left the Visa Office and glanced at a shop window. Then she noticed a new coffeehouse which looked inviting. She went inside and ordered a cup of cappucino. She took out her mail, and glanced at a letter from her sister. The handwriting on the other letter was stilted, and unfamiliar.

Beth was full of the gossip of her busy social life. The spring semester was going well, and the classes weren't all that demanding. Beth wanted to know about her sister's "glamorous diplomatic whirl." In THIS town? In THIS job? Maureen had seen more glamour in the bio lab in high school.

Well, the next assignment would be different. If not Paris or London, then Brussels. The thing to do was to decide where you wanted to live, and then plan your assignment bids to get there.

Given her druthers, Maureen would really like to go to Vienna. She knew just a little bit of German. Vienna from her family's tales seemed like such a nice place, full of music and fine scenery and wonderful food and wine. Maybe the easiest way to get there would be to volunteer for the visa line in the Embassy's Consular Section.

That was a new thought. She decided not to face it until she had to. Glancing around the room, Maureen saw her first two visa applicants happily sharing coffee and croissants at a back table. They didn't see her. They were obviously a couple.

Maureen frowned and took another sip of her cappucino. What did she expect? They were all cons anyway. Some were better at it than others. That was the only real difference.

She took out the second letter. The initials in the return address were no help. Did she have any relatives in Pennsylvania?

Maureen opened the letter. It was from her Aunt Magda, more properly her mother's first cousin. Maureen had rather liked Aunt Magda when she had unexpectedly showed up at her college commencement two years ago. She was really Old World, though. A hat with a veil suited her well.

Come to think of it, it had been Aunt Magda who had told her stories about Austria that weekend. Odd that she should reappear now, just as Maureen had had the idea of applying for a job at the Embassy in Vienna.

Her letter was short and formal, like the writer. She had had some success in tracing the family, and now she was distributing momentoes that she had found. She thought Maureen would like to have this picture. Great Grandmother Nussbaum would have been so proud of her great granddaughter, in the American diplomatic service!

As Maureen knew, Aunt Magda wrote, the family had fled Austria just in the nick of time. Following the death of Great Grandfather Nussbaum by a beating in the streets of Vienna when he had come to the defense of two young Jewish girls being attacked by brownshirted thugs, Great Grandmother Adele Nussbaum had taken charge.

Somehow she had managed to get the family out of Austria to safety, one by one, selling the family possessions over time to do so. When it had finally been her own turn, there was neither time nor money left. Hitler had annexed Austria, the borders were sealed, and hope had gone. There were no visas available. The doors were slammed shut.

Enclosed with Aunt Magda's letter was a sepia toned snapshot of Great Grandmother Nussbaum alone, looking weary, resigned, but at the same time dignified and proud.

The picture had been sent to her family in America, Aunt Magda noted. On the back of the picture, there was a message. Aunt Magda had translated just below Great Grandmother Nussbaum's formal German gothic script what the old lady had wanted to say to her family.

"My children, be good Americans. You are the hope of the world. Never forget those of us who could not come. Adele Nussbaum, Vienna, November 3, 1940."

CHAPTER 24

▼

THE GOLDEN YEARS

Roger Irvin looked around the lounge, now filling up as people left their tables in the adjoining dining room. The after dinner crowd was larger than usual, for there would be a speaker today. People greeted each other with rehearsed formalities and practiced smiles, recalling the diplomats they once had been, and tried to remain during their retirement.

Just like Paris during the French Revolution, he decided with a smirk. Keeping one's rank as an innoculation against reality. In those days a marquis simply wouldn't be seen talking with just anyone, even if the marquis were in prison and the nobody were holding the list of names for the next trundle cart to the guillotine.

Here in the retirement home things seemed much the same, as past diplomatic rank still ruled. Over there, for example, a retired consul was greeting a former political counselor obsequiously, as though still hoping for an invitation. An aging ambassador entered importantly, preceded by retired junior diplomats like tugs for an oceangoing vessel.

Fred Gammon entered the lounge and sat down on the couch next to Roger. Fred was a retired Cultural Affairs Officer and, Roger suspected, a reasonably successful one. Basically he had been a scheduler, an arranger of programs. He had done his job well as long as the money had lasted. He had retired when the Congressional appropriations for cultural exchanges had dried up.

Now he had a problem. Fred was the program chairman for these monthly retiree get togethers. Usually, at this stage of the game, he would be shuffling a paper or two, preparing to introduce the featured speaker. There was the podium, over across the room.

"They just called from the airport," he said to Roger. "Socked in. Lousy weather. They'd told me about the delay. That's why the Assistant Secretary wasn't here for dinner, of course. But now, he can't come at all. All very apologetic and all that, but I'm stuck for a speaker. Not even a suggested alternate date."

"That's tough, Fred." Roger didn't exactly value the confidence, or Fred's conspiratorial tone. He spotted danger on the horizon.

"Help me out with this one, will you Roger?" Fred pleaded. "The topic was going to be Cyprus, after all, and you're the only one here that actually served there, I think. So you'd be up on it, and we could discuss the topic everyone was prepared to hear after all. What do you say?"

Roger Irvin hadn't served in Cyprus in fifteen years. He pointed out at least three other people in the room who had also served there. The Cyprus network was, like most Foreign Service networks, a rather small one. You knew just about everybody who had the same specialty. But the others were not any more current than he was on the Cyprus issue, the island's seemingly unsolvable division between Turkish and Greek Cypriots. That was part of the interest in hearing what the Assistant Secretary would have had to say on the topic. They could then have recycled his remarks for weeks before that topic petered out.

He said as much to Fred. "Sorry, I'm just out of date. Everybody's heard my war stories."

"Well, that's still better than nothing."

"Not much, I suspect."

Fred didn't give up easily. "I bet everybody here has a favorite story or anecdote they haven't told. If enough would do that, we could have a program after all. Why don't I just tell everyone what has happened, suggest that we all tell a story from our experiences, and then introduce you to lead off. Everybody knows you're a great storyteller. Is that okay, Roger?"

Put that way, Roger Irvin could see no objection. As a matter of fact, it might be rather fun after all. He didn't recall even nodding his agreement when Fred Gammon went to the podium, and announced that the Assistant Secretary couldn't be with them that evening. But programs must go on, he chirped.

Then he announced his plan. Since the topic was to have been Cyprus, he was pleased that Roger Irvin, who had served as Consul there, was leading off. Meanwhile Fred would circulate around and ask others to participate. Half a dozen or so would do it nicely. Everyone would have a chance to speak that wanted to do so, and nobody would be at the podium for more than five or ten minutes.

For a moment, there was a reaction of disappointment. But nobody had a better idea, and who knows, it might be interesting. The Ambassador stood, and thanked Roger for leading off, said that she would participate later, and asked others to do so as well.

Roger stood, and ambled over to the speaker's podium. He cleared his throat, smiled, and began to speak in a low voiced, conversational way. That was for effect. If they had to listen closely to hear what he had to say, they would do so. He would turn up the volume later on, once the audience was hooked. That was what the public speaking class had told him to do, and it always seemed to get results.

He surveyed the audience while he told his anecdotes. He did know everybody, or nearly everybody, even the dozen or so retirees who had come in from their homes in the city, in response to Fred's newsletter. One or two seemed to be strangers, or perhaps, strangers now, but there was something familiar even about them, if he could only place them.

Roger said that if the Assistant Secretary were here, of course, he would bring us up to date on the Cyprus issue, and current attempts to resolve it. His own recollections would be anecdotal and rather personal. When he had served at the American Embassy in Nicosia, there had been the opportunity to travel to the northern part of the island, occupied by Turkish Cypriots and, increasingly, by settlers from mainland Turkey.

Drat. Who was that fellow in the fifth row, anyway? It almost broke Roger's train of thought.

He went on with his anecdote. It was a visit in northern Cyprus to the city of Famagusta. He had gone to the ancient castle, said to be the castle of Othello, the setting for Shakespeare's tragedy and Verdi's opera, which Roger preferred. A melodic phrase from the opera came to him. It was *Salce, salce,* "The Willow Song," Desdemona's aria about poor, doomed Barbara, whose fate foreshadowed Desdemona's own murder.

Barbara. He hadn't thought of her for weeks.

Roger told his audience that the Turks had built a small outdoor theater in the castle courtyard. He had been rather touched by their attempt to pay tribute to that literary site, even if there had been no audiences from the outside world for anything performed there. He always thought they deserved a measure of credit for the gesture.

The man in the fifth row shifted his weight a bit, catching Roger's eye. Of course. It was Alex Simon, now balding and not the dapper, fussy little man he had been thirty years ago. Thirty years ago, when Alex had served in Personnel.

That was when Roger had been seeing Barbara, a vivacious young management trainee in one of the downtown Washington department stores. Those were the days, of course, when one still shopped downtown, rather than at a mall or in the suburbs.

With an effort, Roger continued with his anecdote about Turkish Cyprus. He had been struck by all of those empty hotels along the coast in Famagusta, themselves beached like stranded whales after the fighting. Then a ceasefire line had placed them in Turkish hands, separating the hotels from their Greek Cypriot owners.

From time to time, an attempt had been made to nudge the periodic intercommunal talks in the direction of opening up this region or at least a part of it, as a goodwill gesture, but so far the effort had gotten nowhere. That was a shame, really. Roger wondered whether the expensive hotels were even habitable anymore. Probably they were now wrecked by time and inattention.

Barbara. He could see her even now, and remember their last evening together before he had left for his assignment overseas. He had always regretted not having proposed marriage to her, but then, their relationship hadn't been quite that far along.

At least, he hadn't thought so then. And in those days, one did follow a certain ritual. At least, he did. Roger always followed social rituals. It hadn't mattered that the world moved faster than it ever had in the little southern mountain community where he had absorbed his values, the hometown where kindness endured, and where past wrongs also lasted over the generations, erupting from time to time like a volcano long thought to be extinct. The little community had left its stamp on Roger. That hadn't helped his prospects for promotion very much either. Some supervisors wrote on his annual performance reports that he was too single minded, codeword language for his temper.

Roger remembered now. It was Alex who had briefed him on his assignment. It was a good career move, Alex had said, worth leaving his Washington assignment early.

"No need to thank me, old man. All part of the job."

Roger shifted the locale of his story southward, recalling a dinner party in Nicosia. His hosts and their other guests had been curious about what he had seen in the north, and he described the old castle, and the hotels at Famagusta.

One of the dinner guests, an older man, had let out a sigh. He had owned one of those hotels, he had said.

Roger let that sink in for a while, and he rambled on briefly about life in Cyprus, the Crusader castles, the island of Aphrodite, to set the stage for the end of his anecdote.

A gossipy mutual friend had written him a few months after he left Washington. It seemed that Alex and Barbara had become quite an item. Later, though, things seemed to have cooled down. Roger had checked. Alex hadn't married Barbara after all. He had tired of her a year or so after Roger had left Washington.

Barbara herself had left for the midwest somewhere. Roger never knew exactly where, since they hadn't been writing at that point. Even if they had been, how does one pick up again after all that? Surely she had married and quite forgotten him by now. How was he to know that he would never again meet someone like her? How was he to even guess that the women he would meet would always be compared with Barbara, and never quite measure up?

He returned to the old man in his story. The dinner guest had sipped his after dinner drink, and then confided sadly that he had been raised to pay his debts in full, in cash, no credit. He had been so pleased by the prospect of owning a new hotel along the beach in Famagusta, that he had paid cash on the barrelhead. No mortgage. It had been all that he had. He didn't have to spell out that the fighting and then ceasefire line which had put his hotel in the Turkish sector had ruined him. He hadn't even seen the hotel in years.

The old man had nothing to look forward to. "These should be my golden years," he had said. Instead, he had been the victim of his virtues.

Rather like me, Roger thought to himself. He choked back his feelings.

The story was ending a little more sourly than Roger had expected, so he brightened it up with a quip or two, and expressed his hopes that the new round of negotiations would settle things. The White House was paying attention now, and with the coming election, ethnic votes were at stake. That might be an incentive for a new diplomatic initiative. It always had been.

A nice smattering of applause rewarded his efforts, and Fred Gammon briskly went up to the podium to introduce the next speaker.

Roger acknowledged the applause with a smile and walked over towards Alex. The seat next to him was empty. Roger sat down there, his face a diplomatic mask. For a start, for form's sake, he would first reintroduce himself, when the program was over. Then he would take it from there.

After all these years, he would say, they really must get much better acquainted.

There was lots of time now.
And they had so much in common.

CHAPTER 25

▼

A Glass Of Champagne

The trip towards Reims from Burgundy was its own reward on that bright early afternoon in September, 1815. The flat, lush and now peaceful countryside was most inviting, Major John Taunton thought. Champagne now was so different from the way it had been during the war years.

Local memories were still fresh of *La Grande Armee* racing forth, first to carry Napoleon's offensive abroad, and then, defeated, retreating slowly to delay the invader. Not many of them had made it back alive, Major Taunton reflected, and probably even fewer had ever tasted the region's champagne. Certainly not poor Joel Barlow, his predecessor at the American diplomatic mission in Paris. Barlow had died of exposure and disease during the confused retreat in December three years previously following his consultations with the French in Russia.

In those days the Valley of the Marne had acquired a tragic and sinister veneer. Now, instead, the visitor could admire the pinot meunier grapes raised on the slopes of the Marne Valley for the champagne blend. Further north, past Epernay towards the Montagne de Reims, the pinot noir grapes were grown. From his speeding coach, Major Taunton had already admired ripening in the Cote des Blancs the chardonnay grapes which would complete the traditional champagne blend.

Major Taunton was enjoying a long-postponed vacation.. Following last year's arduous negotiations of the Treaty of Ghent ending the latest war with England,

Taunton had been assigned with Albert Gallatin, now the new nation's Minister to France, to the American diplomatic mission in Paris After the summer's climactic battle at Waterloo, and with the arrival of early fall, at last he had been given a month's leave to see more of France.

He was an older American from a young nation in an old and changing country. A generation earlier, he had been one of those exhilarated young patriots who had risked all on battlefields throughout New England. He carried a reminder of the Revolution with him. His old wound from Bennington, where he had fought as an officer in Colonel Nathan Sparhawk's regiment of volunteers, still gave a twinge from time to time when the weather turned cold.

There was no time to think of fine living then. During that war, and the following years of war and revolution throughout the Continent, with trade blockades involving the United States, Great Britain and France, times had hardly been normal. By contrast his luncheon today at Epernay had been delightful, with soups, meats, a flavorful assortment of cheeses and a fruit tart, which went quite well with the delicious, slightly cloudy champagne.

Major Taunton looked forward in particular to his visit to Reims, the heart of Champagne and home of many of its proudest houses. He hoped that war would never again come to this region. It seemed in many ways a spiritual home for the old ways in France, with memories of the nation's monarchs and history enshrined in the great cathedral.

Now, so much of what attracted him to Reims was underground! He wanted to see the famous chalk caves where champagne was stored and aged, remote from light and disturbance, a chilly subterranean treasure house that extended for many miles.

At last his coach arrived at his destination, a stately colonnaded residence, with servants wearing the old livery, newly fashionable once again. His host welcomed him, and called for glasses and a cool bottle to serve the visitor. Then he speculated, at least half seriously, on the prospect of one day exporting champagne to the United States of America. "Perhaps it will replace the tea that you used to drink before dumping it into Boston Harbor!"

The formal setting was exquisite, and so was the champagne, which Major Taunton was astonished to discover was clear, without any sediment. "How did you produce this?" he asked.

"We call it '*le remuage*.'" His host explained that the sediment that is produced naturally during fermentation is heavier than the wine itself. The trick had been to find a way to make it settle, and then get rid of it. It had been found that if the bottles were placed in a rack, necks angled downwards, and given sharp regular turns, the sediment fell into the necks and could then be disgorged, making the champagne clear.

Major Taunton found it delicious, a delight to the eye as well as the palate. His host said that if only the bottles could be strengthened (for they always seemed to be breaking under the strong built-up pressure from the wine), a larger market could be found. "Who knows? Perhaps sparkling champagne might even become the dominant wine here, rather than just a fraction of the wine we produce in Champagne."

The chateau kept a book of reminiscences for honored visitors. Major Taunton was moved to write that the champagne he had just tasted was even finer than that which he had drunk as the peace negotiations at Ghent had been concluded. "May it always celebrate times of peace," he wrote.

$$*\qquad*\qquad*\qquad*$$

The chateau owner showed her latest visitor the book of reminiscences, and Major Taunton's comments. "Of course we'll be glad to supply several cases of champagne for this wonderful evening," she said. "Take as much as you require. We've all waited so long for the Liberation. It's been five long, long years. It seems even longer. But I thought you would like to see the book first. Someone else signed it one hundred and thirty years ago. Someone with the same name as you. A relative, perhaps?"

Captain James Taunton, Adjutant to General W. Bedell Smith, was arranging an informal celebration for the Allied surrender participants, including British Admiral Burrough, the Russian General Susloparoff, and French General Sevez. Including other high-ranking officers and seventeen war correspondents attached to the headquarters, it would be prudent to be well supplied.

General Eisenhower would not be receiving General Jodl's surrender personally, for reasons of military protocol. But Allied Headquarters at Reims had been set up in the *College Moderne et Technique* ever since February. Now, in early May, 1945, the end of the war in Europe would become official in Reims, and the Allies were looking forward to celebrating "V-E Day."

Captain Taunton looked at the book of reminiscences with a wry smile. He had heard the family stories about Major John Taunton, and now was pleased to see his ancestor's firm handwriting and account of his visit. Family lore had it that Major Taunton was pleased with his stay in France, but too set in his ways to stay abroad. His descendant had different ideas. Perhaps now he could even start thinking about the end of the war, going back to school and—who knows?—even have a diplomatic career.

He toasted the thought with a glass of champagne as he added his name to the chateau's book of reminiscences. The sparkling champagne was cool and refreshing. It didn't need further chilling. It had been brought up from a special private hidden cellar in the chalk caves, where it had been kept safe from the invaders these five years. "Perhaps one day I'll return as a diplomat," he wrote and signed his name.

✳   ✳   ✳   ✳

Marcia Taunton looked up from the book of reminiscences and didn't even try to brush the tears away. She had asked to see the book, mentioned in a letter home that her father had written to her mother, shortly before his transfer to the Pacific Theater, a transfer from which he had never returned home.

It was a newer world, over fifty years later, and Ambassador Taunton looked forward to her first posting as Chief of Mission. She had never known her father, having been an infant when he left home for the war. But she had heard the stories, and read and reread the old letters. It was a great pleasure, here in Reims, to retrace his footsteps, and those of Major Taunton as well. She drank a glass of the special house *cuvee*, or blend of the finest selected grapes. Her own Foreign Service career was a source of family pride, and when she had taken the oath of office in the Benjamin Franklin Room on the Department of State's Eighth Floor, she had promised her mother that she would stop at Reims on her way to her new post in what used to be called Eastern Europe.

Major Taunton and her father had both celebrated milestones of peace here, in Reims. Perhaps they would have been pleased with what she had accomplished, she thought as she sipped her glass of champagne, savoring its balance and its elegance. There was so very much to be done now, as she prepared to represent the United States far from home. There was comfort in realizing that for the future, a glass of champagne would now always remind her of Reims, her family and her country.

She signed the book of reminiscences and smiled.

CHAPTER 26

▼

SPIRITS

Rick Hanson glared across his desk at George Fan, the Embassy's leading contractor for administrative chores. Window replacement, air-conditioning repair, minor traffic pool fender benders and tuneups, just call George Fan. That had been the advice given to Hanson by the previous Embassy General Services Officer. "Don't forget, a GSO is a jack of all trades. You'll need all the help you can get," had been his parting advice.

Everyone knew that Fan overcharged. But his work was reliable, and he didn't overcharge by very much, just a shade over his costs and commission. It's not that anyone cared. Hanson knew that he was low man on the Embassy totem pole. If everything was done just right nobody would say anything, and he just might get invited to a reception, a large one where numbers were needed, and probably one where he had had to do most of the work anyway. No matter, Thelma liked receptions.

The problem was that this estimate from Fan was outrageous. It was so inflated that it called into question other jobs that Fan had already completed for the Embassy. Ordinarily Hanson wouldn't care very much, but he had heard in last week's staff meeting that there would be a full-dress inspection of the Embassy next spring.

Come to think of it, that was an odd notion, "spring" in a tropical morass like this place, which boasted just two seasons, steaming hot and soaking wet or steaming hot and pop the sockets dry. Take your pick.

An inspection meant that the blue eyeshade boys from Washington would be all over his books, questioning every item. That's why this outrageous bid from George Fan had to be straightened out. If it had gone through, or anything like it, that would be a red flag to the inspectors to question everything the General Services Section had authorized for months, perhaps even years. Since it was one of the few perks of the job that the air conditioning in his section always worked, Hanson knew that the inspectors would hardly need encouragement to stay in an Embassy office that was always comfortable.

That was a chilling thought. But Fan wasn't talking. Not that Hanson could understand much of what Fan had to say anyway. The man's command of English was decidedly shaky. Hanson did get out of him a reaffirmation that he would charge $1,500 in American dollars to do some fairly standard tree surgery. And that was a new estimate, down $100 from Fan's first bid. Really, the man was getting greedy. This had to stop.

The episode was particularly annoying because Hanson had decided that if he ever stood a chance to get on with his career, and graduate from a dull series of grimy fingernail GSO jobs and become an Administrative Officer, he had to show a little initiative. And so he had taken a tour of all of the Embassy's housing to see what if anything needed fixing, or better yet, preventive maintenance.

That was a good front-office phrase, Hanson had decided. Administrative Officers used expressions like that.

And so he had talked with all of the wives who were at home, and the *amahs*, or house servants, of those who were not. He heard complaints and misgivings. One out of ten thought to give him a cool drink.

All, or nearly all, had complaints. It was the usual series of laments that he heard. Rust, mildew and the island litany of things falling apart in the tropics. What did they expect?

One or two of the women had good suggestions. And then at the Economic Officer's residence Hanson had noticed a large tree on the lawn shading the patio. The trouble was that it was off-center, with several large branches above the trunk juncture leaning rather precipitously towards the house's picture window. It didn't take much imagination to see that in a storm, a stiff wind could send one of those heavy branches right through the window, causing property damage or worse.

The Economic Officer had been pleased by Hanson's discovery and said so. Encouraged, Hanson then wrote a paper giving his findings and extolling the merits of preventive maintenance. His boss the Administrative Officer then said encouraging things about Hanson's initiative in staff meeting. So far, so good.

And then George Fan had spoiled everything with this ridiculously inflated estimate! Hanson had been forced to try a new contractor, William Chop. Perhaps Chop would be more reasonable. In Hanson's experience general contractors always were quite reasonable, at least for the first six weeks, while they learned your operation and the limits of your forbearance. Then they recouped what they had lost on earlier jobs, over a period of time. All part of the GSO game, he reflected.

Hanson walked out of the Embassy into the late morning heat. It was a fairly slow day, and so he might as well walk through the island's teaming noonday streets for a while before lunch. He was meeting William Chop, and it would be dutch treat of course. Hanson expected that there would be a battle over the check, but that was the only way to do business. Besides, he liked to size up people, and luncheon was a good opportunity to do that.

This island was supposed to be a model of modernity for SouthEast Asia, but the traditional good luck charms were everywhere. Red paper charms, oranges, slogans, and many other tokens that Hanson saw but would never recognize. As he walked, Hanson thought about the island's building boom. It seemed to be in a perpetual flux of change. But change didn't necessarily mean modernity, no matter what the outside world thought.

Hanson knew that no building, government or otherwise, ever went up without careful consideration of the *feng shui* involved. That was the science of location and which directions a building should face. The considerations were subtle and intricate, and the art as old as China herself, Hanson supposed. A real spirit world.

Sometimes the spirits were quite modern. Everyone told newcomers the story about the foreign-run Ambulance Brigade, which had never had any local volunteers. The reason had been that they had located themselves in what had been Japanese *Kempetai*, or Secret Police Headquarters during the War. Local people could still hear the screams. The Ambulance Brigade had been stuck with a multi-year lease on the building, and the belated knowledge of why they had gotten it so cheaply, and why the building had stood empty so long.

There was a new building on that corner now.

Hanson went down the alley and into a Hokkien restaurant. At least he thought it was Hokkien, since most of the island's predominantly Chinese population came from that part of China. The food however came from several regions. Like most good Chinese restaurants it attracted customers by word of mouth. The restaurant was rather plain, and the air conditioning was set far too low, perhaps to attract Westerners.

Hanson peered inside. There was William Chop waiting for him at a booth near the door. Hanson went over and shook hands, sat down and studied the menu. It all looked good. He was hungry.

They ordered shark's fin soup, sweet and sour pork, a baked fish with almond sauce, and side orders of fried rice. Hanson could do without the stringy overdone scrambled eggs that always appeared in the fried rice, but he wasn't about to make a federal case out it. He blew on his green tea to cool it some, and then talked business with Chop. He wanted good, reasonable estimates and reliable work.

The luncheon was excellent. The soup had that satisfying glutinous quality that Hanson liked, and the sweet and sour pork was enhanced by the pungent Peking sauce. The fish was good too, if you didn't mind being stared at by your luncheon dish. His conversation with William Chop was satisfactory. Chop was fluent in English, and he knew enough about Embassy administrative requirements to make a favorable impression on Hanson.

William Chop was also smart enough to accept separate checks without protest, and he promised estimates within a few days on the several jobs that Hanson mentioned to him. One, of course, was the tree surgery at the Economic Officer's residence.

∗   ∗   ∗   ∗

William Chop lived up to expectations.

So, unfortunately, did George Fan.

Hanson had called them both into his office that afternoon, to review their estimates. Reluctantly he had agreed to meet with them separately after his General Services Assistant had pointed out privately that morning that one or the other would definitely lose face if they met together and there was any sort of confrontation. It was not in the Embassy's interests for official contracts to funnel to just one firm. Far better to engender a notion of real competition. Having them in the same waiting room would suit that purpose. Hanson had to admit that his GSA was right about that.

Hanson talked with George Fan first. He would not budge from his last estimate of $1,500, no matter what Hanson said. They went over the estimate and Fan's costs. Hanson even tried direct confrontation with Fan.

"Don't you know that this is far too expensive a bid? Don't you realize that you make me wonder about your bids on other Embassy work too?"

There was no answer. The man was impassive. Really, this was too much. Hanson dismissed him to stay in the waiting room. Then he had the GSA call in William Chop.

Chop was all written estimates and detailed costs. He had prepared a number of estimates, but the only one that Hanson really wanted to see was the tree surgery estimate. He played his cards with coolness, though, not commenting while Chop went over several other estimates before the tree surgery estimate appeared.

There it was, well thought out. Hanson let Chop ramble on. There were the costs for materials and hauling, plus a rather specialized line item for poulticing the wound to the tree, so that it would not become weakened by infestation, always a consideration in these tropics. Hanson was impressed by Chop 's thoroughness, and also by the quotation. Chop proposed to do the entire job for $175. The job was clearly his. "Welcome to the Embassy's list of contractors," Hanson gushed. "If this job is satisfactorily completed within a reasonable time, there will be other work as well. We'll take this one as the first test."

Pleased and bowing, Chop left Hanson's office.

That left George Fan sitting disconsolately in the waiting room. Hanson let him sit for a while. Of course he would have seen his rival, sporting a big grin on his face, leaving the General Services Section in triumph.

Not that it made a great deal of difference, Hanson thought. They probably used exactly the same labor pool. After half an hour or so, He asked his GSA to call in George Fan. As an afterthought, he asked the GSA to stay in the office while he met with Fan. It would be a nice touch for the inspectors to have a witness for his efficiency. Might as well go all the way and use the GSA as an interpreter, come to that.

George Fan, looking for all the world that he wished he were elsewhere, entered the office and sat down. The GSA sat next to him, and methodically translated Hanson's questions and Fan's responses.

Fan's estimate remained at $1,500. He refused to budge. Hanson told him that was absurd. Didn't he realize that he was endangering any possibility of future work with the Embassy by giving such an inflated estimate?

George Fan remained impassive.

Hanson decided to try a different tack. "Ask him why this costs so much," he said to the GSA. The question was put to Fan, and then the words began to tumble out.

The GSA nodded comprehension. Then he explained to Hanson.

"Mr. Fan is a spirit worshipper," he said. "He has taken a careful look at the tree on the Economic Officer's lawn. It looks perfectly healthy to him. You are asking him to injure that tree, and he believes its spirit will then surely take vengeance on his workers. That is what the high estimate is for, Mr. Hanson. It is a reserve to pay for his injured workers, a kind of medical insurance."

Hanson nodded, understanding at last.

"Tell Mr. Fan that the contract will go to another firm," he said. "But please also tell him that it is a pleasure to do business with a man of principle."

Smiling, the GSA translated.

CHAPTER 27

▼

BURIED TREASURE

These meetings, Arnie Simmons thought, are really eating up too much time. He wouldn't quite say that they were a waste of time. No, not if you wanted your nominees to get a Young Leader Grant for a few weeks in the United States. You just had to play the game and advance their candidacies vigorously in the staff meeting.

Arnie knew all that, but he would still rather spend his time talking with members of the National Assembly, or tracking legislative records, or writing reports on election prospects. That, after all, was what an Embassy Political Officer was supposed to do, he told himself. Besides, this was going to be tough.

The Deputy Chief of Mission, who was presiding, would lay down the parameters. Probably the USIS Counselor should preside, since they were, after all, USIS funded grants, but since USIS itself had candidates this year for grants, the DCM had stepped in.

That was all right, not that anybody had had much say in the matter. DCM Jack Rogovin was known to be fair, and he ran a tight meeting. Everyone got to talk, but no filibusters.

Rogovin reminded everyone that there were only six grants this year. The Ambassador had agreed, as was the custom, that one of those grants should go to a candidate from the Consulate General. That was a done deal. Consul General Clara Simpson was in town for the day, and would with her usual smoothness present her candidate and two alternates, to be named as a sort of consolation prize.

Of course it sometimes happened that the selected candidate got sick or couldn't make the trip. The candidates were busy people after all, leaders by definition, and not everyone could take several weeks off, even for an American grant.

That left five. Arnie knew that USIS would get one. That was all right with him. It wasn't required by the rules, but USIS had informally vetted their candidate, the leading daily newspaper's most promising midlevel journalist, with the Political Section. He would probably be duty bound to be anti-American for a good six months after his trip, Arnie had pointed out, but for the longer run, the grant should be a good idea. The candidate was probably too bright to believe what he wrote most of the time in any event.

That left four. There was also, Arnie knew, a favorite of the Ambassador among the candidates. Well, "favorite" wasn't quite the right term. The Ambassador, a banker by profession, was newly arrived, and had been favorably impressed by a midlevel regulatory official in the Stock Exchange. Previously the same candidate had also impressed the Economic Counselor, who had made a point of inviting him to an Embassy reception, and introducing him to the Ambassador.

After a few minutes of the candidate's exposition of the joys of capital formation and his lifelong wish to see the United States, the Ambassador had slipped into his artful trap and mentioned as a possibility the grant for which the guest was already a candidate. The man had shaken his head and then the Ambassador's hand in appreciation.

That left three. There would be no disagreement that a distinguished young judge should be one of the grantees. Eyebrows had been raised in pleased surprise when Judge Suffiah had indicated a preliminary interest in submitting an application. Given their host country's relatively recent past as a British colony, usually the legal profession went to Great Britain for polishing. It would create quite a stir when this rising and respected jurist went to the United States instead. His application had been discreetly encouraged by the DCM himself.

That left two. And that was Arnie's dilemma.

A well run former British colony, their host country had a two party political system that, in the initial years of independence, had served the young nation tolerably well. The Radical Tories (who were right of center) were currently in power, having won the last parliamentary elections from the Revolutionary Labour Party (who were left of center, if that was what was needed at the moment). The custom was for Leader Grants to be apportioned equally between candidates of the two parties, to avoid any possible accusations of favoritism directed towards the American Embassy.

And so the unspoken custom had held over the two dozen years of the young nation's independence. When there had been a number of grants available, as many as four candidates from each of the two parties had been selected. One from those first grantees was now Interior Minister, and, Arnie knew, a member of the outgoing cabinet had also been an early grantee. Over the years the numbers of grants had dropped, but the principle of their equal allocation had held firm.

Until this year, Arnie thought ruefully. There were of course always candidates who were members of the Radical Tory Party and the Revolutionary Labour Party, and they were deserving. This year was no exception, with promising members of the National Assembly from each party nominated.

Gerald Hosmer, the Tory, was a methodical consensus maker. Sarah Llewellen from Labour was Hosmer's opposite in personality as well as in politics, a new face who forced attention whenever she entered a gathering. A future national election in which Hosmer and Llewellen led their respective political parties was not, Arnie thought, beyond the realm of possibility.

Ordinarily the grant process would create no problem, beyond the vagaries of the selection itself. Someone had to win, and someone would be an alternate That customarily ended the matter. A few alternates did make the grant trips in place of those selected. Usually candidates who were named as alternates faded into the background, but it was sometimes necessary to placate them with Embassy invitations or panel appearances with visiting firemen. There were ways to handle wounded vanity.

The problem was, that this year a charismatic clergyman from the slums of the capital city had also applied for a grant. Arnie had read about Jacob Solmssom of course, in articles in the newspapers, and once there had even been a feature spread on the charasmatic preacher in the local newsmagazine, but Arnie had not met him. And so one Sunday Arnie had gone to Solmssom's church to hear him preach.

The welcome had been extraordinary. Arnie would even say in retrospect that his visit must have been anticipated. Solmssom was far too smooth to acknowledge the American Political Officer's presence from the pulpit. Instead, with a nod at the visitor he switched sermon topics and gave an extemporaneous sermon on reaching out, to help the less fortunate.

When rock stars with consciences could mean the difference between safety and starvation for thousands in Bosnia, Ethiopia, Biafra, and Bangladesh, and when a sophisticated homebased computer network based in rural Vermont could move international politics towards a global land mine ban and earn its instigator the Nobel Peace Prize, Solmssom argued, all could make a real difference. Those who could not operate on the rock star scale could still help. The heads of his audience nodded in agreement. The man could move an audience.

The cadence of the sermon underscored its magic, and the implied compliment to the United States was unmistakable. Arnie could easily see Solmssom as a national leader, the same as Hosmer and Llewellen. Something also told him that Solmssom could turn sour, and it would not be helpful to have the power of his oratory turned against his nation's young democracy, or against the United States, for that matter. No, he should get a grant, and see the United States for himself.

But then, so should Hosmer and Llewellen. "Three into two won't go," was his grandmother's advice about lasting marriage and avoiding temptation. It seemed to apply to grants as well.

A month ago he had consulted the DCM about this dilemma. With the Ambassador's approval, they had sent in a message to the State Department, backed up by private correspondence to several movers and shakers in the Washington grant world, asking for a seventh grant. They cited exceptional candidates and the need to strengthen American influence in their host country. The tut-tut reply was received two weeks later. Do the best you can with what you've got, was Washington's patronizing response.

Arnie and Rogovin did think it through. Clearly, the usual solution to disputed grant awards, making a good candidate an alternate, wouldn't quite fit. Alternates were by tradition from the same political party, so that if a grantee could not go, his group was still represented. Anyway, it was just not politically possible to make either Hosmer or Llewellen an alternate for the other. That would mean in the public eye that the American Embassy was playing favorites. Some would surely write that they were intervening in the local political scene.

Rogovin was equally firm on the allocation of one grant for the Consulate General. That was the expected custom, and the ever watchful provincial newspapers would have a field day if it were not followed. They were suspicious enough of their capital city as it was, and considerable American private investment in that provincial region also dictated the need for goodwill there towards the United States.

The judge and stock market regulator were also done deals, it seemed. The only possibility left seemed to be to make Solmssom the alternate for the journalist with the USIS slot, and see how things worked out. The trouble with that, of course, was that Solmssom was not a USIS pick. They had another journalist in mind, and could make a persuasive case for her.

DCM Rogovin cleared his throat and declared the meeting open. He briefly described the grant structure and then called on USIS Counselor Cynthia Alderton to describe how grants were programmed back in Washington. This gave USIS a role in the meeting, while it enabled those who would be handling the grantees to tell them how the process worked, and what individual programming they could ask for as part of their grant program.

After Alderton's rundown, Rogovin reminded the meeting that this year, there would be just six grants, with a first and second alternate chosen for each grant in addition to the principal candidate who received the grant.

Preferences would be decided by open voting. Each office received one vote, and a total of six votes in the first round, one for each grant offered. Candidates could be selected outright if they received seven votes out of the nine possible. Then there would be a second and third round for grantees. After that, a majority was enough. In case of ties, Rogovin could vote and decide. Alternates were then picked by category, lining up after the grantees, by majority vote.

Rogovin then called for nominations. There were thirty four names put forward. Arnie Simmons groaned inwardly. This was going to take a lot longer than he had thought. Good thing he hadn't scheduled any appointments for the rest of the afternoon. There would be a lot of palaver.

Arnie nominated his three main candidates, Hosmer, Llewellen and Solmssom, and threw in four other names. His preference for the first three was clear. It would soon be evident if there was any elasticity in the process. A little give and take would help a lot. Then, the list of names completed, Rogovin declared the list closed, and asked for short statements on behalf of the candidates. This could take some time, Rogovin said, so we might as well pay close attention and give it our best.

Arnie looked around the room. Sitting around the table facing DCM Rogovin were Consul General Clara Simpson, USIS Counselor Cynthia Alderton, Economic Counselor Owen Thornton, Consul General Jon Watkins from the Embassy, himself, the Defense Attache, Army Colonel Marvin Timkins, CIA Station Chief Glenda Miller, and Administrative Counselor Jim Wainwright. That made nine votes, excluding Rogovin, the chair. The Ambassador had decreed that every principal member of "his" Country Team would participate fully, including Defense and CIA, even though they could put forward no candidates themselves. Other officers, more junior, filled the remaining spaces at the table, but they were only there to prop up their section chiefs.

The list having been closed, the actual nominations started. This was a two-tiered process, for everyone had favorites, and there was a real preference order in each nominator's mind. The speeches were all short (and cut off after three minutes by Rogovin in any event), but those for second tier candidates who were destined to be alternates, or not make the cut at all, tended to be perfunctory.

Time passed, notes were taken, and Rogovin asked for an initial vote. Judge Suffiah received eight votes, as did Consul General Clara Simpson's candidate. The USIS journalist got six votes, the stock exchange regulator five, Hosmer and Llewellen seven each, and Solmssom three. A scattering of votes went to other candidates.

Rogovin declared that the judge, Hosmer, Llewellen, and the provincial candidate had been selected. No other candidate had received sufficient votes, and it was time for a second round, to decide on the other two principal grantees. With that, there was a much needed break. Arnie was still a confirmed smoker, and he went outside to light up. He saw the Ambassador's Aide conferring with DCM Rogovin, probably getting the bad early news about the stock regulator. This was a bit like a political convention, Arnie had decided. If you didn't win early and were a frontrunner, there was a danger of losing your momentum.

Cynthia Alderton and Glenda Miller joined him. The USIS Counselor was concerned for her candidate. "Arnie," she began, "you know that we have a good candidate for the grant. Ferguson is a rising political reporter. A case could be made that it's as much in the Political Section's interest as it is for us for him to get a grant. Why don't you agree to putting Solmssom down as an alternate for Ferguson?"

This was an interesting point of view. Arnie had been sure that Cynthia would have resisted any such idea, preferring to keep the alternate slots for other journalists. She was in effect advancing what was becoming his own fallback position. "That's very forthcoming, Cynthia," he replied. "I think that Solmssom has the votes, so we'll see how it plays out for a while. But I won't close the door just yet."

He put out his cigarette and headed inside the Embassy. The CIA Station Chief, Glenda Miller, caught up with him. "You're right about Solmssom," she said. "He has a real future in this country. He ought to get a grant. Anyway, you know that he has our vote."

That was an odd way of putting it, Arnie thought.

The meeting began with a dutiful announcement by DCM Rogovin. He thought, ahem, that conferees should be aware that Ambassador Stevens was concerned about the spread and allocation of grants. He didn't want anyone to be affected by his view, of course, but as a banker, the Ambassador believed strongly that it was necessary to cultivate those with direct access to the economic community in their host country. End of message.

"The translation of that," Colonel Timkins hissed to Arnie, "is that you'd all better shape up and vote for the stock exchange bureaucrat that the Ambassador met." Crudely put perhaps, but he had the message right. Economic Counselor Owen Thornton then gave a lugubrious little speech extolling the virtues of his candidate.

The vote was a foregone conclusion. The stock exchange regulator was added to the list of grantees by a unanimous vote.

Then Cynthia Alderton spoke in behalf of her journalist, and Arnie recapitulated the arguments in favor of Solmssom. The vote was seven to seven, deadlocked. Rogovin, unwilling just yet to dictate the result a second time, ordered another impromptu adjournment.

Arnie and CIA Station Chief Glenda Miller had not voted for the journalist, while Cynthia Alderton and the Defense Attache had not voted for Solmssom. "Not that I have anything personal against your man," Colonel Timkins told Arnie. "It's just that people wearing my suit have had to spend a lot of time cleaning up when people like your candidate get into politics."

Well, that was honest enough anyway. One thing Arnie liked about Timkins, come to think about it, is that you always knew exactly where you stood with him. That was a Vermont virtue that they shared, even if Arnie's Yankee accent had been lost over the years. Cynthia Alderton, of course, couldn't vote for Solmssom without ruining the chances of her own candidate.

His own motive in voting against the journalist was the same. What was Glenda Miller up to? He decided to raise the matter with her. Then he decided not to do so. There was the DCM, Jack Rogovin, looking like he could use a cigarette even though he had not smoked for fifteen years.

"This is a tough one, Jack," Arnie said. "Actually, the Political Section wins with either candidate. Any views?"

"When you've been in this business as long as I have," Jack Rogovin said, "you begin to take a charitable view of these things. Anyway, you've got a solid candidate. I expect you'll be sticking with him. We all work for the same government, after all," he said. Then he walked away.

That was an odd signal. If Arnie read it correctly, that meant that Rogovin would cast his deciding vote in favor of Solmssom if he had to do so. What was going on here? He decided to sound out a few more people. Not many except the CIA Station Chief seemed to know Solmssom except by reputation.

"I'm not sure that Solmssom can make it," he finally said to Glenda Miller. "Some of our votes are pretty soft. People realize that these are USIS grants, and it doesn't look good for USIS to draw a blank."

"You're the expert at gauging these situations," Glenda Miller replied. "But I can tell you that we've taken a look at this country and where it is heading, and we share your view that Solmssom would be a good man to have on our side in the future."

So that was it. Arnie took Cynthia Alderton aside and had a hurried talk with her as they returned to the conference room once again. Then, as the meeting began, he announced with her agreement that the journalist would get his vote for the sixth grant. Solmssom, a worthy candidate, would be the journalist's first alternate.

The meeting sputtered out after that. Colonel Timkins raised an eyebrow. "Did I miss something here?" he asked Arnie.

"No, good buddy, but I damned near did," was Arnie's reply.

CHAPTER 28

▼

FOREIGN MINISTRY CALLS

"Might as well share the car," Deputy Chief of Mission Kendall Johnson said. He didn't mean Political Officer Clive Atchison, of course, who was standing next to him. They were after all going on the same errand, a call on Americas Desk Director Dr. Rupert Hendriks. He meant Vice Consul Elliot Murchison, standing with them waiting for the Embassy car to pull up. He was making his first official Foreign Ministry call. Murchison of course was calling on the Consular Department, a separate entrance at the Foreign Ministry, but to use that as a reason not to share the car, when the motor pool was running short as usual, would have been ungenerous.

"First call, Elliot?" Atchison asked, as they got into the car. He was a third tour officer, twice promoted already, with two previous Embassy posts under his belt, and six months' experience at this one. Compared to Murchison, who was at his first overseas post, and indeed had just left the Foreign Service Institute's famed class for fledgling diplomats a few months earlier, he was a seasoned veteran.

"Yes," Murchison answered from the jump seat, facing the other two men. "They've called me in. Or rather, they've finally replied to our requests to see Gilbert and Adams."

"Important stuff, that," nodded the DCM. "Marijuana possession, wasn't it? They've been in jail for over half a year now. Nobody's seen them for most of that time, and their families must be frantic. Her father called me from Idaho just last Wednesday. I hope they're finally ready to grant access. If not, let me know immediately. It might be the Ambassador's turn to take the matter up personally once again with the Foreign Minister. Anyway, this must all get sorted out before the Secretary's visit, if there is to be one. Come to think of it, that's probably just what's going on."

His thought trailed off, and he turned to Atchison. Their topic with Dr. Hendriks was the Secretary's projected trip. It was all in the planning stage, and nothing had been announced. The idea had been broached in Washington and the timing was good, but no hard and fast commitment had been made on either side.

"Is there anything new on whether the trip is really on?" Atchison asked.

"No. It's still up in the air. The air over Capitol Hill, I mean," the DCM added. In other words, the trip would be sorted out when State's budget had made it through the Congressional grinder, freeing the Secretary from strategy sessions and calls to butter up wavering appropriations votes.

"If only we were part of the national security package on the Hill," he snorted, startling his young associates, who were bright enough, but not mind readers. "Stupid business, putting State with Commerce and Justice. We lose every time. No domestic constituency to back us up. If State were part of an overall national defense budget, things might be different. The money spent on diplomacy would be seen as a kind of insurance policy to prevent conflicts. Maybe that's a little visionary for the Hill, but it's the truth. Anyway, we've got to do some contingency planning to flesh out the Secretary's proposed trip. If there is going to be one."

The car rumbled across a bridge, named for a monarch from the old days, which was adorned with Victorian era gaslights in flamboyant *art nouveau* style. They crossed the sluggish river which bisected the capital, the three passengers looking from side to side to catch the view, one of the best in the city. So many of these European cities were on two banks of a river, Murchison thought. Probably related to early commerce and tribal settlements. Places like this couldn't have been very defensible, though, in the early days. Just pay off the Vikings and hope they'll stay bought and leave you alone for a while, must have seemed the wisest policy. The car entered a cobbled square, and came to a graceful stop at the Consular Department entrance of the Foreign Ministry. "Good luck, Elliot," the DCM called after him. "We'll see you back at the Embassy."

Murchison nodded his agreement. That made good sense. Surely their meetings wouldn't break up at the same time, and it would be a pleasant walk back on this early spring afternoon. Rain seemed unlikely. Maybe there would even be time to fit in a glass of good local beer at one of those quayside tables.

Murchison entered the building and found himself in a reception room, decorated by flags of the constituent provinces of this nation, and portraits of the current leader, in uniform. He approached the desk, where a clerk dressed in a rumpled three piece suit looked up at him and attempted to gauge the appropriate degree of politeness the visitor was due. "Yes?" he offered hesitantly, the effect of guessing that English was the visitor's language somewhat broken by the hesitation, and by his distracting sibilant *s*. The letter trailed the word with a touch of menace, like a snake lagging behind a bush in search of a victim.

"Elliot Murchison, American Embassy, to see Dr. Johanss, Assistant Legal Advisor," Murchison announced.

The clerk negotiated with his telephone and ventured a smile. All things considered, Murchison thought, the smile made the clerk's welcome less inviting. "Dr. Johanss will see you directly," the clerk announced. "Please take a seat over there."

If he's going to see me directly, Murchison thought, why do I need to take a seat? He looked at the flags and portraits around the room for a moment, and then was agreeably surprised. "Mr. Murchison? Follow me please." She was young, pleasant, and her smile was full of real charm. Roger that, Murchison thought. He tried vainly for memorable small talk while following her through the metal detectors and into the main corridor that led to the elevator and, following a ride to the seventh floor, to the office of Dr. Johanss. "I'll see you later, Mr. Murchison," she purred, depositing him with Dr. Johanss's secretary.

*   *   *   *

"Ah, Counselor Johnson. Always a pleasure to see you. And Mr. Atchison. I hope you find our small country pleasant?"

The quote from *My Fair Lady* came to Atchison, as Dr. Rupert Hendricks "oozing charm from every pore, oiled his way across the floor." The DCM returned the pleasantries, shaking hands and emphasizing Hendricks's title. Then they sat around a handfashioned mahogany table while some coffee and and glasses of mineral water were served.

"We don't have official word from the State Department yet," Johnson began. "Still, I hear from our Country Director that several days have been blocked on the Secretary's schedule for a trip to our region. That would be three weeks from now. Let's hope that the budget process goes forward quickly enough."

There it was, the diplomatic bureaucrat's opening gambit, a basis for preliminary discussion, but at the same time a disclaimer in case the trip didn't come off. I wonder if there is a diagram for that, like opening moves in chess, Atchison thought. He had taken a small notepad from his jacket pocket, but thought better of recording the disclaimer, which might offend Dr. Hendricks. He would fill it in later, of course. Hendricks smiled at him.

"It would be an honor, of course," Hendricks began. "We haven't had the pleasure of welcoming the current Secretary yet." Nice jab, Atchison thought. Their own Foreign Minister had been in Washington so many times over the years that he should have taken out a time share in a Foggy Bottom condominium. It would have saved this little country some money. "In three weeks, you said? Everyone should be in town. That would be too early for vacations."

"That's the time frame we're looking at now," Johnson confirmed. "Late afternoon arrival, one full day, two nights and a morning's sightseeing."

"Yes, the timetable almost writes itself. We could virtually give it now to Protocol," Hendriks said. "Full dress arrival ceremony, escort to the official residence—he's staying there, I suppose? Yes, well then, evening reception and dinner given by the Foreign Minister. Working meetings the following morning and afternoon. Courtesy call on the Prime Minister, of course. Working luncheon, I assume? Yes. Then, your show for the evening. Dinner at the residence, surely, a parallel for our gala the night before. Then after all that, the visitors would I think appreciate having their final morning off. Nothing official. We'd be glad to put some expert guides at the party's disposal."

Johnson nodded his appreciation. This was all pretty standard, but it meant that the hosts had been through the official visit drill so often over the years that the chances were excellent that there would be no slipups.

They sipped their coffee, as Johnson and Hendricks went over preliminary agendas for the meetings. First, he ticked off something the host government wanted: a social security agreement, so that local residents who were married to American pensioners, or entitled to Social Security through their own work, would receive their dollar checks here. That would also be a selling point for local efforts to get Americans to retire in the countryside here. That wouldn't cost this little nation much to reciprocate. Very few of their checks would ever be mailed to recipients in the United States. And as they prepared their case to join the Economic Union, this would be another bit of western-looking evidence in their favor.

Then came intellectual property. A tougher matter, since it would close down a lucrative local sideline. The issue involved the protection of the work of American artists—was "artists" the right word for those decibel pounders?—from local cutrate CD knockoffs.

"And then we have our consular worries," Johnson said.

"Ah, yes?" Hendricks affected surprise.

"Two young American citizens, a Ruth Adams and a Sherman Gilbert, are in prison here, as I'm sure you are aware, Dr. Hendriks," Johnson said, his voice showing a bit of an edge for the first time. "It's been six months. We've only seen them once…"

"Twice," Hendriks corrected him with a smile.

"Ah, yes, then twice, but not for the last four months. They haven't had a trial date set. They haven't even been formally charged wth anything. We're hoping this matter can be sorted out quickly. It would set such an encouraging tone for the Secretary's visit."

"I hope so too," Hendriks replied, with just a touch of self-satisfaction. "I believe that Dr. Johanns of our Consular Legal Department is speaking with your Vice Consul about this matter at this very moment." Another move on the diplomatic chess board, Atchison thought. If the visit fails for that reason, it's something the consular people failed to sort out properly.

"More coffee?" their host asked.

*   *   *   *

Elliot Murchison savored his coffee and he and Dr. Johanss exchanged pleasantries while the server closed the door behind her.

"Wonderful coffee," Murchison said. "I prefer it to what we usually get at the Embassy."

"Yes, well, it's one of our leading products, as you know. We always make sure it is freshly brewed for our visitors."

"I was pleased to receive your message, Dr. Johanss. For two reasons. First, this is my first Foreign Ministry call, and I've been looking foward to it. Second, the subject matter. You had some news about Sherman Gilbert and Ruth Adams." He leaned forward with anticipation, all coiled energy, like a high-scoring forward expecting a basketball pass down court from a teammate.

Dr. Johanss sipped his coffee. "Yes. Well, I believe we may have some good news for you there. As a special favor to the United States, and in view of the forthcoming visit of your esteemed Secretary of State, we have decided to put them at liberty as soon as the visit is formally and jointly announced by our two governments. By 'at liberty' of course we don't mean turning them loose. We would be returning their passports to your Embassy a day or so ahead of their release. Adams and Gilbert then must be picked up and taken immediately to the airport for direct return to your country. No press interviews."

"I hadn't quite realized that the Secretary's visit was definite." Murchison was thinking out loud, trying to create a bit of elbow room if possible without misleading Dr. Johanss.

"Oh? Well, those are my instructions. I believe that details for the visit are being formulated even now by your Counselor of Embassy Mr. Johnson and Dr. Hendriks of our Americas Department."

Murchison shifted gears. "Let me make quite sure that I understand, Dr. Johanss. Are you saying that in the event of the Secretary's visit, Adams and Gilbert are to be released, as a sort of goodwill gesture?"

Johanss nodded, his thin smile unreadable.

"And if the visit is postponed? I understand it is budget season in Washington, and although we expect a resolution soon of State's annual budget, still that's never a sure thing, and the Secretary's presence may be required longer than we hope or now foresee."

"These matters are up to your government. We quite understand. But I have no instructions regarding the matter of a postponement. You must know that our Justice Ministry is anxious to prosecute this case. We didn't win them over very easily. In fact, we didn't win them over at all."

Murchison thought fast, and decided to try for as much as he dared. "Surely, then, you would have no objection to a consular visit to see them? They've been in custody for over half a year, and it's been months since we've had consular access."

"That long? Well, send over a formal request. I'll argue in favor of it."

One other matter to try. "You mentioned their passports, Dr. Johanss. As you know, they are the property of the United States. We have asked for them in the past. That would be a gesture of cordial intent, I'm sure, for them to be returned to us now."

Johanss thought for a moment. "You may have a point technically. But it's our state practice to keep passports in these circumstances, for safekeeping, you understand. Perhaps if this were formally raised? I can't say what the reaction would be, but there seems to be, as you Americans might put it, no downside in trying."

"We will be glad to do so with a diplomatic note, Dr. Johanss." Murchison realized that this wouldn't cost them very much. The United States could simply issue another set of passports and force the issue. They were our passports, after all.

Murchison took a taxi back to the Embassy. He was anxious to confer with DCM Johnson about what Johanss had had to say. Before going upstairs to Johnson's office, he stopped by his own and ordered up two draft diplomatic notes, one requesting consular access to Ruth Adams and Sherman Gilbert, and the second requesting the return to the Embassy of their two American passports.

*   *   *   *

Johnson heard Murchison's report, and then called in Atchison. "Include what Elliot reports, Clive," he said, "and give me a draft, please. It looks like our local clients are playing games. My own inclination is to let them do it, up to a point. Go ahead and get consular access, Elliot. I'll sign those diplomatic notes over this afternoon. At least we should get that while they are waiting to see if the Secretary's visit is really on. If they do let them go, we could note the action informally, something like that, without being part of it. That's all Washington would need, a precedent requiring prisoner releases from the 50 states when a state visitor is in town! This ups the stakes somewhat for the visit to come off as planned. If it doesn't, and Adams and Gilbert have already been released, I'd hate to be the next American in a local jail!"

The answering cable from the State Department three days later was as DCM Johnson had surmised. Washington was having none of the release officially, but would welcome it as a goodwill gesture informally. The text of a joint announcement of the visit, with dates, was enclosed for coordination with the local host government. An e-mail from their Country Director in the State Department passed along deadpan what H, the Bureau of Congressional Relations, had predicted on the timing of passage of the Justice/State/Commerce Appropriations Bill, based on their latest soundings on the Hill. It looked good. It was encouraging, but no sure thing.

"What on earth do we do with this?" Atchison asked.

"We work it out," Johnson said.

*   *   *   *

Elliot looked around the prison waiting room. After less than a week, the Foreign Ministry Consular Department had called giving him official permission to visit Spencer Gilbert. He drove to the prison in the country's southern province the next morning. A closely shaven, sallow complexioned American in his early thirties wearing khaki pants and shirt approached, accompanied by a sullen uniformed guard, who retired to a corner chair and lit a cigarette.

"How is she? Have you seen Ruth?"

"I didn't get permission yet. They are just letting us see you for the time being. I'm the Vice Consul at the Embassy, Elliot Murchison."

"I'm Spencer Gilbert, of course."

"How's your health, Mr. Gilbert? I brought you some sandwiches, fruit, chocolate bars and a couple of packs of cigarettes. If you don't smoke, they must be worth something where you are now. Go ahead and eat if you're hungry. They won't take anything away while I'm here."

"That's for sure. Thanks. I'm OK. But how's Ruth? Some honeymoon we had. Just in this lousy country a week, and we get picked up. For nothing. Just a little pot. Who cares about that, anyway? We weren't selling the stuff."

"Evidently they care. Marijuana possession is a serious offense here. But what's that you said about a 'honeymoon'?"

"Sure. It was a vacation trip. We'd done that before. But Ruth is just great. I'm not sure what she sees in me. Anyway, we were touring together and just the other side of the border, we got married. That was a great idea. We thought about our future together, a family and everything. The lousy idea was to cross the border for some sightseeing, and then get caught smoking pot. I suppose they are going to try us now. Don't we get a lawyer or something?"

"You certainly do. Also, they may be trying to clean up their act. You and Ruth are the only Americans in jail in this country. Let me share with you that the Secretary of State may be coming on an official visit. I don't think they want the embarrassment of having you and your...wife...in jail. Certainly without even having been tried."

"Do you think there's any chance of getting us out? I mean, as I told you, we weren't selling the stuff, or anything."

"I'll do my best. Take it easy, Spencer. My best is damned good."

*   *   *   *

"You're sure about this, Elliot?"

"Yes, Mr. Johnson. Why else would they have kept them in jail without letting us see them both, for months? It's an embarrassment. They are, frankly, looking for a way to release them. The Secretary's visit gives them that chance. They'll do it if you give them that fig leaf, whether or not the Secretary actually comes. If he doesn't come, they've exchanged a problem for the moral high ground, sort of, and we'll hear about it for a while. Big deal. Either way, they see themselves as winning, as getting out of a problem situation they didn't anticipate and don't want to have. Not with their membership in the Economic Union pending, and the Human Rights Commissioners breathing down their necks every step of the way.

"The only thing that would louse it up would be too many conditions from our side. I say, call on Dr. Hendriks, say it's firm, give them the joint announcement and press statement as final, and get a time and place for me to pick the two of them up real soon. Meanwhile I'll get ticket authorizations from the Department. And either we'll get their passports back immediately, or we'll issue them new ones. Piece of cake. They'll be out of here and on their way home in a couple of days."

"I'll call our Country Director on the secure phone and let him know what's going on."

"Good idea, sir."

"Anything for him to pass on to the family in the States?"

"Yes. Tell them to get the cradle and bassinet ready. I think they're going to need them real soon."

CHAPTER 29

▼

LITTLE BROWN JUG

Sure, Embassy Economic Counselor Larry Carter was known as a good fellow. Anybody would tell you that. Perhaps it was the feeling of bonhomie that he exuded when American trade missions were in town. It might have been the ripple of fat that caused him to perspire ever so readily, particularly in staff meetings in this benighted third world capital, when the Embassy's operating budget was in the red and air conditioning was rationed. That still happens by the way, the air conditioning being shut off, or breaking down, I mean.

For whatever reason, if you wanted a graceful little speech for your transferring junior officer, or a birthday party to be arranged for a lonely single secretary, Larry Carter was your man. That was why the Ambassador had asked him to pick a farewell gift for his right hand man, Deputy Chief of Mission Trip Holland. Not that Carter and Holland were close, you understand, even if they were both New Englanders. For one thing, Carter had spent a lot of time working his way up, grade by grade.

Holland on the other hand was one of the Secretary's fair haired boys. A Seventh Floor special assistant, he had been parachuted in as DCM after troubleshooting for the Secretary. Really he didn't look as young as he was. It must have been the haircut and that air of authority.

It couldn't have been Holland's expensive schooling, not in today's Foreign Service, that had gotten him so far so fast. But that used to grate on Carter anyway, in a quiet sort of way. He'd earned everything he got, he used to say, to nobody in particular, and sometimes even when nobody was asking.

Now, I'm not a New Englander, but I've been around the type. Those Yankees have more castes carried around in their baggage than you'd find in New Delhi. They don't talk about it but they surely do. They can put on that regional "Ayuh!" twang that sets them apart from the rest of us anytime they want to, or talk about the Boston Red Sox and the old Boston Garden. At least, Carter and Holland would, as though it were some sort of private code. Maybe it was.

Anyway, you were asking about Carter. This was his last chance for promotion before mandatory early retirement. We all wished him well. Everyone said that he worked very, very hard. Our Ambassador tended to rubber stamp what his DCM wrote. He wanted it known that that was because of his great trust for Holland's judgment, and his own busy schedule. The truth more likely was that the Ambassador then was a political appointee who didn't understand the Foreign Service codewords.

Carter gave a reception for a trade mission just before the last efficiency reports were due. He had put together an excellent schedule, and taken a lot of the representational work onto his shoulders too. All Trip (John Standish Holland III you see, hence "Trip") had to do was show up. He did, just in time to hear Carter's inflated little attempt at a humorous welcome. Never trust a middle aged bureaucrat to be humorous, I always say. It didn't go over very well, and the guest of honor, a ranking Congressional staffer who tended to confuse his importance with that of his elected boss, didn't laugh.

That incident found its way into Carter's annual efficiency report, in an understated, regretful sort of way, you understand. That was only natural, since it was fresh on Holland's mind when he was writing up the report. Lots of good things about Carter's work set forth and quantified, and then the telling anecdote.

The promotion list wouldn't be published until much later, but Carter could already see the handwriting on the wall. At least that is what he said to me one Friday night when we had both had enough beer at the Marine Bar to forget the third world. He seemed resigned and angry at the same time. I could tell that it was eating him up.

Now, we all know that there are rules against buying gifts for superiors. All very bluenosed and all that. But everybody chips in anyway, at a little post like this, for some token when somebody leaves the post. It goes with the territory. Carter, though, knew that Holland was a stickler for the rules, and so did we. So

Carter came up with an idea. If we'd arrange the necessary for Trip's farewell party, he'd provide the gift.

The whole thing, he said, would be like a church supper back home in New England. Everyone would make something to bring, and he'd donate something he had. No need to actually go out and buy a farewell present. The idea was unusual and a touch of home. We found ourselves actually looking forward to it. That was also better than forming committees and stretching matters out, because Trip Holland was needed back in Washington yesterday, if you know what I mean.

Holland had kept up his high level contacts and I guess had punched his DCM ticket. Now he was being rewarded. Senior Officer Personnel had tipped him off a while back that he was in the running for his own Embassy. Then the call came. The President, on the Secretary's recommendation, was going to send Trip Holland's name to the Senate for confirmation as an Ambassador. He'd get fast track confirmation hearings, the works.

Nothing fancy, you understand. Trip Holland sometimes used to talk about the Embassy in Brussels. Everybody knew that was his goal. Certainly this posting wasn't Brussels. It was actually one of the Stans, somewhere just west of Mongolia, which would be an interesting assignment, long on local color if a bit short on plumbing and up to date medicine. Holland could always punch a ticket there and aim for Brussels later.

But I was telling you about the farewell party. Well, one of the things that Carter and Holland used to joke about from time to time was Yankee cooking. For the rest of us, that was a little oblique. I mean, a New England boiled dinner never was my idea of four star cuisine, and I can take or leave Boston cream pie. Carter and Holland, though, used to talk as though French or Chinese cuisine should take a back seat to what was produced in New England. It was their Yankee code again. My distinct feeling was that the farther away from New England they got, the better they remembered that cooking to have been.

Anyway, they did agree on Yankee baked beans, and there, they had some company. If beans are to be on the menu I prefer a good French cassoulet myself, but I will grant you that real, slow cooked baked beans made from scratch are a treat on a cold winter evening. Not that we have any cold winter evenings here, you understand.

They even agreed on the recipe. Take a pound of beans (they would specify that it had to be King of the Early beans, a sort of kidney bean), sort them, and then soak them overnight. Add salt pork, a touch of salt, a large onion diced in medium sized chunks, a bay leaf, a diced tomato, and a teaspoon or two of dried mustard. Cover with cold fresh water and slow cook half the day.

Oh yes, I almost forgot their one disagreement. Carter would say, add half a cup of unsulphured molasses. Trip Holland used maple syrup instead, the amber kind. The recipe didn't need much tending, just stir from time to time, and adjust the water level. In a slow cooker, you could count on flavorful baked beans by dinner time.

Real Yankees, though, would push the envelope a bit farther. Larry Carter used to say that a slow cooker was just the modern way of substituting for the way that baked beans had been made in New England for generations. The proper way was to use a baked bean jug. Trip Holland agreed with him on that as a matter of principle, although Carter once told me that the only time Holland had ever seen a baked bean jug was at the Durgin Park Restaurant in Boston.

You know what they look like, I suppose. They are round and potbellied, tapering towards the top. It's said that the thickness of the pot is needed to retain and disperse the heat produced during hours of unattended cooking in an oven, say at 300 degrees. That way the beans won't burn, and evaporation is controlled.

Larry Carter had an old fashioned New England bean pot. It had been in his family for years. He got it after a family picnic some twenty years ago. Hadn't been used since. It was made of clay, he said. The real thing. You can't get them anymore. Much more authentic than the stoneware jugs you buy nowadays. It had a nice brown color to it, that was set off by the painted glaze around the edges and the interior. They even called it redware. Clayware is porous, of course, so those old pots were sometimes glazed, to waterproof them. Stoneware doesn't need that.

Anyway, we had a nice farewell party for Trip Holland, and wished him well. The Ambassador said some nice things, and so did Larry Carter We all had a good time, and I must say that the covered dish supper theme was a hit. The high point was when Trip Holland unwrapped his farewell gift. It was Larry Carter's brown baked bean pot.

Carter had scored a direct hit. Holland was so moved that, I understand through the grapevine, once back in Washington he dropped an informal word here and there about Larry Carter. Whether that really happened or not, or was just Holland's matchless way of taking personal credit for good things, I can't say. But we were all pleased when the promotion lists finally came out, and Larry Carter's name was on the list. Then Larry got reassigned somewhere up the ladder in the Department. I guess things worked out for him after all.

By that time, of course, Trip Holland had already taken up his ambassadorship. He was a bachelor, not much time for a family anyway I guess, so he traveled a lot, particularly on those rare occasions when a ranking visitor came to his remote capital. When that happened, a picture of Ambassador Trip Holland in the *Newsletter's* back pages was sure to follow.

I saw several of them. In the first one there was Trip as we all remembered him, big as life, posing with a visitor in a local bazaar. Trip was smiling with that pleasant smile of his for the cameraman, as he leaned towards the important Washington visitor. Good old Trip. You could almost supply the caption, "What Trip Holland Did While Waiting For Embassy Brussels."

Pictures in later issues of the *Newsletter* were a different matter. The next one appeared a few months later. At first, I thought that the photographer had missed the focus. Trip looked a little shaky, not like himself at all, rather like a convalescent who has gotten out of bed a day or so too soon, if you know what I mean.

The next time I got more concerned. That was six months later. Nobody would have guessed that the old man in the photo was the young Trip Holland that we had all known. Or if it was Trip Holland, it was a Dorian Gray version of the man that I'd known. So I guess you can put me down as shocked but not really surprised when I read Trip Holland's obituary last month.

So it was lead poisoning. Well, you can't be too careful, as you fellows in the Medical Office know. It's a good thing that you were sent out to look into Trip's death. I hope that you can trace what happened, and come up with something useful. People serving in backwater countries like this one, or the place where Trip Holland died, need to take every possible precaution.

It's not like we were home, after all.

CHAPTER 30

▼

<u>HOME LEAVE</u>

Ambassador Bob Clanton walked up to the crowded bar at intermission and managed to get two gin and tonics in just enough time for Lucille and him to wet their whistles before the second act began.

Lucille had liked the Lakes Region Playhouse immediately. Bob was pleased that his lure had worked, and that she had agreed to spend some of their precious home leave in New Hampshire after all. She enjoyed the theater. As she had told him more than once, but less frequently since he had received his ambassadorship, she could have had a fine theater career.

It was a playful revival of *The Seven Year Itch,* well performed and, like the Velveteen Rabbit, liked even for its worn places. He turned and saw that Lucille had found a table. They sipped their drinks and chatted about the play.

"Say, aren't you Bob Clanton?"

Clanton looked up and saw a gangling tall man in a worn Madras sports jacket looming over the table. The man looked familiar enough for Clanton to rise from his seat. Then it came to him. "Kent…Kent Clayburn, isn't it? Sit with us, won't you?"

Clayburn accepted the invitation, and Clanton introduced him to Lucille. "Honey, this is Kent Clayburn. We used to know each other when I was growing up here."

Lucille turned on the charm. "You're also from this part of New Hampshire, Mr. Clayburn?"

"We're from Boston, really. But we've summered in New Hampshire as long as anyone can remember."

Lucille wondered aloud about the "we."

"My wife Ann will be up on Thursday. It's up to her to open the house. Say, why don't you come over and see us this weekend. You'll be here that long, won't you? Let's say Saturday evening about seven. You remember the place, don't you Bob? Just over the bridge, second right, third left."

Clayburn was a stockbroker, Clanton remembered. Perhaps that was why his idea of social chitchat sounded like a rushed and confidential telephone conversation. If this kept up, the stock quotes would surely be next. Not that he couldn't use a few tips in that department. The warning bell sounded and they hastily finished their drinks, then went back into the theater for the second act of the play.

✳   ✳   ✳   ✳

Lucille was intrigued, as they dressed for dinner with the Clayburns. Their host had stressed the informality of the evening. That meant for Bob to wear an old sports jacket, which would be immediately taken off, not to be seen again until they left the house.

She compromised with light blue linen pants, a navy blazer and a white shirt with the crested insignia of the Sarawak Yacht Club. That was an in joke, since the Sarawak Yacht Club didn't exist, and the reference was to the Dyak habit in previous years of cannibalism on the folks they caught while on their longboat excursions.

The American Chamber of Commerce of North Borneo had presented Lucille the shirt, and she had promised Bob, who considered it in dubious taste, that she would not wear it until they were home. This seemed a good opportunity to do so.

"So tell me about the Clayburns, Bob." She lit a cigarette and settled in with her preflight drink. "Was he a particular friend of yours?"

"Actually, no. 'Friend' isn't the right word at all. I worked for his father for several summers, when we were living in Lochmere. We were New Hampshire people, as you know." Lucille did know. They had driven past the former family home that afternoon, on their way to visit his mother in the nursing home.

There weren't many New Hampshire connections left now, and this time his mother had not even recognized her only child. It was sad that she never realized that he was now Ambassador Clanton. Come to think of it, there was nobody left up here to talk over the old days, Bob had said as they drove away from the nursing home. Lucille guessed his train of thought, and tried to change it.

"Tell me about Governor's Island. It sounds rather grand."

"Exclusive is the word, rather than grand. It is a small island close to the Lake Winnepesaukee shoreline. The style is clapboard beach houses, good sized, and very well kept, with caretakers for the off season. In the old days, there were all sorts of restrictive covenants, not written down, you see, to keep New Hampshire people out. The island was discovered in the nineteenth century by Massachusetts people, and they bought up all the land."

Lucille was intrigued. "And they've had it ever since?"

"Yes. It's always been a sort of '*Golden Pond*' for Boston folks in the summer. An idyllic place, with canoes rather than motorboats when I was a boy. A few places then didn't even have telephones. They preferred it that way."

"What were the Clayburns like?"

"Kent's father was the definition of oldtime Boston. Even when he wore a bathing suit he looked like he was presiding over a board meeting at First Boston Trust. His mother was really old money, charming and very softspoken. Kent and his sisters had the run of the island and most of this part of New Hampshire as well. We thought they were kind of wild."

"He seems to have settled down now."

"Yes. It goes with the territory. First sow the wild oats, then enter the bank or brokerage firm." Unlike diplomacy, where the reverse happens, she thought.

They finished their drinks and drove the rented Lincoln along the lakeshore, turning left over the bridge onto Governor's Island. No guard was necessary, even now. This was the only entrance and exit to the island. A sign announced that the road was private. It didn't add that trespassers should turn back. It didn't have to. Most people who stumbled upon the island obeyed that injunction instinctively, and turned around. The island's isolation seemed to command that sort of self-policing behavior.

They were early, so Bob drove around the island for half an hour. It was calm and secluded, without clutter. Each house had been carefully placed to take fine advantage of its lakefront location. There were well tended gardens everywhere, it seemed. The island radiated old money rather than opulence. This must have been what the Vineyard had been like before it had been discovered, Lucille thought. She hoped to be the last person to discover Governor's Island.

"Welcome home, Bob." Kent came towards them smiling broadly. He unlatched the gate. Up along the walkway Ann Clayburn stood, a mannequin for

Talbot's summer catalog. The two couples walked together around the house to the patio just beyond, which overlooked a secluded Lake Winnepesaukee cove. The pine trees shading their lawn were enormous. They must have been there always. It was impossible to think that they had ever been planted. In fact they had been by Kent's grandfather sixty years earlier.

There was no beach, just a mossy bank set off by the fragrant pines, and an adequate boathouse. "It saves hauling the boat down to Massachusetts when the season is over," was the traditional semiapologetic explanation, if anyone cared. A kayak and a canoe were held by brackets on the boathouse wall.

"We prefer using them when we aren't going far. It seems such a shame to start those motors and spoil the quiet of our cove," Ann volunteered. "Bob knows all about that," Kent interjected. "This was his special responsibility, this boathouse, many summers ago."

Ann quickly added, "I'm sure that was because you were so hopeless, Kent, that your father was lucky to find Bob. I remember that he used to say so, when I first came here." Kent picked up his cue. "Tell us, Bob, what you've been up to all these years. Foreign Service, wasn't it? Aren't you retired by now?"

"Some in the State Department might wish it, but no, I'm not. We've specialized in East Asia, and over the years we've lived in Taiwan, Japan, Djakarta and Hong Kong. I was twice in Saigon, of course."

"Do you speak those languages?" Ann wanted to know.

"Japanese is my best foreign language," Bob replied. "We've had several tours at the Embassy there. Oh yes, there was also an out of area tour in Accra. That was when Kissinger was Secretary of State, and we all got sent to different regions, for 'broadening,' he said. I hated it. It just made me homesick for the Far East. Enough about me. Tell us about your own career. Always with the family firm?"

"Yes," Kent said. "I meant to try something else from time to time, but the work always interested me, and with the bull market that kept on roaring for so long, there never seemed to be any good reason to do anything else. You should come and see the firm when you're in Boston."

Lucille was enchanted by the setting. Gesturing with her gin and tonic as the steaks broiled on the outdoor charcoal grill, she asked Kent about the island and its inhabitants. "I'm a convert," Lucille said. "It's, well, so permanent here. I can imagine coming here year after year. It's so different from the rest of the lakes region, as far as I can tell. Does any of this property ever come up for sale?"

"Rarely," was Kent's dry rejoinder A slight intake of breath from Ann was missed by Lucille, but not by her husband. Lucille was used to taking people at face value. For Bob, more attuned to the sinuosities of diplomacy and what lay behind the masks he encountered every day, that was one of her most appealing, he would even say, one of her most American traits.

When the steaks were ready, they ate their dinner on the patio and watched the setting sun over the lake. Bob's gift, a vintage Bordeaux, was a perfect match for the steaks. It was idyllic. Even the mosquitoes kept their distance.

The buzz from Bob's cellular phone startled them all. For a while he had even forgotten that he had it with him. The phone was in the pocket of his jacket, draped over an armchair on the patio. "Sorry," he said to Ann. "Damned nuisance really. The desk insisted that I carry it with me throughout this home leave. Trouble in Kuala Lumpur."

He quickly retrieved his jacket and took the message from his phone. "Yes, Bart. No, you were quite right to call. They've taken over the Embassy, you say? How many and when? Yes, put him on."

Kent, Ann and Lucille watched him and monitored the conversation, an easy task in the stillness of the lakeside evening.

"Good evening, Mr. Secretary. Yes, Bart Stevens has filled me in. Of course, I'll return immediately." Bob's click signalled the conversation's end. He gestured towards Lucille, then consulted a typed card in his wallet, and quickly called his Country Director. Then he rejoined the others.

"It's just what we thought might happen," he reported first to Lucille. "Terrorists have taken over our Embassy in Kuala Lumpur. A task force has been set up, and of course I must get back to Washington."

"Can't the Country Director honcho this? Do they really have to bother an Ambassador on his long delayed vacation?" Lucille asked petulantly.

"Not with the Secretary due in Singapore in a month. Too much is at stake."

"Was that the Secretary of State you were talking to?" Ann wanted to know.

"It was the Assistant Secretary for Far Eastern Affairs. That's our home bureau, so to speak." Then he turned to Lucille. "There's no need for your vacation to be spoiled as well, dear. This will probably only be on the front burner for a few days, one week at the outside. You can stay at the lodge and finish out our rental. I'll be back as soon as I can."

Lucille hesitated, but Ann did not. "We wouldn't hear of that, Lucille. You are going to stay with us here on Governor's Island. I can't imagine anything worse than a single vacation on Lake Winnepesaukee, with all those crowds of tourists."

And so it was settled. "And when you've solved that crisis, Bob, come on back home," Kent added. "Now that you've returned to Governor's Island, you really ought to explore having your own place here. You always did belong. Say the word and I'll smooth the way with the Homeowners' Association. We can have an informal get together when you return. Someone may well know of a good property coming vacant, even if I don't. Not every family likes to keep up the old traditions."

Bob smiled in satisfaction. The manipulation of crisis at short notice was his specialty, and the morning's New York *Times* had told him all he had needed to know about the terrorist incident in Kuala Lumpur. An afternoon call to his Country Director had done the rest.

"It's good to be home," was all that he could say.

▼

THE OLD MASTER

The elderly couple looked at Gene Cranston with pride and dignity. The American Consul smiled at them in return. It was a little game he played, trying to figure out his visitors before their business was announced. It didn't take long, and often he was right. Let's see. Pride, he guessed, because they were American citizens. That would be something they had looked forward to and planned for as a goal. They weren't born in the States. Reflugees once, he bet, people who wouldn't give up. People who knew how precious American citizenship was. There was also the slight accent that would never go away for a clue, so the deduction wasn't very hard, but it seemed right.

Dignity was a mixed clue. Very old world and all that. It was often misinterpreted as having wealth, or at least the assurance that comes from knowing you will not be in want. The investment portfolio and the retirement package would cover reasonable expenses, and the insurance would do the rest. In Cranston's experience, though, a sense of dignity often didn't mean that at all. It could in fact mean the reverse, having very little money, but taking care not to ask for help. It usually did mean that. He couldn't be sure about this couple.

"Mr. Consul..." Cranston leaned forward in his chair as the old man spoke. None of this "Call me Gene" stuff. He was a consular officer, not a waiter. "This is hard to say," the visitor went on, "but we need your help." The old lady took out their American passports from her purse and passed them across the desk. Cranston looked at them. Not to have done so would have been most rude.

The passports announced that Anton and Silvia Svoboda, American citizens aged 81 and 79, respectively, had both been born in what was now the Czech Republic. Her birthplace was Prague, while her husband had been born in Plzen, where the best beer still came from. Cranston knew the town slightly. Years ago he had had a tour as Vice Consul at the Embassy in Prague, and had returned recently, driving through the Bohemian region on his way to Prague from Budapest for a Consular Officers' Conference the previous year. It was his third year as Consul at the Embassy on *Szabadsag Ter* (Freedom Square), and he was beginning to feel very much at home in Budapest and the region.

Now, having seen their passports, he was sure of his original assessment. The Svobodas had been refugees. Come to think of it, they were very well dressed, nothing flashy, not that he would have expected that at their ages, but excellent quality. He ought to have seen that before. The man's suit was the best worsted wool, probably tailored. He was less sure about Mrs. Svoboda's clothes. The only jewelry she wore was her worn golden wedding ring, and plain golden earrings.

He handed the passports back to the lady. "Thank you, Mrs. Svoboda. You were saying, sir?"

The old man started again. "We came back for a visit, Mr. Consul. It was painful for us, but we did go back to Plzen, where as you see I was born and lived before the war. Then the Nazis came, of course, and plundered everything. They just stole our things in front of our very eyes, and what they didn't steal or didn't want or couldn't carry, they burned, laughing while they were doing it. We were ordered out of our houses and into a ghetto."

The words tumbled out. Mrs. Svoboda sniffed back the beginnings of a tear as her husband spoke. Many scenes were flashing in front of her eyes, none of which Cranston wanted to share. But she reflected a quiet dignity, and great pride in her husband. Cranston found that beautiful.

"We were wealthy. Bankers. Or rather, my family was. The beer producers always needed money for expansion, and business was always good. Silvia was studying music in Prague. She hoped to attend Charles University and become a concert flautist.

"Then one day the trucks came to Plzen. My parents were sent away. I never saw them again. I guess I was the lucky one, if you can call it that. Since I was young and very strong, I was sent to a work camp. That's where we met, Mr. Consul. Silvia somehow had survived and also was not sent to a death camp. It was our miracle. Instead, she played for the work camp orchestra that the Nazis had assembled in order to give an illusion for the newcomers of what they faced. Or maybe they had some idea of fooling the Red Cross, I don't know. Somehow Silvia and I found each other and lived through that camp. We met again in a refugee camp, afterwards."

Mrs. Svoboda patted her husband's hand. "Yes, you're right, he doesn't have to know all this," he said to her softly.

Anton Svoboda gave a wan smile and went on. "As you will understand, we couldn't stay long in either Plzen or Prague during this visit. It was just too painful. But we had remembered Budapest. I had come here together with my family as a boy, you see, and I loved the city. We have a nice suite at the Hilton looking over—overlooking—the Danube. And our Senator is a good family friend. He told us to let the Ambassador know if we were coming to Budapest. So when we arrived yesterday I called his office. There had, apparently, already been a letter. Your Ambassador was kind enough to invite us for coffee, and we were there this morning. Nice house.

"As a matter of fact, we have just come from there." He fell silent, trying to assemble his thoughts. Cranston knew that the Ambassador often arrived at the Embassy in the late morning. He liked meeting visitors at the official residence, dawdling over morning coffee. "'More cordial than an office meeting," he would say to the staff, which had gotten used to it. In Cranston's experience, Embassy staff usually got used to an Ambassador's eccentricities quite readily.

"Ambassador Sullivan and his wife had greeted us, and we were seated in their morning room," Mr. Svoboda went on. Cranston knew the room well. Its picture windows faced the morning sun, which flooded into the room. "We had just begun our conversation when it happened," the old man said. "We were having a nice visit. We felt welcome and at home. Ambassador Sullivan puts a visitor at ease, and Mrs. Sullivan is charming. We sat on a comfortable couch and chose pastries to go with our coffee. A few minutes later I looked over the Ambassador's shoulder as his wife went to the door to answer her telephone in the next room. And there, on the far wall, protected from the sun, we saw the picture."

Cranston nodded. "I think I know the one you mean, the Matisse. It's wonderful, the pride of the Ambassador's collection."

Svoboda stolidly went on. "The last time I saw it, that painting was hanging on the wall of my father's study in Plzen. My father liked French paintings, and he had a small collection. But that included a Picasso, a Cezanne and this Matisse. He was a banker, as I've explained, and he and my mother visited France occasionally in the nineteen twenties. When they did, sometimes he bought a picture. How many he had and what they were, I'm not sure. I wish I had paid more attention. There were at least six or seven fine paintings.

"With my own eyes I saw the Nazis take them from our house. I never thought I would see any of them again. But this picture is unmistakable. It is our property, Mr. Consul, and we need your help and that of our Governrnent, if necessary, to get it. It was stolen from us, and now we want it back."

Cranston was stunned. His usual consular bonhomie deserted him. He poured a glass of water from the carafe on the table behind him, the carafe that was filled with fresh water by his Hungarian secretary each morning and which he was now using for the first time in three years. "Did you tell the Ambassador?"

"Yes. Well, almost. He saw how startled I was. I said the painting reminded me very much of a Matisse that my family had owned before the war. He said this was a grand period, the artist's paintings during his long residence in Nice, very colorful, full of life and light, comments like that. He said that there were similar themes that the artist used from time to time. He seemed to be implying that I was mistaken, that I had taken his painting for a similar one. We let it go at that. But I remembered, Mr. Consul. We were a well travelled family. My father bought the painting in Paris shortly after it was finished. This was—IS—our painting. Of that, I have no doubt. None whatsoever." He nodded in affirmation and total certainty.

Cranston fumbled for words. "You said you wanted the painting back, Mr. Svoboda. That is understandable." He stalled for words, trying to show sympathy but maintain a little distance. What a bombshell. "Can you prove your ownership?"

"I suppose that is next," Svoboda said. "If necessary, yes. But I hope we don't have to get lawyers involved. All that expense. All that publicity. What I want to do now is talk frankly with the Ambassador and explore the prospects for the return of our painting. And I want you to be present at our meeting with him."

"You put me in a difficult position, Mr. Svoboda. May I ask why?"

"You have a good reputation. We found that out last night, when my wife mentioned to a friend in the American resident comunity here that we were visiting the Embassy this morning." That wasn't enough, but Cranston let it go. Probably he wanted a witness. Yes, that was surely it.

"How long will you be in Budapest?"

"We're flexible. Please leave a message at the Hilton, suite 762, when the meeting has been arranged. And thank you for your efforts, Mr. Cranston."

They shook hands. Svoboda held the Consul's hand longer than customary, and looked him in the eye. "I know you will help us, Mr. Cranston. After all these years, justice must be served." Mrs. Svoboda smiled with pride at her husband as they left the Consul's office.

*   *   *   *

"I think I'm out of my depth here. Better let me tell you about my visitors this morning, and I'd very much appreciate some background." Cranston's first call after the Svobodas had left his office had not been to the Ambassador's secretary to arrange the requested meeting. It had been to Fiona Macready, the Embassy's Cultural Affairs Officer. They sipped their drinks, while waiting for their luncheon at a game restaurant across the square from the Embassy.

Fiona listened carefully as Cranston told her about the Svobodas' visit, and the old man's certainty that the Matisse had been stolen from his family.

"To begin with," she said, "this can't be dismissed out of hand."

"I was rather afraid that you were going to say that. By the way, this is a genuine Matisse, not a copy of some sort?"

"It's a fine example of his work in Nice. Sometime around 1926, I'd say. And it's definitely not a copy. I spotted it as soon as the Ambassador came last year. My Master's degree was in French post-Impressionism. I spent a lot of time with Matisse. The only thing that intrigued me was that I didn't know this painting. It's an *Odalisque*, of course, a reclining woman on a sofa. Lots of color, patches of sunlight playing off different fabrics throughout the scene. And the red robe she is, partly, wearing gives it the title, *Odalisque Rouge*. Ambassador Sullivan discussed it with me in some detail one evening at one of those receptions that he gives. It's obviously a painting in which he takes a lot of pride. And yes, it's genuine. It just creates a mood. I'm quite fond of it. His joy in owning the painting is understandable. It's the sort of painting you enjoy living with, and it's a fine work of art."

"Now, Fiona, please give me some background. What about their story that it had been stolen by the Nazis when they went into Czechoslovakia?"

"Unfortunately, the scenario is entirely plausible. It happened time and again, first clumsily, then in an ordered fashion as the Gestapo assembled lists of works of art that they wanted to steal. Some of the bigwigs, Hermann Goering in particular, fancied themselves as art connoisseurs. They even had lists of works by what they called 'degenerate artists,' that they would seize and sell, then use the proceeds to buy other paintings."

"And were the paintings returned after the war?"

"Some were, but for the most part, I don't think so. For events that took place so long ago, Gene, the effort to match owners with stolen art is really just getting underway." The waiter served their order and refreshed their drinks, Fiona's white wine from the Balaton region and Gene's Pilsner Urquell beer.

"You make it sound like a difficult process."

"It is. Very. For one thing, many of the owners are dead. For another, the paper trail of ownership, what we call the *provenance* is extremely hard for the former owners to put together. Nobody saved ownership papers when they were sent to the camps."

"What happened after the war?"

"The problems got compounded. Many governments just took over the looted art. There were statutes of limitations for filing claims. It took years and years for former owners to get into a position where they could begin to assert claims for their property. Survival was their issue then, not reclaiming works of art. And a lot of art just made it to the United States."

"To the United States?" Cranston sensed a danger sign.

"Yes. That's where the money was, after all. Still is, for that matter. Paintings went to the great museums. And some went to private collectors. The dealers, by the way, stayed in business. Some of the very same people who had been go-betweens for the Nazis were back in business, or had never really left the trade. Now, they were the sophisticated Europeans, with showrooms to match in the finest sectors of their capitals, showing magnificent works of art."

"…to people like the Sullivans."

"Exactly."

Cranston thought for a moment. He seemed to remember something from his reading, when law school had been an option. "In case of a dispute, I suppose the original owners would win. I think the principle is that a thief can't convey any title to property."

"If they could prove it, yes. But that requires a chain of title, or excellent, compelling circumstantial evidence of ownership. Something a jury might buy. But if the buyers exercised what's termed due diligence, and researched the history of the painting's ownership, or *provenance*, that might be a defense. But most buyers haven't done that. They just don't want to know. They often take what the dealers give them on faith. The documentation often looks good, although nowadays sometimes it's forged.

"It does get complicated. The fact that the buyers have not looked more closely at the *provenance* then becomes something that the former owners can explore in court. Why didn't they? That's particularly true when the dealer turns out to have been one of those nasty types with a bad past. As a rule of thumb, where the painting during the time of Hitler's power, 1933-1945, is crucial. These art thefts were an early Nazi priority, starting in Germany with the Nuremberg Laws in 1935, before the war was even launched. That began the dispossession of the Jews, their property, everything. They kept up the same pattern in other countries, of course. So as a rule of thumb, if there is a period that is sort of glossed over, and if the *provenance* includes dealers who dealt with the Nazis, you've got grounds for suspicion. Buy something else. At the very least, check it out thoroughly."

"Where does this leave the Svobodas? It doesn't sound like they are in the driver's seat either."

"No. It's harder from the standpoint of the former owners, I think. After all, this can become a very expensive matter. Lawyers' fees, depositions, expert testimony. That all costs a great deal of money. The present possessors are often wealthy institutions, and highly respected in the community. Or they are like the Sullivans, prominent families with private fortunes. The people trying to prove ownership can't match those resources."

"I think we're at the beginning of a long process. Obviously, I've got to go and see Ambassador Sullivan now, and tell him about the Svobodas."

"I don't envy you."

"No, but I'd like you to stay involved, Fiona. On the sidelines, if you prefer. Your expertise might be a great help."

"Glad to help, I think." She didn't sound sure of that in the least. "What did you have in mind?"

"Well, the Ambassador will be looking into this as well, I'm sure. The *provenance*, I mean. He probably already has the proof with his private papers in a lawyer's safe somewhere in Manhattan, for all we know. But he can't really ask you to do it in any event. I mean, this is essentially a private matter, and you are here for the USG."

"Yes…"

"The problem is to handle this as fairly as possible. I don't have your background. I'd like to know as much as your research will tell you, if anything, about this painting. Let me see if I have this straight." He counted on his fingers as he spoke. "Who owned it, and when? Where was it exhibited, if ever? Any gaps during the war in the ownership documentation? And, of course, which dealers handled any sales of the painting, and just who were they?"

"Gene, are you taking sides in this?"

"That's just what I am not doing. I expect that it will all sort itself out. If not, I'm going to document every step that we take. Hell, I'll be doing that anyway."

"And I'll join you, to that extent. I'll do some research. It's an interesting problem. In a way, you're pretty lucky. Not everybody will do this for a luncheon, you know."

He smiled at her. "My pleasure, Fiona," he said. "Of course I'll pick up the check. It's the least one poor bureaucrat can do, and the most I can afford, for that matter."

*   *   *   *

Cranston was waved into the Ambassador's office by an executive assistant, who closed the door behind him. Ambassador Sullivan, ebullient and smiling, came forward to greet his Consul. He shook hands, and then waved Cranston over to a sofa and chair to the right of the entrance. Ambassador Sullivan took the chair, with its telephone within easy reach. Cranston looked over his shoulder and noticed the plaque on the wall, which commemorated Cardinal Mindszenty's exile in this room for fifteen years. A different era, Cranston thought.

"What's all the mystery, Gene?" Sullivan asked. "My secretary said you wouldn't give a reason for the meeting. Not that I need one, of course. Always an open door for key members of our Embassy staff."

"We both had visitors earlier today, Mr. Ambassador. The same visitors, an elderly couple, Anton and Silvia Svoboda, pushing their eighties."

"Yes. We had them over for coffee this morning. They had had Senator Wharton send along a courtesy letter. He does it for a lot of folks. Still, it's best to be on his good side. Never know when he really is recommending someone who's a personal friend, not just a constituent."

Cranston returned his smile. Ambassador Sullivan had wonderful political antennae. And as a political appointee in a new administration, there was a possibility that he might even get another embassy in a year or two. A larger one, farther west. Yes, the Ambassador specialized in creating a cordial atmosphere. He was no dummy. No need to alienate people who could be helpful. In an odd sort of way, that might make him rather vulnerable, too, Cranston realized.

"Yes, sir. He told me about it. He also had something to say about a painting that you have hanging on the wall of the morning room at the residence. It's a Matisse, I think you once told me. Beautiful thing. I've noticed it myself when you and Mrs. Sullivan have had the Embassy staff over. *Odalisque*, I think it's called."

"*Odalisque Rouge*, to be precise. Matisse painted several on a similar theme. Full of light and life. Susan and I are very fond of it. That's why we chose to bring it with us. We couldn't imagine leaving it in storage with our other paintings during our stay here in Budapest. What did Svoboda have to say?"

"That's why I'm here, sir," Cranston began quite unnecessarily, stalling for time, a few more seconds. Perhaps something would occur to him. Perhaps Ambassador Sullivan would say something that would save him. But he didn't. He waited with an appraising look.

"The Svobodas were refugees after the war. He told me just a bit. It was a horrible story; family murdered, the camps, property stolen. He and his wife had both lived in what was Czechoslovakia. He was from Plzen, in Bohemia, south of Prague, where she was a music student." Sullivan nodded. "He said that his father was a banker in Plzen there before the war. Apparently they were well fixed. They even had their own art collection. He said his parents used to visit France before the war. They bought paintings there. One of them, he is convinced, is your *Odalisque Rouge*."

Ambassador Sullivan recoiled. "So what is he saying?"

"He's saying, sir, that it was his family's painting. He says that the Nazis stole that painting, which he specifically remembers, along with half a dozen other fine paintings. He was there when they did it. We didn't get into the others, what they were. The upshot is that he saw your painting, Mr. Ambassador. He says it belongs to him, and he wants it back."

"Why did he come to you?"

"A Consul is kind of a family figure, sir. It's someone within the Embassy that the local community often feels comfortable with. He and his wife probably didn't know what to do when they left the residence. He says that last night, after they arrived, he met someone at the hotel whom I had helped. That's always possible. There's always a lot of consular work to do with the local American comunity, both resident and tourist. It was probably someone I helped with a notarial. Anyway, he had my name, and probably didn't think he could either call you directly, or ask for another appointment after he and his wife had just been to the residence. Also, he strikes me as on the up and up. That's my first impression. Sometimes I change it, but that's the way it seemed to me. I almost thought he didn't want you to be blindsided, sir. It was perfectly obvious that by talking with me, he would be sure that you heard the real reason for the requested meeting, in some detail, and that it would be handled discreetly."

"So you think I should see him?" The question was really rhetorical, Cranston thought. He's already made up his mind.

"I think you would look bad if you didn't see him, sir."

"What do you know about art, Cranston? Particularly, art from this period?"

"Some. You can't get through a liberal arts curriculum without taking an arts survey course. And if you can, you shouldn't. Matisse with Picasso and Cezanne is one of the greats of this century. His paintings are worth huge sums."

"That's well said. Does Mr. Svoboda know anything about the paintings that his family lost, what happened to them? Has he tried to trace them, I mean?"

"He didn't say, and I didn't ask. I almost have the feeling that he would have blurted it out if he had been on any sort of search mission."

"Sounds reasonable. All right, Cranston, Tell my secretary that I'll see the Svobodas here at the office the day after tomorrow. Can't do it before then. I've got that factory visit in Debrecen tomorrow. Have her pick a time that's convenient for all concerned. I want you to be on hand as well. Oh, and between now and then, see what you can find out about this general subject. I'll alert my lawyers at home, of course, but it would be good to find out what we can here as well."

That sounded insufficient, and so he walked Cranston to the door. "Don't worry, Gene," he said. "It's my painting, and this will sort itself out. My father bought it from Rohmer Brothers in New York in 1953. The *provenance* is quite in order."

Cranston left the Ambassador's office, and told the waiting secretary about the Svoboda appointment. She still had their hotel and room number from their previous call. "I'll let you know as soon as it's all arranged, Mr. Cranston," she said. He left the ambassadorial suite and walked down two flights of stairs to his office, pondering the fact that Ambassador Sullivan was so confident about his ownership of the painting, even to the year his father had bought it. A cool sort behind all that bonhomie, Cranston thought. Oh well, he reflected, you don't get to be CEO of a Fortune 500 company without knowing how to roll with the punches.

∗   ∗   ∗   ∗

The next day he met Fiona Macready for drinks after work. She had done some research, and was bubbling with enthusiasm to share what she had learned.

"I haven't been able yet to trace this particular painting, Gene. I need some details regarding *provenance*. But there is a very clear pattern. Major works like this one must leave tracks. It would help to know when and where the Sullivans got it."

"As a matter of fact, he told me. He said that his father had purchased it from art dealers in New York, the Rohmer Brothers. He even knew the date. It was 1953."

"That fits a pattern. The Rohmer Brothers are a well-known firm, but they have been cited in several cases of disputed ownership. Now they've cleaned up their act. I'm not sure they even deal in this period anymore. But for years, they were leading go-betweens for American art purchases of European paintings. Often, the *provenance* might have been questionable."

"So the bill of sale doesn't end things."

"To the contrary, it just opens them up. Furthermore, this entire area of restitution, particularly for Holocaust victims, is opening up. You know about payments from the German Government, of course, and the mess the Swiss banks have been in. Ditto insurance companies who dishonored claims made by Holocaust survivors. Now the state archives are beginning to open. It's not an edifying scene. The French Government, amongst others, has begun to make more documents from the period public. And there have been meetings of various nations to make clear the principle of returning stolen Holocaust era works of art as a moral obligation."

"Still, there are burdens of proof."

"Yes, and they remain high. However, there have been precedents, and they are recent. I've found out that the National Gallery of Art in Washington has returned a 17th century painting by the Flemish artist Franz Snyders to its rightful owner. That's not all. The North Carolina Museum of Art and the Chicago Art Institute have had to return paintings. Even the Museum of Modern Art, 'MOMA' as we call it, is in litigation over an Egon Schiele."

She sipped her drink. "Here's the zinger, Gene. More to the point, the Seattle Art Museum in June, 1999 returned a Matisse, a 1928 *Odalisque*, to its rightful owners. In that case, the museum is now suing the gallery concerned that had sold the painting to the man who later donated it to them. He had bought it forty or fifty years ago, just like Ambassador Sullivan's father. So that may be a direct precedent. That Matisse, by the way, is appraised at $2 million. At least, that is what the Seattle Art Museum is trying now to recover.

"You make it sound like there is a momentum going here, one that doesn't favor Ambassador Sullivan. And, the fact that his father bought the painting some fifty years ago may be no defense?"

"That's exactly what's going on. And potential claimants are beginning to have some powerful allies. The Seattle affair was helped by *provenance* research done by the Holocaust Art Restitution Project. They're good, and they're professional."

"And Ambassador Sullivan, if he wants another post, or at least wants to finish this one honorably, cannot afford to blow the claimants off."

"Not unless he wants to hear early from the White House, he doesn't. Fortunately for him, there are extenuating circumstances. He's a victim, too, of a sort. His father bought the painting, after all. He didn't. All he did was inherit the painting. If he handles the Svobodas well, he'll still be all right."

*   *   *   *

The meeting opened without rancor or pleasantries. Ambassador Sullivan, all business, sat behind his desk. Gene Cranston sat in an armchair beside the desk, determined to take as many notes as he could. For all he knew, this could end up in court. Might as well try to get it right. He remembered hearing that when Henry Kissinger was Secretary of State, he had required Foreign Service Officers to take vebatim notes of his meetings with foreign officials. Just monitor the action and be quiet. This was similar. The Svobodas faced Ambassador Sullivan across the desk, seated in a pair of armchairs with a coffee table between them.

"Thank you for seeing us, Ambassador Sullivan. This is a painful and difficult matter for me, particularly because of your hospitality a day or so ago." Sullivan nodded.

"You have a painting hanging on the wall of the morning room at your official residence. It is *Odalisque Rouge*, the original I am sure. Do I assume correctly that you brought it with you, and that it is not the property of the Government?"

"The Art In Embassies program does not extend to issuing Matisse paintings, Mr. Svoboda, regret it though we may. And yes, it is the original. It has been in my family for over fifty years."

"My family did not possess it for that long, Ambassador Sullivan. They weren't allowed to by the invading Nazis." He paused. Cranston had the impression that he had carefully gone over what he was going to say next.

"For it is our painting. Make no mistake about that. My father bought it during one of his periodic trips to France before the war. He was a banker in Plzen, as I told your Consul, Mr. Cranston. He has perhaps explained to you what happened next."

"I understand what you have told him, yes."

"If we let the lawyers handle this, Mr. Ambassador, all questions of *provenance* will become known shortly. Why not save time, and share what we know? After all, you are not to blame in this matter, not in the least."

"I have no problem with that. I've already called my attorney in New York, who is getting the papers together. As I recall, there was a detailed *provenance* outlined at the time my father bought the painting. That was in 1953. But the records conveyed went back much further, including a few times when it was publicly exhibited. I may be wrong, but I seem to recall that there had been exhibitions in Paris and in London prior to its sale in the late nineteen twenties."

"From whom did your father purchase the painting? Was it directly from an owner?"

"No. Actually, it was from Rohmer Brothers, the New York gallery. Very well established and reputable."

"I'm sorry to say, not always and not for this period."

"Tell me about your claim of ownership, Mr. Svoboda."

"First of all, of course, the claim is one of emotion and memory. I remember the painting well from my boyhood. I even remember when my parents returned from France, excited about their purchase. I must have been about ten years old at the time. It was shipped from the gallery in Paris, of course. Perhaps they even have the records of shipment to the Svoboda residence in Plzen. I'm sure they must. The French are great record keepers."

He paused, and went on. "The picture used to hang in my mother's sitting room. We had other paintings, too, but that was our favorite. So full of emotion and light, and so, well, womanly. I used to see it often. When the Nazis plundered our home, it was like another murder of our family"

Ambassador Sullivan asked in a low tone. "And your brothers and sisters, Mr. Svoboda?"

"I had two brothers and one sister. Like my parents, they did not survive the war. As a matter or fact, I'm not even sure they all survived that first horrible night, when I was taken away. My eldest brother tried to resist. He was very brave. But it made no sense. I heard shots."

The old man's voice fell silent.

"You make a compelling case, Mr. Svoboda. And so as far as you know, you are the last surviving member of the Svoboda family, and therefore, the rightful owner of the Matisse? Everyone else is dead. Did I understand that is the basis for your claim?"

"Yes."

"Clearly," Ambassador Sullivan began, "a great injustice has been done here. I don't think I ever really understood the position of someone like the Svobodas until now. You, after all, were a refugee, Mr. Svoboda. You have these terrible experiences and memories. I do not. I was born in the United States. We all have our bad memories and our injustices, but I simply cannot imagine being so surrounded by hatred, with plunder and murder part of one's own family history."

He stopped, and Svoboda looked at him, with a thin smile. Cranston thought, well at least this is going to have some sort of civilized resolution. The Ambassador doesn't need the negative publicity that a court fight would involve, and Svoboda couldn't afford a lawsuit anyway. They'll come to some sort of a deal.

"Supposing that this was the property of the Svoboda family in Plzen, as you say, and suppose also that there was a problem in the *provenance* of the picture. What does that mean now? I think there are some interesting legal issues to be raised. For one thing, my father was a very shrewd businessman. He would not have purchased a painting in which there was the least doubt of ownership. After all, he founded one of America's biggest corporations. He was no fool. I'm sure that he looked into the matter most thoroughly."

"Come, come, Mr. Ambassador. One cannot be an expert in all things. Paintings are a matter of love and possession. He saw it and wanted it. And to be fair, the standards of the time—did you say the early fifties?—were not what they are now. And so he bought it. The adequacy of the *provenance* is now the issue. And it is inadequate. Totally inadequate."

"Have you any idea what the Matisse would now be worth?"

"That is a secondary matter, Mr. Ambassador."

"Not to a potential thief, Mr. Svoboda. There was a very recent case in Seattle. It involved the return of a Matisse, like this one an *Odalisque*. The value of the painting was set at two million dollars."

"That much! Well, I can't pretend that sentimental factors are all that are at stake here. Should the painting be sold, the money realized would cover many injustices over the years. Yes, it would."

"But that, of course, could take a long time, if ever. You are not a young man, Mr. Svoboda. You would have to sell the painting yourself. Why, you couldn't even afford the premiums to insure the painting. And if you could, do you have any idea what protections the insurance companies would require before they would even consider issuing a policy?"

That stopped Svoboda, and he began formulating another proposition. "I hadn't really considered all that, Ambassador Sullivan. Perhaps the painting should remain with you, after all. Taking the most generous view of the matter, you have grown up with the painting. You love it as much as I do, and no blame attaches to your ownership."

"Go on."

"Instead of pursuing this claim, it occurs to me that there is another solution possible. If you would be interested in purchasing my claim to the painting, I would let it go at that. No no, my dear," he said, patting his wife on her arm. "That might be the right thing to do."

"But Anton, you've spent so many years dreaming of recovering your family's property."

"Yes, my dear, but sometimes the best way to keep a dream is to let it go."

Ambassador Sullivan leaned back in his chair and looked at the ceiling for a moment. Then he faced Svoboda again. "Have you thought of an appropriate price for this settlement?"

Svoboda's voice grew regretful and ponderous. "Not specifically. We could talk about it. There is no particular hurry." He paused. "But you asked a question and deserve some answer. I should think, all things considered, that half a million would be fair. I'd like, by the way, for that to be a net figure. Perhaps your lawyers could explain to us how the income tax laws would apply in this situation."

"So that's the bottom line," Ambassador Sullivan said softly, lighting a rare cigarette.

"This has been very educational, Mr. Svoboda. I only wish my father were alive to hear it. He died a few years ago. He was a wonderful man, Mr. Svoboda. He taught me the value of family. I'm sure that was because he had lost his own family. He was raised in England, where he had been sent for safety in one of the few *kindertransport* before the war. He was added at the last possible moment. That wasn't generally known. The rest of his family died. But my father was raised by a business associate of his father. George Wyckham, a barrister, was the man. He was also something of an art connoisseur. When he visited my grandparents in the 'thirties, he kept a diary of the trip. Room by room, it describes my grandparents' paintings, and their setting. I think it would prove most persuasive as evidence in a court of law.

"When my father changed his name to Sullivan, it was because he thought it would be better to sound American in his new country. I also have a letter from Mrs. Wyckham, which was notarized and witnessed. It is a short note, but she mentions her husband's travel diary. She was pleased that her foster child Anton Svoboda had done so well as Andrew Sullivan in his new country."

He rose, red faced and menacing. "It isn't a crime to buy back your own property, as my father did. But extortion is a crime. I'm sorry I don't speak Czech. If I did, I could tell you in that language too what I really think of you and your contemptible extortion scheme. Get the hell out of this Embassy and do it now!"

The old woman looked at her husband with blazing eyes and began to scream.

Cranston translated. "Liar! Bastard! Lying bastard! Who are you? WHO ARE YOU?" She yelled again and again as, with failing strength, she struck at her husband with her frail arms.

CHAPTER 32

▼

NOTHING TO LOSE BUT YOUR CHAINS

Alice Hamilton had enjoyed her husband Frank's Foreign Service career, really she had. From Dakar to Brussels, the change of scene every few years had been invigorating. She even liked the interim tours of duty in Washington. They were opportunities to catch up with her college classmates, many of whom seemed to have managed careers of their own.

She knew that Frank was a good husband. That was settled in her mind. But it was a good thing that she enjoyed his career nearly as much as he did.

Of course, he had his debatable points. For one thing, Frank was never under foot when it came time to pack the house, and make those agonizing decisions about what went to the next post and what stayed in storage, but she had come to expect that. Frank usually agreed with her assortments anyway, although there was the occasional comment.

The gradually increasing responsibilities that Frank had enjoyed as a commercial and economic specialist had taken so much of his time, that Alice had raised their daughters almost by herself. Not that Frank wasn't a fine father, always ready to see the lacrosse match at their school, or quiz the girls about their homework. It's just that he always seemed so preoccupied.

That is one reason why Felicia and Nancy had always felt closer to their mother. Now they were gone, living back home, educated and with families of their own. They kept in touch dutifully. They were good girls.

Now that Frank was a Commercial Counselor, with several officers in his section, one would think that he would let up a bit. In a way, he did. After much prodding and reminding, he had finally scheduled a nice vacation in England, something they had always wanted to do. It would be their time to be together and have a nice holiday. They had carefully poured over schedules and resort brochures. They knew London of course, but the countryside was less familiar to them. They decided not to visit British diplomatic colleagues at home, after all. This would be their own getaway.

Frank was a walker and Alice loved poetry, so they decided to combine their interests, and stay in the Lake District. It was early summer, and a very nice June at that, a blessing, the locals around their favorite pub in Windermere had declared.

Their days were pleasantly spent on walks around the region, through charming towns like Ambleside and Buttermere, with occasional easy climbs through the scenic hilly country surrounding the lakes. Frank bought nobbed walking sticks, but they were more pleasant affectations than necessary to their walks. Alice delighted in discovering Wordsworth's Dove Cottage in Grasmere, and Beatrix Potter's home. They were more at ease on this holiday than they had been for years.

The village church at Grasmere, Wordsworth's resting place, attracted Frank's interest. They could easily fit the service into their visit, he said. Alice began to get a bit uneasy. She was not churchy, and Frank was. Not that Frank went to church very often, mind you. But when he did, it was to atone for past and future lapses, it seemed to Alice. He would then over Sunday dinner discuss the sermon that he had heard, asking her for comment. Since she had invariably not heard a word of the sermon, her comment was often predictably short.

And so the following Sunday morning saw them among the village church's parisioners. The church interior was surprisingly large, with pews reserved for leading squire families. It was cool and pleasant as they entered.

The church was nearly full. Everyone seemed to know each other, Alice noticed with approval. There were tablets on the walls to the fallen in Britain's wars, and occasional statuary evocations of the past. The choir was excellent, their choice of hymns a selection from the remembered childhoods of their American visitors. That added to the charm of the service.

Frank listened closely to the sermon. Alice tuned it out fairly quickly, only returning to listen from time to time, as the curate droned on. And how he did drone on! Frank seemed enthralled, but to Alice, it seemed that the sermon had little coherence.

Finally—FINALLY—it ended. Alice thought that a quick escape to that nice tea shop on High Street around the corner from the church would be just the thing. But they must be quick about it, before the Sunday tour buses began to arrive.

Frank had other ideas. He led his politely protesting wife in the opposite direction from the tea shop, towards the parsonage, having seen in the program a notice that coffee would be served there after the service. Really! Frank, Alice was sure, could be counted on for a soliloquy on the sermon that she had not heard. It was all too much bother.

The ladies of the congregation had set long tables in the parsonage, and Frank and Alice got their coffee and milk, and sat down at a table, which filled rapidly. They introduced themselves as American tourists on a holiday visit to the Lake District. Then, as Alice feared, Frank started to talk about the sermon, which he had found particularly edifying.

"Are his sermons always so long?" Alice asked sweetly. Her neighbor nodded in agreement, and replied that they really didn't know. This was a guest curate. Their own spiritual leader had been in Grasmere for many years, but was getting on, and had retired. His own last sermon had been delivered the previous month. Now there was a series of interim religious figures, plucked doubtless from administrative obscurity and sent to Grasmere, each in turn, for a weekend's excursion by the diocesan authorities.

Some excellent coffee buns were passed around the table, and a lady whose pin proclaimed her to be a member of the Sunday Welcoming Committee poured refills of coffee. It was surprisingly good for British coffee, Alice thought. She chatted with her neighbor a bit about the village and its church. She was beginning despite herself to feel quite at home.

"I don't suppose you'll select this curate, will you?" she sallied forth. "He seemed pleasant enough, but that sermon was rather long, and I noticed that a number of people were nodding off. I'm rather afraid that I did myself for a moment," she confessed. There was a quizzical look from Frank. Where could this be leading?

Her neighbor was intrigued. "No, he has duties assigned elsewhere, we understand," she said "We don't have to worry about his sermons on a regular basis." Then her voice dropped, and she looked at Alice closely. One would almost have thought they were conspirators. "What's that you said about selecting a new curate?"

"At home," Alice innocently volunteered, "there is always a selection process when there is a question of changing ministers. We wouldn't dream of not taking part."

"You mean to say that you don't just accept whoever may be sent to you by the diocese or whoever decides such things?" The woman's eyes opened wide.

"Not in the least," Alice replied. "It's our congregation, after all. We should have the deciding say in who should be our minister. After all, he'll be with us for years."

Soon a small group of ladies gathered around Alice. Frank's attempts to talk about the sermon, lacking the oxygen of an audience, sputtered out. He looked with amazement at Alice. Then he remembered. This was the spark of a look that he had noticed when they had been at college together, the first few weeks, before the young women students had absorbed that their careers were their families. Alice had learned that lesson well over the years. What on earth was happening now? He didn't seem to recognize her for a moment.

Frank could just catch the flow of words, questions and points of view being exchanged. Alice put forth the suggestion of a committee to consider the appointment of a new curate. There was not, it seemed, any great rush. After all, there had been no appointment yet, so the diocesan authorities had not publicly committed the post to anyone in particular.

As time passed a few husbands dropped by the table to pick up their wives from the coffee. They remained to hear the conversation. It wasn't entirely to their liking. Several of them in fact aimed some very queer and appraising looks in Frank's direction. Having not been there at the start of the conversation, now they had a very difficult task in attempting to divert its flow. Some tried, but soon gave up. It couldn't be done.

First, as Alice suggested, a committee was formed on the spot to consider all of the ramifications of the appointment of a new curate for their village church. Then an interim committee to plan for services presided over by parishioners was formed. The next week's visiting curate had already been notified to them. Well, he could still come. Rather than wait to hear who would be sent to them in two weeks, the parishioners themselves would organize the service, and so notify the diocese.

And so the coffee had evolved into an impromptu strategy and organizing session to consider the issue of a new curate. The ladies buzzed and bustled, their husbands wondered what this all meant and hastily conferred with each other with averted glances behind cupped hands, wondering whether this movement could be stopped or whether it had gone too far and must be joined. From the evidence of buzzing conversations spreading from table to table, it seemed like the ranks of parishioner revolutionaries were swelling.

Frank and Alice left the parsonage to return to their hotel for Sunday dinner. Alice had the idea that this time, she would be spared the inevitable rehash of the morning's sermon.

Frank looked carefully at Alice over the dinner table, in case further revolutionary ideas were brewing. That didn't seem to be the case, but after the morning's events, he could not be quite sure.

Then Frank remembered other moments from their Foreign Service career.

To start with, there had been the countless times that Alice had put up with bores at dinner parties that they had given in furtherance of Frank's career. She even had liked it, he had told himself at the time. But sometimes she hadn't.

He thought of that time in Singapore when a visiting Senator was scolded, he later heard, by an Embassy wife for attempting to buy Chinese antique goods and smuggle them into the United States in his luggage, at a time when such purchases were illegal for American citizens. It hadn't dawned on him that it might have been Alice doing the scolding.

There had been the time in Dakar when she had organized a health group in a local slum, to teach some of the local women about sanitation matters. That had been a busy time at the Embassy, and so Frank hadn't paid much attention. But he had noticed the many visitors that he hadn't known from the local community seeing them off when they had left Senegal.

There had been the shipment of clothing that Alice had organized for an orphanage near Saigon during his unaccompanied tour of duty there. It had been very much needed and appreciated. He couldn't imagine how she had managed all of the logistics, but she had.

He smiled fondly at her.

"What gave you the idea of organizing those ladies?" he asked. "I have the feeling that things will never be quite the same around here ever again."

Alice returned his smile and decided not to answer directly. Her own world was the more valued for having its occasional secrets. "I must tell Felicia and Nancy about this lovely little town," she said. "I'm sure they would love to see the Lake District one day themselves."

CHAPTER 33

▼

CONTROL OFFICER

Wendy Saunders was settling in nicely, a fine addition to the Central European Office, her Office Director Harry Mills observed to himself. Linda Morrison, his secretary, heard him, but took no notice of his mutterings. Increasingly, Mills did value himself as an audience. It must have been his tropical posts catching up to him at last. "Tropical neurasthenia" was the all purpose term used at State. Still, he was right about this, Linda thought. She liked Wendy Saunders. Everyone did.

The wonder was, that they had taken something of a risk in approving her assignment—or rather, asking the European Bureau's man in Personnel to put in a word for her at the weekly assignment panel that decided mid-level postings. She was a consular officer after all, not a political or economic specialist. She also had no experience in Central Europe.

Still, during her two previous overseas assignments in Africa she had gotten fine annual reports. These had been capped by the Secretary's Award for Heroism after her last assignment, when she organized an evacuation of American citizens during the rioting that had wracked her landlocked host country, then drove around the capital picking up frightened stray citizens who hadn't made it to the airport.

That was enough to mark her as a comer in the diplomatic service, and the cachet her actions conveyed would be an ornament for any office she joined.

Mills was convinced as soon as he saw that she had bid on a desk job in his office that she would handle the stresses and unfamiliar substance of her new job just fine.

It had been time for her to return to Washington for her first assignment in the Department of State, and when she chose to broaden her career by requesting the Central European Office, not many hands in the office had objected. Those that had, were redeeming their outstanding pledges to officers in the field, who knew the territory and its ancient history and antagonisms. They were outvoted by Office Director Mills, the only vote that counted. He had thanked them for their views and picked Wendy.

After reporting in, Wendy had soon become absorbed in learning the basics about the Department itself, how it worked, what the channels of communication were, how to greet visitors, accompany them to Sixth Floor meetings with the Assistant Secretary and then write memos regarding those meetings. Corrections for her work were usually in the form of suggestions, which she learned to absorb without comment. After all, she was the first to admit that she had much to learn.

Gradually she also absorbed the views of her superiors regarding the state of official relations with her client states. In time, there was less to learn about the relations themselves than to see which officials agreed with her, and when those who did not might be on annual leave, so that her occasional memos advocating action or a policy corrective might go forward unimpeded.

The embassies under jurisdiction of her desk were Hungary, the Czech Republic, and Slovakia. She enjoyed visiting them on festive occasions such as their national days, and was always welcomed personally by the respective Ambassador. There wasn't time to learn their languages, of course, but English was universally spoken in any event. After she had been in the office for about a year, Harry Mills called her in, with news that delighted her. It was time, he said, for her to visit her charges. The bureau's liaison with the Congressional Affairs Bureau had just called, with a notice that a Congressional delegation, "CODEL" in the State Department's jargon, would be visiting Prague and Budapest in three weeks. She could help with the preparations, go along, and then peel off for a visit to Bratislava. There would be a lot of work to do, but it would immerse her in the diplomatic workings of her nations in a practical and immediate way.

Wendy was delighted. She scheduled an afternoon on Capitol Hill with staffers for Congressman Lem Stark and Senator Evan Billings, Co-Chairmen of the Joint Congressional Committee on NATO Expansion, who would be making the trip together with several committee and personal staff members.

"We're flying commercial this time," Sam Perkins, Congressman Stark's Administrative Assistant, told her. "There's not enough fire power to fill an Air Force plane. Between you and me, this recess is just too close to the fall elections. Most Members will be back home politicking, instead of hitting the road. But Stark has a safe seat, and Billings isn't up for election for four years."

Perkins outlined some briefing requirements for her. More were added later by Senator Billings's chief committee staffer, John Moley. "Nothing too fancy. You can skip most of the paperwork. Both Stark and Billings know the territory pretty well. But updates would be useful. They'd appreciate a briefing before the trip starts."

That didn't sound like heavy lifting. She would arrange their briefings shortly before departure. The trip cable requesting appointments with the Czech and Hungarian Governments had gone out, and control officers had already been picked by the American Embassies in Prague and Budapest.

Wendy made a note to follow up vigorously with both, and then sent an e-mail to the two control officers announcing that she would be along for the trip. She asked to sit in on the CODEL's official meetings wherever possible. As an afterthought, she sent an e-mail to the Embassy in Bratislava announcing her trip, details and timing to be sent later.

The pace of work in the office suddenly picked up. It seemed that her clients were again the center of attention, as problems with future NATO expansion including the Baltic nations, fueled by Russian objections and sabre rattling, became a fashionable topic on the Washington television talk shows. This trip, Moley had said, would survey how well the first entrants into an expanded NATO had already done.

Wendy wrote briefing papers not only for the Assistant Secretary of State for European Affairs, the office's usual Sixth Floor principal, but also for such ranking Seventh Floor officers of the Department as the Under Secretary for Political Affairs. He had become a fixture on the Sunday morning talking heads circuit.

She arranged for the briefing of the CODEL and for the safe delivery and management of classified briefing papers to Capitol Hill. All in all, she was looking forward to the trip, and began to feel confident about the preparations that she had made. Wendy even realized with a smile one afternoon that six months had gone by since she had thought to call her predecessor on the desk for advice on how to play a policy issue. She had nothing against calling him, but now it would be to fine tune a point with another knowledgeable colleague. Service on a Central European desk was, she was coming to realize, rather a small club. She was glad to be a member.

Soon enough, the day of the trip arrived. Wendy met Senator Billings and Congressman Stark and their three staffers in the VIP Lounge at Dulles Airport. It was a night flight, and they would be in Budapest in the morning, met by Embassy cars. Piece of cake.

Wendy greeted Sam Perkins, John Moley, and Bob Ratigan, whom she had not met before. "I'm the press type," he said. "Can't have Members of Congress flying about making news without a press type. Cannon shot in the desert, you know."

Wendy knew, and had notified the field, that several other staffers had cancelled at the last minute. Press of official Congressional business, she had been told. A Joint Committee hearing had been scheduled for directly after this short recess. They had to stay behind and prepare for it. Luck of the draw.

Senator Billings was attractive in a laid-back, Southern sort of way, Wendy decided. True to type, he was relaxing with a bourbon and branch water. It dawned on Wendy that in a previous decade he would probably already have made a pass at her. Not so Congressman Stark, whose rigid Yankee demeanor made one wonder how New Englanders had ever reached the current generation. He sipped what looked like herbal tea and went over last minute scheduling with Perkins. Stark saw Wendy and gave her a courteous acknowledging nod. She went over to his chair to say hello, just as he shook some pills out of a small case, and took them with the last sip of his tea.

"Nitro," he explained, "for the old ticker." He smiled. "That's funny, come to think of it. Half a century ago I was in demolitions, and used this stuff to blow bad guys to kingdom come. Now they keep me going." Wendy was at a loss for words. She decided to keep an eye on Stark, to make sure his scheduling did not get out of hand.

A courtesy limo took them out to the commercial plane. They settled in for the flight, and Wendy looked forward to the sight of Budapest in the morning.

∗   ∗   ∗   ∗

It was an overcast morning at Ferihegy Airport outside of Budapest. The Control Officer, Jon Allerton, had come out to whisk them through customs. Then two Embassy cars and a baggage truck guided the party through the city to the Budapest Hilton, on a prime hillside location on the historic Buda side of the Danube overlooking the modern city.

Wendy rode with Allerton, going over last minute details of the schedule. She decided that she liked him. He would be good to work with on this trip. He seemed knowledgeable without being a know-it-all. And he had nice clear blue eyes. "Don't you usually wear two earrings?" he asked. Then with a grin he produced the missing one, which had fallen on the car seat. She decided they were going to be friends.

As the CODEL checked into their rooms, a worried John Moley caught up with Wendy. "Senator Billings doesn't like these changes," he curtly began, waving in her face the revised copy of the schedule that Jon Allerton had given them at the airport. "He wants a meeting with the Defense Minister today. Get on it."

Wendy conferred with Allerton. "The Defense Minister isn't in town today," he said. "Change of plan. He got called out by the Prime Minister to check on force readiness near the Southern border. He'll be back Wednesday."

"Should I offer to try to go ahead with the number two in the Defense Ministry?" Allerton was concerned.

"I'll put it to them. What is he like?"

"Very solid, but cautious. Also, his English isn't quite up to that of the Defense Minister. Might be better to wait."

"Thanks," Wendy said. "Let's put it to them."

"We better do it quickly. They are supposed to start their schedule soon." This was said in a collegial, not bossy way.

They met Moley at the small accommodation exchange office that the Embassy had set up in the hotel. Given the alternatives, Moley agreed that the schedule was best left alone. He'd square it with Senator Billings, he said.

She smiled at Allerton, who then left for the Embassy.

"Whew!" she said upon reaching her room. She savored the luxury of two hours of freshening up before the Embassy briefings, and then the Ambassador's luncheon at his residence.

What could be next?

What was next was a concerned Sam Perkins knocking on her door. "You're not going to believe this," was his cheery opener, "but Stark left his topcoat on the plane. His heart pills were in the pocket, too."

"Next crisis," she said, adding under her breath that this was turning out to be worse than Africa. At least there, English was spoken. She put in an immediate call to Jon Allerton in his Embassy car and spelled out the situation. He suggested that she call Perkins back and get the Congressman's coat size and physician's name and telephone number in the United States.

They were in luck. Just as Wendy was conferring with Perkins over calling the doctor as a measure of prudence to get a duplicate prescription, Jon Allerton called back. The plane hadn't left Ferihegy Airport yet. There had been several hours of cleaning and maintenance scheduled. In any event, a sweep of the plane after the morning arrival had produced the topcoat.

Congressman Stark had left it with a stewardess upon getting on the flight. She, in turn, had put it on a rack. There it was, unclaimed, in the airline's office at the airport. Yes, Allerton was picking it up immediately, and would meet them at the Embassy.

An hour later, the travellers assembled in the lobby, awaiting transportation to go to the Embassy. Wendy looked quizzically at Moley. "He's not happy, but he's calmed down, Moley said. "The schedule can proceed."

It did, except for the press type, Bob Ratigan, who was "not feeling well." Perkins filled Wendy in. "Don't worry. He'll catch up with us at the luncheon. Better have a car pick him up here directly." Wendy shook her head, puzzled but agreeable. Why wasn't their press officer going to their briefing?

They crossed the Danube and arrived at the Embassy in Freedom Square. Downstairs waiting for them was Jon Allerton. He handed Congressman Stark's overcoat to Sam Perkins, and deftly gave the box of pills to Congressman Stark. The travellers were all in a better frame of mind now, and listened carefully as Ambassador Mellon and her staff briefed them on relations with Hungary, emphasizing defense aspects.

"Aren't we missing somebody?" Allerton asked Wendy in an aside. "Yes, Bob Ratigan, the press guy. Said he was 'not feeling well,' but that he'd catch up with us at luncheon," she whispered back. "Sounds like a drinking problem. I'll alert the Consul," Allerton said.

And so it was. The Consul, a congenial teller of tall tales, had no problem finding Ratigan in the Hilton bar half an hour before the luncheon. It must have been the flight and time changes. Surely he couldn't have gotten that looped that fast otherwise. Wendy later remembered that it had been rather bumpy at times over the Atlantic.

"Happens more often than you would think," Allerton said, when the Consul's report had been relayed to Wendy. She noticed the quick aside to Ambassador Mellon, and she had a quiet word with Sam Perkins. Meanwhile, Allerton called the Ambassador's residence and rearranged the seating chart for the luncheon.

Wendy was not quite sure whether protocol or luck had decreed that on the revised seating, she was next to Jon Allerton. But she decided that she liked the coincidence. There was time between courses for a little exchange of biographic data. He seemed to know all about her. What he wanted to know about was her family, how many brothers and sisters, where they had lived, what she liked to do for vacations, and that old favorite, why had she joined the Foreign Service?

He had been, he said, a Foreign Service Brat, and had spent as much time outside the United States as in Washington—kindergarten in Singapore, elementary school here in Budapest, where Dad had been Economic Officer at the Embassy, and then high school in Ankara. In the Foreign Service, following a consular services tour in the State Department, Budapest was his first overseas assignment. He had spent over two years here as the Embassy Vice Consul, and she outranked him slightly.

He already spoke three foreign languages: colloquial Turkish "because if you are playing soccer in Turkey you'd better speak Turkish." The other two were Hungarian and German, "hardest of the three, because I had to learn it out of books." He made all this sound natural. Wendy realized that from his standpoint, it was.

He was easy to talk with, and several minutes went by before Wendy realized that she had completely neglected the Foreign Ministry man on her right, as well as losing the thread of every story that Ambassador Mellon had told. She was sorry when the luncheon ended.

She was sorrier still when, following their whirlwind schedule, the CODEL left Budapest for Prague the following afternoon. She had seen Allerton a few more times, but only briefly. He had not been included in the meetings at either the Defense Ministry or the Foreign Ministry. "I don't have the rank for that," he said sheepishly.

That would change, she assured him. Early Foreign Service promotions were reasonably assured. What was necessary was a string of good assignments.

*   *   *   *

Wendy took a deep breath, and then gave an informal knock or two on Harry Mills's door.

"Come in, Wendy. I've heard good reports about your trip. Apparently everything went smoothly?"

Wendy wondered about her boss's sources of information. It could have been a call from their Embassy, or a staffer on the Hill that he knew. Whatever, her boss was clearly plugged in.

"The Assistant Secretary was particularly pleased about your fast handling of Congressman Stark's problem. The overcoat and heart pills. He does have a serious heart condition, you see, although we're not supposed to know about it. That could have been very bad news."

"That was really the Control Officer, Harry. It was Jon Allerton who bailed us all out." She filled him in on the various emergencies that Allerton had handled during their short stay in Budapest.

"Interesting fellow. Good Foreign Service background too. I knew his father slightly. Retired now, I suppose." He stared at her, wondering what was coming next.

"Actually he seemed like one of our sort. We could use him in this office, Harry. He handles a crisis situation well. Defuses it before it gets out of hand. True, he's had only one overseas assignment so far, but that is in Budapest. He speaks Hungarian, and has a good flair for the area."

"If I understand this correctly, you'd like to see him in our office in the Department?"

"He'd be a good asset, I think."

Mills nodded tentative agreement.

She let the matter drop. It was time to fill him in on the substantive parts of the trip, and go beyond the memos to relate how the visitors got along with their hosts.

Mills listened carefully. Wendy made a note to herself to send a message to Jon Allerton about openings in the office. He should put in a formal application with the Office of Personnel. It would be just the right assignment for his future, she had decided.

CHAPTER 34

▼

THE EXTRA

"Time to get up, Josh!"

He could just hear, beyond Marge's voice, the alarm clock winding down. Four o'clock in the morning. Josh pecked her on the cheek, got up somehow, shaved and showered, struggled into a suit and began the drive from his Northern Virginia home into the District. At least there was no traffic across the 14th Street Bridge at that hour.

Being a movie extra was by definition unreal. He arrived a few minutes early at the designated parking lot, and already the lot was nearly full. None of that Foreign Service stuff about arriving ten minutes after the designated hour. The first time he had ever been an extra, he had arrived right on time, only to see the Central Casting bus pull out of the lot as he arrived. He'd had to waste precious time and money finding a cab to get to the set Then he'd had to talk his way into the holding area. No, now he was early every time.

This wasn't a second career. There wasn't enough money to be made, and the work was too irregular. Maybe if he ever qualified to join SAG, the Screen Actors Guild, he would take it more seriously. Also the pay was better. But the up front entrance fee, even after you qualified to join, would be a stretch on his Foreign Service pension. Meanwhile this got him out of the house, widened his circle beyond the retirees he knew, and was sometimes fun. He could always, at a film opening, search the screen to see if his scene were cut or included, and if included, whether he was visible.

Sometimes he was. Then it would be fun to rehash the experience. Once he was on center screen behind Jack Lemmon for several seconds, clearly visible in a reception scene, not made indistinct the way they often did. He and Marge had rented the video and had some friends over, savoring that one.

Reception scenes were his specialty. With a good Foreign Service wardrobe, he probably saved the casting company some money anyway. He was on their list, Josh supposed, because he always showed up, never called attention to himself, worked the long, long hours without complaint, and had a good wardrobe. Also he had mentally cataloged the sins of neophytes, and never stared at the camera, made suggestions to an assistant director, or tried to insert himself into a scene.

It was a reception scene that was being filmed now, at Meridian House, up 16th Street Northwest. The seventy or so extras hadn't been called to the set yet. It was now six o'clock in the morning, and they were in the holding area. Odd to see so many people at that hour so well dressed. Josh wondered how the women had managed to get their hair done so early. They really looked like they were going to a reception.

Josh knew the drill. First, of course, get there. Then get in costume if you weren't already. Some men went from jeans to a suit in minutes. Then go through wardrobe to make sure your clothes were appropriate for the scene. Most were, but the wardrobe people seemed to have a fixation on ties this morning. They had brought others, if your tie called too much attention to yourself, Josh supposed. His passed muster, a good State Department rep tie.

After wardrobe, a second check for hair and makeup. That wasn't a problem for most people. However, there was a makeup station and emergency hairdresser in the staging area in case repairs were needed. Then, the pay cards were handed out. You kept them throughout the day, noting meal times (if any), breaks, and whether you were SAG or not.

Josh barely heard the instructions. It was all pretty routine by now. The SAG representative was introduced and gave a little spiel about the benefits of membership. On this set, that seemed to be rather marginal. Union members had lunch sooner and the food was hotter. But that wouldn't be for hours and hours. They'd just have to wait and nosh in the meantime.

Josh went over to the snack table, poured himself some juice and some coffee, and took a cherry danish. Not even his usual breakfast time yet, and he already felt starved. People were beginning to open up a little. He sat next to a young fellow whom he thought he recognized from a previous film. They shook hands, and it turned out they had worked together a few months earlier. The shared memory was a good one. The shoot hadn't been too long, the weather had been pleasant, and the food had been good.

Josh's acquaintance Antonio was, like many of the extras, sort of semi serious about acting as a possible career. He had a cheap printed edition of a play that he planned to audition for, and he was memorizing a few lines of dialogue from time to time. The play was in Spanish. Josh remembered enough Spanish to agree to help him, and they spent half an hour on the play. Josh would give the prompting line, and Antonio would answer. When he got it wrong, Josh would repeat the line. It got tiresome after a while.

Josh looked up and saw that they had been joined by four young women. He grinned and said "Don't look now, but I think in this scene we're reading this young man just asked me to marry him!" He was rewarded by forced smiles. Might as well humor the old duffer. Time was when they would have exchanged names by now.

A young, intense and humorless Assistant Director stood up and called for silence. She listened on her cell phone to directions coming from someone on the set and announced that they would be leaving the holding area in a few minutes, and going over to the set. "Please keep the noise level down, and you will be placed in groups around the set when you get there. For now, pair up, with someone about your height and age." The extras finished their coffee, put the paperbacks and playing cards away, and noiselessly formed a line, two by two, waiting to cross the street and walk to Meridian House. "Just like the Army," someone muttered. "Hurry up and wait."

Going onto a set always gave Josh a rush. He liked walking past the gawkers on the street, and he liked taking in the set, trying to imagine what the director had in mind. It was, for one thing, much messier than he would have imagined. There were cords everywhere, chalked in blocking marks on the floor where people were supposed to stand, and a whole series of cameras and special lighting. That was a specialty in itself.

He paired up with a lady who looked like she wanted to change her mind and go to the mall after all. "It's tiring, of course, but it gets interesting as the shooting goes along," Josh offered. She smiled back, and they walked together over to the set, once nearly tripping over the tangle of cords.

Josh knew Meridian House, of course. He had been there for several receptions in the past, and had once served as moderator for a panel discussion there on the concerns of foreign students in Washington. It was an elegant structure, with high ceilings and expansive reception rooms, just the place for a movie set.

Josh realized that many people who had never been to a real diplomatic reception would be seeing this one in a movie. Might as well get it right.

Josh and his partner were placed near the piano by one of the production functionaries. Then the Director introduced himself and gave them some basics on the film. The working title was *Affairs Of State*. It would star Jack Nicholson and Demi Moore, both of whom would be in this scene. There was a rush of excitement amongst the extras. They were filming a diplomatic reception given by a foreign embassy during a state visit, at which the Secretary of State (played by Nicholson) is pursued by a newspaper reporter (played by Demi Moore) who has crashed the reception.

That was all they needed to know, apparently. It left open some interesting possibilities, which Josh and his partner, Helen Gibbons, amused themselves by speculating about, filling in the blanks. "Perhaps," Josh volunteered, "Demi Moore's character had dug up some dirt, and was trying to get a confirmation or denial." "Perhaps instead," Helen countered, "she was having an affair with Nicholson's character and he was trying to dump her."

Interesting, but not, Josh decided, at Nicholson's age very likely. "Which?" Helen asked. "Not likely that he would be having an affair, or that he would be dumping Demi Moore?"

"Quiet on the set!" the Director barked. He sketched out some action for the extras, some movement here and there, providing some interaction with the waiters who would be passing drinks. Josh was always surprised by the improvisation that was possible. You didn't have to just stand there, unless the action of the main characters required that. Sometimes they would come onto a scene, and your job as an extra was to stay rooted in place and register surprise, or recognition, or whatever was appropriate to the main character's action.

Usually though, some flexibility was possible. If you looked assured enough, for example, you could walk across the room and join a group. They, then, would embellish your bit by welcoming you, shaking hands and so forth. Once done, it would be polished and endlessly repeated along with other bits and perhaps make it onto the finished scene. You got it just right when it started to bore you to tears. But improvising certainly beat standing around like statues, and it added realism to what was, after all, supposed to be a diplomatic reception.

"Where are Nicholson and Moore?" Helen wanted to know. From experience, Josh knew that they probably wouldn't show up until later, when the cameras and lighting had been adjusted, and the Director was satisfied that all of the props, including the extras themselves, were in position for the shoot. Meanwhile, their stand-ins were there, blocking their positions.

"Just like an embassy reception," Josh offered. "You get the staff together, brief the Ambassador on who is coming and then make sure that ranking guests are not shunted aside like wallflowers at a school dance. Everyone has assigned tasks, and nothing is left to chance."

Josh had certainly been to enough diplomatic receptions in his time. More than hundreds. Thousands, most likely, at posts around the world. A few stuck out in his memory, even now. It occurred to him that Meridian House somewhat resembled the Consul General's residence in Singapore.

Singapore had been his first diplomatic post, when it was not yet an Embassy and when he was a beginning Vice Consul. There, for the Fourth of July, he had helped arrange his first diplomatic reception. As a junior officer, he had been stuck with six months of grunt administrative chores in the absence of a General Services Officer. Actually that wasn't so bad.

Josh had liked the work better than he would have imagined. He got to know local contractors, largely Chinese, and all of the mission's property. He had even cataloged that property and its furnishings, wedging that precious information slowly from a reluctant longterm local Foreign Service employee, a White Russian who had found his second refuge in Singapore decades earlier when Mao's People's Liberation Army had overrun China.

The Consul General's residence at 53 Grange Road would have been a perfect setting for a Somerset Maugham novel. Sweeping grounds leading up to the mansion, high ceilings, and a veranda on the second floor front where the Consul General and his wife could enjoy drinks under the ceiling fans, while looking out over the lawn and the bordering bamboo and palm trees and see their guests arrive. Josh supposed that his lifelong fondness for ceiling fans had come from those days. So much more fitting to the summer than just air conditioning. Artificial climates for artificial people.

He remembered that Fourth of July reception. "If you think this movie reception is hard, just try arranging a reception in the tropics for five hundred people," he muttered to nobody in particular. The drinks, the waiters, the *hors d'oeuvres*, the valet parking, and that nightmare of the time, the outdoor microphone with its attendant cords for the Consul General's Fourth of July toast, all had to be arranged. Not to mention the lighting and a tent, flaps raised to keep the mugginess down. He had even had the lawn sprayed for bugs and mosquitoes that morning. And he had done it all within the budget allowed.

Josh chuckled, remembering that the Consul General never did find out who had left the lawn sprinklers on all afternoon, to keep the dust down. The result was that lady guests had their high heels sinking into the lawn throughout the evening!

More than at any other Foreign Service post, Josh supposed, you could sense things in Singapore. There was for example the murder. That was, after all, how he and Marge had secured the services of Ah-Long, probably the most skilled house servant they would ever employ. Josh sometimes thought how good it would be to take the very best from each Foreign Service post and transfer it to the next one. That was a pipe dream, of course.

Ah-Long had been the number two *amah* at 53 Grange Road, and she was efficient, intelligent and loyal. She also knew about spirits. The murder had taken place in the servants' housing, back of the mansion to the right. Some said the ghost of the philandering husband would appear from time to time. It had been enough to make Ah-Long quit. She was looking for work just when Josh and Marge arrived, as luck would have it. Josh wondered whether Meridian House had any resident spirits.

*   *   *   *

Three hours passed, as the extras rehearsed to varying lighting and camera angles their background bits for the scene. The Director and someone on his cell phone carried on a continuing and rococo argument about the scene they were filming, and everytime the Director's voice was raised the scene was reshot. Josh lost count of the takes and his movements became more and more mechanical. Finally a coffee break was announced and the extras filed back to their holding area.

This time, the extras were more relaxed and more tired too. The early morning rush of adrenalin had long since gone. Perhaps some coffee would perk them up again, if it hadn't turned to battery acid by this time. The newspapers scattered about had all been read, and people traded gossip about this and previous sets. Josh listened in. A number of people, it seemed to him, had made good money on the set of Homicide, the regular television series that had been filmed in Baltimore. They were lamenting the end of the series, and wondering what if anything might replace it for local filming.

As to the rest, Josh couldn't help but wonder how they got by. Since this extra work was so irregular and so badly paid, they had to support themselves somehow unless, like himself, they had retirement checks. Some others were probably doing this with the idea that it would be a lark, like his partner Helen. Some lark!

Josh wondered about the younger ones, who were the majority of the extras that day. They were surely just starting out. What about their day jobs? Could they just take off from them, with short notice, to work as extras? It must not be easy paying one's dues, starting out. Josh supposed that most became discouraged. That was probably why every six months or so, the Washington *Post* announced open casting calls for extras. More fresh faces were needed, as people just got sick of it and quit.

On the other hand, discoveries did happen. Robert Mitchum had been an extra. More recently, so had Matthew McConaughey. If you weren't there on the set, you couldn't get discovered. And there was a pride in seeing things through. The tougher the day, the more some people dug in and did their best. Josh hoped that those were the ones who got discovered.

People began to swap horror stories. There was the day of filming *Murder At 1600* on Pennsylvania Avenue in front of the White House when the rain poured all afternoon. Sometimes there was snow and freezing cold. Josh had seen t-shirts with the inscription, "I survived *Mars Attacks.*" They meant the film shoot, which had taken place in a March snowstorm.

There were good memories too. Occasionally you got to see one of the stars up close. Perhaps that would happen today. Sometimes they got the shoot right rather quickly. Josh remembered that his scene at Union Station for *My Fellow Americans* had gone quickly and was interesting. He had also seen both Jack Lemmon and Walter Matthau close up. Marge had been intrigued by that, and pumped him for details. And he had once even managed a friendly chat with Jane Seymour on the set of *The Wedding Crashers*.

Years ago, when he was just starting this, Josh had been pleased to be in two scenes in the television series, *War and Remembrance*. Wardrobe had put him in an army officer's uniform from 1940, and Josh had been amazed that the costumer had actually guessed correctly both his service (Army) and branch (Signal Corps). Those were good memories.

On the other hand, there was that all nighter behind the White House for *Air Force One*, for the prayer scene for the hijacked President. Josh hadn't realized that it was going to be an all nighter, and he didn't have a cellular phone. The extras had finally had their "luncheon," jargon for their meal whenever it takes place, after midnight in the nearby DAR headquarters. Marge had not been amused when he got home at seven o'clock the next morning.

The lucky ones had passed into legend. In *No Way Out*, a Kevin Costner remake of the Fred MacMurray film noir *The Big Clock*, one extra had ended up with a day contract and a few lines to say on screen as a cabdriver. Josh himself had almost received a day contract while filming another cocktail reception, for *The Jackal.*

They had picked someone else. Too bad. That would have given him his eligibility to join SAG and make some better money out of his extra shoots. SAG members working as extras got twice the nonunion minimum wage, with extras for delayed meals and overtime bonuses that tended to mount up fast. If you were eligible and could afford the hefty entrance fee, then you would be in the next edition of the SAG film book and start making some better money. It wasn't easy to join SAG, however.

On *The Jackal* Josh had been paid at the SAG rate. That happened when the entire day's shoot was covered by a union contract, and there weren't enough SAG members on the set. The casting company would fill in, and nonunion extras got paid at the same SAG rate. If that happened three times, you were eligible to join SAG. Two down, one to go. He heard a rumor that they were getting SAG rates on this set. Of course, if you got a day contract on a SAG set, you had immediate SAG eligibility.

He wondered if Marge would put up with this foolishness much longer. She had noticed that a day on the set was usually followed by two days of crankiness and assorted aches and pains, and she was not above the occasional remark pointing this out.

The chirpy Assistant Director announced the end of the coffee break, and the extras filed back out of the holding and onto the Meridian House set. Everyone took their places. Assistant Directors quickly swept through the set, taking Polaroid pictures of the extras in their little groups, then taking the names of each extra after the pictures developed.

The Director began his cues. "Quiet on the set. I said QUIET! Lights! Action! BACKGROUND ACTION!"

The call for background action was the extras' cue to start their own movements. Josh began his routine, bowing slightly to his group and then walking across the room, from the piano area to the *hors d'oeuvres* table, stopping to mouth pleasantries with another threesome. Then he took the second lady from that threesome by the arm, as they had done fifteen times that morning, and looking towards her, meandered closer to the *hors d'oeuvres* table.

Just at that moment the principals joined the scene, and Josh made extra history by backing straight into Jack Nicholson. Amidst the gasps Nicholson, amused, stuck out his hand and said "If we're going to meet like this, we might at least introduce ourselves. I'm Secretary Ravenal." So he was keeping it in character. So did Josh. "Pardon me, Mr. Secretary, I'm Josh Upshaw." Nicholson grinned, turned and continued with the scene.

The Director yelled "Cut." Josh hadn't even realized the cameras were still rolling, but the cameraman had been so fascinated by what he had seen that he hadn't stopped the action. Nicholson turned to the Director and stopped him cold. "Leave it in," he said.

The scene wasn't filmed twice, so Josh realized he'd just have to wait and see whether the filmed scene would stay in the movie. He hoped so, but rather doubted it. But it would mean extra money now, Josh realized, as an accountant for the production company came up with a preprinted day contract for him to sign. Josh remembered the last time he had jolted a ranking guest at a diplomatic reception, that time in Saigon, when he had been a Second Secretary in the Embassy Political Section.

Everyone Comes to Rick's. That had been the original title of the play on which *Casablanca* was based, Josh had once read. Well, Everyone Came to Saigon, too, in those days. Working first in the Political Section, and then for a spell as Aide to the Ambassador, Josh had met them all.

National heroes, celebrities, celebrity seekers, you name it, they all came. Now, it was a war that everyone tried to forget or excuse or qualify. Then, in the early days, everyone came. And they all supported the war. Every single one. Those who couldn't found excuses to stay home. Charles Lindbergh, General Omar Bradley, Ann Landers, a gaggle of visiting media pundits, half the Congress, Cabinet officers, everyone came.

Lindbergh was the most famous celebrity that Josh had ever met, or really ever expected to meet. He looked just like his pictures. While they waited for Ambassador Lodge, Josh had told him a family story.

His uncle and grandmother had been visiting Paris in 1927 at the time of Lindbergh's flight. They were having dinner at the *Tour d'Argent*, the family legend had it, one evening during that frenzied week when Lindbergh was the only news story on two continents. His uncle was tall, thin and had dark hair, and the restaurant owners chose to believe that the celebrity was dining incognito in their midst. The check was waived.

Lindbergh had been amused by the story. "Imagine getting a free meal at the *Tour d'Argent*," he had said. Josh hadn't volunteered that, at $500 per couple for dinner, the family hadn't been back to the restaurant since then!

General Omar Bradley, Josh knew, was the greatest person he had ever met.

When Bradley and his wife came silently and without fuss into the Ambassador's reception area, both Josh and the secretary had stood up. It was just an automatic reaction. The odd thing about it was that Bradley was so soft spoken. He seemed to dote on every word that you said, as though you were the celebrity, not Omar Bradley.

He thought again of that reception at the Ambassador's residence. Ambassador Bunker had replaced Lodge, and he was in top form, cool as usual, as though he weren't really in the tropics at all. Josh had helped coordinate the final invitation list. What had bothered him, what had really bothered him, was the presence of General Loan on the list.

He remembered that it was within a week or two of the publication worldwide of that famous picture, that showed General Loan, revolver in hand, killing a Viet Cong prisoner. That picture, Josh supposed, had joined the famous pictures of Buddhist monk immolations and the little girl fleeing a napalm attack in undermining the American position in Viet-Nam. And here was General Loan invited to the Ambassador's residence.

It wasn't a very brave gesture, but it was all that he could think of at the time. General Loan came in with his escort, through security, and approached Josh, who stood just before the Ambassador, performing introductions. Bunker's head was, Josh remembered, slightly turned the other way, exchanging a pleasantry with the Japanese Ambassador, when General Loan stuck out his hand to Josh.

Josh had thought this through when he had seen the final list of acceptances for the guest list that afternoon. He was not going to soil his hand by shaking hands with this murderer. Josh nodded formally, and with a gesture swept General Loan's arm towards Ambassador Bunker, who shook his hand as though he were someone of value. General Loan briefly glared at Josh, but that was that. It wasn't much, perhaps, but it counted. For Josh it had preserved honor and a sense of perspective.

$$*\qquad *\qquad *\qquad *$$

The filming continued. Amazingly, the collective fatigue seemed to lift and the crew of extras started to get further into their roles. The first timers were tired too, you could tell, but theirs was a fatigue tinged with sheer annoyance. Why is this taking so damned long! Why didn't they do it right in the first place…or even on the tenth take? Why is it taking ALL DAY? You could read it on their faces easily.

By contrast the pros, the more experienced extras, those who hoped to go somewhere in this game, were showing something else, a sort of stamina. Let's get it right this time, seemed to be their attitude. Let's work on it and improve the take. It was a sort of teamwork. Josh wondered whether the stars of the film were aware of it. He hoped so.

The scene now included Demi Moore. She entered from the opposite door that led to the terrace, and made a beeline for Nicholson. The action called for a diplomatic security agent to try and stop her until the agent was waived off by Nicholson's press aide. Then she charged forward and, with lowered voice, demanded a private interview. Nicholson agreed, excused himself, and they left the room. The press aide tried to join them, but was waved back by Nicholson, who shut the door behind them.

That was the scene. The background action for the extras now became two tiered. The Director wanted those closest to the Secretary, who included Josh, to react with some surprise to Demi Moore's abrupt entrance, and to Nicholson's equally abrupt departure with her. Other extras, farther away, were to continue as cocktail party guests in the background, oblivious to what Moore and Nicholson were doing.

The scene was shot repeatedly, as Demi Moore entered the room from different angles. Somebody repeated Josh's blunder of getting in her way, ruining one take. A waiter dropped a tray, stopping all action for a quarter of an hour while the mess was cleaned up. There was discussion between Moore, Nicholson and the Director at one point, which Josh couldn't quite overhear.

Oh well, these film sets were not the only times when he had been around film stars. Far from it. Josh conjured up a memory of Budapest. It was unreal, but it had happened. At that point the Berlin Wall was still in place, and Hungary had some reputation for easing up politically, some twenty years after the 1956 Hungarian Revolution. The West was then beginning to rediscover Budapest, and that included film production companies.

Elizabeth Taylor and Richard Burton were in Budapest for the filming of *Bluebeard,* starring Burton. It was also Elizabeth Taylor's 40th birthday. Josh remembered it all, step by step. He could rewind it in his mind like a film. Josh and Marge had once even been interviewed by a writer doing a biography of Elizabeth Taylor, but they had kept their silence.

The British Ambassador was giving a small dinner party to celebrate Elizabeth Taylor's 40th birthday. It was a party of ten. There were the British Ambassador and his wife, the Swiss Ambassador and his wife, Josh and Marge from the American Embassy, Elizabeth Taylor, Richard Burton, the Director Edward Dmytryk, and the actress Joey Heatherton.

Josh sat between Joey Heatherton and Elizabeth Taylor. Across the table, Marge sat between Dmytryk and Richard Burton. The conversation from Burton was right out of *Who's Afraid Of Virginia Woolf?*. Burton was soon drunk, but he elicited concern rather than contempt. He was clearly very upset about the death of a recent friend. He kept saying, over and over again, in that superb rich voice, how very easy acting was, as though he despised his craft. Elizabeth Taylor tried to bring him back to the occasion, but Burton wouldn't cooperate.

At one point, he made a pass at Marge. "Don't you find me attractive?" he hissed at her. In her plummiest Radcliffe tones, Marge replied "Frankly, not when you are drunk," and removed his hand from her knee, plopping it on the table. Burton then went around the table, attempting to summarize the other guests, his comments laced with insults. His hostess asked him to leave the dinner, and he did.

Elizabeth Taylor had stayed behind to tend to any collateral damage. Marge agreed with Josh that she was just superb. She talked about her life and films and her children as with old friends. Everyone liked her. Josh also remembered with a grin that as they drove home Marge had talked about Elizabeth Taylor's enormous diamond ring, a famous present from Richard Burton. Josh had confessed that he hadn't even seen it. "Those violet eyes" had captured his attention instead.

*   *   *   *

The luncheon break finally arrived, and the extras walked back to the holding area. One or two checked their messages on their cell phones as they walked. Josh wished that he had one, although he had no idea how they worked. He really should call Marge. Perhaps he'd have time after lunch to locate a pay phone.

Luncheon was hot and tasty, and there was plenty of it. There were *boeuf bourguinon* over rice, hot vegetables, roast beef slices, and broiled chicken. Worried by his high cholesterol, Josh settled for the chicken and a salad, and some iced tea.

"Is it always this tiring?"

Josh located the voice, halfway down the table. It was Helen, picking listlessly at her food. "Actually, this is one of the better days," Josh answered. "It's always tiring. Today, though, the action was explained to us. That doesn't always happen. Also we got to see the two stars. That doesn't always happen either. Not by a long shot. And the luncheon is worth the eating. So it's been a good day."

"That sounds like the ending of *One Day In The Life Of Ivan Denisovitch*," she said. "Will we be reshooting the same scene this afternoon?"

Nobody seemed to know for sure. The young man with the Spanish play volunteered that he had seen the day's shooting schedule over an Assistant Director's shoulder, but the paper had been too general to get a clear idea. He went back to reading his play.

"I'm tempted to leave right now," Helen said. "Wouldn't advise it," Josh said. "Very bad form. We all signed up for the day, and that's the way it is. Walking off is mortal sin in this business, and there's no absolution. Besides, you wouldn't get your fifty bucks."

Helen snorted in amusement. "Why are you doing this, anyway?" Helen asked. The question seemed aimed at Josh. "Marge says it gets me out of the house," he replied. "Besides, like half the people in this town, I've got a screenplay in my computer. Being around a set gives me some idea of how action comes across in filming. Screen action and dialogue are very different from writing a novel. Being on a set from time to time helps me gauge that."

She put the same question to the five others at the table. Two were lost in their newspapers, and one was falling asleep. The play reader said that he wanted to make acting his career. Any practical experience would help him do that. One other woman, like Helen, was doing it for the day just to see if it was fun. "It isn't," was her sour verdict.

"Back to the set!" the Assistant Director announced.

Another Assistant Director came through and started rearranging the extras, who had settled into the same places that they had started in that morning. There were new partners, too. Also, for the men, different ties handed out by wardrobe, with new accessories for the women. It looked like they were going to do a different shoot entirely, and get two scenes filmed instead of one. Helen was standing near Josh, and he explained that.

"How can they tell where we all were standing this morning?"

"Remember those still photos, those Polaroids they took of us on the set this morning? That was to fix everyone's place, so that we could be reassembled in exactly the same groups if they wanted to reshoot a sequence."

"Uh-huh."

"Now they are going to use those photos for a different purpose, Josh went on. "My guess is that they are going to vary our places so that those who were near the principals in that first scene would now be in the background, while the others are moved up."

"So that it looks like a different crowd."

"Exactly.

"Do you suppose that it's supposed to be a different reception?"

Josh mulled this over. "Could be," he said, "but probably it's at a different stage of the same reception. Let's see if the Director is going to explain it to us."

They spent an hour being moved around, like cards being reshuffled. No cameras filmed anything. It seemed to Josh that the Director really didn't have any clear notion of what he wanted, and was just trying out various ideas.

Well, in a few hours the overtime would start, a pittance for the non-union people, but for SAG members that would be the beginning of some serious money. As far as they were concerned, of course, the shoot could last from now until next weekend, the longer the better.

Josh tried to summon up the best acting performances that he had witnessed. The two best actors had been French. When he was a student in Paris, he had once wangled a half price ticket to see Jean Louis Barrault doing Kafka's *The Castle*. The performance had been riveting, so much so that the pain from an infected root canal that had lacerated his jaw had seemed to disappear with Barrault on stage. He had simply forgotten it.

Then, years later, on July 14, 1989 to be exact, the 200th anniversary of the taking of the Bastille, there had been a free performance at the *Comedie Francaise*. The play was Beaumarchais's *Marriage of Figaro*. Josh remembered that during the intermission of the play, he had seen displayed at the theater the very notice posted on July 14, 1789 . . "*Relache* (closed today) *a cause des troubles*."

It was after the performance that the glorious moment came. Richard Fontana, who played Figaro, stepped forward. He recited "*La Marseillaise*." It was as though nobody had ever said it before, the words were so vivid and fresh. It was said that Sarah Bernhardt had done the same thing at her theatrical tryout, and those who claimed later to have been present on that occasion could have populated a province.

As for great actresses, there were two that Josh had seen. He had gone to the final afternoon of the annual reading of *Ulysses* at the Joyce Festival at American University in Northwest Washington. Ordinarily Josh didn't care much for Joyce. However it had been reported that Siobvan McKenna, in Washington for a performance of a Sean O'Casey play at the Hartke Theater at Catholic University, would be reading. So would another fine professional actress, as well as a celebrated amateur, to complement the volunteer readers. That was worth hearing.

Although he was early by an hour and a half, it had still been difficult to find space in the crowded lounge. But there was room. The readers were not announced. They merely replaced each other. The long Molly Bloom soliloquy was feelingly read. And then the reader changed, and the new depth was immediately apparent This must be Siobvan McKenna. What a treat. Josh listened so closely that he could hardly breathe. Then, the readers changed once again and for the last time, as McKenna took her place and began her reading of the final portions of the soliloquy.

It was as though Bjoerling or Pavarotti in his prime had replaced a competent professional tenor for the last act of *Otello*. The reading acquired unfathomable depth and layers of meaning, and the audience was struck dumb with the awe of the occasion. This was hardly acting. It was closer to sorcery.

The same might be said of the performance that he and Marge and Katherine had seen together at Epidavros when they were posted to the Embassy in Athens. Josh was Deputy Political Counselor, and had learned enough Greek to follow the ancient plays, performed in their original settings in modern Greek translation.

There were the famous theaters of course, Delphi and Herod Atticus in Athens. There were also the small, hard to find places, like the theater on Euboia where the trap entrance onto the stage began, and the seats which still existed at Dionnysos, marking the religious celebrations which, under the actor Thespis, had evolved into the first theater. It amused Josh that the paired carved stone seats had double width armrests between them. The comfort of the theatergoer had been important then, if not now.

At the ancient theater of Epidavros on the Peloponesi the acoustics were still perfect. They also transmitted sound in reverse, from the audience towards the stage. Josh remembered a late arriving couple sitting down in the last row. Their argument was clearly audible throughout the entire theater before the patrons shushed the quarrel.

It was there that they saw *Medea*, and Eleni Hadjiargyri's performance of the doomed heroine. The chorus intoned with ghastly hollowness *"Min ne skotosis ta paidia,"* ("Don't kill the children") to no avail. Only O'Neill was close to Euripides in American drama, Josh thought, O'Neill and sometimes Arthur Miller. It clearly was a catharsis, or emotional cleansing, as the Greeks had intended.

Katherine was their only child, and they had had a bit of a tussle over her name. Marge had majored in French literature, and Josh in English and American drama, so they had compromised on the name of the French princess from Shakespeare's *Henry V*. The onset of her illness from some tropical disease had been swift and her decline so immediate that even now, years later, they wondered how it could all have happened so suddenly. Was it a school trip to Egypt, or an infection from this Mediterranean seaport capital? They would never be sure. Their friends at the Embassy had packed them up as they left that overseas posting that had begun with such promise.

Life had gone on, with whatever meaning he and Marge had forged into it, day by day. Josh sometimes thought that he had then become something of an extra in the diplomatic world, as he waited out his retirement. Without the scrapbooks that Marge had assembled, with letters of commendation, pictures and souvenirs of their various posts, he would have had trouble even remembering that he had ever handled behind the scenes negotiations in assignment after assignment, sweating out deadlines. That must have been someone else. But Josh and Marge were content. It had been the right thing to do to continue, even if their hearts were not there.

*　　　*　　　*　　　*

"QUIET on the set! Lights! ACTION! BACKground action!" In the background now, Josh took a champagne glass from a passing waiter, sipped the soft drink and mouthed conversation with his neighbors. Two supporting leads came in and started an argument. They were playing two Members of Congress. Josh recognized them, sort of. He must ask someone who they were. Marge would be interested.

The scene was reshot, again and again and again. It was not possible, from his vantage point, to tell exactly what was going on. They were probably just trying ideas out. What he could hear of the dialogue sounded rather improvised. It would all come together later in the editing room.

Josh knew from experience that a good performance was as necessary now as it had been earlier, when he was up front, close to Jack Nicholson. For one thing, it was entirely likely that the faces right around Nicholson would be blurred, so that he would not be seen then, but he might be glimpsed in a pan shot when he was in the background. That is, if either scene was used at all. Luck, colors, contrast, lighting, camera angles, it all depended on so many things. He looked around for Helen, and could not find her.

His last post had been as Consul General in Lyon, France. He had, as a matter of fact, closed the post, which had been a reward for his earlier assignments, when it could no longer be saved for budgetary reasons. Josh always thought that was too bad, really. The Foreign Service needed Consulates General to train its officers in management, and give them some breadth.

That had been possible at Lyon. He had enjoyed the city and the famous consular district, which ran the length of Burgundy. With Raymond Barre, a former Prime Minister and still a regional political power, there was someone with national scope to offer a political perspective, one that the Embassy heard with real respect.

There was good theater to attend, including opera and plays, and a fine orchestra which attracted famous soloists. Josh enjoyed the Guignol, an outdoor traditional Punch and Judy performance, in the pleasant months. He had envied the French retirees who could enjoy a performance in the springtime, accompanied by the laughter of their grandchildren.

Josh remembered a reception at the residence of the Ambassador in Paris, on the *rue du Faubourg St. Honore.* Every year the Consuls General came in from Lyon, Strasbourg, Marseilles, Bordeaux and Martinique for a conference on pending business, to learn the latest in the sometimes fractious bilateral relationship betwen Paris and Washington, and to swap experiences with their colleagues, whether it was visa fraud patterns or cultural affairs grants.

This was the top of the line, many would say. It was our most elegant diplomatic establishment. Just getting there at all was an accomplishment. Josh knew Foreign Service Officers who had sweated it out tour after tour in Francophone Africa paying their dues, in the hope that they would get a chance some day to serve in Paris. Some were able to do so. But there was much more to diplomacy than glitter. Those who had toughed it out in hardship posts, or around the negotiating table trying to separate groups that hated each other, were the best in the profession, even if there wasn't much credit for their efforts publicly given. And now, the Secretary had decreed that assignments in Western Europe were being curtailed. What a shame.

The reception had concluded with a smaller dinner in the formal west dining room, the light from dozens of candles reflected over and over in the gilded mirrors around the room. Fine wines had been served, from the Ambassador's personal collection. Marge had looked particularly nice, and they had both been surprised by the Ambassador's graceful little after dinner speech, which praised their service. Josh tried hard to hold the memory. Not many farewells in the Foreign Service had such an elegant aspect. Coffee, a plaque, and out the door were the norm in Washington. But the Paris scene slipped away.

*   *   *   *

"CUT! Thank you very much! Return the ties and accessories to wardrobe. The bus will take you back to the parking lot in fifteen minutes." The Assistant Directors were everywhere, busy and chattering. Josh left the set with the other extras and walked back to the holding area. He gave the tie back to wardrobe.

Dreadful thing, really. It was certainly not one that he would ever have bought. Josh filled out his time card, marking his non-union status. Well, after today's day contract, that should change. He'd know for sure when the check arrived next month from Central Casting. There should be enough eligibility now for him to join SAG.

A group of onlookers lined the street as the extras climbed onto the bus. They were curious, and looking for celebrities. Josh wondered how their day had gone. He was sure that each had probably earned far more than the extras had, and probably not worked so hard.

That was part of the game, after all. But he would remember this day and the set long after they had forgotten the details. It would be relived from time to time, and then recycled after the film came out. He hoped that this time he would be lucky, and would actually appear on screen. But the important thing was that he had participated. Marge would be pleased. He made a note to stop on the way home and buy a nice bottle of white wine for them to savor while he told her the story.

CHAPTER 35

▼

Les Revenants

Ronald Parkins settled back into his easy chair upstairs at the City Tavern Club and relaxed. The lecture had gone well, and dinner had been convivial. Then his audience had drifted away, and Parkins himself had walked upstairs to his favorite alcove to digest his dinner and savor the evening.

Who would have thought that such a large number of club members would be on hand on a Wednesday evening? Well, it was the middle of a dreary Washington winter, the price of the evening (with dinner) was reasonable, and attending "A Tasting Lecture on Single Malt Scotch Whiskys" delivered by former Consul General to Edinburgh Ronald Parkins had proved an irresistible attraction.

Parkins smiled in satisfaction. There had been six sample whiskys, Highland, Lowland, Speyside. He had shared anecdotes about visiting the distilleries of each whisky served. With such high quality, your preference, he had said, depended upon individual taste. He had gone over the various flavors and qualities. There was the smoothness of Glenlivet, of course, and the pleasantly smoky quality of Glenmorangie. It was a bit like fine perfume. All were good. You should choose what you liked best.

The highpoint had come when that obnoxious Larry Carter had tried to trip him up with an unknown, near the end of his remarks. The waiter had apologetically brought him the glass, while Carter rose to give his boorish challenge. Of course, it hadn't been Scotch at all. Parkins could tell that right away. It tasted like fine single cask Bourbon. Specifically, it was Maker's Mark. Parkins had identified it, to a nice supplementary round of applause. The chagrined look on Carter's face had been worth the extra stress that Parkins had momentarily felt when the challenge had been issued.

Parkins cradled his cognac and looked around the room. It was fine cognac, smooth Hennessey, from his own bottle of *Le Paradis* that the club kept for him. Parkins remembered visiting Hennessey at Cognac in the Charente region of western France, and seeing the storeroom, *Le Paradis*, where the most treasured cognacs were kept. He had even been privileged to taste a *fin bois* from 1864. There might even be just a trace of that very cask of *fin bois* in his glass now. The cognac seemed still alive and evolving, when every person that had known that Civil War year had long been dead and gone.

Parkins stared at the log fire burning in the fireplace, transfixed for a moment. It warmed him, along with the cognac. When was the last time he had been in this room? Oh yes, it had been that evening when ghost stories had been told. That had been fun. It had not been too hammy.

The City Tavern Club, with its eighteenth century beginnings and associations with the earliest days of the planning of Washington, had its resident ghost of course. She hadn't been seen for some years now, but of the many who passed by on bustling M Street, how many would ever guess that the unobtrusive tavern sign for the *Sign of the Indian King* masked a private Georgetown club with origins that predated the White House?

There were Civil War ghosts talked about that night as well, which Parkins always considered rather gloomy. Slave ghosts were always a desperately sad story. The ghosts of murderers he could do without. They were for those of weak imagination.

Then of course there were the contemporary haunts, such as the Capitol Cat, an enormous feline, which appeared after hours, usually to Congressmen who had had several too many. It was huge, fat and not overly threatening once you faced it down. Just like that former Speaker, Parkins thought.

The *revenant* better fit his notion of romance: one who returns to a place where great conflict was experienced. Parkins remembered the story of the ghosts from General Braddock's doomed force who had marched through Georgetown from Alexandria across the Potomac River on their way to the frontier. The stress on them as they marched away from civilization to face Indians and a French Army must have been great. They must have all known that many would not come back alive. Those who had survived the Braddock expedition, Parkins recalled, had been fortunate to have had George Washington to bail them out. Otherwise they might all have been massacred in the forests.

He savored his cognac. This French notion of ghosts neatly fit the Braddock expedition. Come to think of it, the *revenant* implied not just a return. It was more than that. The spirit had to repeat an action, over and over again, one that recalled unresolved emotional stress, just as Braddock's men were said to repeat their doomed march every year.

Parkins stared at the fire, and turned off the light near his chair, so he could better catch the flames from the fireplace, and see them cast shadows around the room. He began to feel a little warm, and somewhat drowsy and heavy in his limbs. His mind wandered to his foreign service posts. Let's see. There had been Budapest, Lahore, London, Saigon, Rawalpindi, and Edinburgh, with, of course, a number of interim returns to the Washington ladder.

Edinburgh had been the last one, and he had fully enjoyed it. His audience tonight could certainly tell that. His joy in Scotland had been catching. The scenery was grand, the fishing superb, and the people companionable.

That was what he had missed, companionship. He had never married, and the joys of a domestic animal, a dog or a cat, had been denied him. Not that he hadn't tried from time to time, but his allergy to their fur flared up whenever an animal was near. It was too bad, really. He knew that a dog or a cat would have been good company. He would have liked that.

Once, he had been serious about a woman. Eileen was her name, and she was Irish, the wife of the British Commercial Attache in Budapest. It had been more than forty years earlier, not long after the Hungarian Revolution.

Eileen had had flaming red hair, red like that fire, and green eyes, and her laughter still could be heard in his imagination. "Ach, Ronald," she would tease, "why are you so afraid to live?" And then he had realized that her teasing was very serious, the product of frustration in a marriage that had turned sour.

The British Embassy residence on the *Rozsadomb*, a hilly section on the Buda side of the Danube, had been where he had seen her last. It was all so melodramatic, really. He wasn't going to break up her marriage. She did after all have three small children. He was a bachelor. But in those days, the wrong notation in an annual evaluation report, one that you would never even see, could ruin a career, and he knew that the American Minister was straightlaced. And so the moment had passed, and after a long time, a very long time, the wanting had eased and then vanished.

He wondered whether roses still bloomed on the *Rozsadomb*. They had bloomed for over four centuries, since legend had it they were first planted during the Turkish occupation by the poet Gul Baba, "Father of Roses." He also wondered with a smile, and not for the first time, what laconic sense of humor had led the British Embassy in Budapest to assign its most romantic location, the residence on the *Rozsadomb*, to house its most prosaic substantive officer, the Commercial Attache.

He sipped his cognac and tried to cross his legs, but they were too heavy. The glass slipped from his fingers and made no noise as it fell on the rug, the remaining drops of cognac spilling. He thought of Eileen, and the old longing came back once more, rich and fresh and new.

$$* \qquad * \qquad * \qquad *$$

Cecily liked the early dawn. She had always been full of energy, and this uninterrupted time of day, before Nigel and their children had risen, was her time. She had her little rituals, and would enjoy fresh juice and a bun and the first cup of coffee of the day. This was the time also that she saved to read the London newspapers that Nigel brought from the Embassy on *Harmincad Utca* in downtown Pest, plus any letters from home.

It was her own time, and often a time to write as well. The rest of the day would be sandwiched into routine, pleasant routine, but routine nonetheless. There would be the bustling of the children off to their school, surely an Embassy luncheon or a visitor to show around, and always a reception to attend. Cecily enjoyed all that, she really did. That was a good thing, because the wife of the British Commercial Attache had a full schedule. It went with the territory.

Sometimes though she wondered if the life she were leading were quite her own. It was fun, even thrilling sometimes, but it was also not quite what she had pictured of the diplomatic life, when she had been at that dreary school in Hampshire. She did see that Nigel was the last man on the Embassy pecking order, not included in the Ambassador's charmed circle. She tried hard to affect an interest in his trade missions, and their dreary businessmen. She really did.

Cecily knew but rarely admitted that it was getting harder and harder to be interested in such things, and sometimes she even had the passing thought that life, real exciting life, was passing her by. Just fancy. One of these days she might even speak more personally to that attractive fellow from the Austrian Embassy. He would understand. Heaven knows he had stared at her often enough.

Nigel had turned rather dour over the years. That turn of his personality had also been, Cecily was convinced, an element in the slowed rate of his promotions. Nigel's chances for his own diplomatic mission had diminished accordingly. Cecily knew intuitively that she was the family diplomat, had she but had the opportunity.

Work with the material at hand, her teachers had said. For a while it had been a matter of covering for Nigel. Then even that had stopped, and she had long ceased pointing out, however obliquely, his social errors in the hopes that he would mend them. It wasn't kind, and he was a good father, after all.

She looked out her front parlor window in the early dawn. The sunlight was just beginning to light their *Rozsadomb* street, glancing off the snow from last Friday's snowfall. She saw, or thought she saw, the figure of a tall man at her gate. Then he seemed to be actually inside her gate. That was either her imagination, or again the gate alarm is not working properly, she thought crossly. She hastily made a note to Nigel to send a memorandum to get it rewired.

Cecily looked up again. To her surprise the man was definitely within her grounds, and now a woman was hurrying along the walkway, from the house it seemed. It was hard to tell. The woman had flaming red hair.

The man started to run towards the woman. They were only a few feet from each other, when with the first full rays of the sun striking the walkway, they vanished.

FINIS

978-0-595-39100-4
0-595-39100-1

Printed in the United States
69075LVS00007B/40-45